She held the
in her hand before plugging it into the side of her computer. Black rubber surrounded the stick like the rubber on an underwater camera. *Here goes.* She watched it upload. *Let's see what this is all about.*

Ten documents labeled by date flashed on her computer screen. Six documents dated years before Tim and Kendall met; the other four ranged from the beginning of their relationship to one dated three days before Tim died.

Inhaling deeply, she touched her mouse, pulling down to the right and clicking without hesitation on the last icon, a video file. She squeezed her eyes to hold back tears as Tim's face filled the screen. The background was the upstairs office over the garage. She hit play.

~*~

Praise for this book...

"*A DEEP THING* by A.K. Smith is a high concept thriller—think *The Da Vinci Code* of the deep—that grabs you from the beginning and doesn't let go. A roller coaster ride of romance, suspense, mystery and intrigue, this page-turner surprises at every turn and offers a stunning ending you'll never suspect.

~*Marilyn Baron, author of Stumble Stones: A Novel*

Acknowledgments

This book would not have been possible without a hike around Lookout Mountain in Phoenix with my husband, Darrell Smith. He listened to the entire outline of *A Deep Thing* and said, "I see it as a movie." He is my biggest fan, and his support means more than words. Special thanks to my family—my mother, Grace, who believes I can do anything. My sister Lisa Rafferty who encouraged me to write this novel, (she never heard of cenotes and found them fascinating), sorry it's not the horror novel you envisioned. My sisters Coleen Martin for advice and Iris Kaltenbaugh for encouragement. My brothers Peter and Mark Kaltenbaugh, who believed in me, as did my father.

Thanks to Judy Brinkhurst, my very first reader, and to all my beta readers for their advice and excitement: Cheri and Darrin Jones, Carla Engel, Marcia Brockmeyer, Julene Pinto-Dyczewski, Dan Dyczewski, Michelle Kaltenbaugh, Lynne Trailov, Susan Cardillo, Dennis and Weezie Thomas, and Corb Harding. Thanks to Elisabeth Hallett for her proofing skills. Three of my life mentors passed away while I was writing this book; thanks to them for everything: Bud Crawley, Betty Moore, and Mitchell Alexander.

Thanks to Paolo of Diving Cenotes Tulum, Ed and Diego for the magical cenote dive. If you've never witnessed the unworldly beauty of a cenote, go to the Yucatán.

Special thanks to The Wild Rose Press and Ally Robertson for believing in me and my story. Thanks to the Las Vegas Writers Conference for allowing such introductions to happen. I'm so thankful to have met Ally.

A Deep Thing

by

A. K. Smith

A Deep Thing

Cover Art by *Debbie Taylor*

The Wild Rose Press, Inc.
PO Box 708
Adams Basin, NY 14410-0708
Visit us at www.thewildrosepress.com

Publishing History
First Mainstream Thriller Edition, 2016
Print ISBN 978-1-5092-1048-0
Digital ISBN 978-1-5092-1049-7

Published in the United States of America

Dedication

For my brothers Pete and Mark
and all my friends and family who fight the battle.
May we find the magic cure.

Notes from the Author

To all new writers, don't give up and don't forget the small presses. The Wild Rose Press, Inc. has been voted the best small press for the last seven years by Predators and Editors and is a wonderful publishing house to work with.

~*~

To my readers, join me in an experiment! *A Deep Thing* is my debut fiction novel. Publishing experts and literary agents state the secret to a break-out novel is simply one thing: word of mouth. If you enjoy this book, please tell five people and ask them to tell five people. Take the trip, join the journey.

~*~

Cenotes are magical underground caves that exist in the Yucatán Peninsula...Deep holes under the earth filled with crystal clear fresh water containing minerals found nowhere else in the world. *A beautiful sinkhole.* The Maya discovered them centuries ago, calling them "dzonot," translated by the Spaniards to the word "cenote" meaning in Spanish "a deep thing."

Chapter 1

Were they still following him? Tim Jackson
scanned the canopy of the lush jungle as the damp and
musty scent of the wild eased his anxiety. The birds
chirped in rhythm with the incessant buzzing melody of
the insects creating an organic symphony. He turned his
head slightly to the left. No, they weren't out there yet,
but eventually they would be. An acquisition of
memories played in his mind as he rubbed a hand over
the tightness in his chest.

"Tim, the boat is fixed, you ready?" Adam
emerged in the light and held Tim's gaze. "Everything
fine?"

Tim stood, brushing a hand through his hair. "Yes,
everything is fine. Is Colton ready to go?"

"Everyone's ready."

The chop hit hard, bouncing the thirty-four-foot
Boston Whaler on the turquoise water for the first forty-
five minutes. As the boat entered the reef, it welcomed
twenty minutes of a smooth ride and a race with a pod
of playful dolphins. Their slick, pointy faces broke
through the water with a smile, only to head downward
in a rhythmic motion of up and down, daring the boat to
follow. Colton and Adam, Tim's dive buddies on many
excursions, cheered the flippers on from the front of the
bow. Sheer joy highlighted their facial features. Back in
the open water, the chop returned, and the men settled

in silence, taking in the vastness of the azure sea. Soon they reached Lighthouse Atoll, home of the Great Blue Hole in Belize.

Seen from above, the Great Blue Hole resembled a pupil, a large deep indigo circle surrounded by a ring of turquoise looking up as if beckoning to come closer. By boat, the almost perfectly circular reef with a diameter of 980 ft. and a depth of over 480 ft. painted a different picture. The sideways viewpoint created a kaleidoscope of luminous variations of blue and green, but it was not the magical glow of water that intensified the moment, it was the overwhelming feeling it created—the energy in the air charged, as if the intensity of the color was a mysterious vortex.

"It never gets old—I'm a pixel on the screen." Adam said. "Just look at it." Hundreds of shades of aquamarine color exploded in the vastness as far as you could see. Incredible beauty surrounded them. They were anchored now inside the reef in calm waters. Tim stopped writing in his logbook, captivated as always by this wonder of nature.

"You know, 10,000 years ago it was above ground, a limestone cavern, a cave at the center of a tunnel. The ceiling collapsed, and now it is an undersea mountain." Tim spoke softly clutching the dive book. He pulled in then slowly released a deep breath, staring at the sea. "It is amazing, in the scheme of it all. We are just a ripple in the water." He placed the dive book carefully in his bag and picked up his scuba equipment.

Adam and Colton joined him adjusting their gear. Their excitement was contagious. "You ready? Let's do this!"

The dive in the Blue Hole was the first of three

dives for the day, this one ten minutes long at 140 feet.

Three divers plopped into the water. Only two would surface.

Chapter 2

Kendall Riggs unscrewed the cap off the prescription bottle, hand shaking and heart beating erratically. A voice hidden somewhere deep down was fighting to surface in her fuzzy mind. She blocked it out instantly with the intense biting of her lower lip and exhaled a deep breath.

Why stop? Who really cares? Just as she was placing the pill on the back of her tongue and reaching for her water to wash it down, the door to her College Activities office opened and in stepped her boss, the President of Western Maryland College, Frank Alexander.

"Is everything okay, Kendall?"

She swallowed the pill. Frank looked straight at her. "We missed you in the meeting today."

The meeting. Kendall got that sinking feeling in the pit of her stomach. She ran her fingers through her long, light brown hair and stood up from her desk. She tucked her wrinkled black blouse into a black pencil skirt, looser than it should be. Her eyes focused on Frank with the best smile she could muster. "I'm sorry, Frank, I completely lost track of time."

Was she slurring her words? Her tongue felt a little thick and she thought she might be talking too quickly. She saw the look in his eyes. He was thinking the same thing everyone else was thinking—get over your

4

husband's death already, it's been a year and a half, you need to pick up your life and move on.

Kendall hated that look from friends and colleagues more than the sympathetic look from strangers when they heard her husband had been killed in a horrific diving accident. Everyone seemed to know what happened. The story ran on the *Today* show and *Good Morning America* with a follow-up story, and plenty of pictures of her Reality star stepson, Ryder, who was left behind after the tragic death.

Frank took his glasses off and cleaned the lens of each side with his tie, an annoying habit. "Okay, get the minutes from Mitchell to see what you missed and the updates on your committee report." He stopped, paused, as he put the rimless glasses back on the perch of his nose, peering over them once again to stare at her. "Kendall, I know it's hard to move on, but some day you'll realize everything happens…"

With a tightening inside her chest, she forced a fake smile. "I'll get with Mitchell right away and catch up. I'm sorry I missed it, it won't happen again."

She could bring the horror up clearly in her mind. It only took an instant. A flash, a deep guttural inside pain, quick to surface.

The pain was sharp each time she replayed the phone call that changed her life. It was like a scratched DVD replaying the same scene and she was watching herself.

"Hey handsome, how was the dive?" she purred into the phone.

After a series of clicks, rustling, and static, a deep calm voice spoke. "Kendall, this is Adam Matthews."

"Adam, what's wrong? Where's Tim?" When

Adam didn't respond, her voice rose. "Where is he?"

"Kendall, I'm so sorry, there's been an accident…."

She swallowed again, her cluttered desk coming into focus, her hand holding the file folder trembling. The small pill stuck in the back of her throat. It didn't matter. The slight uncomfortable feeling of an object lodged sideways in her esophagus was nothing in relation to the glass shard stuck in her chest every hour of the day for the last sixteen months. How could he die?

****

Her eyes lift up to the round circle on the wall with numbers. Hours have passed and she realizes she needs to go home and check on Harvey. Harvey is the one companion who never let her down.

Putting the key in the lock reminds her of what isn't inside; with a twist of her hand, she turns the knob. Harvey springs into the air, clearing more than a foot off the ground, paws outstretched, almost like he's asking for a dance, or leaping to a rim shot off a basket. The springy dance is repeated in a melodic beat.

Almost three years old, this fifty-pound wheaten terrier-poodle mix is the only being on the planet to stir up a microscopic bit of the once-known emotion of joy. Perhaps it's another being touching her skin and licking her face. For a split second, her lips turn slightly upward.

It doesn't last long. Harvey runs to the pantry door and then settles down to feast on his food, carefully eating in sections. After a spin out the doggy door, she dreads what happens next. He goes immediately to the small white couch in front of the picture window by the door. With his head resting on his paws on the back of the couch, he sits upright staring out the window, turning his head every few minutes, looking for a response. He is waiting to hear the rumble of the engine of a Ford F150 truck pulling into the driveway. He knows the sound, but it never comes. This nightly vigil tightens the tourniquet around her heart as she coaxes him to bed his movements slower and his head nearly touching the ground.

She hated the lines everyone spouted at her: *It will get easier over time. Time heals all things. Everything happens for a reason.*

Kendall really liked that last one. She used to tell people that all the time. In the past, she sincerely believed it.

What was wrong with her...how dare she say that to people in pain. Who was she before? Some glass half-full, eternal optimist full of love and life, stupid woman, naïve to the pain or reality of life?

She had the picture-perfect life with Tim, little or no heartache, minimal stress, much warmth for others, and a desire to make the world a better place. She actually thought she was qualified to spout philosophical advice she had no right to give to those in pain. Who was she to tell people anything about the pain of suffering...how they should feel inside or will feel in the days ahead? She had never experienced pain like this, hot searing pain like a knife stuck in your stomach.

That person was gone forever; she didn't even know that foolish individual she used to be. But if she were here right now, that gullible optimist, she would scream at the top of her voice, directly in her face,

"Okay, Miss Sunshine, you want to know the reason things happen? Here's the reason…. I'm going to put twenty pills in my mouth at one time." *Because the love of my life is gone.*

Gone forever. She never got to whisper goodbye, kiss his sweet soft lips one last time or wrap her arms around his broad chest and tell him how much she loved him. She will never get to feel the warmth of his body next to hers in their bed, their legs wrapped together, and the soft sound of him breathing by her ear. His sweet smell, musky, masculine, and his.

The reason? How many do you want?

"There's your 'everything happens for a reason.'" Kendall tilted her head back and swallowed a cluster of tiny white pills in one gulp, in one blind moment of pain.

Chapter 3

Ryder picked up the Turkish oil lamp, staring at the tarnished brass and threw it across the room. An angry thud and a gaping hole in the drywall verified his rage. He remembered the day his father, returning from a business trip, unwrapped the little lamp and carefully placed the shiny object in his hands. To a ten-year-old, it smelled old and magical, just like an Aladdin lamp.

"Is it magic?" He had asked, captivated.

"Maybe, if you live a good and purposeful life, maybe someday your wishes will come true."

He had watched Aladdin so many times; he knew if you rubbed a magic lamp, a genie might appear and grant three wishes.

For most of his life, his three wishes never changed. Just like Tony Stark in Ironman, he wanted a huge mansion on the ocean, and he wanted to be filthy rich and famous.

Well, he was on his way to being famous—sort of—with his new job on a reality TV show. The show focused on Dr. Ian Grant's patients, women and men having plastic surgery. Ryder just happened to be one of the real characters, a receptionist, cast in the mostly scripted TV show, titled after the prominent, upscale, steamy desert it was filmed in, *Paradise Valley*.

The real story was in the office dynamics, the clients' spectacle and performance before and after surgery and the clients—male and female—who became obsessed with their dreamy surgeon. A reality soap opera, filled with drama, and clients flirting with everyone, including him.

He wanted fame; it charged him up, gave him power. However, in addition to money and fame, he wanted two more things. His father to be alive, and to shake off this revolting anxiety that wrapped its sickening stranglehold around his heart. It pissed him off as he wiped the sweat off the back of his neck. Some call it stage fright or performance anxiety. He never even knew what anxiety meant until he experienced it in the second season of shooting *Paradise Valley*.

He remembers it clearly. One minute he's joking around with the catering staff complaining about the lack of healthy foods and flirting with the hot blonde in the crew, giving him the "I want to have sex with you now" look and the next he walks onto the set and seconds after the camera's light turns red, he is covered in sweat and running off camera. He remembers his heartbeat rapidly pounding out of his chest, pain, tightening of his gut, and the overwhelming desire to be anywhere else. He thought he was having a heart attack.

He tried to work through the anxiety, swallowing a few Valiums before filming the last few episodes of Season Two. It didn't matter. When the camera turned on, so did his anxiety. Night after night, he would find himself covered in sweat, dreading the next episode. Embarrassed to tell anyone—afraid it would leak out in the media—he hid it from everyone. If they found out, he was convinced his career of being a reality star and dreams of being rich and famous would be over. He woke up obsessing about it and went to sleep worrying when it would happen next. It controlled his life. He couldn't tell his publicist and now with Season Two over, he hid from management until he figured out what he could do. He missed his father so much. A voice inside his head kept asking, "Why, Dad, why did you have to leave me? I needed you so much and you left me." He had planned to talk to his father when he returned from the trip that took his life. The only one he could talk to and now he was gone.

****

He was eighteen, a legal adult his father would never know. He slammed the door on his silver BMW 325i and walked toward the park, nicknamed "the DUN playground." Thankful his father didn't know this Ryder.

The DUN playground stood for the "drugs u need" playground. He needed more Valium, or Xanax, some type of antianxiety medication to help in front of the camera. He swallowed his last one. He pulled his hat down wearing dark sunglasses. He hadn't showered since the gym, hoping this helped him smell and play the part of a strung out druggie. He glanced past the puffy block letters painted in various colors declaring territory on the warm cement. He hoped the pimple-faced blond surfer-looking dude on meth would appear.

His iPhone vibrated. He blinked at the display, the drugs making everything hazy. Kendall. He spit on the sidewalk. He wouldn't answer. Talking on the phone, even texting irritated him. Old school. It reminded him of his mother, all she did was talk on the phone.

Kendall. His father left her everything in the will, his half of the bar in Gettysburg, the house in Maryland, everything except a scholarship fund for Ryder, only payable if he went to college, and another lump sum when he graduated. He didn't need the money that bad. It pissed him off. Kendall had offered for him to move out to Maryland where he could go to school at Western Maryland College, and work part time at the bar, but he wasn't interested. Leave Scottsdale? Live with Kendall? He had no reason to speak to her. She was nothing to him. Nothing. He did not love her, not even a little bit. His father was dead, and she was no relation, just a bad reminder of his father.

Gripping his phone, he thought back to the day when he did answer. Kendall sobbing, as she uttered the words his father was dead in Belize. He hated her. He threw the phone against the wall, the glass shattered.

Chapter 4

Water was all around her, transparent turquoise water. The liquid warm and clear. Floating seemed so natural. When she looked out, she could see miles ahead, incredible visibility with high definition. Then she saw him, his blue-green eyes and dark curly hair, his cleft chin and his white enchanting smile. She wanted to swim toward him but he was shaking his head. Wait…a vibration came out of nowhere, irritating, she could hear a buzzing in her ear, it hummed, pulsed and then she felt wetness over her eyes and face, like a warm rough rag being dragged across her skin.

Kendall gasped, tried to lift her eyelids, separate bottom and top lashes. Her head swayed, as a jackhammer pounded in her skull. Nausea washed over her. The rough wet rag swiped her mouth and cheekbone. The buzzing sound again and then presence of breath next to hers. He looked concerned, staring at her eyes, three inches from her face, and he whined, glancing back at the pill bottle lying on the bed. Nudging her face, whimpering, Harvey licked Kendall until she responded.

Clarity hit Kendall like a sharp paper cut. *The pills.* The buzzing sound continued this time in short bursts. Harvey continued to whine and nudge her until she sat up. She barely made it to the bathroom, vomiting her insides in the toilet. Harvey never took his eyes off her. What seemed like hours later, Kendall washed her face, brushed her teeth and returned to bed.

She pulled Harvey to her chest and hugged him with all the energy she had left in her body. He lay there with her, letting her hold him in her arms and cry. She couldn't stop the tears. She moaned, she cried, she yelled out Tim's name. Gasping for air, sobbing, the air sealed so tight in her chest burst, finally the anguish escaped.

She had no idea how long they lay there. A woman and her dog mourning the loss of a man like Tim Jackson. Every so often, the vibration of the phone would add to their sounds of sorrow. The level of light changed. The oversized photo canvas of Tim and her on their wedding night in the sunset on the beach of Puerto Morelos, Mexico, was coming into focus. Reds and oranges of the sea reflecting the sun's warmth, and their love for each other explosively glowing on their faces. She in a white halter wedding dress, Tim in white long-sleeved shirt and white pants.

She used to like waking up faced with the two of them first thing in the morning. Sometimes, depending on the sun's path, especially in the early spring, the light from the window would create an illusion of the surf moving in and out on the sand. She raised her head. He was staring at her. Tim's loving face and wind-blown dark hair with his arms wrapped around her, his gentle white smile, and the water dancing on the surf appeared to be turned to the bed. Normally, they were both looking at the sunset. The picture fell to the ground.

She never much believed in signs, as her pulse

quickened and she inhaled to catch her breath.

Why didn't the pills kill her? Kendall's heart froze then pounded. Tim would never have understood her desperate action. He wanted her to live, to pick up the pieces and experience life. As weak as she felt, something unfamiliar stirred inside her. A small glimmer of hope.

It was time. She bolted out of bed, it startled Harvey and he went flying across the room, panting with his long pink tongue hanging out, kind brown eyes staring at her. Somehow, things were going to change. She couldn't go on like this.

She used the house phone and left a message at the college about taking a personal day. It was six a.m., Thursday morning, almost sixteen months to the day when she lost the love of her life. Time to start living again, even if it was without Tim.

She didn't stop. Like a severe OCD patient, she packed up the bedspreads, the sheets, the pillows. She went through the cupboards in her kitchen carefully removing the photos of Tim she had taped inside every cabinet. Next, the doors, she had his photo attached to the back of closet doors, the bathroom door and her bedroom door.

Most of the photographs were duplicates, shots of Tim taken in the past six years, but only a dozen different pictures. A few from his childhood and several face shots of the two of them when Tim held up the iPhone. He had been an avid photographer of others, but avoided pictures of himself. Removing the photos off the refrigerator, she placed them in a large old Dunhill cigar box of Tim's. Like a robot, she methodically peeled photographs off every surface until her fingertips wanted to bleed. Every recorded copy of his face placed in a box except the canvas print in the bedroom and one beside the bed. She rearranged furniture, removed paintings from the wall which reminded her of him and yanked out nails and picture hooks. Simple, clean, bare walls. She moved rugs and relocated the white couch to face the fireplace. She scoured the house, packing everything up in boxes and bags. Systematically, pulling, folding, and making piles. As if it were anybody's clothing. Underwear, sweats, and shorts in one bag, T-shirts and button-downs in another. Jackets, sports coats and suits in a large box and two bags full of jeans and khaki pants.

She kept one worn sweatshirt from a bar in Evergreen, Colorado, holding it against her cheek for a brief moment and a shirt he loved from Ireland with a four leaf clover on it, and shoved them in the bottom drawer of her dresser as if she didn't want anyone to see. Flip-flops, dress shoes, boots, running shoes all thrown into a garbage bag. Her face glistened with sweat and dirt as this freaky adrenaline pumped into her veins.

When she finally stopped, the front room full of garbage bags and boxes, her gaze lingered on the liquor cabinet. She hesitated, opened the door, grabbed the dozen or so bottles of tequila in various stages of fullness and placed them in a box. She had tried to find solace in tequila—Tim's favorite liquor—a remedy to dull the pain. It never worked. She decided to move everything to the upstairs of the detached garage. Making a dozen trips back and forth, she carried the load to the bottom of the steps, Harvey on her heels watching every move. Kendall found the key, climbed the stairs like a superhero and without a second thought juggled the first load, opening the door with her arms holding three oversized bags.

The door swung open with a kick from her foot. Sweet musty tang filled her nostrils, a little cologne, hints of Ralph Lauren Polo, and a trace of a cigar. It was as if someone slapped her. She dropped to her knees hugging the bags, then with a shove a football coach would be proud of she moved them away placing her forehead on the dusty wooden floor, she extended her arms straight out. Unintentionally, she lay in Child's Pose, a position of rest in Yoga, powerless to move from his smell.

At six p.m., she stood, walked down the stairs, and took a shower. Mechanically, she leashed Harvey for a quick walk down the path, behind the house, through the woods, her legs on autopilot. As the falling light silhouetted the branches of the trees and the sounds of evening birds chattered, Kendall chose to live.

By eight p.m., she was driving back to the house in her black Saab with plastic bags filling the backseat full of white fluffy towels, soft sheets and a white down comforter. One solitary white vanilla candle from Bed Bath and Beyond sat on the seat beside her.

What seemed like moments to Kendall passed and the house was transformed. She lit the vanilla candle and turned on some classic John Mayer. She liked listening to him before knowing Tim; it was pre-Tim music, a safe choice, no images appeared in her mind.

Her stomach shouted at her, grumbling. Ready to order some won ton soup from the Chinese delivery place around the corner, she searched for her cell phone. Between the vomiting and the marathon clean-up, she was washed out. Adrenaline had taken over for the past fourteen hours, an inner force ecstatic she was alive had helped her survive a day when most people would not be able to function or crawl out of bed.

It was then Kendall saw the three missed calls and a message from Puerto Morelos, Mexico.

Chapter 5

"Hello, this is Scout Whitman. I'm calling for Tim Jackson. I'm following up on a letter I sent to an address in Westminster, Maryland. Umm, I've tried to email Tim over the past couple months and the emails are returned. Probably my email service in Mexico. I've been having issues with my server down here." Long pause. "I'm hoping this number is a way to reach him. I called before and didn't know if I should leave a message but, umm...this number was listed in the initial paperwork as an emergency contact for the trip."

Slight pause and clearing of the throat. "Please call me back as soon as possible. As I said in the letter, everything is arranged for the trip, the gear, the Sherpas, and the trespassing approvals. I wanted to confirm for the first week of May. Okay then...thanks."

Another pause; the caller was not done. "I'm calling from Puerto Morelos, Mexico, so please leave me a message at this number, someone will get it to me and I will call you back. From the US dial 011 638 5319987."

With her iPhone in her hands, Kendall kept replaying the message. Her exhausted mind created different scenarios of what the message could mean. *What approvals? What trip? First week of May?* Tapping the touch screen again, Kendall leaned her head nearer to the phone as if she'd missed something crucial; if she listened closer, maybe it would make sense.

Puerto Morelos, Mexico took Kendall back to a place of wonderful memories. They married, honeymooned and fell deeper in love with each other on the Riviera Maya coast of Mexico. In ten glorious, freeing days, they made their way from Cancun to Puerto Morelos to Playa Del Carmen to Tulum.

Just thinking about their honeymoon moved the corners of Kendall's mouth upward, a gesture she hadn't practiced in a long time.

They had rented a luxury beach villa. Days and time jumbled together as they took long walks on the beach, drank wine, made love, and sipped irresistible buttery tequila. White soft sand, flip-flops and bare feet, bright warm days with happy blue seas and bubbles from the waves hitting the shore stayed trapped in her mind forever. She wished she could be there right now, holding his hand.

Exploring the local towns, they had walked and talked for hours each day. Their skin glowed with warmth, her hair curly from the humidity, his black hair unruly and wavy from maneuvering in soft sheets. They tasted like salt. They constantly touched each other, his hand on her waist or her fingers running through the dark curly hair at the nape of the neck, no schedule, no appointments, and no agendas. They fed each other ceviche, lime-cured fish with fresh avocado, and kissed after each citrusy taste. Sipped hot sauce from raw oysters and dipped warm fried chips into mashed-up roasted tomatoes, drank *cervezas* on ice with salt rimming the glass and sampled private reserve tequilas. Mariachi music filled the air and local merchants' voices yelled out one-liners selling their wares.

Days and nights blended. They slept in the day; they lounged on the beach at night. She had dreamed of days like these. Although Tim had been married for twelve years, she had waited her whole life to meet him.

A husband. She remembered waking up looking out at the brilliant sparkly blue water, twisted in soft white sheets with Tim's arms wrapped around her naked body. On his left hand, she could see the platinum wedding band; joined together forever.

At night on the roof deck, completely private from another living being, they stretched out on the euro lounge chair made for two, counted falling stars, shared wishes, made love and slept breathing the sea air filling their lungs.

It was when they finally decided to put real clothes on and explore outside their newly created private sensual world in Puerto Morelos they discovered the Ruta de los Cenotes, Spanish for the "road of the cenotes."

"What is it again?" she remembers asking, never having heard the word before.

Tim poured her a sipping glass of tequila, Clase Azul, a wonderful buttery tequila discovered in Playa Del Carmen. They toasted and he wrapped his arms around her waist.

"A cenote is an underground cavern of fresh water. A beautiful sinkhole. A deep thing."

She was astounded by the cenotes. The fact, they were unknown and unfamiliar amazed her. The guidebook mentioned they were sacred to the Maya as they were the only resource for sweet fresh water in the

Yucatán jungle. Some believed the crystal-clear water had magical qualities; others believed they represented the entrance to the underworld.

Kendall read everything she could find on her iPad; she discovered the majority of cenotes were owned by private families. Certain cenotes would allow visitors access so they could zip line across, snorkel or swim. She would read to Tim from her research, "Did you know there are rumored to be over six thousand cenotes in the Yucatán Peninsula but less than a thousand are registered and only a few hundred marked on a map?" Or, "Did you know cave diving was strictly forbidden in the private cenotes unless authorized by a private guide?"

"Have you been inside one?" she asked.

"Yes, many times."

"Are they as magical and mysterious as they look?"

He kissed her and smiled at her eagerness. "Yes, they are as magical and mysterious as they look. Steve and I came down here during college and did some cave diving. Why, you want to explore one?"

She squealed and jumped up to hug him wrapping her legs around him.

She found it fascinating so many were on private land, inaccessible to the outside world. She remembered thinking how cool it would be to have a cenote in your backyard.

The picture of the Chichen Itza cenote, owned by the Mexican government, looked like a gaping hole or large well that opened in the middle of the jungle with rocks and trees lining the rim, descending deep into the earth. The color of the water mesmerizing. Here tourists could swim, but Tim stated he would take her to a more intimate cenote. She agreed with joy.

The day they visited the road of the cenotes, she was entranced with the clarity of the water and the brilliance of the colors. The freshwater holes formed by the rivers flowing underground in the Yucatán peninsula were made up of limestone porous rock, so where water gathered it formed spectacular caverns underneath the land. Sunlight hitting the water on the open cenotes shimmered and created a color that transfixed her to a land of make believe.

Before Tim's death, she had loved the water and scuba diving. Open-water certified, she surprised Tim with a vacation to Bonaire when they first started dating. It was in Bonaire where she noticed Tim and the water had a special connection. He seemed to be more beautiful in the water, glowing. In the cenotes, it was indescribable.

Tim had become a certified scuba diver when he was a child. His Uncle Dan, a strong force in Tim's life, took him to Mexico for two weeks when he was twelve. When he came home to Arizona, the joke his uncle told was, "Tim grew fins."

Tim's love of water continued, his summers spent in the little town on the Sea of Cortez in Mexico called Puerto Penasco with his Uncle Dan. Only a four-hour drive from Phoenix, Arizona, his uncle's work and connection with CEDO—Intercultural Center for the Study of Deserts and Oceans—fed Tim's desire and fascination with the sea.

Tim, his passion for the water and admiration for his Uncle Dan, surprised everyone by enlisting in the ROTC his senior year in high school and joining the

Navy. His brother, Tyler, one year behind Tim, followed in his footsteps, joined the ROTC as a sophomore and signed up for the Navy by the time he was a senior in high school. Tyler and Tim both made the first levels of acceptance into the Navy SEAL program at the same time and were determined to make it through the program.

The Navy SEAL era in his life was never discussed. He didn't want to talk about it. But on the honeymoon, he woke up yelling and crying out in the middle of the night. She woke up, holding him, wiping tears and kissing his cheek repeating, "It's okay, Tim." She heard him whisper, "Tyler", before he woke up.

Tim didn't talk about the nightmare.

It wasn't until the next night under the stars on the roof deck, with his arms around her, sipping tequila, Tim whispered the story, until the sun peeked out from the ocean horizon.

"It was after the last phase of Navy SEAL training we were both home for two days and that's when it happened. He drowned." His voice was a whisper. "Tyler and an old high school friend, Max, had been drinking all day and they were swimming laps underwater to see who could hold their breath the longest. It didn't make sense. He was a SEAL, an amazing swimmer. Tyler died holding his breath too long. My parents died thirty days later in a small plane crash."

That was all she ever heard about his SEAL days and of his parents' death.

Tim retired from the Navy and on the G.I. Bill attended Gettysburg College. He didn't ramble about college days or share ex-girlfriend stories. All she knew was his Uncle Dan lived in Gettysburg, Pennsylvania, and he helped his uncle out with his old local bar, during college.

It was in graduate school Tim met Tricia, his first wife, in a bar. She was visiting from New York and became pregnant right before Tim was due to graduate. Tim experienced graduation, marriage, and having a child like ordering a meal with the appetizer, entrée and dessert all coming to the table at once. Days after graduation, he moved to Scottsdale, Arizona, securing a job with an innovative Engineering, Science and Biotech firm.

Tim never talked about his ex-wife. Good or bad. All she knew was she cheated on him after twelve years of marriage. To make it worse, it was with her friend's husband. After they divorced, he moved back to Gettysburg and re-opened up the bar he inherited from his Uncle Dan, restoring and remodeling it into a contemporary speakeasy called "Jackson's Easy." She knew the dissolution of marriage had hurt him deeply, but he never discussed it.

****

Kendall lit the vanilla candle and sank back on the white cushions, when a black creature tried to climb into her lap. Even though Harvey weighed fifty-four pounds, he still thought he was a lapdog. He coiled his body into the littlest ball possible and curled up in her lap. As she stroked his soft black hair and patted his stomach, the exhaustion of the day took over.

For the first time since Tim died, Kendall skipped the glass of tequila and Harvey skipped his nightly vigil of waiting for Tim by the front window. Instead, he curled up and lay beside Kendall, both falling into a deep sleep.

****

Kendall woke up, Harvey beside her, sleeping on his back with his paws in the air, and the lone candle still burning. The scent of sweet vanilla filled the air, grounding her in the present and she recognized the gnarly pain in her abdomen. Her mind, still a little foggy from the day's events, she remembered the telephone call from Mexico. Did she dream it? She was certain she didn't as she went into the kitchen searching for food. She took two slices of wheat bread, some homemade strawberry jam and a jar of JIF peanut butter and made a sandwich for herself and a bowl of dog food with peanut butter on it for Harvey.

It was four-thirty a.m. when she and Harvey crawled into the new white sheets. The plethora of pictures of Tim on her bedside, gone.

A change was going to come. Her heart seemed stronger, her mind clearer. She needed a wake-up call. It was hard to believe she had actually tried swallowing all the pills. Before Tim's death, suicide would never have crossed her mind, never…but she had a feeling, call it an intuition, call it strength from above, change was coming and someone was looking out for her.

And for the first time in a long time, change didn't scare her or make her incredibly sad.

Chapter 6

With strong arms, he lifted his body up and out of the crystal turquoise liquid with little or no effort. He gently shook off the beads of water, flung his dark, wet hair out of his face, scaled the limestone ledge to the ladder, climbed up, and pulled himself up to the edge in a simple gesture.

She was waiting for him when he walked out of the lush green jungle and into the clearing. He smiled as he moved toward her. Her gaze roamed appreciatively over his body. She'd told him he had the body of an Olympic swimmer with the grace of a male ballerina.

"It will be here before we know it." Her long brown hair was wavy in the humidity, her body toned and petite under a colorful flowing Mexican sarong, her skin tan from days of sunshine. Her gracious smile enhanced her face.

"I know," he said, smiling. "We've waited a long time. Perhaps this time it will really happen."

"Do you think it will happen?" she asked.

He clasped her warm hand in his. "We can only hope and believe."

Chapter 7

Kendall could tell by the brightness in the room, and how the light hit the canvas print of Tim and her on the wall, it was late. The waves were not moving. She had overslept. She surged out of bed feeling remarkably energized; Harvey jumped dramatically as if to emphasize how late it was, and barked. Twenty minutes to shower and make it to her office. Stripping her clothes off, she walked into the bathroom and turned the hot water on.

Grabbing a black pinstriped skirt and black blouse, she was ready. She looked in the mirror. Behind her in the reflection were the new white comforter and the clutterless dressers void of all the pictures, except one. Her fingers fumbled with the buttons of the black blouse as she peeled it off and put on a light blue one instead. She liked black; even before Tim died she sought out cute black outfits, but in the last year and a half, it had become a uniform. *Time for a change.* Adding a belt and boots, she kissed Harvey on the nose and was off.

Grabbing her iPhone, she took a sharp intake of breath...*the message from Puerto Morelos. She didn't dream it.* She would barely make it to the nine a.m. Director's meeting. *I'll put it out of my mind until the meeting's over, then I'll make the call.*

****

Kendall's foot moved up and down against the bottom wheel of her chair. As hard as she tried to keep her mind focused on the upcoming graduation ceremonies at Western Maryland College, she could not stop thinking about Mexico, and the message left on her inbox. Staring at the hands on the clock, watching Frank Alexander's mouth talk about Commencement services, back to staring at the hands of the clock, back to his mouth. Gripping the bottom of her chair, she tried to calm down, taking soft deep breaths and holding her foot still, she did her best to appear interested in the meeting.

Finally, the meeting ended. Her heart raced and she stood up. Pulling her phone out of her skirt pocket, she headed for the outside.

Kendall concentrated on each stair. She didn't want to meet anyone or have any discussions; she just wanted to make the call. She rushed down the four flights of stairs and escaped into the outside air.

Like a newborn opening his eyes after a nap and realizing the wonder of light in the world, for the first time in what seemed like forever, she noticed the warmth of the sun and the prisms of light shining through the towering trees on campus. Western Maryland College was a picturesque campus, filled with green leaves, spring flowers, and a party of old sturdy trees dancing in the wind and leaning against old buildings. Built on a hill overlooking the town, it was covered with emerald grass sprinkled with a gardener's dream of crayon box colors of flowers lining the walks. Peaceful and inspiring; anyone could study here. Sidewalks meandering through the campus, either of bronze earthy cobblestone or red brick pavers, completed the canvas. Only 1500 students had the privilege of attending this small, private liberal arts school. It was the oldest co-ed college south of the Mason-Dixon line, started in 1867 after the Civil War. WMC quietly touted an alumni roster of unique, prominent men and women, not well known to most, but whose actions made a difference in significant outcomes in military and government history. Its strong PhD program in biochemistry and bioscience was in close proximity to the nation's capital, Gettysburg, and the mountains of Catoctin.

The sounding of the bells in the church tower indicated it was eleven a.m. She headed down to the park bench on the golf course pond to make the call. The phone was ringing. Kendall knew she was calling Mexico because of the long ring tone. A woman answered the phone, *"Buenos dias, Scout's Dive Shop."*

Her heart beating rapidly, she said, *"Buenos dias, hola, Señor Scout Whitman por favor?"* She was out of practice on her little known Spanish. No response. "Do you speak English?"

"Si. Yes. Mr. Scout he is not here, I take messages for him. Would you like to leave a message?"

"Yes, this is Kendall Jackson."

"Sorry, Chango Jackson?"

"No, ummm, Tim Jackson's wife returning Scout's call about the trip. He left Tim a message, I mean he left a message on our phone about a trip…Are you a dive shop?" Her heart was pounding like a fast drum. *Tim had scheduled a dive trip? When?*

"Yes, this is Scout's Dive Shop."

"Could you ask him to call me at this number today after four?"

After repeating the phone number twice, and spelling Tim Jackson as the contact name, as the name Kendall made no translation in Spanish, she put the phone back in her pocket and wished, with every jumping nerve in her body, she had not dumped what was left of her pills into the toilet last night. Her skin crawled with sensation, itchy, tight with pulsating blood. She was anything but calm, and the idea of holding onto something regarding Tim was probably the wrong road to lead her mind down. *When did he plan a dive trip...he has been gone for sixteen months?*

It was an excruciating, long day at work. The Student Government Association last year, had selected the founder of Twitter, Jack Dorsey, to be their Commencement speaker and arrangements were finalized. Now due to a schedule change and a court battle over Twitter IPO, they were left with finding someone two months before graduation.

The task of securing a speaker was the highest priority to the administration. It was the final event of each student's career at Western Maryland College and the message was of the utmost importance. After the students reluctantly agreed to give up on Mark Zuckerberg, the top three names on the list were all technology-driven.

Generation Y and Z heroes. With over a billion users on Facebook, the world was tech crazy and social media obsessed. The students had even suggested the Commencement speaker be on a webcast or Skype. The committee insisted on an in-person speaker.

Time was running out to secure a speaker at this date. The fourth backup speaker was the only one who was an alumnus of the college, well, sort of an alumnus.

After taking Mark Zuckerberg off the list, it consisted of Tim Westergren, founder of Pandora Radio, Connor Pope, founder of 'What is it?'—a website and hot phone app that helped users identify objects such as insects, plants, trees, animals and food—and Conrad Nathaniel, a thirty-something alumnus biologist who was working on a scientific process whereby humans could breathe underwater.

She studied his bio. The Conrad Nathaniel family, one of the biggest benefactors of the college since its inception in 1876. Numerous buildings named after his grandparents and great-great-grandparents. But unlike his ancestors, Conrad attended his freshman year at Western Maryland before transferring to the University of California, Santa Barbara, majoring in Ecology, Evolution, and Marine Biology. The amazing thing about Conrad, not only did he graduate with honors from UC Santa Barbara, he completed his remaining credits from Western Maryland online, and successfully graduated with degrees from both schools. Now, based outside of Baltimore, he was a prominent figure in MCDB—Molecular, Cellular, and Developmental Biology—leading the world in underwater technology.

Kendall remembered a conversation with Steve, Tim's partner at the bar, stating Conrad Nathaniel came in Jackson's Easy last year, after Tim's death, and expressed his sympathy for the loss, leaving Kendall a card with a sizable donation made in Tim's name to the college. When Steve handed her the donation card, she remembered wondering how Tim had known him.

Well, if I can't get the other two tech wizards to speak...maybe the connection with Tim will help me secure Conrad Nathaniel. Kendall was sure she had sent him a thank you note, the donation was quite a large sum of money, but she had never met the man.

Her iPhone vibrated. An exceptionally long line of numbers flashed on the screen; it was Mexico calling.

Chapter 8

Scout Whitman turned off the key to the Jeep and let out a deep sigh. Looking up to the sky through his polarized Ray-Bans, he could see the gray outline of the rain clouds rapidly covering the blue. He stretched back, grabbed anything that shouldn't get wet lying on the backseat and stuffed it into the long yellow dry bag.

He had just completed teaching a three-day training course for cavern diving with four seniors from Arizona State University. Four different dives in three caves in three days. The guys had done a great job and had been easy to work with. He burped. Maybe he should have stopped at the fourth Negro Modelo Especial beer and fifth shot of tequila. The ASU guys, twenty years younger, were diving and playing hard. He tossed the age difference aside like a wet bar napkin and kept up with them drink after drink. When he left the Palapa Bar, the four guys waved, bleary-eyed, as he walked sober as a Christian woman coming out of church. He could hear them as he hoisted his body into the jeep, cheering each other on as he pulled out of the parking lot and drove the short drive to his dive shop.

Lily was sitting on a stool behind the counter, with her legs crossed, staring at the computer. Petite with doe-brown eyes, she had lovely black hair, which sometimes turned red and once purple, but now sported blond ends. Scout noticed she spent quite a bit of time today applying her makeup and extra-long black lashes. Red lips, red nails, and black eyeliner with silver shadow completed the picture.

"*Buenas tardes*, Scout." Lily flashed her dazzling new white smile, since just recently her braces had come off. She held out a phone message slip on hot pink paper. She had copied hundreds, perhaps even thousands of these "while you were gone" notes on fluorescent sheets. Scout had fifty calls a year.

"You have a message, from a gringo, someone you called calling you back." Her mouth went back to a line as she stared at the computer.

He was relieved to see the message was from Tim Jackson. It had been a long time, almost two years, since he had contact with Tim. In the last six months, he had emailed him repeatedly, tried numerous phone numbers, and finally left a message on his wife's phone yesterday. He was looking forward to the cave diving trip with Tim and his son. Tim visited him almost two years ago, rented a few tanks, and paid him to take him out for a day of diving.

He remembered the day distinctly. Tim had a commanding look but a sincere, gentle demeanor. Women would find him attractive with a movie star quality, some famous actor sort of resemblance. He was confident enough in his manhood to notice when a man possessed something special and he knew to most women Tim was something special.

He had enjoyed the day as if he were diving with an old friend who was part fish. Time flew by with easy conversation and stories about cave diving. As a leader in cave diving expeditions, with more cave dives under his belt than anyone in the Western Hemisphere they discussed his explorations and mapping of various cenotes in the Yucatán which were the first English published books on cenotes. Tim asked him intriguing questions about certain dives and the stories flowed easily.

Packing up the gear and closing up the boat, Tim pulled two beers out of a cooler and handed one to Scout. "Buy you a beer?"

They sat down on his little deck under a beautiful leaning palm tree, looking out at the sea with the color of the sky turning orange, a warm hue signaling a day's end. Tim pulled out a long round cylinder out of his backpack.

"I want to hire you as a guide for a diving trip for my son's eighteenth birthday."

He presented a hand-drawn map, noticeably old by the writing and numbers on the scale, but preserved and in excellent condition. Scout didn't recognize this area or underground cavern system. Cenotes for the most part were privately owned and the cenotes in the area Tim wanted to dive were definitely off limits and had been for as long as Scout had been in the area.

"It's a difficult area to access by any vehicle and it's private property." Most unexplored cenotes were unexplored for a reason, they were passed down with the land from generation to generation with no access to the public.

"I understand. I have permission from the land owners." Tim presented a letter in Spanish signed by the owners of the land, sealed with a *notario* stamp allowing Tim Jackson and his son Ryder and three guides access into the area. Attached to it was a much smaller copy of the hand-drawn map, barely readable.

"It's a special present for my son. I want him to be part of a discovery on his eighteenth birthday," Tim said. "This trip is confidential. I know you are in the cave diving circuit, but no one should know. I promised the owners I would not bring in any tourists or public interest. Between us. Understood?"

Scout nodded as Tim handed him his credentials which showed he had the highest level of DiveCon, Master scuba diver and various certifications in cave diving training, as well as advanced rescue diver. Scout, who had logged more than 5000 cave dives, was impressed.

Tim pulled a large envelope from his backpack. "I want to hire you to arrange this trip for me and my son. A ten-day trip of cenote diving, with time in the beginning to refresh my son on cavern techniques. He's certified open-water, rescue diver, and has a cavern certification from Florida, but has never dove a cenote."

The bulging envelope was a lot of cash to be carrying around in Mexico.

"Let me know if you need more money, but this should cover all the transportation, camping equipment, diving equipment, and food for all three of us. I'm thinking same time next year, May first is my son's eighteenth birthday."

Without counting it, he knew it was more than enough. Intrigued by the cash, Tim Jackson's character, his vibe, and the chance to explore an unknown cenote that until now had been unheard-of and off-limits to the diving world he happily agreed.

"One more thing," Tim said as he pulled out a letter. "Can you sign this?"

It was a brief nondisclosure clause about the

confidentiality of the map and the residents' privacy, a paragraph in Spanish in one column translated in English on the next. Scout read it, signed the letter and wrote up a quick receipt for the trip. He stumbled on the amount; he hadn't counted the money but knew there was a lot of money in the bag. Rolls of hundreds with rubber bands around them.

Tim stopped him and said, "I don't need a receipt, just your word and your confidentiality." He stuck his hand out and as their hands and eyes met, Tim asked, "I trust that should cover everything?"

"Everything," Scout answered, thinking two things—one, this would really help him out, and two, he could finally publish his film and photography book on cenotes. Scout remembered contemplating how one moment can change your life.

After he had taken all his information, email, and specifics they agreed to keep in touch to finalize the date for next year.

"Do you have a safe?" Tim asked.

"A safe, yes, I will keep the money locked up."

"Put the little map in it, keep it away from wandering eyes and don't let anyone see it. I need your word on this."

Tim held out his hand again, they shook on it.

Over the next year, he gathered everything he needed for the trip, sparing no expense as he had been paid more than ten times what he would have normally charged. He emailed Tim twice with updates.

One year later, the only response from Tim was a quick email:

From: Tim Jackson
Subject: Puerto Morelos Trip

Date: November 10, 2014
To: Scout Whitman
Scout,

I apologize for the short notice but I need to reschedule my son's dive trip. My son Ryder has become involved in a contract job with a television show and he is unable to take vacation until they finish the second season. My thoughts are to reschedule it next year, same time in May. I will make it his nineteenth birthday surprise. I hope he will not be prohibited from taking vacations from any new job. I'll tell him on his eighteenth birthday so he has a year to plan time off. Again, I apologize for the change in schedule. Please let me know if you see any issues with waiting a year. I will be in touch with the exact dates closer to next year; I'm still thinking beginning of May. Thank you in advance for postponing this trip for me, I will be in touch as soon as I know more.

Best,

Tim Jackson

Scout took a weekend last year to drive out near the cenote Tim wanted to dive with his son. He tried to follow the small copy of the hand-drawn map; Tim had kept the large one in the cylinder and taken it with him. The little one was difficult to read. His attempts to follow it faced him with locked gates. The entire area fenced in with angry barbed wires and a natural jungle barrier, with old worn small signs in Spanish, "Warning, Private, NO Trespassing" hanging everywhere.

He found himself in the middle of nowhere. One hundred fifty miles away from any town of significant size on rugged roads might as well have been five hundred miles away. His cell service was nonexistent. It was on that trip he decided to buy a satellite phone for emergencies on the upcoming excursion. He also decided, given the remoteness of the place, it might be worth renting a boat for a drop-off and pick-up.

The satellite phone sat in the box in his jumble of an office. Since he didn't have a phone in his beach house, he would have to shoo Lily off the computer. Tim Jackson had not responded to him for over a year. Well, he still wanted to see the cavern system, and Tim paid him a lot of money, so better late than never.

"Lily, can you dial the number for me on Skype?" Scout held out the pink piece of paper.

She pretended she was so engrossed in whatever she was reading she didn't hear or see the paper four inches from her head. "Lily, por favor, dial the number for me…" She looked up, showed her white teeth in a fake smile, handed him the earplugs, and her hand flew across the keyboard.

"It's ringing, Señor Scout."

Chapter 9

"I'm sorry, is this Tim's wife? Mrs. Jackson? I thought I was calling your husband back, my assistant Lily said Tim Jackson called."

Kendall took a deep breath; at this point she didn't feel like explaining.

"No, this is Kendall Jackson, his wife, I called back this morning, after you left a message on my phone yesterday, regarding a trip my husband planned in Puerto Morelos?"

"Yes, does your husband want to reschedule the trip for this May? I guess that would be your son's nineteenth birthday? Since he postponed it on his eighteenth birthday?"

"My husband postponed a trip last May?" Her heart picked up speed—as she knew this was not possible—it was seven months after Tim was declared dead.

"Yes, in November he emailed me and said your son had a contract with some television show or something like that and couldn't take any vacations." Scout paused, "Would you rather have me call back when I can speak with your husband, Mrs. Jackson?" Scout cleared his throat. "I think I should wait to speak with him, can you please have him call me?"

"November of last year?" Kendall whispered.

She wasn't sure if he heard her and her tone

became a little higher-pitched and louder. "November of last year, my husband emailed you about a trip he had planned for this coming May?" Kendall's voice quivered as she asked the question.

"Umm, no Ma'am, sorry, it was November of the year before, he emailed and said the May trip for last year would need to be pushed back to the next year, which is next month, so I just wanted to check in with him and see if he wanted to postpone it again or take his son next month. I have everything ready to go even a satellite phone." Scout paused again. "Is there a good time to talk to Mr. Jackson?"

Kendall silent for what seemed like five minutes, couldn't say the words.

"Hello, Mrs. Jackson, are you still there?"

"Yes, I'm still here...it's my husband that's not...here...at all." Kendall's voice cracked, and she let out a gust of air she was holding in her lungs, she swallowed and held the tears back. "My husband is dead."

Scout was a bit slow to reply.

"I'm sorry, Mrs. Jackson, I had no idea...ummm, my deepest sympathies to you and your family." A long minute of silence filled the air. "I'm very sorry."

"It's been eighteen months, but it still feels like yesterday." Kendall took a deep breath.

"Well, Mrs. Jackson, I could still take your son and a friend on the trip, since your husband wanted him to go...it's a cenote dive trip, private and comfortable, all the gear, lessons included or I can...refund the money back to you, somehow, umm...I mean your husband paid in cash and he wanted it to be a surprise for your son. Seemed very important to him." He sounded like he was rambling.

****

Kendall touched the end button on the screen of her iPhone, her phone shaking and her finger still paused on the screen. Her eyes locked on some point as if frozen in place. She put the phone down and ran her left hand through her hair replaying the conversation in her mind.

Chapter 10

Ryder tried to move his arm on the chair rest, biting the inside of his cheek. He disliked Southwest Airlines because they didn't have First Class. Head down, shades on, he acted immersed in the Netflix movie playing on his iPad. He didn't want to be recognized. East Coasters seemed to be glued to the show *Paradise Valley*. He liked the crowds in Scottsdale, most girls and guys were self-centered enough to not make such a big deal of a reality star as they did on the East Coast.

His publicist/manager, Courtney Clay, was in his space. She was accompanying him to a paid appearance at some sixteen-year-old's birthday party in New Jersey. The father willing to pay $12,000 for Ryder to go to his daughter's sweet sixteen party. From the picture, she looked hot and not so sweet for turning sixteen, probably why Courtney was tagging along with him.

As long as there are no cameras filming at the party, I'll be fine. He tried to swallow, as his pulse picked up.

He still hadn't confessed his social anxiety phobia. When the camera light turned on, the nausea, sweating and rapid heartbeat made it difficult to breathe. It seemed to be getting worse. Lately, he avoided any situation where there might be a video or movie camera. Something about a piece of film capturing parts of his life made him instantly feel a taut squeeze on his chest. He knew it was irrational.

He so wished his father were alive to ask his advice. If he could just talk to him, explain to him what was happening in front of the camera. He would be the one person who would understand him. He would not overreact and he would keep it private.

His father was a private person, never talking much about his Navy days or Uncle Tyler who died. Unlike his mother, who couldn't keep anything personal or private. "What's on her mind is on her lips," his father had said under his breath many times. She would gossip, as if she were stating a fact. Any secret or issue would be shared with the whole family, sisters, mother, father, and cousins, who would then blab it to someone else and post it on Facebook.

Last year his future had seemed so bright, he finally knew what he was going to do with the rest of his life, and now this stupid phobia was making everything a disaster. Just thinking about it tightened his stomach. It was getting worse.

****

After the birthday party, Ryder returned to his hotel room, stating he was tired. He searched the Internet for information about social phobias, phobias in front of a camera, social anxiety…anything that would give him some advice on how to get a handle on this anxiety. He needed a grip on this. At the party, a young girl was shooting a video with her iPhone and he started sweating. He wasn't going to get rich or famous with this phobia.

Glancing at his phone, he noticed three missed

calls, all from Kendall. Kendall was the last person Ryder wanted to talk to. He gritted his teeth. *Stay out of my life. Stop calling me.* Just speaking to her reminded him of his father's death, he wasn't going to call her back. He didn't have to, she wasn't family and he wasn't going to listen to the voicemail blinking on his phone, which he was sure was from her.

Not finding much on the Internet on social phobia anxiety, he lost interest. He found a few books, counseling options and possibly, hypnosis. He watched a YouTube video on hypnosis therapy and bookmarked it for later.

Bored, he decided he would listen to the voicemail he had ignored for the last three hours. He knew who it was from...not that he had any intention of calling her back.

The voicemail as he suspected was from Kendall. A long message explaining she needed to talk to him right away and to call her back as soon as he got the message. She had ended with a sad little stupid voice stating, "Ryder, I hope everything is going good in your life, I miss you and I love you...I really need you to call me back as soon as you get this. It's important. It's about your father. Please."

He wasn't going to call her back. Even though it was about his father it was probably something she found and wanted to give him. Or it could be about the college fund, which was the last thing Ryder wanted to think about right now. She was probably trying to persuade him to move back to Gettysburg and go to Western Maryland College, work at his father's bar, which should have been left to him. His face became rigid and he clenched his teeth. Kendall only knew his father for six years, and he left her everything.

He would never, ever move back to Western Maryland College. He had a future in television. He just had to get over this phobia. He loved the atmosphere of television, film, the studio, the whole environment; he did not need to be in front of a camera, as long as he made the big bucks. Screenwriter or a director, he thought as he closed his eyes. Screenwriters were millionaires and famous.

****

The knock on the door jolted Ryder from a dream about diving with his father. His flight home was in less than two hours. Great, he'd forgotten to set the alarm. Jumping up, he opened the door with a sheet wrapped around him. Courtney, ready to snarl at him for being late, stopped in mid-sentence. Her expression changed from angry to embarrassed with a little hint of flirty in seconds. Her eyes ran down Ryder's towel-clothed half-naked body.

"Sorry, Courtney, I guess the hotel never put in the wake-up call…I'll be right there, just give me ten." He shut the door and dropped the sheet, before he could hear Courtney's response. The look in her eyes surprised him; he forgot how even good-looking girls responded to him.

In the car on the way to the airport, he noticed Courtney stealing glances at him. Oh, please do not hit on me, just give me space. He flipped open his iPad and noticed several new messages on Facebook and a text. One text and a private message was from Kendall, they read exactly the same: Ryder please call me back today. It's urgent. I need to speak with you about your father.

Ryder did not want to call her back and wouldn't.

He didn't want to talk on the phone, especially to Kendall. He replied on Facebook. *On a plane flying back from New Jersey to Arizona. It's been really busy, just text me or message me what you need to tell me.*

Somewhere in the air space above Kansas, Ryder got the reply from Kendall.

He couldn't believe it. His father had planned a diving trip to Mexico for his eighteenth birthday, and postponed it a few days before he died, because of Ryder's commitment with *Paradise Valley*. She wrote, "Ryder, this was obviously very important to your father, he planned and paid for it almost two years ago. Will you go with me on this trip next month for your nineteenth birthday? Do this one last thing for your father?" And, for the hundredth time she asked him to call her when he got home, no matter what the time.

He used to love diving; it was something he did with his father since he was ten years old. The water a soft warm blanket wrapped around him and the closeness of his father created a happy place. For the last six years of his father's life, they had managed to do ten dives a year. Their special bonding until he married Kendall. He tried two dive trips with his dad and Kendall, after they were married. Their special bond vanished with Kendall along. Diving, he was not interested in diving, especially with Kendall.

Ryder recalled the conversation with his dad in November. It wasn't just any conversation; it was the last conversation with his father. He replayed it a thousand times in his head. He wanted to go on the Blue Hole dive trip with his father, but he was prohibited time off for the next year because of his contract. Ryder had never seen the Blue Hole and he wanted to experience it with his father…together.

"Can you save the Blue Hole dive for me?" Ryder had asked. They were eating pizza at their favorite restaurant in Scottsdale called Humble Pie.

"Save the Blue Hole for you, huh?" His dad smiled at him and grabbed his shoulders jokingly. "Now that you're a big movie star, I have to be on your schedule…is that how it works? Now, I see how it is." He grabbed a piece of cheesy pizza and paused before taking a bite. "Sorry, son, it's too late, we have the dive all set, I'm really sorry you can't make it. How about we do some special diving next May? Just the two of us." He smiled with excitement like a little kid about to tell a secret. "Celebrate your birthday, somewhere extraordinary."

"Can't do May either, Dad, the contract states I can't take any vacations until the following year."

"Wow! Even for your eighteenth birthday. You must be serious about this acting thing. You'll be an old movie star by then." Tim slapped the table. "So, Mr. Ryder Jackson, do you like this television work, that's taking all your time?" His one eyebrow arched high as he did when he was trying to look inquisitive. "Are the movies in your future? I mean is this what you want to do with the rest of your life?"

"I think so, Dad, it comes easy to me and the money is not bad—or the girls."

His dad was quiet for a long minute. "Well, when you're rich and famous, you can take me to the Blue Hole and we can dive it together."

The smell of garlic and loud cheering from the patrons diverted their attention to discover the Arizona Diamondbacks had scored, getting closer to winning the

World Series. The rest of the night, laughs and one-liners passed between a father and a son. Like nestling back in an old leather chair, cozy and comfortable, all was right with the world.

Ryder had to be on set first thing in the morning, so they called it an early night. His father dropped him off and hugged him. If Ryder had only known. There in the concrete driveway of his mother's house, it was the last moment to gaze upon his father's face and feel his loving strength, he would have never gone to bed early. He would have hugged him harder; asked him his thoughts on breaking into movies or what he thought about celebrities. He would have discussed hot girls, sex and asked all the questions of the universe he needed answers to.

At seventeen, not for a minute did he imagine this would be the last time he laid eyes on his father. He struggled to replay the moment. It was getting more worn and fuzzy each time he tried to rewind the conversations in his mind. He asked himself the question a hundred times, what would have happened if he had gone on the Blue Hole dive with his father, would he be here right now? Would his father be alive?

It was a crazy accident, the probability of being struck by lightning or winning a billion-dollar lottery card would have been higher. His father was diving with two other experienced divers and a boat captain in the Blue Hole. One moment descending slowly together to 110 feet and suddenly at breakneck speed, his father plummeted.

How could his weights be so heavy? Both divers stated one minute they were descending slowly together, clearing out every ten feet, and then his dad dropped past them, as if he were a balloon full of air and someone punctured it...falling. All they could see was his bubbles, lots and lots of bubbles. One minute he was in their field of visibility, next, he was gone.

Frantically they looked for him, trying to descend slowly in their panic. When they spotted movement, both divers realized it was a group of large steel-gray sharks swimming in the hazy depth. Ryder couldn't imagine the deep black water full of fins, and searching frantically for your partner while trying to dive at appropriate speed with the sharks swimming below you. It seemed horrific. When he dove with his father, they were always in constant sight of each other. His father was a master diver. How did it go so wrong?

They found his regulator hose, bitten off and floating. The damage on the equipment confirmed to be made by sharks, great white to be specific. The Belizean Coast Guard was called immediately for the search and rescue. They had jurisdiction over the Blue Hole and, unfortunately, this was not a unique occurrence.

The BCG continued to search for the body, Thursday afternoon and all day Friday. There had been several shark attacks in the past, in the Blue Hole, but none reported recently. Kendall and his dad's business partner in the bar, Steve, flew down to Belize on Friday and assisted in a private search until dusk on Sunday. The BCG had the final jurisdiction and after searching and spotting a great white shark in the area, the balance of probabilities ruled "accidental death" based on the two diving companions' matching statements and the overwhelming evidence when parts of his diving gear surfaced.

Kendall buried an empty box. Ryder had a hard time understanding the sense of the empty box, but his father's diving gear rested inside beside his Uncle Dan in a cemetery plot not too far from Jackson's Easy. He squinted his eyes remembering the piercing shots of the twenty-one-gun salute from the Navy and the burning smell of gunpowder.

Dive trip? Dive trip with Kendall? Kendall was crazy. He certainly wouldn't have anything to do with it or with her. She was really losing it. Maybe he should get her some medication. Take her to the DUN playground. She needed help.

Chapter 11

It had to be around here somewhere.

Kendall's tired arms threw the black garbage bag, heavy with clothes, against the others in the corner. A layer of fuzz filled the air, covering the floor, windowsills, and furniture.

Even with the dust, a lingering smell of Polo and musk, mixed in with a hint of cigar and wood climbed up her nostrils. Inhaling, shoulders raised and released, Kendall's eyes moistened, and a familiar sharp pain in her stomach made her slump to the office floor.

Where was Tim's dive bag? It was hard for her to remember what she brought back from Belize after Tim's death. Steve had been there helping to arrange another search in the Blue Hole. It was a fuzzy time. When the Belizean government ruled the official death, she couldn't comprehend much of anything. Everything felt wrong, and she tried to wake up from the nightmare going on in her head. What she packed, what she wore, or if she packed anything was lost in her mind. One item she remembered, Tim's vintage leather traveler bag.

Like a child carrying a safety blanket close to her heart, Kendall would lower her nose to the clothes inside his bag and inhale his scent; she hugged his leather traveler bag like a pillow the whole way home. It was all she had left. When she packed everything up

53

in her marathon cleaning day, she left his leather traveler in the bedroom closet, unpacked. It was the last thing with him; she liked having it in her closet.

Sitting on the floor, Kendall noticed something catching the light under the bookcase. Sticking her hand underneath the bottom shelf, she could feel a suitcase of some kind wedged in under the shelf, a tight fit. She had a sudden flash of a steel-like briefcase sitting in Tim's office when they first started dating. She remembered making a joke about his titanium burglar-proof briefcase, "so strong even you cannot get in it." She could not recall noticing it after they got married.

Well, maybe it was stuck under the bookcase, all this time. She tried to pull it out but it caught in the shelf's legs. She yanked it with all her strength, bracing her body with her feet. She soon realized to get it out she would have to move all the books off the shelves and the bookcase. *Must have been here a long time,* she wiped her dusty fingers. It was as if the bookcase were built on top of it. She would deal with the briefcase later. Right now, her focus was on finding the dive bag, hoping something was relevant to the Puerto Morelos trip Tim had planned for Ryder.

Dive bag, where are you?

She hadn't thought about it since the funeral, was it left in Belize?

That's it, Steve has it. Steve is the one who put his mask and snorkel in the empty coffin.

Grabbing her phone, she touched Steve Crawford's name and face on the iPhone screen. It went directly to an impersonal mailbox. It exasperated her most people did not have a personalized voicemail message. Most of the students on campus rarely checked voice messages.

She and Tim used to laugh about technology, make jokes how the world would evolve into humanity where people lost their voice because no one talked to each other—only texted, blogged, or updated their status. Children would be forced to take classes to learn how to talk and socialize. It made her think of Ryder and how she couldn't get him to pick up the phone and just talk to her, call her back and have an actual conversation.

Kendall mumbled out loud, "Doesn't anyone answer their phone anymore?"

She looked at her watch. eight p.m. Steve should be behind the bar at Jackson's Easy.

****

When she pulled into the parking lot, she had the strangest feeling. Kendall had been here hundreds of times to meet Tim, but tonight she had a sensation at the back of her neck, as if someone was watching her. Impossible. She looked around the empty parking lot.

Only a few cars were left on the street and in the small lot adjacent to Jackson's Easy. Most folks driving by would not have given the dim lighting on the old stone blasted building a second glance. No neon bar signs, no loud music blaring out, nothing to make you think it was the local watering hole. She parked beside Steve's black Carrera2 soft-top, the sight of it stirring up memories of happy road trips. She was glad Steve was at the bar. She decided to tell him about Tim's birthday dive trip for Ryder. Maybe Tim had mentioned it to him; perhaps he could supply a little more information.

Staring at the door to Jackson's Easy, she closed her eyes, biting her top lip. *If only he would be here when she opened the heavy old door, as he was a thousand times before.* Her heart ached. The lump reappeared in her throat and the moisture clouded her eyes. Time did not ease the pain. The want, the desire to have someone here with her was so overwhelming she wasn't sure if she could step inside.

She thought of the night when it all began: Jackson's Easy had been voted in the Top 10 Best Bar category of *Washingtonian Magazine* and she had persuaded her co-workers to come check out this historic landmark. The article stated the bar, a tribute to the 1920s, was at one time a cigar shop from 1922-1933, but it was a front. The basement had a cabinet built behind a masonry wall, rumored to be a hiding place for the Underground Railroad. It also had a wine room with a fake wall, where ancient cupboards held the once illegal potions, now available at any 7-11.

The work group was in good spirits, it was Friday, a chance for everyone to blow off steam and de-stress. They barged in laughing, stumbling in the door, after figuring out how to enter from the not so obvious outside bar entrance. First, they had to push a button, really a buzzer, and speak the password in order to gain access. Candles, low lighting, and a mellow luminosity created an ambiance of soft conversations and privacy. A fireplace was burning in the back, casting a soft glow on all who walked in. This was not a bright, crowded, loud sports bar. No, this was historical casualness with Washington politicians who lived in the bedroom communities of DC mixing with local Gettysburg residents. Some relaxed in their T-shirts and jeans, and others with ties undone and suit coats on the chair beside them, happy to be out of the limelight. It was the spot for those who wanted a drink in a quiet, cool, and comfortable place with character.

The house rules of Jackson's Easy were printed on the entrance wall:

Speak softly or easy—thus "speak easy"—a term coined in history to speak quietly, not draw attention to yourself, especially if you are asking for liquor…

No yelling at your bartender,
No use of cell phones,
No photography,
No loud dancing, and
No actions to call attention to yourself.

Al Jolson's melodic voice filled the dimly lit room accented with dark wood and cozy lighting. It was impossible to know who settled in the ultra-comfortable high back chairs, quietly going unnoticed. The main floor of the bar was much bigger than it appeared, and several small cubbies tucked into the back corners.

Kendall and her colleagues congregated at an empty round pub table in the corner. Kendall read the house rules on the wall out loud, and before her burly colleague Ken could yell his typical husky voice to the bartender, she grabbed money and went up to the bar to order the table a round of drinks.

Tim was talking to someone at the bar, with a pen behind his ear and a devilish look. He looked at her, kept talking and looked again. He had smiled at his friend and said, "Excuse me, Skip, let me help this patient lady with a drink."

His smile was contagious and confident. In the low light, his eyes grabbed her attention; they were an unusual color. Instantly she was racking her brain for whom he resembled…Rob Lowe meets George Clooney with light eyes? Is that a possible combination? Not quite, he had his own unique look, she decided, a very interesting combination. Uncomfortably handsome. Her heart raced as she ordered and he made eye contact. She went back to the table empty-handed and a little self-conscious at her physical reaction.

"He's bringing the drinks over," she said to the group. Her heart beat at the surface of her skin as if you could see it thumping from the outside, and she could feel the attraction, way down there. She had hoped no one noticed.

****

Ready to open the heavy old door again, she knew one moment, so long ago, changed her life forever. Hindsight, perfect all the time.

Taking a deep breath, she pushed the button and repeated her password, "bourbon," and the door unlocked. One hundred different words would open the door during business hours; most of them names of liquor. Tim and Steve used to change them every so often just to keep the patrons guessing.

The smell caught her off guard making her dizzy. She loved that musky, earthy smell of an old place, especially one with liquor. She would catch a whiff of it on Tim's hair or clothing when he would come home and instantly, as all smells do, her senses brought her a memory.

She remembered a Sunday helping Tim stock the bar; on most Sundays they were closed. He told her to select the music on the iPod and she had picked an old favorite of hers by the Rolling Stones, "Satisfaction." He laughed as Mick Jagger came blaring out...and asked her, if she couldn't get any satisfaction? She had answered, Yes, but I try, and I try…She continued to help put the rest of the case of beer in the cooler. She felt Tim grab her from behind and the music changed to Frank Sinatra's "I've got you under my skin." He moved her slowly in a circle, then a waltz-like move to the hard wood floor and slowly unbuttoned her shirt, and he whispered softly in her ear, "Dance with me naked…oh, I've got you under my skin, Kendall." She had never danced naked with anyone, definitely not in a bar. She had known then he was under her skin. Later in bed, he had whispered he loved her, right before she fell into a deep sleep.

Shaking away the memories, she pushed her shoulders back and walked toward the back bar area. Steve's face lit up and he came out around the bar to give her a hug.

Steve and Tim were polar opposites in looks. Steve had an all-American boy look even in his early forties. His blond hair darkened over the years, almost touched the low ceilings. He bent down and gave Kendall a big hug and led her to the back room.

"Hi!" He hugged her again. "Everything okay?" Steve inspected her as if he were checking a basket of fruit to see if any were bruised. "I mean it's so good to see you…wouldn't have expected to see you tonight. But it's so good, really good, you look great!" His handsome looks accented by a large white smile.

"Yes, Steve, everything is fine. I just thought it was time to come in here." She smiled, something she hadn't done in a while. "I wanted to ask you something, are you busy?"

"Never too busy for you, never…it's been a slow night but steady, did you read the monthly sheets from last month?"

"Yes, well…no, I didn't read them but I got them, thanks. It's not about the business. I know you are doing a wonderful job. Tim would be happy the way you have kept everything going so well."

Saying his name aloud made the room shrink and grow quieter. The office had changed. This was a very organized office, no clutter, and a new oversized painting took up most of the space on the main wall. Her eyes stopped on the painting. She had never seen it before. It was a picture of the ocean, a giclée, high quality print, the color of the sea so radiant it was hard to take her eyes off the painting and her mind instantly went to diving.

"Do you know what happened to Tim's dive bag?"

Steve turned around, his brows raised. "Tim's dive bag, yes…it's here somewhere."

"Great, I looked for it everywhere; I figured it must be here. Where is it?"

"I think it's in the storage closet, let me get you a drink while I look for it. Pinot noir? Or a beer?"

"No thanks, Steve, I'll just take the bag, I'm a little tired."

Steve chewed on his lip. "Seriously, Kendall, it's so special you are here…at least have a drink with me." He rubbed his neck. "Just you coming into the bar is a reason to celebrate." He walked toward the wine rack. "What will it be?" he asked, reaching for a bottle. "Wine?"

True, she walked into the bar and her heart wasn't in her throat. It would be a normal thing to do, visit with an old friend and have a glass of wine, rather than storm in for a minute to get something of Tim's and leave. *It would be normal.* She was trying to change, as she flashed back to the night of the pills.

"Pinot sounds great, thanks."

She stood by the print of the sea. "This is new, Steve, I like it, where did you get it?"

With two glasses of wine in his hand, he offered one to Kendall. "Uum, Belize." His face turned various shades of red and he clamped his lips tight. Puzzled at his expression, it dawned on Kendall, it was a close-up photo of a section of the Blue Hole; *what a beautiful place to die.*

Steve turned and retreated into the closet, Kendall could see the handles of the dive bag, he unzipped a side pocket. Kendall wished she could make him more comfortable, she walked over and smiled. "He loved that bag, went all over the world with him."

Steve extracted something shiny out of the pocket.

"What's that?" Kendall asked.

Steve swallowed, his adams' apple quivered. "I don't know, it's some sort of old key, thought maybe it went to the bar." He hesitated, clutching the object tightly in his hand before he opened his palm.

She took the not so typical key; it felt substantial, some type of heavy metal. She couldn't read the imprint, the letters intricately tiny; embossed, a circle with an elaborate wing on it, maybe a bird.

She handed it back. "Well, try it out on the old doors back here, or maybe it's an original key to one of the fake wooden doors downstairs." Kendall focused on the dive bag. "Let me know…it looks pretty unusual."

"I will, I spotted it when I picked it up at the police station. It was on the list of items in the bag. I just now remembered it." He looked uncomfortable again, as if he hated bringing up Tim to Kendall.

She sympathized with Steve; he lost his best friend, college roommate, and business partner. She hoped the day would come when mentioning Tim didn't make the air so thick. She was part of the problem. It was up to her to change and now she possessed more strength and the desire to live again.

"I got an unusual call the other day."

Steve lifted his eyebrows, his arms crossed over his chest.

"Apparently, Tim had arranged a dive trip in the cenotes in Puerto Morelos for Ryder. An eighteenth birthday present. Did Tim tell you about the trip?"

Steve shook his head slowly. "A dive trip for Ryder's birthday? No…I knew he wanted Ryder to go to the Blue…" Steve caught himself mentioning Belize, and stopped. "No, I didn't know anything about a Puerto Morelos trip, how did you find out?"

"A man named Scout. Some cavern diver in Mexico, called and said Tim had prepaid and arranged for this dive trip and in November postponed the trip till May when Ryder turns nineteen." Kendall took a breath, "I guess Ryder was filming *Paradise Valley* on his eighteenth birthday and couldn't take vacations, so he postponed it to this year."

"Wait? He postponed it in November? Of last year?" Steve's eyebrows arched.

"No, November the year before. It must have been right…" Kendall chose her words carefully, "before the trip."

"Okay, so why the call now? I'm confused."

"Because Tim postponed the trip to this May; I guess he was planning ahead. I thought maybe he talked to you, 'cause he never said anything to me."

Silence filled the space between them, Steve's eyebrows bunched together. Kendall attempted a smile. "So, I'm trying to reach Ryder and persuade him to go on this trip, convince him I'm going to take him for Tim. That's why I was looking for the dive bag," Kendall said. "I think it's what Tim would have wanted. I really have a feeling about this...I need to do the trip in his memory and for Ryder."

"Really?" Steve hesitated before continuing, "Do you think that's a good idea? I mean..." Steve stumbled over his choice of words. "What did Ryder say, have you talked to him yet?" Steve didn't even give her a chance to respond as he continued speaking, "Are you sure you want to go, Kendall? Do you want me to go with you or take Ryder? And, where is the dive exactly? I want to know details." Steve shook his head. "I'm not sure it's the right thing, I mean...diving...seriously." His tone gritty.

She stood up, sucking her cheeks in, the room becoming hot. "Well, thanks for the wine, Steve, I better get home to Harvey, he gets so anxious lately if I'm too late." She gave him an awkward hug, ending and ignoring the conversation. A skill she had refined since Tim died. If anyone made a comment she didn't want to hear or respond to, she would simply paste her fake smile on and change the subject. She picked up the dive bag, wondering what else of Tim's personal effects remained in the bag, turned around, and headed for the door.

Chapter 12

After leaving the bar, she carried the dive bag up to Tim's office over the garage and, sitting on the floor with Harvey, dumped everything out going through each item. An extra snorkel, mask, fins and gloves, miscellaneous dive gear, nothing special. His favorite dive equipment—the gear he had worn that day—were the remnants buried in his coffin. It was when she unzipped the hidden pocket under the bottom of the bag that she found his dive log.

A three-ring binder, book size, enclosed in a metal waterproof case. She remembered diving in Bonaire, how he was old-school and still logged in the hand-written notebook. He also maintained a computer log with detailed information and they had joked it was good he was transferring to the computer logbook or his dive book might weigh down the boat. Tim logged at least 600 dives since he was twelve years old. This journal looked fairly new, it had 200 pages in it and each section recorded the following:

Date, dive # or cave dive #, location, diving buddies, basic equipment info, time in and out, total dive time, water temperature and visibility, maximum and average depth, mix, air used, and a short narrative about the dive. In his neat handwriting, he included a short commentary about each dive, dive shops' names and numbers and instructions in the event of an accident.

Kendall flipped to the last page of the dive book. Tim had started recording the beginning of the Blue Hole dive. She sucked in her breath as she read his last completed entry.

Date: November 10th, 2014, Dive # 681, Location: Blue Hole, Belize

Divers: Adam Matthews, Colton Evans, Wanderlust Divers Belize, 34 ft. center console Boston Whaler. Captain Arturo Chavez

Time Out

Total Dive Time:

Water Temp & Viz

Max and Average Depth

Tanks used

Mix

Air Used

Remarks:

Instructions ICOE—Contact Kendall Jackson 410-723-4567, tell her to take the trip with Ryder. KILY—UWMA

She couldn't believe what she was reading. Instructions ICOE—In case of emergency.

No one had bothered to check Tim's dive log after the accident. But there it was in Tim's handwriting, *Tell her to take the trip with Ryder*???

She knew he meant the birthday trip to Puerto Morelos. Deep down inside she knew it was a message for her. KILY was how he signed any letter or card she had ever received. It was their secret language…KILY for Kendall I love you. She used to write back TILY. They had always used letters for messages to each other. Sometimes on the bottom of cards or in the return address, they would send a message; it would take each of them days to figure out the secret message. It was way before texting or LOL was even invented. It was their secret code.

UWMA was used once before by Tim, after the first night they met at Jackson's. At the college, Kendall had received a dozen startling, unique orchids. The card had read, UWMA, your secret admirer. One of the students figured it out in a second,—it should have been a sure sign students would love texting and abbreviations in the very near years to come. UWMA stood for "Until we meet again."

She gasped. She had to book a ticket to Phoenix, show Ryder the logbook and persuade him to take the trip to Puerto Morelos. It was what Tim wanted. Kendall hugged Harvey. "Come on, pup, we have so much to do before I leave." Kendall threw the dive equipment back in the dive bag, and a round cylinder rolled out of the hidden pocket. Harvey sprang into action and instantly went to chase it. With one swift motion of his black paw he knocked it under the bookcase. Head down, butt up in the air in Downward Facing Dog pose, Harvey frantically tried to get the object, scratching the floor.

On her knees on the floor beside Harvey, she put her hand under the bookcase, and hit the briefcase. *Oh yeah, Tim's briefcase...* She remembered it was under there, she just didn't know how to get it out without moving all the books off the bookshelf. It hadn't seemed like a priority.

Moving her hand behind the briefcase, she pulled out the tin canister Harvey was chasing. It resembled a mini Altoids canister, two inches by two inches.

Embossed on the front of the box a small stamp, a bird or wings. She had seen it before. The canister did not open, but her memory did, as she realized where she had seen the stamp before. She was almost certain.

Chapter 13

"Kendall," Steve turned around at the bar not able to hide his surprise, "twice in one week, I feel like a lucky guy." He smiled, left the bar rag and walked around the bar.

He leaned in to hug her. "You know, I didn't mean to be negative about the dive trip with Ryder, it just threw me off guard. I've been thinking, I'd like to go with you guys, it would be fun, the three of us. Before you say no, I could really use a break from this place and I would like to do this for Tim." He flashed his best smile, leaning forward. "Why don't you give me the guy's name and I'll call him and see if I can add another diver and help you figure it all out? I'll take care of it. We can do this together."

He studied her unreadable expression. For the first time since Tim died, she looked alive and healthy. Her pretty features were resurfacing in a soft, kind way, losing the lost puppy struggling in a face of hopelessness. However, something else was present, right on the surface of her emotions; something that wasn't there the other night.

"Thanks Steve, really, thanks, I appreciate your offer, I do, but this is a trip Ryder and I need to take together. In fact, I am flying out to Scottsdale on Friday; I just need one thing from you before I leave."

Steve sighed rubbing the back of his neck. "Sure,

Kendall, anything you need, you know that...but will you just consider me going with you?"

She ignored his question. "I need the key you pulled out of Tim's dive bag, I think I may have figured out what it goes to."

He cleared his throat, finding it difficult to swallow. "Really? What?"

"Possibly an old briefcase of Tim's, I found it under the bookcase in his office. It was kind of stuck under there, probably for a long time but when I finally pulled it out, I'm thinking the key fits the lock." She shrugged her shoulders. "I might be wrong, but let me try. I'll give it back to you, if it doesn't work and it belongs to the bar."

She stood up, waiting for Steve to get the key. He froze, seconds seemed to float in the air. The pause unusual, even uncomfortable as he slowly took a breath and stood up, opened the lock box in his desk drawer and took the key out. Handing it to Kendall, he forced a smile, trying to calm his emotions. "Well, let me know if it fits, if not, like you said, it might go to one of the old doors down in the cellar. I haven't even tried it yet."

She took the key. Her eyes showed puzzlement. He knew she was wondering why the situation turned so awkward. He wanted to ask her a hundred more questions but he gritted his teeth and forced a smile.

"I better get back to the bar, let me know about Ryder or if I can do anything to help you."

****

Kendall placed the small Altoid looking canister on the outside seam of the briefcase. Click. A portion of the seam slid back revealing a lock. The key from the dive bag slid right into the newly exposed opening and turned the inner locks on the titanium latches. Her instincts confirmed, she studied the symbol on the little box. Using Tim's magnifying glass on the end of a letter opener he always kept on his desktop, she read the tiny initials "DNA" above the embossed pair of wings. She had no idea what they stood for but it reminded her of some official government seal.

Chapter 14

Kendall inhaled and let her breath out slowly, staring out the window of the plane. She had four hours of flying time to Phoenix and she desperately wished she grabbed the strange maps and papers out of Tim's briefcase. She would have missed her flight if she went back for it. One of the items in the suitcase was a cylinder, with the same electronic latch opened by the small tin box. In it a very old map on unusual paper. A map of what, Kendall could not figure out. It was hand drawn, with lettering in Spanish, or at least it appeared to be Spanish. The other document in the briefcase was also a map of some kind, this one not old, resembling a computerized blueprint of a structural or industrial system. Possibly a piping layout or utilities map.

In her haste to make this trip, time was of the essence. She had so many things to do, she didn't want to jeopardize her already shaky career. After finalizing the Commencement committee plans, contacting Scout Whitman in Mexico and arranging for her neighbor Lizzie to take care of Harvey, she accidentally left the briefcase locked in her office.

Running late for the flight, she had no choice but to leave it. She would examine the strange contents when she returned. The trip Tim wanted her to take was the priority. Now, faced with four hours of flying, she could not get the contents of the briefcase off her mind.

She wished she had grabbed at least one of the documents.

Besides the map in the cylinder and the blueprint, there was a computer zip file and a leather passport case. Inside, she found a black credit card she had never seen before, a white key card, the business card of a physician from Johns Hopkins, and a government ID from the Navy. The ID was not old; it had a holograph seal on it, and a very current picture of Tim. The minute she looked at it, she knew it was recent. Tim had a small cut on his face. That cut happened on a ski trip in Breckenridge, in 2012. Tim had got caught in a white out skiing a black diamond and a tree branch cut into his face; Kendall was thrilled he missed the tree and didn't go over the edge. She couldn't stop wondering how Tim could still have ties to the Navy and not tell her. She felt sick to her stomach.

And there was the business card from Johns Hopkins Medical Center, a neurosurgeon. The aching pit in her stomach was new. She would have bet a million dollars with anyone Tim would never lie to her, or keep secrets. Secret life? Seriously? Could it be something classified he couldn't tell anyone? Neurosurgery. Could he have something medically wrong in his brain?

She got out her iPad and made a list of all her questions, trying to put the confusion down on paper to help her make sense of what she had discovered.

There had to be a logical explanation. Obviously, as she had first thought, the briefcase had not been under the bookcase for any length of time. Images, ideas and thoughts raced through her mind. The unknown conjured up frightening speculation.

Fatigue took over, and her head dropped. In what felt like seconds she heard the pilot joke about the high temperature in Phoenix, laughing over the speaker, as he said, "But it's a dry heat." They were ready to land.

Kendall stretched, pulling her hair back into a ponytail. Ryder. She needed to focus on getting Ryder to agree to the dive trip. She had called his publicist, Courtney Clay, and cleared seven days off his calendar. She gave little explanation but firmly explained something important had come up, a private family matter associated with his father's death, and she needed to ensure Ryder's calendar was clear for the next seven days.

****

Flying into Phoenix, she took in the rugged, towering rocks randomly placed around the city, thrown in clumps as if an angry toddler threw rocks in different directions. A widespread abundance of freeways and houses dotted the landscape in every direction, with tiny circles and geometric shapes of blue water scattered behind the majority of buildings. Courtney confided Ryder had tickets to the Phoenix Coyotes game tonight and with the team's winning record, she had arranged for a publicity shot at the hockey game. Ryder would be home by ten or eleven p.m. since he was going with Dr. Ian Grant from *Paradise Valley* and generally, they did not make it a late night without dates.

She did not care what time he arrived home. She would wait outside his house, however long it took, all night if she needed to. She decided she would attempt to explain the situation to Ryder's mother, and see if she would help pack his clothes. She pictured the tense conversation, but she was ready. She was not leaving Scottsdale until he agreed to go with her. She wasn't going to take no for an answer.

Tim's ex-wife, Tricia, was usually cordial to Kendall. Their contact minimal, she didn't have a reason not to like her. At Ryder's middle school graduation, a birthday party, and at the last event where they all met, a night out watching the premiere of *Paradise Valley*, Tricia was pleasant. Her actions toward Tim on the other hand were not so civil. Perhaps it was a little show of trying to act as if she did not miss him, but somehow it did not come off right. She always ended up feeling sorry for her; she couldn't picture the two of them together in any scenario.

Desperately hoping Tricia would understand the importance of the journey for Ryder, and help encourage him to take this trip, she debated asking Tricia about the briefcase. Keeping secrets and living a low profile was not one of Tricia's dominant traits. She knew in her heart of hearts if Tim needed to keep something private, he would never share it with Tricia.

****

She gripped the steering wheel of the rental car. It was ten p.m. and she knew from the stats on the iPhone the game was almost over. Biting her lip, she decided she would risk talking to Tricia, before Ryder arrived home. She hated showing up unannounced.

She rang the doorbell.

The blinds on the window beside the door pushed back and she could see Tricia's face.

"Hi Tricia, it's me, Kendall. I'm sorry to be knocking on your door so late, it's regarding Ryder. Can we talk?"

The sound of several locks opening made her stomach twist. Tricia stood there, no makeup, her jet black hair pulled in a ponytail, wearing a black and pink workout outfit. For a minute, she caught a glimpse of a young Tricia; perhaps one Tim met so long ago. Without all the heavy makeup piled on and false eyelashes, Tricia looked pretty. A softer and even kinder look.

"Kendall, what's happened? Did something happen to Ryder?" Her sharp smokers' voice spoiled the image.

"No, no, nothing happened to Ryder, I'm sorry for showing up at your house at this late hour. Nothing is wrong."

Tricia pulled the door open and stepped back, running her fingers through her long ponytail. She looked relieved for a second. She studied Kendall and then a hardness passed over her face, her mouth set in a straight line. "What's going on?"

"I need to talk to you about something. It's important. I wouldn't have come here if it wasn't. I just…Ryder won't return my calls. I have emailed him, sent messages on Facebook, texted him, and now I'm here to explain to him in person why I so desperately need to talk to him." She knew she was rambling and for the first time questioned her snap decision, flying out here and putting all the plans in motion for the trip.

Tricia's eyes showed confusion, but her botoxed brow was smooth. "This couldn't wait? It's late."

Exhaustion threatened to overwhelm her. She lifted her chin. "It can't. I'm sorry. Can we sit down for a minute? We can sit outside, if you'd like, I just want to explain to you why this is so important. Why I flew all the way from Maryland to talk to Ryder tonight."

Tricia stepped back and Kendall moved past her through the doorway. She had never been inside the home Tricia and Ryder had once shared with Tim. He had paid it off in the divorce, with explicit directions when Ryder turned thirty or if Tricia was going to sell it before then, it became the property of Ryder Jackson. He wanted stability in Ryder's life.

Inside the foyer gigantic modern glass pots filled with a mix of curly sticks loomed to the ceiling. A large mirror rested up against the wall.

She remembered an old photo of Tim with Ryder. Ryder must have been six or seven; they were standing in front of a beautiful rock fireplace with an animal rug on the wood floor, possibly a cowhide, and a portrait of a cowboy in a blue denim shirt hanging on the wall to their left. To Kendall it epitomized the essence of the Southwest; she used this memory every time she thought of Ryder, Tricia, and Tim living in this house. Obviously, the house was stripped of everything Western and warm. The painting was nowhere to be seen.

Tricia led her to an ultra-modern kitchen, with black granite countertops and wood cabinets. She pointed to the chair by the table, and Kendall sat. "Would you like a cup of coffee or water or something?"

"No, thanks. I'm fine."

"So, what's this all about?" Tricia stared at her nails and then back at Kendall.

"Tim had planned to take Ryder on a special eighteenth birthday trip, a cave diving trip just for the two of them. It's with a cave diver in Mexico and Tim set everything up, it looks like right before…" She paused, "the accident." He postponed the trip until Ryder's nineteenth birthday, next week." She rubbed the palm of her hand with her thumb, drawing a circle. "It was one of the last things he did before he died, and in his logbook, his diving logbook, he left me a message. In case anything happened to him, he wanted me to take Ryder on the trip. He left the message the day he died." Crossing her legs, she clasped her hands in front of her and took a deep breath. "I told Ryder about the trip, but he won't respond to me." She sat up straighter and spoke with authority. "I have two tickets leaving Phoenix tomorrow to Cancun with a car picking us up to take us to the resort. I've cleared Ryder's schedule with his publicist, and we will be gone for the next seven days. The dive master, Scout, has everything ready and set up to do the trip." She knew her face was full of emotion but, unwavering, she did not lose eye contact. "I was wondering if you would help me...help me pack Ryder's dive bag and help me complete Tim's last wish." She paused. "I've never asked you for anything, Tricia, but I'm asking you for this."

****

Ryder threw his car keys on the counter, headed directly for the refrigerator, opened it and looked inside. He pulled out a bottle of Rock Star energy drink and flipped the tab back, and just as he was tilting his head back, out of the corner of his eye he noticed Kendall standing in his kitchen.

"Kendall?" He swallowed, clenching his jaw. He put the drink down on the counter and waited for her to speak, the hot dog from the hockey game wanting to come up.

Chapter 15

Looking out the window, Ryder sank lower in the seat and pulled the hat over his eyes. At Security, Kendall had handed him his boarding pass and he had been shocked she booked First Class. *Thank God. At least on the way home, which can't get here soon enough, it will be comfortable.*

He closed his eyes, and involuntarily shook his head as he replayed the scene from last night. He almost spit his drink out when he noticed Kendall standing in his kitchen with his mom. She just stood there with a stupid smile on her face. His heart tightened when he spotted his suitcase and dive bag by the front door.

Kendall had caught him by surprise with her question.

"Ryder, if you knew what your father's last wish was—the last wish before he died—and you had the capability of making it come true, would you do it?"

His mother leaned against the kitchen counter, with a bottle of water in her hand wearing a look Ryder was unfamiliar with.

"Of course I would, what a stupid question." He grinded his teeth. "What's going on, what's with all the philosophical questions?" He met Kendall's eyes. "What are you doing in my house?"

Now, here he was, on a plane headed for Cancun,

Mexico, his last two painkillers stashed in his backpack and the majority of his clothes packed by his mother.

He wished he were taking this trip with his father, not Kendall. Thinking about it pissed him off even more. It was his birthday present, he should get to decide who he goes with. It didn't matter he didn't know anybody who was cave diving certified except for Steve Crawford, he was still angry. How did he agree to this?

The same questions kept running through his mind, *why did his father write in his log book right before he died? Why did he write Kendall should take Ryder on the trip? Perhaps, he didn't even mean the cave diving trip; maybe he meant another trip to the Blue Hole? What is so important about this trip? Why did I agree to do this?*

The last time they were together, they discussed a future Blue Hole diving trip and then his father went without him and died. Strange, all of it, the postponed trip, the logbook. He didn't understand any of it, but because of the entry in the logbook, well, it meant something. Knowing the last words his father wrote down on a piece of paper included his name. Just that simple gesture. His father thinking of him before he died, comforted him. He knew no matter what or how he acted toward Kendall, deep down inside, he was going on the trip to honor his father's wishes.

Listening to his headphones, he doubted his mom had packed everything necessary for seven days of cave diving and he wondered if he could actually survive the jungle with Kendall and this guide. He had been to Cancun with his father six or seven years ago right before his father married; it was the last one on one dive trip with his dad. They had stayed at a beautiful resort in Playa Del Carmen called Hacienda Tres Rios, a spectacular Nature Park, not too far from where he passed the rescue diver certification.

Was Kendall certified as a basic cave diver? Was she even equipped to go on this dive in a cenote?

He had snorkeled in a cenote waterway; a striking turquoise river and tunnel with rock formations with his father. At times, it went on the surface and then below. They had followed the above-ground river to the sea. It was an epic adventure and Ryder was mesmerized as they treaded water in the last cave and swam with manatees. He remembered his father telling him a story he hadn't thought about for years.

His father explained Mexico had the largest underground cave systems in the world, hundreds no man had ever seen. Once the cenotes were a series of tunnels that ran under the earth, but as the limestone became saturated and time went on, the tunnels filled up with fresh water. They were sacred places to the Maya people; treasured because it was the only fresh water in the Yucatán. Fresh water from the cenotes held a magical quality because of its mineral content and luminescent color.

His father described in detail a dive that contained giant caverns, stalactites and stalagmites falling and rising from the limestone walls with underwater passageways of crystal-clear water. A hidden paradise, his father had said. He remembered asking, "Will you take me there, Dad?" His father had smiled and said something like, "I hope so, when the time is right, maybe someday we can go there together. It will be our special trip." He realized the time would never be right since he was gone…but maybe this cenote exploration was the place he wanted him to see.

The flight dragged on. Ryder kept his music loud, pretending he was sleeping, avoiding conversation with Kendall. He kept repeating the same little chant in his mind, *I'm going on this trip for my father, Kendall just happens to be here.*

Chapter 16

It was apparent to Kendall, as Ryder stared at the glimpses of the beautiful blue water hugging the road to Puerto Morelos, he loved the ocean as much as his father did. She had never noticed the resemblance so distinctly. Ryder carried the same glint in his eyes as Tim around water, his eyes reflecting light from the sea; even from a distance, it turned his eyes fifty shades of color.

Ryder did not utter a whole sentence to Kendall on the plane. His one-syllable answers to various questions were not the conversations she had pictured in her mind.

It was enough; he was here, and this was a big step in their relationship, she knew to take it slow. Tonight she imagined getting to the hotel room and going out to dinner and having something that resembled a conversation. Tomorrow, they would meet Scout Whitman and find out all the details of the dive trip Tim had planned.

Scout Whitman, she assumed, had reserved a suite for them at a beautiful resort, Zoëtry Paraiso de la Bonita. It had two master bedrooms, two baths on opposite ends of a large living room/dining room, with an individual terrace separated by a large shared outdoor lounging and eating area. A gorgeous oceanfront boutique resort. Even Ryder's jaw dropped driving through the manicured lawns and exotic jungle surrounding the road leading to the beach where the resort was located. He smiled for the first time when greeted at check-in by an exotic, beautiful young hostess and given a hot towel, cold drink, and a selection of fresh fruits.

The resort was beyond a doubt spectacular, ninety suites nestled on fourteen pristine acres of breathtaking talcum-powder-white sand and turquoise-blue water. Located next door to a well-preserved National Marine Park, which boasted the largest barrier reef in the Americas, it appeared as a mirage, taking form in the middle of the empty, rugged coastline.

The room had marble and stone in every direction in warm sand colors, and deep rich wood, tranquil and luxurious in a sparse contemporary way. An ultra-large terrace was situated in the middle. The suite large enough to have a blowout party if you wanted and yet it maintained privacy from neighboring suites with outdoor dining, a lounge area, a great white soft-sheeted bed and a dead-on straight view of the water. A long wooden pier ran out into the water and a beautiful catamaran was moored out in front. She wondered if Tim had selected this place or if Scout had picked it. It was simply magnificent. Her heart ached, wishing she were experiencing this with Tim. She shook her head as if to knock away those feelings from her brain.

The all-inclusive resort had several restaurants to choose from or the option to order room service on their scenic terrace. Tonight, she and Ryder could have a nice dinner on the terrace, talk about his father, the diving adventure, and Ryder's life with *Paradise Valley*. She had no idea what was going on in Ryder's life. She had little contact over the past year except for a few cryptic texts. Her mind raced back to the original thought regarding the entry in the logbook. Maybe Tim told her to take Ryder on the trip because he knew if something were to happen to him, Ryder would lose all contact. His way of keeping them connected.

Lost in thought, she heard the door open. Ryder walked out of his master suite and opened the door to the outside.

"Ryder, I thought maybe we could order a little dinner and talk about this week? Maybe sit on the terrace and call room service or maybe you would like to pick a restaurant on site? They have several, and they all look delicious, your choice…"

He turned around, the beautiful eyes with shades of color reflecting the water disappeared. Anger filled them. "Well, it is *my* birthday trip, so let's say I do a little celebrating the way I want to." He walked out letting the door slam behind him.

The back of the door held her focus. Even the sunset sneaking into the terrace, the rays painting a kaleidoscope of light and shadows didn't turn her head. All the beauty of a place could not hide the ugliness of hurt.

Chapter 17

"Ryder, you need to get up, we're meeting Scout Whitman in fifteen minutes." She knocked again, hurting her hand as she pounded harder. "Ryder, answer me, or I'm coming in...you need to get up now. We need to leave here to meet Scout."

Kendall let out a deep breath, looked up at the ceiling, her hands on hips, shaking her head. "Ryder, are you in there?"

She debated whether she should turn the knob and open the door. Suddenly, the suites' outside door opened.

"What are you doing?" He walked toward her, scowling, staring at her hand on the doorknob to his room. Kendall had a fine sense of smell, most times annoyingly so. The liquor smell emanated from Ryder's body, and something else, sweet perfume hit her square in the face. He looked like an old Tom Cruise movie with retro black matte Ray-Ban sunglasses, white T-shirt and jeans. His clothes unwrinkled, she wondered if he even slept or what he slept in.

"Seriously? You're asking me what I'm doing." He was eighteen, but what were the rules? Last night, she woke up every hour to check whether he had come home, thoughts racing through her mind about calling resort security. Finally, in the last hour she had fallen hard into a deep sleep, dreaming of blue waters and

Tim swimming toward her. She was angry, tired, and sad and definitely unsure if this journey was the best idea.

They stood in silence. Kendall put her sunglasses on and threaded her ponytail through the hole in the back of the baseball cap. "See you out front in ten minutes, bring everything you think you'll need...or don't bring anything at all. I really don't care, if you're not there, no problem." Heat crawled up her neck and face. She took a deep breath, paused and lowered her voice to a soft, calm tone. "You know, Ryder, we can end it right now, pack up and go home, it's entirely up to you." A long pause again. "Like you said, this is 'your birthday present', and yes I know it's from your father who is not here and I am instead, and yes, I wish it were different, Oh God do I wish it were different." Her throat tightened, and her eyes watered. "You work it out. You're over eighteen, an adult. Figure out what you want to do, so I know what to do...and by the way...you smell like a brewery. Good luck with diving today," she paused again, "that is if you still want to dive." She picked up Tim's old dive bag, a large green duffel, and walked past him out the door. *Now, we will see if this journey is going to start or not.*

****

As soon as the resort van pulled up to Scout's Dive Shop, a sporty shack-like structure in bright blue with a yellow porch, a tall, tanned, muscular man with a baseball hat and short blond ponytail opened the door.

"Hola, you must be Kendall. Scout Whitman. Nice to meet you." Kendall smiled and stepped out of the van. Scout walked around the back of the shuttle where Ryder was climbing out. Scout held out his hand, trying

86

to maintain eye contact, but Ryder kept his black sunglasses on and offered a limp handshake. "And, you must be Ryder…"

Scout had gear lined up in large piles on the ground outside the shop.

"Is this all for us?"

Scout took off his hat, pulling the ponytail loose and ran his fingers through messy medium-length blond hair. His sun-kissed skin was a warm bronze. "Yes, and there's more in the rover," he said. "First, let's go sit down and discuss the trip." Scout pointed to the small porch with a few chairs and a swing. "I really don't know how much you know regarding what your…er, husband planned."

"Well, not much. Actually, we don't know anything…just that he wanted to take Ryder on this dive trip. So, why don't you show us where we are going?" Sleeping bags and tents lay on the ground. Taking a deep breath, she reminded herself she could do this for Tim. "Oh, with such a nice resort reserved for us, I didn't realize we would be camping for a night…"

Scout raised his eyebrows. "Not exactly for a night…but the next five nights, it's a pretty remote location, not accessible in a day, the Sherpas will help us carry our packs in and out," Scout paused, his eyes going back and forth on Kendall and Ryder. "Sounds like I need to bring you up to speed."

Sherpas?…I thought they were only at Mt. Everest.

Chapter 18

Scout could see the resemblance to Tim as Ryder lifted his hat off and ran his hand over the top of his head. It would be difficult to say Ryder Jackson was not a fundamentally handsome kid. His pretty-boy characteristics and muscular, rugged physique were undeniably striking. He looked like he could be in the movies. He carried a scowl and a presence of entitlement, a trait his father didn't pass down. His good looks were obvious, made more evident as Lily, Scout's assistant, who barely looked up from her computer for anyone, was blushing under her heavy makeup and tongue-tied trying to introduce herself as they walked onto the porch to sit down.

Rubbing his chin, wondering for the hundredth time, why it had been so damn important for him to get in touch with Tim Jackson, why he couldn't let it go after not hearing back from him, he sighed. No one would have known. Scout had been teetering back and forth in his mind, questioning whether he should take Kendall and Ryder to the specific cenote Tim Jackson had shown him on the map. It would be a difficult excursion for any experienced cave diver and the journey was deep into the Yucatán. There would not be easy access; it was unlikely it had ever been explored, and it involved a demanding expedition to get there and no accessible roads within twenty-five miles.

Within ten minutes of talking to them, Scout knew it was definitely going to be a difficult challenge with these two. He also knew he had to make a quick assessment on whether or not they possessed full-blown cave diving skills. He excused himself from the porch. He needed to think.

Since cave diving officially began in the mid to late eighties, over four-hundred people had lost their lives. Scout had a clean record, no deaths under his watch and over 7000 logged cave dives. Most open-water divers had the mindset if they could open-water dive, then with a little course or reading up on cave dives they could easily cave dive.

Wrong thinking….that was where most of the deaths occurred—inexperience and lack of education. Cave diving wasn't for everyone. It required good balance, good buoyancy and confidence in the ability to deal psychologically with any predicament that could occur in a cave. Unlike other diving, if you needed to surface you couldn't. Most people couldn't deal with that constriction.

He analyzed the two of them through the window. You also needed to get along and have respect for each other, clearly something which did not exist with the mismatched pair in front of him. Tim's wife repacked her bag assessing the large mound of supplies on the ground. With her hair pulled back in a ponytail hanging out of a black hat, she looked fresh, a classic look, much younger than her age and slightly uncomfortable. Her eyes held a haunted look. Ryder stood, arms crossed, facing the water, earplugs in, his fingers flying on his phone. This attachment to technology, was a tribal marking of American teenagers. He would give

Ryder a few more minutes of his obsession, a pleasure soon to be short-lived, as they would be going off the grid. He had to make a choice.

Even the most experienced and trained diver, in one second, could be separated from his buddy and a newfound anxiety could take over his sanity. All it took was a little bit of low visibility due to silt or organic debris stirred up in a tight space, and losing one's sense of direction. Any unknown incident could create mental anguish, which could lead to accidents. He had experienced this as a team of one of twelve divers who recorded and mapped the longest underground cave system in the Yucatán. Accidents happen even when everyone had the same goal in mind.

Here he was taking a widow and a son who obviously had a problematic relationship, on a diving trip. Would they know the difference if he took them diving to another cenote, not the one on the map? *How could they? They didn't even know about the trip.* It was the right choice. He would take them to a somewhat remote cenote, one he knew by heart, and could safely lead two beginning cave divers through the cave system.

He convinced himself it was in their best interest, the smart thing to do. His mind made up, he formulated a plan.

A loud angry voice carried to him. "I just didn't realize we would be camping, I mean maybe I thought we would be camping for a night, two at the most..." long pause and then, "but I didn't realize we would be camping for five nights." Ryder's toe kicked a canvas duffel with a sleeping bag showing through. A childish reaction, his eyes showing darkness underneath, the corner of his mouth turned down, arms crossed. A boy in a man's body.

Tim's wife was standing around the equipment with a look of uncertainty. "Well, let's talk to Scout, I know your father planned this trip, so let's get a better understanding of what's going on."

Scout joined them. "Let me show you what I have planned, your father wanted a day or two of revisiting cavern diving and basic cave diving for Ryder here and then…" He swallowed. He hated liars and prided himself on his honesty. Still, somehow this seemed like the best play of action. "He wanted to explore several beautiful cenotes that very few have seen." He gripped his chin with his thumb and finger. "What we can do to cut down the camping time, is to go out today and tomorrow to review cavern diving and basic cave diving. I can change our destination to something close by. You can return to your rooms for the next two nights. Then I can take you to the cenotes which will require a little bit of hiking, crossing a few rivers and a night or two of camping." Scout paused, waiting for the questions regarding the cenote Tim Jackson wanted to show his son. *Did they even know he had the map?*

Kendall looked at Ryder. "What do you think?"

Ryder huffed, dropping his shoulders slowly, his back turned. "Fine, whatever, when do we leave?"

Chapter 19

"Okay, we are going to wash off, no body oils, suntan lotions, no bug spray. We want to really make sure nothing is on the outside of the tanks...stickers, peeling paint, anything that could fall off into the cenote."

Scout helped rinse everyone's skin before they tugged their wet suits over their slippery muscles. A little awkwardness filled the air, the estranged pair barely acknowledging the other. Scout continued to explain the fragile environment of the cenotes, as he went into a lengthy monologue of the Yucatán's valuable assets and the efforts to keep the unique cenotes protected from humans. His voice filled the tense empty silence between Kendall and the kid. "There are many countries where fresh water is worth more than gold; I think we are living on top of a treasure. Here in the Yucatán, we have an enormous shelf of land perforated with fresh water running underneath, we just need to make sure it stays that way."

The perimeter of the large crystal-clear pond, was surrounded by lush green vegetation and curvy wooden trees. The sides, the darkest of wet browns resembled a beaver dam stacked full of twisty branches and twigs tangled together, forming a spectacular natural circle around an intense, unnatural blue-green color.

"This is the cenote 'Naharon', meaning Crystal; it is only 45 feet or 14 meters maximum depth, there is no permanent guideline. Once we go over a review of cavern diving safety and techniques, we will work together on using a guideline and reel in the water. The cavern entrance is on the west side of the cenote and down below visibility is excellent."

They were standing over a deep hole, luminescent water reflecting back an unreadable expression on both their faces

"It's beautiful." Kendall's head bent over the edge. "The color seems fake, it doesn't seem real."

Scout studied her profile. "It definitely is real but it's unlike any other water I've ever seen in my life." He whispered. "There's something about this water, the color, the feel of it, its mysterious beauty gets inside you." He turned his head catching her eyes. "That's why I had to move down here, to the Yucatán, all because of the cenotes. The damn cenotes."

****.

After an hour of instruction, and being quizzed on use of reel and line, lights, propulsion techniques, problem solving, and practice sharing equipment, Scout wondered if they knew he was testing their ability. Kendall had her cavern certification and Ryder was both cavern and cave certified. They had both explored caverns in Florida.

"The Florida caves are unique in their own right, but you will be astonished at the clarity and beauty of the Yucatán caves," Scout said. *This is a cavern on steroids—wait until they see this.* It didn't matter how many caves he dived or how many cenotes he explored, this underworld electrified him.

"Are you ready?" he asked. "Remember the signals, keep your distance and follow me. He flicked the flashlight attached to his suit on and off. "Light check."

The steady beat of breathing underwater filled his head, like a drumbeat it both relaxed him and pumped euphoria into his bloodstream. The decorations were a magnificent work of art. Scout involuntarily smiled even with the regulator in his mouth. He pointed the light on a formation which resembled a drinking straw. Cave decorations came in all shapes and sizes; they grew from the ceiling and from the floor; resembling rippled sheets or even twisted worms. Stalactites and stalagmites were the most commonly known, but decorations in the cenotes were outstanding. His light illuminated the magnificence of the cave.

Light blue, deep blue, emerald, turquoise, a hodgepodge of hues resembled the mixture of colors of a kaleidoscope. They were inside the wheel and someone was turning it, blending all the colors together. Clear, crystal, crisp and sharp...depending on which way you looked, natural light from the sun spotlighted the water. With every different angle the view and vibrancy changed. Remarkable. Inexplicably brilliant. Hues so full of luminosity it appeared there was lighting underneath.

The day flew by. The beauty in the underworld, possibly impacting the bitterness between Kendall and Ryder and the rugged terrain. The caves were only accessible by traveling back a dirt road, climbing over a fence and paying a small fee in pesos to the always present landowner.

The second cenote, nicknamed Carwash, was like

pulling up to a large lake. Wooden platforms provided easy entry to the water. Attached to a large rock at the beginning of a passageway was a sign in English:

Prevent Your Death
Go No Further
Unless Trained
in Cave Diving
Many Open-Water Divers
(even Instructors) Have Died
Attempting to Dive Caves

Scout pointed to the sign. "Underneath there are several rooms with different passageways leading in opposite directions away from the entrance. Divers enter rooms, lose orientation, and die without having enough air to make it back to the entrance." As soon as the word die left his lips, he wanted to swallow his words.

The silence in the air became thick like layers stacking themselves on top of each other creating a distance between all three of them,

Even the two Sherpas, Enrique and Roberto, who knew no English, knew something changed the group's attitude.

Scout, fluent in Spanish, had short private conversations with Enrique and Roberto throughout the day. He had worked with them before, and respected their local knowledge, their kindness, and work ethic. They were both good men, working hard to take care of their families. Enrique, part Maya, handled the paying of each cenote owner, answering a few questions in a Spanish/Mayan dialect, Scout couldn't decipher.

At the last cenote of the day, the landowner exchanged a few words with Enrique gesturing toward

Ryder. Enrique translated. "He wants you to take your cap and shades off," Scout said to Ryder. An odd request. Scout attempted to analyze the expression on the landowner's face. His body language rigid, his face strained under a pair of sunglasses. Why?

Kendall flashed a beautiful smile, and said, "See what happens when you bring a reality TV star to the jungle, Ryder, you're famous even in Mexico." She watched Ryder stare at the old man. She laughed and said, "Perhaps they have satellite and watch your show."

The landowner never smiled. He ignored Kendall. His body turned toward Ryder, beaten-up black sunglasses perched on his nose. Shirtless; his years showed on the sagging of his skin, his hair long and straggly, gray even on his chest, and a face full of time lines. Ryder took his cap and glasses off.

In slow motion, he removed his slightly bent lopsided glasses. The old man's eyes grew larger. Intense light blue eyes in caramel-colored skin, mesmerized by Ryder. After a few seconds of staring, the glasses went back on and the landowner stood up, turned and retreated back to his shack.

The curious moment passed in silence. Kendall attempted a joke. "Ryder's fame follows him everywhere." No one laughed.

As they hiked back from the last cenote, Ryder stuck his earbuds in, blocking out any chance of conversing.

"So, it's a reality show about plastic surgery?" Scout wanted to understand.

"Yes, but it's more like a soap opera, with the patients falling over the plastic surgeon and even hitting on Ryder. It's interesting, I guess…if you like Reality television."

"And, it's popular, people want to watch it?" From behind, Scout analyzed Ryder's physical features.

"Yes, it's one of the highest rated reality shows for the last two seasons." Kendall raised her palms. "Crazy world we live in, right?"

****

The last cenote caught the late afternoon sun. The escaping rays broke through the canopy of jungle creating a thousand pinpoints of circles on the water. Ryder was still thinking about the man at the entrance. He sensed a connection when he took his glasses off, like the calm and serenity that filled him as he entered the cenotes. Weird.

"Well, I think it's time we should be heading back to the resort. It's been a great day. You have all done an excellent job. Tomorrow we'll explore a few more cenotes in this vicinity, and I think you will be ready to try some passageways. Wednesday we will head out for the camping trip exploring an unknown cenote off the beaten path."

"Seriously?" Ryder looked at Scout. "So the cenotes we visited today are not off the beaten path?"

"No, not really, the cenotes we explored today anyone can find if they research it. They have all been explored and mapped and the majority have miles of mainlines." Scout put his hat and sunglasses on. "The one I'm going to take you to involves a journey just to get there, not accessible by cars or vehicles."

"Sounds mysterious." Kendall grinned. "And I don't know how to thank you, Scout, it felt incredible to get back into the water again. The cenotes really are magnificent, spectacular…especially down under. It's like another world." Kendall paused. "I can see why Tim loved diving in them so much." At the sound of Tim's name Ryder lost the feeling of peacefulness, wondering for the hundredth time today, why he was here with Kendall.

The special moment had passed. They were no longer simply divers, enjoying an adventure, exploring an unusual unknown land together.

The Sherpas loaded up Scout's vehicle and they were on the road heading to the resort. For an old guy who seemed to be removed from technology, Scout pulled out the latest version iPod, scrolled through the music with a flick of his finger and landed on a playlist. Soon the sounds of the Rolling Stones' "You can't always get what you want" filled the quiet space.

The lush, thick jungle settings slowly turned into low-density shrubs as they left the mostly uninhabited area of the Yucatán and headed toward civilization where beautiful resorts decorated beachfronts at the end of long dirt roads. Kendall and Scout were laughing in the front seat. He couldn't stand her happiness another moment longer. He popped in his ear buds, shutting everyone out.

****

Kendall took in the picturesque scenery and glanced over at Scout noticing for the first time his uniqueness and his rugged good looks. *It has been so long since I recognized another human being as a man…even thought about someone as a member of the opposite sex. There's something charming about him. He has kindness in his eyes.* She had always been attracted to kind but rugged men. What was his story?

How did he end up here? Everyone had a story.

Looking out the window she tightly clutched the side of the seat. It was eighteen months since she had thought of another man. Almost two years since a member of the opposite sex held her tight, looked directly in her eyes or stirred up any old feelings of attractiveness. She realized the difference with Scout Whitman. He didn't have pity in his eyes. Steve or any other man who knew Tim back in Maryland projected pity every time they conversed. Scout met Tim, but he didn't know him. He didn't know the two of them together. Somehow, it made a difference.

She took a deep breath and let out a loud sigh without even realizing it. Ryder was sitting in the backseat with his ear buds, oblivious to anyone else. She turned her head to the left to sneak a peek at Scout. He was staring at her, and smiled. "It wasn't that bad of a day, was it?"

Kendall's mouth turned up involuntarily. He seemed so sincere as the sunlight lit up his face. "It was a great day, Scout; it was really a great day."

****

Upon returning to the resort, Ryder jumped out of the rover before Scout barely had it in park, pushing down his ear buds and stretching.

"How about we take a look at the menu and order a delicious meal and get our rest tonight?" Kendall faced Ryder, but he averted direct eye contact.

"I've got plans." It was an unkind, snappy retort. Ryder pulled his hat off and ran his fingers through his hair, never glancing her way. He walked over to Scout. "What time are we leaving tomorrow?"

Scout studied the body language of both of them.

"I'll be here at seven o'clock, it's a big day tomorrow. Rest up, I'll need all of your mind, body, and energy to be there."

"Sure, see you then." Ryder nodded and walked away without glancing at Kendall.

Kendall watched Ryder's back. "Thanks, Scout, it was a great day—He just misses his dad. I thought maybe this would bring us closer together, but well, we've never been close…but I'm still hopeful." Her smile did not reach her eyes.

Scout's heart went out to her. Ryder was making it tough. "See you at seven a.m." With a heavy slow pace she walked back to the entrance of the resort. He knew hurt, he had a front row pass to that emotion. Scout hoped she would turn around, but she never did.

Chapter 20

Five words.

Ryder uttered only five words since they woke up this morning.

"Four days left to go."

Not spoken to her, but tensely enunciated with grit, as he strutted out the door to their room. This was not what Kendall had pictured when she envisioned the trip Tim wanted her to take with Ryder.

At least the dives were spectacular. Scout, an excellent instructor, continued to test their ability. Yesterday, they stayed in the limits of natural sunlight and did checks, making sure they exited with two thirds of their air supply. Today, they each carried two battery-powered lights to go deeper. An experience of being pioneers, explorers in a non-commercial world untouched by humans.

As they left the natural light and followed the guideline, they were immersed in an underground maze of fragile decorations and majestic formations. Scout was teaching them to respect the delicate limestone, showing them techniques that would not damage these amazing natural wonders. The visibility good, the dive incredibly beautiful and both Kendall and Ryder proved their ability to follow safety techniques, showcasing their skills to maintain a parallel swim and not stir up silt or damage fragile creations.

The last cenote of the second day called "Ponderosa," meaning Eden was up a dirt road on a very steep hill. Organically wild, she envisioned this resembled the Garden of Eden, with wild green and brown twisted trees, fluorescent foliage and fauna. The smell delightfully fresh and pure. The landowner had spent quite some time in the cenote, decades, by the age of the structure. A curvy large stone stairway was built into the rock, leading down into the earth, ending with a ladder and a fifteen-foot drop-off into the cenote.

Looking down was like discovering a magical entrance to a secret underworld. The water so clear the reflection of their souls might bounce back. The air cool, crisp and clean. Scout explained the cenote water contained a rare quality of minerals or ingredients that made the particles in this space feel different in the nose, mouth, and skin. The change in the air unexplainable, but the impact of something different was noticeable.

Scout placed a hand-drawn map on the clipboard. There were several cavern zones, most marked with an installed gold permanent cavern line leading the way through the tunnels.

"We need to follow the line, no deviating, one area of the cavern has depths over 70 feet, and at about 33 feet a halocline. That's the depth we should stay at—33 to 40 feet," Scout explained.

"What is a halocline again?" Ryder asked, excluding Kendall, by standing in front of her.

"Halocline comes from the word 'halo' meaning circle and 'cline' meaning change in continuum." Scout moved to the side to create a circle of conversation. "The halocline occurs when saltwater meets and interacts with fresh water. Because the limestone of the cenotes allows saltwater to penetrate, the two will merge at some point. It's like mixing oil and water, when a diver swims through the halocline it almost seems like they are coming out of the water into a dry cavern." He added with a smile in his eyes, "Depending on how the light hits the halocline it can be illusionary, enchanting, creating an underwater experience reflecting unusual colors. You have to experience it for yourself." Scout stood on the stairwell leading into the earth.

"Cenote diving is much like going to church for some divers, it's majestic, eternal and all-encompassing. The peacefulness of the dive is calming and then you're surrounded by spectacular artistic formations, not made by any human hand, but by time…stunning decorations of art, enormous and breathtaking, more than any piece of artwork I can imagine. It's powerful." Ryder appeared mesmerized; finally something had caught his attention.

Scout descended the ladder and plopped into the water, with a grin on his face he yelled, "Let's go to church."

Eden was a fitting name for this cenote. One would never take a bite of an apple from any sea creature in this underwater garden, for fear one would be banished. A privilege one would not easily give up. Tranquil like a dream, a magical land, the clarity of the water creating an illusion one was suspended in air just drifting through colors. Kendall was reluctant to surface and face the tension of Ryder.

****

Scout glanced at Ryder. The all-day scowl he

brought with him had completely left his face. Scout understood how the television cameras could make him a pop star, especially if they caught this side of Ryder. In the cenotes Scout noticed the strong resemblance to Tim. He remembered diving with Tim, noticing the same thing he detected regarding Ryder today, something uniquely visible happened to each of them in the water, something changed. He couldn't quite put his finger on the difference with Tim, he had even mulled over it later, but looking at Ryder outside the water, he knew the difference became apparent inside the water. Ryder's essence was on fire, the water brought his skin, eyes, and personality to life. Scout shook his head, *maybe Ryder was just happy diving and living underneath the world instead of being on the surface with his stepmother and me*. A thought not too far removed from Scout's own mind in various stages of his life. He escaped life in the waters of the cenote; he might have to give this teenager a break.

Kendall, on the other hand, was very attractive, in the water and outside of the water. Scout tried not to notice her blue eyes reflecting the water and her soft sexy smile. She looked tired at times, but it didn't affect her natural beauty. She carried a soft beauty, nothing distinctive, but the averageness of her face and eyes created a classic picture one wanted to look. At least he did. A story was caught in her eyes, like reading a good book that couldn't be put down, a mystery yet to be discovered. The more he was around her, the more he liked her company. He wondered if she noticed him at all.

Enrique and Roberto helped Scout, Kendall, and Ryder pack up everything they brought in and provided a tasty snack of nuts, berries, and fruit rolled up in a tortilla of sorts. After a long day of diving and hiking, the fresh water and foods tasted incredible as they watched the sun fall into the water and the sky turn tangerine to bloody orange on the ride home. While Scout played one of his favorite tunes by Stevie Ray Vaughn, "The Sky is Crying," the vibrant red, orange, and pink colors painted the sky.

His thoughts drifted to the real reason Tim Jackson had arranged this trip. Not being truthful was an uncomfortable and unfamiliar feeling for Scout. They had no idea, it was evident, but he hated lies.

Chapter 21

After an interval of silence, he entered the dark empty house. He walked a slow pace, with confidence, even after hearing a double beep of the alarm code. He knew the layout of the house; he had been here before.

In the bedroom, his flashlight illuminated the painting of Kendall and Tim on the beach in Mexico. The light paused on their faces for at least thirty seconds. The house engulfed in pure silence as the man stopped and stared at the oversized canvas photo. His eyes locked in on their faces. Abruptly, he turned away and the search began. At first drawers were opened with a gentle touch, contents not disturbed. Gingerly touching a few items a little longer than necessary, gloved fingers unbolted closets and cabinets, going from room to room.

Time passed, and he found himself back to the photo on the wall empty-handed. Rapid movements developed into slamming drawers and cabinets, tossing contents on the floor, pushing furniture out of his path. Destruction became an outlet, he threw furniture and knocked over lamps. He picked up a picture he had thrown on the floor. On the back, he spotted it. Someone was listening. He searched for hidden cameras and found none.

Silence once again filled the empty house as he made his way stealthily to the garage and slowly crept up the staircase to the room above. He turned the knob; the door was locked. He hesitated and then with adrenaline force tried to kick the door in. Once, twice, the noise pierced the quiet air with pain. Silence again filled the heavy black night until the sound of a key entered the lock on the upstairs garage door.

Five minutes later sirens filled the air.

Chapter 22

Kendall gazed at the incredible view from the patio she shared with Ryder, her eyes filled with water, a single flow of moisture on her cheeks. She wiped the tears with the back of her hand. Thoughts of Tim consumed her, wondering how things would be different if he were here. She imagined an environment where her stepson actually enjoyed her company and they communicated. Tomorrow, she and Ryder would embark on the overnight camping trip and she hoped it would prove to be exciting and adventurous not disastrous and painful.

Ryder spent every night outside of the two-bedroom villa they shared. Eventually, by morning, he would end up in his room but for hours he was out of sight, hidden in a bar somewhere or hooking up with a girl he met or strolling with the handful of eighteen to twenty-one-year-olds that inhabited the resort. A strange dynamic, an adults-only resort, with an unusual pack of unattached single adults generally under the age of twenty-one, traveling with a parent. Attracted to each other like the little Scottish tricky dog magnets, chasing each other in the wee hours of the night. The electric energy of each seemed to draw the others out. Somehow, they found each other in the late hours of each day, traveling in packs and congregating in places not populated by couples or older adults.

Upon their return from diving, Ryder briefly chatted to several different guys and girls. As they passed each other they provided the slightest up-tick to the chin to acknowledge each other.

She thought about staying up until dawn to confront Ryder, but as soon as the thought entered her mind, she knew it was the wrong thing to do. He was over eighteen; therefore, at least on paper even if not in maturity, he was a legal adult.

The idea of burning the midnight oil night after night and then diving all day seemed impossible. She remembered a time not so long ago when staying up all night talking, listening to music and just being in close proximity with the one you love, gave you energy of a different force. It was electrifying. She had many nights with Tim, when sleep wasn't even on the radar screen. She wished they would have stayed up more nights.

Was this the trip he envisioned for his son? Probably not, it would have been a guy's trip. She wouldn't have been part of it. Her mind went to the briefcase. Was there a part of Tim she didn't know? It seemed impossible but what she found made it factual. *He kept secrets from me.*

She rolled over, staring at her beautiful hotel room with its dark beams on the ceiling and billowing canvas woven in between the wood. Luxurious and romantic but the giant king bed seemed half empty. Lonely and sad, two emotions not part of the six years with Tim, now were her closest roommates.

****

Kendall awoke, once again dreaming of Tim, a tranquil peace washed over her. She fought the pressure to open her eyes. For in that moment she was filled with joy and she wanted to stay asleep to see what would happen next.

She heard the noise again and looked at the clock on the nightstand; it was the first night all week, Ryder was home before midnight. The click of the door and the sound of Ryder running the water allowed her to close her eyes and for the first time in a long time, she slept a peaceful sleep.

The wake-up call jarred her. She bounded out of bed, took a long hot shower, picked up the room service menu, and ordered a breakfast for two to be delivered, full of eggs, protein drinks, and fruit. She smiled in the shower, a little residue of last night's dream still playing in her head as she enjoyed the hot water running over her, the last for the next three days.

Her dream of Tim still playing in her mind, even though the details were fuzzy and fading with every drop of water. She loved dreaming of him; for a moment he was alive and they were together again.

"Good morning."

Ryder didn't look up and greet her good morning, acting entrenched in whatever he was reading, shoveling eggs and bacon in his mouth, headphones on.

Kendall pretended another human being ignoring your morning greeting was typical.

At least they were together in the same room, not fighting. As much as she wasn't a camper, Kendall was determined to enjoy this last leg of the journey. Perhaps it was last night's dream, giving her a sign saying everything was going to be all right.

She hoped so, her thoughts unwillingly flashed to the contents of the briefcase, the Navy ID, and the neurosurgeon's card. One thing at a time.

Chapter 23

Scout noticed something different as Kendall walked over to his Land Rover.

"Good morning, Scout, I think everything on the list is in this duffel." She let the heavy duffel slide off her shoulder. "And I have a backpack as well." Kendall placed the overstuffed backpack on the ground next to the duffel. "Is this too much to take?"

The extra-large duffel, bursting at the seams, couldn't hold another pair of socks. He had stayed in the jungle with a third of her luggage for forty-five days when they laid the eighty-mile line underwater, but Tim had paid for the Sherpas and as long as Ryder didn't have double the load, they should be okay. *Women always pack more.*

"It looks okay, let Enrique repack it if you don't mind and we can see if we can use this dry pack to fit it all in." He held up a yellow bag half the size.

"Okay…dry pack, will we be taking it through water?" she asked. "My Kindle is in there."

Kindle? He had no idea what she was referring to, and in an attempt to not embarrass himself, in case it was a private woman's thing, he nodded. "Okay, we can put it in the dry bag."

"So, will we be walking through water to our camp spot?" She still looked puzzled.

Scout started to answer but his attention moved to

Ryder as he dumped two bags, both the size of Kendall's, on the ground.

Ryder's duffel's were grossly oversized. Thank God, they weren't trekking to the original cenote. They would never make it with this weight. Never. This confirmed his doubts, he made the right choice. "We have to cross six rivers to get to the site. We can take the Land Rover through the first three rivers but the other three we will need to swim through as they are too deep for any vehicle. It's a one-day hike to get to the cenote, we will arrive at dusk, set up camp and explore the cenote the next day. Then another night of camping and the third day we will head out and return home."

He had their attention; he continued, "To answer your question, yes, we will need to pack everything in a dry bag otherwise it will get wet and we will definitely have to reduce the load."

His voice sounded gritty even to him. He spoke softer instead of scolding. "Really, we just need suits and something to sleep in and clothes to hike in. The jungle is thick, and some of the plants can cause rashes, I would recommend layering a thin long shirt over a T-shirt, long pants and hats. If you think there is something you can take out of your packs please figure it out, we have Enrique and Roberto to help, but remember they will be carrying food, water, and the diving equipment, that means tanks and all the supplies."

Kendall immediately went to her pack, face flushed. "I'm sorry. I don't know what I was thinking, I didn't realize about the rivers and traveling all by foot." She smiled at Scout. "I can definitely get rid of some things."

Ryder knelt on the ground pulling items out of his two large duffels.

Thirty minutes later, the contents of the three large duffel bags were down to two dry packs. Kendall and Ryder, with layered light clothing and hats on, both had backpacks in smaller dry bags slung over their shoulders. They looked as if they knew what they were doing; the scene could have been a cover photo in an adventure magazine. Scout was reminded how easily looks could be deceiving.

The roar of the Land Rover opened up to the raw nature, soaring through the scrub, birds flying with the vehicle. A lush, wet and shiny jungle scene flashed out the back windows, a green explosion, in every shade imaginable. They were on their way.

****

The fourth river caught them by surprise. The first three river crossings had been relatively easy and strikingly picturesque. Three hours and three river crossings later, after traveling 78 miles through dense jungle on narrow, bumpy roads, they hit the fourth river.

Ryder, desperately in need of a Manners 101 class, kept his headphones on the entire three hours, while Kendall and Scout easily slipped into conversations regarding a variety of topics.

She listened and asked simple touristy questions. Scout adored this part of the world and was full of useful information. What she really wanted to know was more about Scout. The more they talked, the more she found him intriguing. His wild straw-colored hair pulled back in a ponytail, and his fluidity of the English

113

language reminded her of a college professor. A professor all the young girls would be in love with. She wanted to ask, where he was from, if he lived alone, and of all the beach towns in the world, why here? Questions which seemed too private in front of Ryder, Enrique and Roberto, so she said nothing.

In the small shadows of silence her mind escaped to Tim and the briefcase. Analyzing why he would keep this from her. She pressed on her temples with both hands closing her eyes.

"Is it something I said?" Scout had stopped in mid-sentence and looked sideways at her; she was caught not paying attention.

"No, I was just thinking about stuff back home, you know, work stuff." She smiled apologetically.

"Not really," he replied. "This is my work, my home. I gave up all that busy stressful city life a long time ago."

"What city?" She studied him curiously.

"D.C."

"Wow, I would never have guessed you were going to say D.C., so you were born in our nation's capital?"

"No, born in California, Northern California." His gaze met hers. "And you, Maryland?"

"No, a small town in Western Pennsylvania, outside of Pittsburgh. Soap Hollow, and yes that is seriously the name."

He laughed. She decided to ask the questions she wanted to ask all day. "What made you move to D.C.?"

Scout laughed. "Usually, I get the question, what made you move to Mexico?"

His laugh was contagious. "That's my next question."

He revealed he loved growing up in Northern California, mentioning—more than once—it should be a separate state from Southern California. He went to the University of California, Santa Barbara, and studied environmental issues focusing on climate change.

"Climate change?" she asked. "Did they even call it that back then?"

He raised his eyebrow, his attraction level shining through. "Back then?" He smiled. "Not everyone, at first it was climate modification, because that is all we knew, then the term global warming was used. I hooked up with an organization and they relocated me to the nation's capital to assist in publishing research on the warming climate. Lots of politics and stress. Can you imagine the frustration in trying to attach importance to research no one wanted to believe in? Powerful corporations were succeeding at disproving it. In their mind, they had no choice but to protect their bottom line. The lies, the oil industry advocates, the politics of those trying to discredit scientific consensus for political reasons and greed." He took a breath. "It was exhausting. What I know is this, in the decades ahead the consequences of carbon and other greenhouse gas emission by humans and their activities will cause irrefutable dangerous developments." Scout continued in a serious calm voice. "We can expect without a doubt major droughts, polar melting, coastal flooding, and severe weather. Just watch the weather channel for any extended length of time and it's not hard to see what's coming."

She sat up, listening intently to Scout speak, he was much more than a cave diver who owned a dive shack on the beach of Mexico. His green eyes full of a passion and conviction mixed with the same enthusiastic look he exposed to her when diving the cenotes.

"One day all nations will fight over scarcity of land and fresh water. In many countries, the war has been on for centuries. Arable land, land that can be used for farming, growing crops, land which we can live off, survive on, there will be a shortage even to Americans. We are polluting our waterways on a daily basis with EPA leaks, oil leaks." Scout paused. "It's all about the water." He turned to look at her as he repeated, "It truly is all about the water, your husband and I had this same conversation."

Before she could shake the surprise off her face, Scout slammed the brakes. She hadn't even noticed the wide-ranging river in front of them. The fourth river. A river they could not drive through.

They parked the Land Rover and got out to stretch their legs. Her mind was trying to wrap itself around the picture of Scout and Tim having a conversation. The dense bush and jungle cradled the river. As far as the eye could see, there were no signs of civilization, no cell phone towers, no buildings, roads, or signs of life. "It feels so removed, like we are the only ones on the planet. Who owns this land?" she asked Scout.

He stopped stretching and started placing the packs and gear on the ground. "The people of Mexico. Most of this land is owned by many families together, for centuries it has been passed down."

Scout, Enrique, and Roberto sorted out the packs, tanks and gear with surprising ease, and explained where and how they would cross the river.

"From here on out, the rest of the trip is on foot, our real journey starts now, so take a break and get ready to cross."

She was disappointed their conversation would have to wait until another time. Scout pointed to a small clearing up ahead surrounded by dense bush. "If you need some privacy go there, but watch out for the pizza plant I showed you yesterday. If it touches your skin, it will swell up and produce hives and blisters. Trust me you don't want to touch it."

After a small break, careful not to touch any pizza plants, the group prepared to cross the river. Scout took the lead with Ryder, she was in the middle, Enrique and Roberto in the back stepping slowly through the swift flowing river. At the deepest part of the river, the trekking turned into swimming as the depth, higher than their shoulders, went over their heads.

In less than ten minutes, bags and supplies made it safe to the other side, including the tanks carried on the Sherpas' backs. Regrouping on the other side, they took a short break, dried off as well as they could, laced up their dry hiking boots, and continued onward.

****

The jungle terrain of the Riviera Maya was lush, thick, tropical vegetation, creating an illusion of Amazon jungles and primitive lands untouched by humans. Enrique, now in the lead, held a machete high above his shoulders, chopping the path with an up and down motion, two tanks on his back.

Ryder had finally become present. Still ignoring Kendall, he marched through the low canopy, fascinated with the portable GPS. For the first time on the trip, Scout was impressed with his intelligent questions.

"So, this cenote we are trekking to, is this the

cenote you took my father to?" Ryder asked.

Scout's heart rate accelerated, and with a slight hesitation, he answered, "No, your father and I went ocean diving together. We never went to any cenotes or cave systems. He planned this trip to do cave diving with you." Scout swallowed, trying to stay as close to the truth as possible.

Soon, they faced the next river, a somewhat quiet, meandering river. The crossing went smooth. Everyone knew the drill and worked together as a team; now, they only had one more river to cross.

The trek continued with conversations regarding the hard work and pride of the local people, until they came to a dense spot of scrub in the middle of the trail. The roar of rushing water reached his ears. Enrique and Roberto helped machete their way through a particularly dense area. Their next crossing came into view.

The last river was much wider and faster with power behind it. Dark gray-blue water made up the waterway, resembling a snake twisting and crawling its way across the wild, unruly jungle, complementing the canvas of dark army greens, shiny lime-green leaves, and sage-colored scrubs mixed in with dark brown. The palette created a feeling of rough edges and toughness. Unlike the cenotes, there was nothing calm about this tributary or the masculine scenery before their eyes.

"This is the last major river crossing. Let's go over in pairs." Scout lowered his packs and knelt by the edge. "One part of the center has a pretty swift current. I'll go over first with Ryder, then come back for you, Kendall. Enrique and Roberto will float the tanks."

Kendall sat on the ground carefully taking her

hiking boots off and putting her wet socks on. The muscular silhouette of her leg, accented her toned physique. He ignored the stirring in his abdomen. He tried to shake off his thoughts. "You and I go next. Leave your hiking shoes on for this one, we are only a couple miles from our camp spot, and I think the traction from your shoes will be needed for the bottom of this river."

Kendall nodded, took her wet socks off, and put her hiking shoes back on. She wore sparkly blue toenail polish, and it made him smile. At first glance, one might get the wrong impression, write her off as a girly girl, but she was really a rare combination of a tomboy with grace and beauty, not shying away from outdoor adventure.

He was attracted to her, more attracted than he wanted to recognize, his thoughts consumed by her essence. They slowly moved through the river. It happened in a flash. Kendall slipped, and the force of the river pulled her under.

Chapter 24

Sloshing shoes, mosquitoes, and humidity added to the harshness of the last few miles. The river crossing left them quiet. Kendall was still recovering from the current that buckled her knees and knocked her down, fully submerging her under the water. In a flash Scout grabbed her tight and held her against a tree branch growing out of the river. The closeness of his embrace seemed to linger a moment longer than natural. Pressed against his warm body, she met his green eyes. The connection was electrifying, it took her breath away, the adrenaline surging through her being.

No one else seemed to notice the intense moment in the river, but she was fiercely aware of it and certain Scout was too.

Ryder seemed indifferent, not even asking her if she was okay.

She suppressed a grin at his appearance. If any jungle trekking reality fan ran into Ryder Jackson that day, they would have thought he walked right out of a scene of a jungle adventure movie. His wet clothes stuck to his sculptured body and the dirt overlying the tan on his face intensified his blue eyes. He was striking. But, attractiveness took more than a pretty face. Ryder was sometimes cold, self-absorbed and cruel. Kendall wished he was more like his father.

****

Kendall moved in silence after the river grabbed her. Ryder didn't wish her any physical harm, but he couldn't deny the pleasure from her panic. A change in the air was noticeable, but he could not pinpoint it. Was she sorry she forced herself on this trip? He hoped so, she didn't need to be here.

He liked Scout; he respected his knowledge and his diving skills. He understood why his father chose Scout to take them on this journey. Talking about his father was difficult. Going a day without any drugs was also something new in his daily ritual. He was successful in smuggling a few Vicodin in his Tylenol bottle, but he only had one left. His hands hadn't shaken all day. He felt remarkably well without them.

He agreed to take this trip for his father. Every time he looked at Kendall he desperately wished it were his father instead of her. He'd been trying to figure out all day, why his father made that entry in the logbook. Perhaps, when he was on the boat at the Blue Hole, he was thinking about him and the upcoming trip he had planned. Did he actually have a feeling something tragic was going to happen that particular afternoon in Belize that would make him ask Kendall to take him?

He'd never know what his dad was thinking that day, but at least he was thinking of Ryder and this was the place he wanted to show him. *I'm here, Dad, is this what you wanted? Why?*

****

Enrique and Roberto stopped dead in their tracks, faces turned to the jungle behind them. Enrique lifted his hand and Roberto held up a finger to his lips, silencing the group.

Roberto motioned to Scout and pointed to the left.

Kendall, her long wet hair falling down her back, still looking like a drowned rat, appeared years younger than her age. A baseball cap shielding the truth in her eyes, he wondered if she felt the same electricity he did as he held her in his arms in the river.

Scout held up his hand signaling 'stay' and put his finger to his lips.

Several minutes passed, the background music of the jungle increasing in volume with the sound of insects and birds.

Scout whispered to Enrique in Spanish, and Roberto nodded his head in agreement.

"It's okay." Scout said. "It might have been an animal. Enrique and Roberto both heard something in the woods."

"What kind of animal?" Kendall asked.

Scout cast a glance at Enrique and Roberto and back to Kendall. "Well, it's hard to say, if it was a howler monkey we would usually hear their calls. I'm sure you'll hear them tomorrow, they are quite communicative and travel in packs." Scout paused. "And we would see them swinging in the tree. But there are smaller animals out there, like your raccoons or skunks. One called coatimundi can make noise as well."

Everyone surveyed the jungle.

"It's quiet now…so whatever it was is gone."

He smiled and moved next to Kendall, pulling out his GPS. "We are not too far from where we will set up camp, it's up ahead, should be an open area."

Ryder kept walking. "There's jaguars in the Yucatán? Right?"

He turned around and gave Ryder a penetrating glare. "There could be, but man has really chased them away to certain areas, if they were in this area, they would keep their distance…from us."

Chapter 25

The canopy of trees formed a swaying umbrella over their campsite. They passed an amazing pumping spring spouting clear water out of the middle of a mangrove forest, and walked through thorny green scrub and low-level palms. Suddenly, a captivating clearing with a carpet of thick green moss, emanating a feeling of an enchanted forest filled with fairytale characters, appeared. A place from another world. This would be their camp.

Scout helped lay out the camping equipment from the packs, remarking Enrique and Roberto were experts at setting up a campsite. He pointed straight ahead looking at the GPS. "Just a little farther is the cenote we will be exploring tomorrow." Scout tilted his head. "It's still light, we could check it out now, it's a great way to rinse off after our long hike."

Ryder sat on the ground. "I think I have had enough walking today." Peeling off his hiking boots, he revealed a few blisters. "Count me out."

"You okay? I have some ointment you can use." She dug around in her pack, brought out a tube, and handed it to Ryder.

Ryder reluctantly took the ointment from her, but then continued to look away. "I'm fine, I just want to lie down and listen to some music." The ear buds went into his ear.

Scout turned to Kendall. "You want to go check it out?"

"Sounds like a plan, even this big jungle can feel small." She smiled.

****

She watched him as he released his ponytail and casually ran his fingers through his hair. Grabbing her camera she followed, snapping a few pictures of the back of him walking in the jungle. She bit her lip as her heartbeat increased. She was stimulated by his presence. He was at ease in the middle of the tropics. The wildness complemented him as his energy and excitement picked up his pace.

She let out a loud sigh, a habit she had picked up from her mother over the years. It was not a sign of unhappiness or frustration, it was a sign of relaxing, taking a deep breath and letting all the stress out. Scout turned around. "Are you tired? I know it's been a long day, but you two are great hikers, you did really well today."

She returned his smile. "No, not really, I know I should be tired, but there's something about this place that gives me energy...a swim in the cenote sounds refreshing."

She hesitated. "Can I ask you something personal, Scout?"

He kept walking.

"Sure, shoot."

"I found some confidential information about my husband before I took this trip." She needed to tell someone. "I would've bet all the money in Las Vegas, I knew everything about Tim, certain he would never lie to me, would never keep secrets from me." She paused.

125

"But I would've lost, lost it all." Another pause. "I found a briefcase of his, it has information he never told me, almost like a secret life."

Scout stopped and turned around.

"What would you do with information like that? Would you tell anybody? Would you tell his son?"

****

Scout was unsure how to respond; he did best when he thought something through, asked questions until he knew what to say. He thought, no, he hoped the question would be about him, revealing a mutual interest on Kendall's part. *How long does it take a widow to be interested in another man*; he had no idea. *But, she was clearly focused on her husband.*

"Well, I guess it would depend what type of confidential information it was. Is it something that involves Ryder?" Scout rubbed the back of his neck, wondering if she knew about the secret cenote; it seemed Tim had more secrets.

She kept walking. "I know I just met you, but Tim liked you, trusted you enough to arrange this trip and quite frankly, I don't have anyone else to talk to."

He couldn't explain why he so desperately wanted to help her. He was compelled to be near her, but it went deeper than attraction. He pushed the untruth of the other cenote out of his head. She probably didn't need any more surprises about her husband. He caught up with her and touched her arm, turning her around to face him. "I'm a good listener, Kendall, and your secrets are safe with me."

Even after almost drowning and hiking through a humid jungle, she glowed with life; she had natural beauty inside and out. Even her sweat smelled sweet.

Touching her seemed electric. "The cenote is just up here; let's sit down on the edge."

She nodded and started walking through the clearing, then stopped still in her tracks.

He could hear the intake of breath as she took in the scene, her voice a silky whisper. "It's incredible!"

In front of them, a scene of sensations exploded before their eyes. A bubbling waterfall flowed down into a deep clear lagoon, creating a sound of soothing water. A small river exited the lagoon, trickling over shiny brown rocks surrounded by soft, fuzzy moss-covered rocks. Freshness crawled inside his nose, a smell that always invigorated him. The depth of the colors in the lagoon were astonishing shades of blue-green mixed together but not completely stirred, creating an illusion of colors to trick the eye. The pool glowed as if there were light underneath and the setting sun hit the leaves and branches of the jungle flora creating patterns on the rocks and branches.

Scout silent, allowed Kendall that special moment he had when he first came upon this beautiful cenote. It was as magnificent to him this time as on his first trek; he was in awe of the sheer beauty of the Yucatán.

He fought the urge to put his arms around her, so instead he crossed them tightly over his chest. For a brief minute, he wondered how it would feel to share exquisite beauty like this, with another human being whom you loved. He contemplated this was the reason Tim requested to take his son to the unexplored cenote, sharing this stunning experience with someone you loved was incredible. He wanted to touch her.

He perched on the flat rock along the edge of the lagoon facing the waterfall. "Come sit down, this is a great spot to take it in."

Her eyes reflected the colors of the beautiful water. It was evident she appreciated this outstanding canvas of nature's work.

"I understand now…I understand why Tim would want to share this with Ryder." She paused. "It may be one of my favorite places on earth."

It seemed the moment had passed for her to confide Tim's secrets. Not wanting to break the spell, he started undoing his hiking boots and taking off his shirt and hat.

He could feel her watching him and she laughed, a happy sound that warmed Scout's heart.

"I finally figured it out; I know who you remind me of."

He stopped, unsure if he wanted to be a reminder of anyone to her. He waited, not looking at her.

"Have you ever seen the series *Lost*?"

"Well, I don't have satellite and I'm not much of a TV watcher, but I have watched a few episodes about the plane going missing on the island. My sister sent me the box set for Christmas."

"Then you know who I'm going to say you look like?…Sawyer." She came closer. "Your sister said the same thing and that's why she sent you the series, am I right?"

He flung his body into the cenote. "Sawyer? Which one is that, the handsome con artist?" He laughed before he went under the water. When he came up, she was walking away toward the group of palms.

"Turn around, I'll be right in."

She emerged from the trees with her bathing suit on, a sight Scout witnessed for the last few days diving in the cenote. It stirred something inside him. This moment seemed more intimate. It was the first time the two of them were alone together, and to top it off a gorgeous waterfall cascaded into a clear pool, heightening the experience.

She hesitated at the ledge, catching his eyes, her mouth turned up. He wished she was his.

Treading water, half floating on his back, he inched closer. He didn't want to break the spell. He was going to let her say the first word. His heart was racing.

She emerged, her eyes catching the sparkle of the water. The moment lingered in the air, with the silence of their voices surrounded by the pounding of the falls and the birds singing in the trees. He didn't want to be anywhere else but here in this moment. He hoped he wasn't misreading her feelings for him.

She broke the seconds of quiet. "You know I was always a Sawyer fan, I much preferred him over the doctor Jack, something about his rugged hard exterior covering up a soft big heart." She smiled. "You saved me today in the river, thanks for catching me."

It seemed natural as he encircled her with his arms and brought his face next to hers. Their lips met. The kiss soft and tender left him wanting more. She kissed him back. The sound of the waterfall was mixed in with their heavy breathing.

She pulled back, went under the water, swam toward the large flat rock on the edge of the waterfall, and pulled herself up. No words were spoken.

He slowly swam toward her. Tears slid down her cheeks. "It's okay, Kendall…"

She continued to look at the waterfall. "I think we let the magic in this place get the best of us. The sun's

going down. We should probably get back."
****

Kendall had not kissed another man since Tim. Confusion and feelings of betrayal consumed her pounding heart. She couldn't look at Scout.

The walk back to the campsite passed quickly even though few words were uttered. Scout tried to make small talk about the next day's dive, she knew he sensed her discomfort.

When the trail ended at their campsite, she was struck with the intimacy of the cozy scene in front of her—two small fires in the center of three tents and six tiki sticks in a circle around the perimeter. The smell of sautéed onions teased her senses, she was starving even though her stomach was a tight knot. Scout gave her a smile as if everything would be okay and started speaking in Spanish to Enrique and Roberto.

Ryder was nowhere to be seen. Scout gestured toward the tent. "Roberto said he is taking a siesta. Dinner will be ready in a few minutes."

She nodded. "Okay, I'll wake him." She focused on his chin, not meeting his eyes.

The dinner was tasty with shucked ears of corn in their husks roasted over the fire, cut potatoes mixed with peppers, onions, and vegetables in a unique spicy sauce to complement warm rolls of bread. Ryder, more awake than before, dominated the conversation asking Scout questions about the cenote.

Darkness fell and soft colors of the fire added to the ambiance of the jungle. The warm food made her sleepy as she sat mesmerized by the fire. Conversations started to slack off.

In one of the silent moments, a rustling noise came

from the jungle. Roberto sprung to his feet, with Enrique putting a finger to his lips.

Her heart started beating irregularly fast for the third time that day, and in a flash, she realized how short life was. Perhaps it was the unknown nature of the sound in the jungle, but when she made eye contact with Scout, security and safety cloaked her like a warm blanket. She wasn't going to be afraid of her feelings.

Scout and Roberto walked stealthily toward the edge of the clearing, and Roberto disappeared behind the closely packed trees. The noise stopped.

Ryder's profile in the flickering firelight calmed her nerves. The resemblance to his father was uncanny. For a second she was looking at a replica of a younger Tim. It pulled at her heart, returning a familiar ache.

Not speaking directly to her Ryder said, "I'm sure it's just an animal, they won't come near the fire."

"I'm sure you're right, it's just an animal." She paused, uncertain whether she should say what she was thinking. "Right now, when you spoke, you looked and sounded just like your father."

Ryder hesitated then he did something he had not done all day, he looked directly at her, his blue eyes catching the light of the fire. "I'll take that as a compliment. But, he should be here, not you."

"I know." Her heart ached, she swallowed the tears back.

The fire cast dancing shadows as the large leaves of the trees arching above swayed gently. *I can feel you, Tim; I know you're with us.*

Scout, Enrique, and Roberto finally returned to the campfire. "It's just an animal, maybe a howler curious about who's spending the night in their territory," Scout said. "Don't worry, they won't come near the fire. The perimeter of the clearing is as far as they'll wander. Roberto and Enrique will be sleeping outside the tents—they will watch over us. You guys okay?"

They both nodded.

"Well, we have a big day tomorrow, three incredible dives, so let's get a good night's sleep." He pointed to the middle tent. "Kendall, you take the middle tent; Ryder and I will be on the outside. If you need to go for some privacy, wake Enrique or Roberto. Don't go alone in the jungle at night."

****

In less than thirty minutes, everyone was down for the night. Even Enrique and Roberto lost the battle of the closing of their eyelids as a gentle breeze blew and the night sounds of the jungle played a relaxing musical score. Scout unzipped his tent and took watch. The dancing flames of the fire hypnotized him. The small hairs on his sweaty neck alerted him. Between the leaves of a palm tree and a twisted branch, blue flashes appeared. His heart thumped. It looked like two sets of eyes. Standing up, he scanned the jungle. Nothing. Was his mind playing tricks on him? For the next hour he watched and listened. Nothing appeared.

Chapter 26

Kendall was swimming in circles, surrounded by clear aqua water. "Tim?" she yelled. "Tim?" Her voice jarred her into reality. A terrifying low guttural howl took her breath away. Her adrenaline spiked and she lost the ability to yell. Her eyelids fluttered, her heart thumping in her chest. She was awake now. The bellow filled the air.

Adjusting to the dark, she focused on the teeth of the zipper on the front panel. Tent. Jungle. Yes, she was camping in the Yucatán. She reached for her sport watch, pressing the side button to illuminate the time. The sun would be rising soon.

She placed her head back on her tiny pillow, squinting tightly in deep concentration. She couldn't detect movement from the tents next to her. The loud chatter of the birds grew in volume. She didn't want to be the only one awake.

Did she dream the ungodly shrieks? She held her breath, again the eerie screams echoed through the primeval forest. The massive noise bolted her back up to a sitting position. Images of a gigantic dinosaur whirling its head howling flashed through her mind. Uncertain what to do, she threw on her hat, slipped her flip-flops on and grabbed a flashlight. Licking her lips and taking steady breaths, she unzipped the entrance in slow motion.

Roberto leaned against the trunk of a tree, legs stretched out on a blanket, his head tilted back resting on the cradle of his hands, focusing on the canopy of trees above. He put his finger to his lips and pointed up.

She lifted her chin to the sky, not seeing anything in the soft light of the dawn except the silhouette of the jungle leaves. It took a minute to adjust to the daybreak. The movement startled her: a graceful swinging motion from one branch to the next. Throat opened to the sky, the hairy beast released its howl. The sound unlike anything she had ever witnessed.

Another one bellowed off to the left, a group of them, calling out to each other shouting to the gods "good morning, world" in their scary, deep monkey language.

She bent her knees to the ground, sharing the blanket with Roberto. Together as the sun released its light, they enjoyed a beautiful show of graceful monkeys swinging across the treetops.

She glanced at Scout's tent, and Roberto uttered a few words in Spanish and motioned to the woods. She pointed at Ryder's tent. Roberto said, "No, *sueños*" and leaned his head on folded hands.

She wished she'd paid attention in high school Spanish. The language barrier sucked. Afraid to speak, she smiled and headed to her tent to get ready for the day of diving. With a little bit of sunscreen, her teeth brushed, her long hair combed back in a ponytail, she was ready. As Kendall zipped up her tent, Scout strolled out of the bush toward her. Unexpectedly—all on its own—her heart did a little flip-flop, accelerating in beats.

A tiny corner of his mouth appeared to rise as he

spoke. "*Buenos dias*, we got some coffee boiling and Roberto grilled up some homemade tamales."

She cleared her throat. "Good morning." Her voice squeaked. His soft lips made her remember yesterday's kiss.

"I heard you watched the morning monkey pageant."

"Yes it was an outstanding show." Frozen like a teenage girl with a sudden crush, she was stumped for words. She took the steaming tin cup out of Roberto's hands as he placed the coffee pot back on the fire. Her hands shook. "*Perfecto*, Roberto! *Gracias*." She was certain her warm cheeks had splotches of pink. She tried to hide the awkwardness invading her limbs. Not looking at anyone in particular, she said, "I can't believe Ryder didn't wake up with the howler monkeys, they have such a crazy shriek."

Stop acting like a nervous teenager on a first date. Having been dormant for so long, the sexual energies Scout stirred up were unexpected. She moved toward Ryder's tent and in a cheerful voice said, "Ryder...coffee's on the fire and tamales are ready...." She waited, no response. She attempted to sit down gracefully in one of the foldable chairs; it collapsed, spilling her and the coffee on the ground. Roberto and Enrique offered her a hand and she shook them off, smiling like a clown. They left with a grin.

Scout dropped to the chair next to her. "How did you like waking up to the roar of the howler monkeys?" He smirked. "They sure have a crazy sound, but you get used to it in the Yucatán. Actually, I never get used to those amazing apes, but it's a special sign. Their presence means it's going to be an awesome diving day.

In fact, I have never been on a successful cenote exploration, without seeing or at least hearing the monkeys."

She was taking dainty bites of her tamale, trying to focus on something other than her beating heart.

"I believe they are the ancient guardians to the cenotes. You won't find them at every tourist cenote, but the ones hidden deep, always seem to have a howler and an iguana defending their entrances. I mean, it never fails, you find a secret cenote and there they are sitting up in the trees checking out everybody who goes into their sacred waters. Some say the Mayas transformed into howlers and iguanas. Now they are watching over us to protect their land."

She swallowed, meeting his gaze with a soft smile. "Really?"

"Who knows, I was just seeing if you were paying attention."

"Well, they certainly got my attention this morning. I was dreaming and it sounded like dinosaurs."

Scout laughed. A happy hearty sound filled the jungle. "You have a good ear, Kendall, they actually used the sounds of the howler monkeys in the movie *Jurassic Park*."

Her eyes widened as she giggled. "Seriously? I was dreaming and when I woke up I was ready to fight off the prehistoric beast T-rex."

She chewed the last bite of her tamale, her nervousness disappearing. She was strangely comfortable, sitting here with Scout, outside the campfire in the morning light, in the middle of the wild.

His knee grazed her leg as he rushed to get the

words out. "Really? A dream of dinosaurs, that's all you got? I had a dream last night—I was swimming in the cenotes and you were in it."

Blood rushed to her cheeks.

Scout cleared his throat. "Not like that, I mean…We were just swimming, maybe searching for something. But the scenery was beautiful…just like yesterday afternoon."

Kendall heard the tent zipper being yanked down, Ryder emerged wearing a tight white T-shirt over long gym shorts. Part of his hair was sticking straight up. Amazing how naturally beautiful and handsome young adults looked waking up.

"What time is it?" Ryder stretched and yawned. Scout stood up, offering Ryder his chair. "It's breakfast time, have some tamales, so we can get started on the first dive of the day." Scout's voice was full of excitement. "You're going to love this cenote, Ryder, it's epic."

****

Brown curly twigs and rock ledges were visible from the crystal-clear water. Depths of color sparkled, bottomless, like an infinity mirror without end or beginning. The banks surrounding the beautiful lagoon were crowded with roots, leaves, and brown moss. Trunks of trees looked eternal, old as the ancient ones, framing this spectacular oasis. Kendall inhaled the fresh earthy smell. It was just as incredible today as it was yesterday.

The picture it painted was like no other. Beams of sunshine created a circle of light reflecting greens and blues on rocks and leaves, inventing a place of enlightenment designed by nature.

Even Ryder froze in the glorious sight, offering a rare glimpse of his face, full of joy.

In seconds his body hit the water with a woo-hoo echoing in the air. Scout met her gaze. Yes, she was thinking about the spot from yesterday, not soon to be forgotten.

Like an hour glass with a wide center, the three dives and the resting time in between flew by at record speed. The perfect weather, the sky as deep blue as the water, and the underground world below was an unbelievable experience as they descended through several tight cave passages, which opened up into magnificent cathedral rooms.

In the last cathedral room, they were able to surface and take deep breaths of fresh air. Heads thrown back to the ceiling, the tiny pinhole of light from the outside world hundreds of feet above them, flickered over each one of them. Nothing else seemed to matter but the beauty of the moment.

"I think I understand why my father wanted me to see this. I feel different in the cenotes, I have some kind of peace or calmness I don't typically have back home." Ryder turned in Scout's direction. "Thanks, Scout, for following through with my dad's wishes, I think somehow he is smiling down on us—happy that I made it."

Scout wiped the water off his face with the back of his hand. His mouth opened up in response, then nothing come out. Kendall wondered what he was holding back.

****

A tinge of guilt intruded Scout's thoughts. He should be happy Ryder was so impressed with the cenote he showed him. What difference did it make if it wasn't the exact cenote his father wanted him to see. He blocked out the annoying voice in his head as he helped get dinner started.

The companies who created freeze-dried meals had jungle dining down to a science. Kendall and Ryder enjoyed two different types of pasta, alfredo and carbonara, while Enrique and Roberto ate some dry packed mixture of vegetables, rice, and beans. For dessert, he surprised them all by singing Happy Birthday to Ryder and providing s'mores with a candle. Enrique and Roberto were unsure of the concoction of marshmallows, chocolate, and crackers, but once tasted their faces lit up like little kids at a candy factory as they had third and fourth helpings

After the food was gone, Ryder was the first one to call it a day. Enrique and Roberto left to set up the tiki torches around the perimeter and he was alone with Kendall for the first time since breakfast.

He memorized her profile in the firelight. "I think Ryder really enjoyed himself today. You two seem to be getting along a lot better."

She continued to focus on the fire. "I doubt it. I think he loved the cenotes, but…it's a start. Tomorrow will be our last day together…for I don't know how long. He doesn't have any reason to come to Maryland to visit, and his mother and I don't exactly see eye to eye, so I don't make too many trips to Arizona. I guess it's up to me to figure out how we move forward."

The silence lingered with the smoke from the crackling fire, a blanket of stars twinkled above them.

"Will you make any more trips to Mexico?"

"I don't know. Maybe…"

"There's something I want to tell you, Kendall." He moved his chair beside her struggling to speak the words.

"I don't think we need to talk about it." Her words cut him off.

He was silent, *I feel so guilty for not taking them to the cenote Tim wanted to show them. She'll probably never speak to me again if she knows I was dishonest.* The lie was eating through him. He liked Kendall, and he never lied. Honesty and integrity were what he lived by and he expected the same things from those he allowed into his life. He wanted her in his life, or at least he wanted to try, see where it went. He knew this like he knew the caves in the cenote.

He stood up and looked over in the direction of Enrique and Roberto smoking cigarettes on the other side of camp; he wanted to say more. "I guess we ought to think about calling it a day." He leaned down and whispered in her ear, "Someday, when you're ready, I would love for you to come back and visit Mexico. My Mexico. With me."

And with that, he walked away.

She stared into the fire's red-orange dancing shapes. The sensation of being watched prickled over her skin. She peered into the surrounding woods. Nothing. She shivered and turned back to the fire, but the sensation of eyes on her remained.

Chapter 27

Once again, the screams of the howler monkeys startled her awake, this time the background music seemed fitting. The hike back to the vehicles seemed much easier than the initial trek to the cenote. The rivers were calmer and luckily Kendall was not pulled under by an undertow. With the cenotes and the jungle behind them, Ryder's mask slid back on, covering his emotions. The light from his eyes gone, the "I'm so bored" expression returned to his face.

"If you're not too tired," Scout said, "I know a great place to grab some delicious local food, not too far from your resort."

Kendall glanced in the rearview mirror, Ryder's eyes closed, earbuds in. She smiled. "Going out to dinner sounds outstanding, Scout, let me ask Ryder. Maybe he'll come if it's all three of us. Eating together in public, something Ryder and I haven't experienced this entire time…would be a wonderful way to end the trip." She laughed at the thought, admiring the masculine, rugged scenery with its multitude of greens and early evening shadows.

She turned sideways to Scout. *He is such a handsome man, and seems so genuine, rare, and kind. Maybe, there is room in my heart. Maybe.*

"Would Enrique and Roberto like to come? It would be my treat."

Scout translated the invitation to the two passengers in the back seat. "They do not wish to insult you or turn down your generous invitation, but they have been gone from their families for two nights and are anxious to see their children and wives. Roberto's youngest son was sick when he left and he is eager to be with him."

"Of course, please tell him I hope his son is doing better." She had spent the last six days with them, never asking anything regarding their lives.

Language really was a barrier, especially if you let it be. She had been too wrapped up in her own little world to think about others. She wanted to ask about his sick boy, but didn't know how to begin the conversation.

Scout pulled up to the gate and she gave her villa number to the guards. Immediately the men's eyes widened and the tallest of the two motioned to the other. He picked up the telephone speaking rapidly in Spanish. Scout got out of the Jeep and walked over to the man, and she could hear an urgent dialogue exchanged in Spanish.

"What's going on?" she asked stepping out of the Jeep.

"The resort has been looking for you two for the past twenty-four hours."

"Looking for us? Why?" She stuttered her words her heart racing.

"There was a break-in at your house the morning you left for the camping trip. Friends have been trying to contact you and the staff became alarmed when you never returned the calls or picked up the messages. Housekeeping informed the manager your beds had not been slept in and the key card showed you never entered your rooms for two days." He kept his voice calm. "Ryder's mother has been frantic, calling every hour, and she notified the local authorities." The guard interrupted, speaking rapidly. Scout answered nodding his head pointing to Ryder in the back seat.

"I explained the situation, but I think you guys have some calls to make." Scout's face softened. "Is there something I can help with? I'm sorry about somebody robbing your house back home." Kendall took a deep breath, shaking her head.

Scout grasped his hands as if holding back his urge to hug her. "Don't worry about dinner; I'm sure you have enough on your plate to clear up this mess. I'm really sorry about everything."

She touched his arm. "Is there a number where I can reach you in a couple hours?"

Ryder, busy on his phone, grabbed his bags and headed toward the villa. Oblivious to saying thank you or good-bye to Scout, Enrique, and Roberto. Scout watched him walk away. "How about if I call your room in two hours?"

She wondered if this would be the last time she would ever see Scout, and even in this mess of the current situation she knew she didn't want to say goodbye, not like this. She shook Enrique's and Roberto's hands, saying thank you, then turned to Scout. "Okay, please call my room number 2021."

Her stomach fluttered, she was unsure whether to hug him. She ached for him to hold her.

"Okay, 2021." Scout nodded and smiled as he awkwardly stood next to the Jeep.

Chapter 28

Phoenix Sky Harbor International Airport Customs area. One place where Ryder's earbuds didn't block out the world. His electronic mask of no use here. The signs stated in five languages: no cell phones, no headphones, and no electronics. The crowded line wrapped around rows of people, a hundred bodies long, of all nationalities, ages, and races, dressed in a variety of clothes, from vacation flip-flops and beachwear to sweaters and boots.

It wasn't a bad thing to stand still for an hour. The last twenty-four hours had been confusing and manic for Kendall, full of phone calls and conversations, which needed to be in person.

Ryder's publicist and his mother alerted the Special Department for Missing Persons of the US embassy, a teen reality star, disappeared in Mexico. Next, somebody leaked information to the internet tabloids, and since there was no current hot topic going viral in the media, a missing pseudo celebrity made a sensational story.

The media continually warned US tourists to stay away from Mexico. Timing was perfect. With graduation approaching, journalists had a good headline to segue into the warning about students traveling to Mexico on senior week or graduation trips. Over reactive, just like Ryder's mother. When she was unable to get in touch with Ryder on his phone, she contacted anyone who would listen about her missing son. It added fuel to the news story.

Of course, savvy reporters instantly made the connection with his father's death in the Blue Hole in Belize, and additional meat added to the story: "Father went missing and now son is missing in Mexico."

Not this again. Lack of sleep and worry added to the ache in her stomach as she studied Ryder flirting with the young charming blonde in front of him. Her thoughts went to last night. Steve. She couldn't believe Steve Crawford had flown down to Mexico. Her sweet widow neighbor, Lizzie, Harvey's dog-sitter, called Steve about the break-in. When he couldn't reach Kendall he contacted Ryder's mother for help. The phone call to Tricia started the whirlwind speculation something bad had happened in Mexico.

Americans missing for more than twenty-four hours—quite a big deal.

Yesterday, Steve was waiting for her in the resort office. He looked frantic, as he hugged Kendall and Ryder, and concern tarnished his playboy face. She could swear he was on the brink of tears when she walked into the office. His words haunted her thoughts. "I've been through this once with Tim and I wasn't going to let it happen again. I knew you two must be diving somewhere...I should have come along."

Tricia's wrath overwhelmed her. Worried about the delicate balance of the relationship before the trip, their connection was nonexistent now. Steve tried to explain what little he knew about the break-in. Apparently, he couldn't determine what theft occurred, but the drawers were emptied on the floor, broken glass and objects strewn around the house. The only forcible entry was to the upstairs office door in the garage.

Steve spent the night in the villa living room talking on the phone, helping contact all those concerned and straightening everything out with the Embassy and the resort. Throwing heavy doses of water on the fire of Ryder's mother's temper and sorting out the false tabloid reports with Steve, almost kept her mind off Scout. Almost. She realized after a few hours, Scout never called.

It's better this way, I'm not ready to start a relationship with anybody anyway...especially someone who lived in Mexico. But in the midst of everything going on, disappointment and sadness clouded her mind, realizing she must be healing because she truly wanted to see Scout again.

On the plane ride home, she tried to wrap her mind around the burglary. Steve said, according to the police, the computer, the flat screens, and what appeared to be a jewelry box were still there. *Could it possibly have anything to do with the briefcase? How was that even possible?*

The briefcase. Something about Steve's questions last night bothered her.

After everything calmed down, the three of them ordered dinner on the terrace of the Villa. Steve remarked about the gorgeous resort setting and looked surprised when Ryder stated his father booked the resort.

Ryder excused himself, halfway through the meal, promising he would be back in an hour. He wanted to take a walk and say goodbye to a few friends he had met earlier in the week. He assured them he would not be gone long, knowing the seriousness of what transpired with his mother. She knew tonight he would come home.

Talking outside on the terrace, the waves rolling in, Steve asked question after question about the trip. How, where, when Tim had planned this vacation for Ryder's birthday before he died. Not being able to answer all his questions bothered her.

His inquisitiveness disturbed her. She didn't notice how much until he brought up the key from the dive bag.

She hesitated in answering. The thought of trusting him seemed wrong. Why? Possibly his voice or body language, reflected false to her and traveled down to her gut. Acting on instinct, she lied to him, and told him she was in such a hurry when she left she never tried the key.

She slept uneasily in the 1200 thread count Egyptian cotton sheets; the jungle floor had been more comfortable. She should have been comforted but she wasn't. Here was a trusted friend of Tim's, his business partner, now hers, sleeping on the couch just outside her room. But she couldn't shake her inner alarm when Steve asked about the key. Questions clouded her mind. Did Steve know about Tim's still being in the Navy? Was he hiding the same thing? They had been partners and best friends forever.

She debated whether she should tell Ryder about his father's briefcase. She didn't want to keep anything from Ryder, about his father, but she wanted to understand more about what it all meant. Tim still in the military in some capacity seemed ludicrous when he never talked about his eight years of service in the

Navy.

****

The Customs line creeped along in slow motion. Most people shuffled a few steps, each time gaining only an inch. She touched Ryder on the shoulder. "Thanks, Ryder, thanks for going on the trip your father wanted you to take. I'm sorry about the scare with your mother."

Ryder was slow to answer. "I'm glad I did it, I'm not sure I understand why this trip was so important to my father, but the cenotes are incredible. I'll never forget them." He was speaking but not really at her. "And, I got some added publicity, being missing in Mexico…publicity never hurts."

"I'm sorry, Ryder, I should've told the resort we would not be staying in our rooms for two nights…I don't know why I didn't think of it. I hope your mother forgives me." She hesitated, then added, "But I'm certain of one thing, your father would be very proud of you for following through with something important to him."

They were finally having a conversation. She continued, "Steve was so happy to see you, I hope you take him up on his invitation to come out and visit, we would both like for you to come to Maryland." She touched his shoulder again. "I know I would." Ryder looked at her hand and didn't move away. Kendall slowly removed her hand. *Perhaps we made some progress after all.*

Just before it was their turn to go through Customs, Ryder turned around and said, "I can't shake the feeling there was something more to this trip. I mean, don't you think there should be more to it?"

Could the vacation be as simple as Tim's way to help them keep in touch and stay close if something happened to him? "I don't know..." She hesitated, wishing she could confide in Ryder about the briefcase. "Maybe we will figure more out later, once we are back. I do know he loved you very much and wanted to share the world with you. Maybe this was his way."

The moment they walked through Security, Tricia and Ryder's publicist Courtney Clay bombarded Ryder; a few cameras flashed, and she realized they were going to make the most of this homecoming for the show. Cameras and lights were on, filming his arrival. She stopped. Ian Grant, the prominent plastic surgeon from the show, and the glamorous producer Hannah, whom she had met at the first screening of the premiere episode, rushed over to hug Ryder.

Tricia, all made up, over dressed, looking fabulous, could have been one of the plastic surgery patients from the show. Dramatically caught up in the scene, hugging Ryder and crying, she moved always facing the camera, careful not to smear her make up.

A few fellow passengers stopped walking and got caught up in the excitement, trying to figure out what celebrity was being interviewed—taking pictures with their phones anxious to Facebook the latest celebrity gossip. Two young teenagers asked for autographs and pictures with Ryder. Sporting a golden tan, and handsome as ever in his plain white T-shirt and jeans, Ryder pressed his instant-on smile, with his blue eyes twinkling.

One attractive young female passerby yelled, "I'm glad you're not missing, Ryder!" and giggled. Ryder rewarded her with a thumbs up and an irresistible flash of white teeth.

Keeping her distance from the cameras, she analyzed the media circus, unsure of what part to play in the commotion, until Ian Grant walked over and clasped her hand. "We were all concerned for your safe return, glad you arrived safely back from Mexico, with our boy." She smiled as Tricia glared at her.

She politely excused herself and walked over to Tricia, who ignored her. She touched her arm. "I'm sorry, Tricia, we should have notified the resort about the camping trip. I never imagined this would happen. I'm sorry I put you through any stress when everything worked out."

Tricia's eyes spoke the truth but she painted on a fake smile for the camera and hissed under her breath, spittle coming out of her mouth. "Yes, you should have told the resort or me you would be gone, that's what responsible parents do. After all we have been through, I would have thought you would know how it feels to think you have lost someone. But then you've never been a mother, so how would you ever understand."

From a distance, a stranger might conclude a pleasant conversation between two women, but underneath her smile, Tricia's anger seethed, hot and vicious. She turned her back ignoring Kendall and put her arm around her son, milking the publicity of the homecoming.

Her connecting flight to Baltimore finished boarding in minutes. She wanted to hug Ryder goodbye—with this crowd it would be next to impossible. Perhaps, the moment at Customs would be enough.

Still, she tried to catch Ryder's eye as she called

his name. He glanced at her; she waved and smiled; he turned his back engulfed in the circle around him. In the thick bustling airport crowd, she never felt more alone.

Chapter 29

Her one-story white wood-framed house, came into view. Large leafy maple trees framed the driveway, and green shrubs, plants, and grass completed a pretty picture of a classic all-American home. Kendall expected vivid signs of the invasion of her sanctuary. However, as Steve pulled into the driveway, the same warm, lovely place she shared with Tim for six years greeted her in peaceful memories.

Eager to get inside, she forced herself to wait for the police before entering. In less than five minutes the local trooper SUV pulled up behind Steve.

"Mrs. Jackson, I'm Officer Heffernan, this is Officer Tosetto. Let's do a walk-through." The large burly men nodded to Steve. "Mr. Crawford walked through the house with us last week, but he could not determine what was missing. We are hoping you can provide some answers. I understand you were in Mexico?"

"Yes." She hesitated and stepped through the front door.

Furniture was upside down, contents of drawers were dumped, and the glass in several picture frames were broken. Either someone was angry or was searching for something. Both the fifty-inch flat screen TV and the forty-two-inch TV were still intact in their places. Steve had an unreadable expression on his face.

She took a deep breath, and sighed lifting a broken lamp off the floor. "I feel so violated. What would kids be looking for in my house? It doesn't make sense…" Her heart raced. "My MacBook and the flat TV monitor, both fit into any back pack…" Running her fingers through her hair, her hands were shaking. "Even my iPod is sitting on the dock on the stereo." She walked over to the liquor cabinet, nothing was missing. "It doesn't make sense."

The police were taking notes. Officer Tosetto crossed his thick arms. "Most kids snatch the liquor and the electronics, unlikely it's the neighborhood juveniles, Mrs. Jackson." He cleared his throat. "Let's sit down in the kitchen. We would like to ask a few more questions for the report."

Her hand shook as she poured coffee for each of the officers.

"Do you have any enemies, anyone who would be trying to hurt you?"

"Enemies? No." She took a few deep breaths to calm her racing thoughts.

"Before you left for your trip, did you engage in a dispute or argument with anyone?" Officer Tosetto continued. "Do you know any reason why someone would want something from your house, something in your possession?" She kept repeating "no", "no" "no" as the officer continued. "Any issues with colleagues or students at the College?"

"Are you in a relationship with someone who may have been angry at your trip to Mexico?" Officer Heffernan finally spoke.

She raised her shoulders, shook her head and exhaled a frustrated sigh. "No, I have no idea what someone would want enough to break into my house!" She paused; she couldn't get the briefcase out of her mind, but she knew it was locked in her office at Western Maryland College. How could anybody know about the briefcase? She wanted to tell them, but instinct silenced her. First, she needed to understand the contents of the briefcase and what they meant.

Steve was leaning against the kitchen counter, his arms folded against his chest. His eyes darted between her and the officer. A wire connected in her mind, intuition settled in the pit of her stomach almost knocking her off balance. Steve was involved. He was the only one who knew about the key.

****

Steve analyzed her, sitting at the table with her legs crossed, one leg moving in a nervous twitch, talking to the police. Her skin golden, her long hair streaked with blonde from the sun. She barely resembled the depressed, lifeless Kendall who emerged after Tim's death. She appeared to have gained an independence, a confidence she lacked over the last eighteen months. The sadness still present in her eyes, but now worn as experience. *Did she open the briefcase or not? Would she lie to the police?*

He wondered, if she did have it, why she wouldn't say anything to the police or to him on the ride over. After talking to her in Puerto Morelos and in the car ride home from the airport, he was almost certain, she had not opened the briefcase.

He searched the villa the night he stayed there and nothing was in her luggage or on her laptop. He was positive if she confided in Ryder, he would have brought it up in a conversation. He needed to know.

In the kitchen, Kendall focused on his face. In a lightning-flash of a second, he recognized what he feared most. *She knows...she opened the briefcase.* He squirmed under the intensity of her gaze, certain she suspected him.

Chapter 30

Ten years ago, Steve realized Tim had secrets.

Unlocking the back door outside the office, he encountered a startled Tim working on a laptop with an enormous rolled out map and a blueprint of some sort. A silver briefcase open next to him. Tim rolled up the displayed materials and closed his computer in one swift motion.

Steve lifted his brows. "Why are you burning the midnight oil?"

"I didn't realize the time. Maybe I should ask you the same? Where are you coming from at this hour, a late date?" Tim stood. The air was thick with untruthfulness.

"Couldn't sleep, thought I'd take a ride and I saw the light on…" Steve said.

"Yeah, me too." Tim stretched. "I've been here since the bar closed up."

Tim did not elaborate. He turned off the desk light and walked over to the door. "I guess we two insomniacs need to go home."

Tim was the brother Steve always wanted. Best friends who shared a pact. It all started one day in the Maryland woods, when they realized they were both part of a classified military reserve program called The Collective.

Could Tim be hiding information from him? Steve

respected the classified research and confidential nature of The Collective, but in ten years of being involved with the program, they always worked together.

Comrades of secrets. Since their college days in Gettysburg, they shielded knowledge from everyone, except each other. Both experts at hiding the truth.

The Collective's inside influence at Gettysburg College, aligned the two ex-military students as roommates, never revealing their secret association to the other. Both out-scored fellow elite soldiers on a battery of tests including aptitude, intellect, psychological, and physical. Both discharged from military service three months before starting their freshman year. To the rest of the world, Steve and Tim were civilians, holding normal jobs; each loyal to the oath never to reveal their classified military assignment.

At the time, the offer presented to Steve, seemed the best of both worlds: a chance to serve his country in the Intelligence area of government, and to enjoy the world as a civilian. A full ride to college, both undergrad and graduate school, and a part time job seemed like winning the lottery.

In return, his involvement could not be divulged, not to family, friends, wife, or children. At the age of twenty-five, living in a 10 x 20 space for four months with his roommate, he never suspected they each belonged to a secret Intelligence division.

****

Steve would never forget the day he discovered the truth.

The thick snow fell in clumps, piling up on tree branches. A wintery mix of snow and ice coated the roads. Winter break started the next day and he needed to drive the back road through the Catoctin Mountain Park to Site R. Inside the park, after going through two electronically locked gates that dead-ended into an old stone tunnel, he turned on the restricted road. Coming around the bend on the unplowed pavement he slid on the ice, fishtailed out of control, and slammed into another car.

Speech escaped him. Standing on the prohibited street with snowflakes falling on his black knit cap, blue eyes peered out at him. Tim burst into laughter and Steve followed. In minutes they figured out the connection.

When other college students partied at fraternity houses, attended sporting events, or recited stories of drunken nights and wild girls, he and Tim studied high-level classes on marine biology and survival skills at what they called "the library."

Tucked in the picturesque countryside of Maryland, six miles from the infamous presidential retreat, Camp David, "Site R," known to the public as the Raven Rock Mountain Complex remained hidden in the middle of six thousand acres of dense woods. Steve nicknamed RRMC, "the library."

Raven Rock's history fascinated Steve. Known as the "underground pentagon," RRMC appeared more secretive than Area 51. It started with President Truman in 1950, even back then, military engineers had the capability to construct elaborate underground cities. Workers blasted deep down into the earth to create a hidden fortress. Old miners and their children told stories of workers being picked up in a van and blindfolded each morning until they reached their work site. Steve believed four three-story buildings existed in the main part of the underground complex and in a threat of a nuclear war, RRMC would be used as a military command post for leaders and high-ranking government officials.

Steve shared all his discoveries with Tim. But, in the last year before Tim died, he wondered why Tim didn't confide in him. He suspected Tim was assigned a classified project without him. He asked Tim, but he laughed it off, claiming Steve needed to stop watching secret agent movies.

When he discovered Tim covering his tracks about several dive trips to Belize, Honduras, and most recently to Mexico, he needed to understand.

He convinced himself—the month before Tim's death—Tim was working with The Collective without him. Their mission, since they joined The Collective, always revolved around the DNA Project. The possibility of being excluded from a big discovery, filled him with anger. The exclusion ate away at him, at first a little at a time but it progressed, the unknown and rejection escalating to high paranoia.

Anxious, a month before the Blue Hole diving accident, Steve reported his concerns to a field operative. They assigned Steve to investigate Tim.

The unexpected diving trip for Ryder alarmed him. He replayed his last conversation with Tim.

Steve walked into the office at the bar at closing time. Tim slid the silver briefcase under his desk. "What's in the briefcase?"

Tim met his eyes, a serious look on his face but remained silent.

"What are you hiding, did you find something?"

Steve moved closer to the desk. Tim blocked him

with his arm.

"Steve, trust me, let it go. It's personal. Nothing to do with you." With the briefcase in his hand, he walked out the back door of the bar and drove away.

****

After Tim's death Steve searched for the briefcase. He ripped apart the bar, the office drawers, old boxes and cleaned out storage closets in the cellar. After a year of investigating random places, he figured the case would never show up, until Kendall came in and asked for the key from the dive bag. The Collective questioned him for hours about Tim's trip to Belize. He never mentioned the briefcase. He thought he would find the briefcase in Kendall's house when she left for Mexico. He hadn't expected his anger to kick in. Why did Tim withhold information from him after all these years? Why didn't he trust him? His rage took over.

Chapter 31

The hands of the clock on her kitchen wall moved slowly, the only evidence time was passing. Curiosity crawled out of her skin. The odds of resting her head on her pillow tonight, in a house that had been broken into, and not thinking about the items in Tim's briefcase, were astronomically unlikely. She dressed, leashing Harvey as if to take him on a walk.

Unlocking her office door, her face felt flushed and her arms were blotchy.

What if somebody was actually observing her right now—her head turned side-to side—waiting for her to show the briefcase. Is that what the break-in was about? Her mind swirled, *why now, why after eighteen months since Tim died was someone looking for the briefcase...* She had not told anyone about its existence except Scout and Steve. Scout lived in Mexico. Steve...well, she wished she could confide in him but...the link had to be Steve Crawford.

She shook her head trying to figure out what Steve would want in the briefcase...True, he was the only other person who knew about the key, but the thought of Steve breaking into her house didn't make sense.

Turning on her office light she prayed the briefcase would still be in her locked drawer. Her hand shook as she fit the key in the lock. Kendall exhaled, her shoulders going up and down as she sank into her office chair. The briefcase was still there. Sweat was lying on her upper lip and under her shirt. Tapping her teeth together, she got up and locked her door.

She opened the briefcase behind the desk and took out the computer zip drive, leaving the maps and IDs in the case.

Her mind fixated on Steve. Had he told someone about her asking for the strange key? Perhaps he told the wrong person.

She put the zip drive in the small front pocket of her jeans. She locked the drawer, sat back down. Unlocking the drawer again, she pulled the briefcase out, opened it and delicately placed all the contents on the floor behind her desk. With her iPhone she took a picture of each item.

Nodding her head in affirmation, she put everything back in the briefcase, locked the drawer, checked it twice, grabbed a binder and headed out the door.

Her secret was trapped inside a box too small. She desperately needed to talk to someone before she exploded.

****

Kendall's house glowed with the brightness of a hundred lights. In her mind, the illuminated house downplayed the secrecy of the briefcase. Light gave her courage.

Harvey next to her, Kendall, sat cross-legged on the bed, staring at her laptop. A glass of white wine, sat untouched on the bedside table. She put her iPod in, selected Jason Mraz and turned it up loud.

She turned off the Wi-Fi. Her mind was battling thoughts of hackers and computer surveillance.

She held the unusual memory stick in her hand before plugging it into the side of her computer. Black rubber surrounded the stick like the rubber on an underwater camera. *Here goes.* She watched it upload. *Let's see what this is all about.*

Ten documents labeled by date flashed on her computer screen. Six documents dated years before Tim and Kendall met; the other four ranged from the beginning of their relationship to one dated three days before Tim died.

Inhaling deeply, she touched her mouse, pulling down to the right and clicking without hesitation on the last icon, a video file. She squeezed her eyes to hold back tears as Tim's face filled the screen. The background was the upstairs office over the garage. She hit play.

"This message is for my wife. Kendall, if you're watching this video, I'm so sorry not to be with you. Obviously, something happened to me for you to be hearing this. I know life's been hard for you. I'm sorry, my love, I'm sorry I kept a secret from you, but I've been sworn to secrecy to protect a division of the US government. I hoped they will share this video with you. I can't disclose the details about my job, but it's not important to us. Something I did, not who I am. You know who I am, Kendall, you're the only one who really knew me." She wiped the tears running off her chin.

"Stay close with Ryder, he's not your blood, but he is a part of me and I want him in your life. UWMA, Kendall, UWMA I love you, Lambie."

Her brows furrowed as tears ran down her face and her open mouth. She gasped for air. A division of the

US government? Some type of CIA agent? The badge said Navy. UWMA. Was this truly happening?

Lambie. Tim sent her a message no one else would figure out. For years, she and Tim joked around calling each other "Lambie" after watching a Lifetime movie about a deranged young girl in love with a married man whom she called "Lambie." "Oh, Lambie," Tim would say…and Kendall said, "Don't ever call me 'Lambie'," but Tim wrestled her on the sectional and after they made sweet, tender, passionate love…he jokingly called her "Lambie." Tim decided right then and there it would be their secret password.

Excited, Tim stated if they called each other "Lambie" in public, or on a phone call or in an email, don't ignore the word, it was their code word. At a large gathering it would signal the desire to leave…on a phone call it would mean things are not as they seem. He said, "If someone snatched you for ransom, and you said, 'I'm okay, Lambie, don't worry,' I would realize it's definitely not okay and call the police."

She laughed like mad and asked if she should be concerned she would be kidnapped. And he grinned and said, "Well, you never know." Over the years, at a party, Tim would come up to Kendall, kiss her on the cheek and say aloud, "I love you, Lambie." Kendall knew he wanted to leave. They used it to their advantage and it became a game. When one of them became stuck in an unwelcome discussion, the other would say, "What do you think, Lambie?" and help create an escape from the conversation. Never used as a term of endearment, only to make a point.

Tim used the word to convey a message to her. She had no idea what he wanted her to grasp. UWMA,

Tim's "until we meet again," also emphasized something important. And he had used it in the dive log as well.

She closed her eyes and yelled aloud, "What are you trying to tell me?" Harvey sat up, came over and nuzzled her face. With a determined look, she got out her notebook and wrote down every word Tim said in the video. Taking notes she opened the first file dated ten years before she and Tim met. A series of numbers, possibly a formula of some kind. She couldn't make sense of it. The next several documents consisted of a series of dates and presidents' names beside them. She Googled the first date and the first president listed.

Abraham Lincoln—March 1865, a month before his assassination. The list continued, comprised of presidents' names, and beside each name a date. All dates linked to a time when they held office. President Obama, the last name on the list included a date from three years ago.

The fifth and sixth documents appeared to be a report of statistics. Possibly a list of temperatures, or pH levels. The seventh record caught her attention. Once again, a series of digits filled the page. Trying to make a connection, halfway down the page, three numbers jumped out at her. Her photographic memory kicked in. She realized she had seen those numbers before. She tried to remember where.

20.83984890 20.83984890,-86.88778710

20 50 23.46

86 53 16.03

The last three documents contained image files. She clicked. It was a slideshow of scanned pictures, a few older black and white snapshots and newer ones in color. The first black and white photo dark and poor quality appeared a century old. Five men in white collared shirts and dark pants stood with a handsome, bare-chested man in a tropical jungle. The man looked familiar, as well as the man in the middle of the group.

Analyzing the second color photo, realization hit her. Dwight D. Eisenhower, stood next to the bare-chested man. She knew Eisenhower from a photograph of him hanging in the Grand Hall at Western Maryland College; she passed by it hundreds of times. He had been a member of the "Friends of the College Foundation" for many years.

John F. Kennedy was clearly recognizable in the next photo, and as Kendall continued examining picture after picture, she found Bill Clinton, Ronald Reagan, George H. W. Bush, George W. Bush, and the most recent image of Barack Obama and the first woman to be photographed, Hillary Clinton. The locations were diverse. Sometimes a jungle was the backdrop, but most snapped next to a sandy beach and a startling blue colored body of water.

Except for Hillary Clinton, men dominated the photos, sometimes in ties and suit jackets, some in t-shirts and bathing suits. The anomaly was the bare-chested man who looked out of place. Maybe a native of the area, a local family member, a descendant of the bare-chested man from the first photograph. This one man stood out from the businessmen and the president.

She went back to each document and printed each page out to her air printer.

She pored over the documents for hours, making notes, trying to make a connection, and then she jumped off the bed and ran downstairs to the front hallway. A beautiful photograph of the night sky from their honeymoon, hung on the wall. Tim surprised her with the image on their five-year anniversary. She remembered a clue written in her anniversary card.

She lifted the print off the wall. On the back of the frame the same three series of numbers Tim had written in her card,

20 ° 50.- 23.46 N

86° 53' 16.03 W.

The beautiful wood-framed gift recreated the exact night sky of their honeymoon in Puerto Morelos. Including a constellation map showing the positions of the moon and stars. The numbers matched 20° 50.- 23.46 N 86° 53' 16.03 W. It was longitude and latitude.

She ran back upstairs, with Harvey following on her heels feeling the excitement. Now realizing one document was a list of different locations, giving longitude and latitude. She sat down again, making notes.

Chapter 32

Kendall bailed from her car and rushed up to the University steps. She was late for her nine o'clock Director's meeting. Again. Tim's secret life consumed her mind, and work seemed trivial. Before she left the house she secured her notes and the briefcase in her safe, the zip drive in her purse.

Most of her notes were locations. International destinations with names she barely recognized; islands or areas next to a large body of water. Typing in the longitude and latitude degrees, minutes, and seconds in Google Earth pinpointed exact locations. Nothing made sense as she marked them on a world map with colored thumb tacks.

The locations ranged from Mexico, Central America, South America, and even Antarctica and to her surprise, right here in Maryland. One coordinate appeared exactly on the college and the other further to the west in the Catoctin State Park, near Thurmont, Maryland. The other curious spot, Puerto Morelos. At first glance, it seemed it marked the location of the cenote she and Ryder just visited, but looking at the proximity of the sea to the coordinates, it was further south of Puerto Morelos.

With everything going through her mind, she needed to focus on her job at least for a few hours.

Kendall groaned as she walked into the Director's

meeting. She was behind schedule on finding commencement speakers.

****

Kendall was thrilled; she could announce Conrad Nathaniel would be the Commencement speaker. It didn't hurt when she called, he mentioned he knew Tim, and after agreeing to speak at graduation, he promised to tell her a story of how Tim saved his life free diving. She hadn't realized Conrad Nathaniel was splashed all over the media headlines while she was vacationing in Puerto Morelos. Apparently, his invention of underwater breathing went viral. A film crew was making a documentary about the Nathaniel family and Conrad Nathaniel's achievements, and a short video was leaked hitting over four million views. Obviously, he was involved in cutting-edge stuff. Both the committee and student body would be excited she had secured him as speaker. She smiled as she hit send on the email with the YouTube video and announcement.

Two voice mails blinked on her cell phone. One from Steve asked if she would meet him for dinner. The next voice increased her heart rate and she smiled. Scout. Something about his voice warmed her heart. He wanted to say hello, make sure she returned safely to Maryland, and hoped everything was okay with the break-in. However, his last line she replayed three times to make sure she understood it correctly. He said, "I understand why you didn't have time to call me back on your last night or meet for dinner, but I really wanted to say goodbye and make sure everything is okay with you and…" a long pause…"And, there's something else I wanted to discuss with you. Something I think you need to know. Please call me back."

Scout must be mistaken, because he never called.

He was off diving and asked her to call tomorrow. Anxious to speak with him, she would have to be patient. She also wanted to ask him about the longitude and latitude numbers she found near Puerto Morelos.

First things first. Her instincts nagged at her. Did Steve take a call from Scout and not tell her?

Why?

Chapter 33

"I'm so glad you decided to go out to dinner with me, Kendall." Steve, wearing a snug-fitting black shirt, and strong but appealing cologne, turned heads. Even the college-age waitress at the trendy new eatery in Gettysburg noticed, and forever the playboy he poured on his charm. When Kendall agreed to meet him at this new upscale contemporary joint, not too far from Jackson's Easy, she had one goal in mind. Get him drunk. Steve, always a heavy social drinker, opened up as he imbibed and if possible, became more charismatic. Truth serum.

"Well, the dinner's on me, Steve. It's the least I can do after you flew all the way down to Mexico for Ryder and me. It meant a lot to us." She paused, then added, "Ryder looks up to you, you know?"

"He's a good kid. I'm always here for him, I hope he knows that. You know, it isn't just Ryder that means a lot to me." Steve touched Kendall's hands, and looked her straight in the eye. "Kendall, I've been so worried about you for the last year and a half. It hurts me to see you in pain. I've always been here for you even if you didn't take me up on it." He released her hands and took a sip from his large red wine glass.

"I know you've always been there, Steve, I just needed some time away from everyone. But I'm in a good place now, the trip was good for both Ryder and me, even with the mix-up at the end." She smiled and poured more wine into both their glasses.

"Well, you certainly look like you're in a good place. Your tan makes you look beautiful and well rested." Steve oozed with charm and warmth, and it dawned on her, he was flirting. She had never seen it before, never noticed his slight advances. Amazing. Before the trip to Mexico, that part of her was dormant. Recognizing flirting was not in her mindset. *Maybe that's why he never told me Scout called.*

The wine flowed and dinner was excellent. With each glass, Steve became animated, telling old stories, dribbling with charisma. She directed the conversation to cave diving spots Steve explored, mentioning several locations which appeared in the documents last night. The majority of the locations she mentioned Steve and Tim traveled together. She laughed at a few memories of Steve and the vast variety of women he took diving. From the outside looking in, it was simply two attractive adults enjoying a night out.

She wanted to discuss the briefcase, but she just couldn't form the words. 'Lambie' kept popping in her mind. She didn't want to change the mood, so she suggested an after-dinner drink, and he gladly ordered his favorite drink, Grand Marnier for two. Eventually the conversation inevitably turned back to Tim. Steve and Tim had a long history, longer than she and Tim. Tim the one link they had in common. But, for the past year and a half Steve had been cautious around Kendall, never discussing Tim and glory stories from the past.

Tonight was an exception, the liquor helped them laugh at old stories and reminisce about the past. Kendall almost forgot her plan until their second Grand

Marnier when Steve made a seemingly casual inquiry.

"So, I meant to ask you, did that key ever fit Tim's briefcase?"

The air drastically changed. The question seemed forced, like trying to push a large dog out of a small cat door. She didn't mean to stop laughing so abruptly, and she clamped a hand over her mouth, the alcohol affecting her. "Oh, I think I have the hiccups," She forced a hiccup and laughed, "Excuse me for one second, I'll be right back."

Standing up from the table, she wobbled. In her efforts to get Steve drunk, she succeeded in getting herself tipsy. The ladies' room mirror reflected a flushed face and chest. She had no idea how to answer Steve's question. She took two deep breaths and ran her wrists under cold water.

When she returned to the table, the waitress placed the black portfolio on the table next to Steve.

"Steve, I'm buying dinner tonight." She reached for the bill as he pulled it away from her and said, "It's already paid, you can buy me a drink at the bar."

Her plan was falling apart. "Thank you, Steve, and I will buy you a drink as well...but I really wanted to buy you dinner." Standing, his scent surrounded her and warm eyes met hers; she could see why a woman would find him irresistible. She smiled and took a deep breath. "I'm buying you a shot just for that."

He put his arm around her shoulder, leading her to the bar, and said, "Only if you're going to do one with me."

They shuffled to the loungy bar area, with low lighting, lit candles, and empty barstools. Alcohol definitely made everything a little fuzzy. Steve ordered up three Don Julio 1942 tequila shots.

"These are on the lady."

It sobered her up—the three tequila shots sitting on the bar in front of her. She realized how much he missed his friend. Tim would have made the same gesture for a close friend who had passed. She studied his face. Definitely a handsome man, but his playboy reputation and his treatment of women in the past marred his outer beauty. She always admired his looks, but never attracted to his cocky personality.

Tonight a softness covered his facial features, the corner of his eyes portraying a lost and lonely look. Perhaps it was the libations, but she actually felt a little sorry for him. He had never married, and rarely kept a girlfriend for more than three or four months. *He must be lonely.*

"So, what about you, Steve?"

"What about me?"

"Do you have anyone special in your life?"

He smiled and looked straight at her, and with a little slur replied, "No, not me. I'm just waiting for the right girl to become available." He leaned forward. It took a second for her to realize his intention, and then, he was kissing her. His lips were soft, warm. Confusion and guilt flooded her. She pulled back, her breath coming in short pants.

She had a choice to make.

Chapter 34

The alarm clock went off and Kendall rubbed her crusty eyes. Harvey shook his head, nudging her, a sure sign he needed to go outside and wanted her to wake up. Fuzzy, or perhaps a little dizzy. She scrambled to think straight. *Last night...*

Steve insisted on following her back to her house, to make sure she made it home okay. He also insisted on coming into the house and doing a thorough check because of the break-in.

She hadn't been able to control her rapid heartbeat; the alcohol and the kiss had her mind zooming. As much as she knew it was wrong, she wanted to feel a man's arms around her. She wanted to be held tight after eighteen months of zero sexual activity. Her libido directing her. First, Scout, and now she felt a strange sexual pull to playboy Steve.

Even in a cloudy haze, Kendall remembered the events of last night, Steve asked about the briefcase again.

"So, you never answered my question, Kendall, did that key ever fit the briefcase?"

The question about the briefcase shut her libido down and woke her up out of her drunken state. As he asked the question a second time; she was convinced, Steve knew.... He knew something about Tim's secret life.

This time she was ready with an answer. "No, it didn't fit the briefcase, must go to some cabinet in the bar, and now I can't figure out where I put it!" Steve leaned against the granite island in the kitchen.

"The key or the briefcase?"

Getting each of them a cup of coffee, her insides jumped as if on a trampoline. The rhythm of her heartbeat accelerated in her ears. She didn't turn. "The key, I can't figure out where I put the key."

Facing him she leaned, on the counter. The distance between them less than twelve inches she wanted answers, and she needed them tonight.

"What do you know about Tim that I don't know?"

Steve was silent, his soft brown eyes almost golden. He hesitated, and then answered, "I know he was taking dive trips, and intentionally lying to me about them."

She was taken aback by his answer; she hadn't expected any answer at all.

"Dive trips? What do you mean he was lying to you about dive trips?"

"I don't know, Kendall. For the past couple of years Tim has been traveling to destinations and lying about them. Did you know where he was going on his dive trips?"

She thought back to the longitude and latitude document with all the different locations, places she never realized Tim visited. She lied, "Yes, I did know where he was going; I figured you couldn't go along, because you were watching the bar."

He ran his fingers through his hair and folded his arms over his chest. "Yes, you're probably right, maybe that's why." He stood and poured himself a cup of coffee. "So do you need help getting the briefcase open?"

There was more Steve was holding back from her. "The briefcase? No, it wasn't really locked. Just some clasp and button you pushed, turns out I didn't need a key after all." Her face and neck were flushed; she was a terrible liar.

Steve seemed instantly awake. "What was in it?"

"Nothing really important, a few things of Ryder's, his divorce papers, just legal documents." She opened the fridge grabbing the organic half-and-half. "Cream, Steve?" She held her hand to the counter to stop it from shaking.

Silence; the swarm of lies hovered in the air, thickening the space. She imagined Steve yelling loud and clear, *I don't believe you.*

He had to know about the briefcase contents…but her gut was yelling right back, *don't say anything*. She used an early morning meeting as an excuse, and practically pushed Steve out of the house.

****

Experts say it takes twenty-one days to make or break a habit. Starting a new bad habit, Kendall realized she was going to be late for work again. She hoped it wasn't her twenty-first day.

Work was the last thing on her mind, but Kendall had to step up and pull her weight if she didn't want to jeopardize her livelihood. Just get through today. She would have all weekend to study the contents of the briefcase and make sense out of Steve's behavior last night.

Four busy hours later, she was ready to take her lunch break. She opened the safe in her office and took out the map that looked like a blueprint. Something was nagging her. She couldn't wait until the weekend. She headed to the faculty conference lounge seldom used by anyone in Sutton Hall. In the past, she used to meet a favorite colleague there for lunch, Dr. Andrew Lunardini. One of WMC's beloved history professors, most including Kendall called him Dr. A. She co-chaired a committee with him several years ago and long after the committee disbanded, they continued their monthly lunch meetings. Lunch with Dr. A was like watching a treasured movie. She would always learn something new. One day, an interesting tidbit about college history, and the next something unusual and exciting about a far corner of the world.

Dr. A's reflections on the past intrigued her the most. His unique perspective, slightly off from the norm, unlocked her mind to new interpretations. Dr. A savored each new idea, like a wine taster. He would take a step back, swirl the idea around, smell it, then taste it. He was inquisitive without ever offending.

Handsome for his age, which he never disclosed, and no one asked, Kendall guessed he was in his early seventies. His kind, hazel eyes always focused. He listened—as if he really cared about the speaker, paying attention to each word uttered.

After Tim died, even when she was not sharing, he was there. His student assistants confirmed their monthly lunch appointment, calling it a standing committee co-chair meeting up until the month he retired.

He taught Kendall the art of listening. She wanted to display that same empathy to students. Because of him, she learned to slow her mind down. Kendall missed their lunches, and she missed being heard.

Walking through the oak grove to Sutton and Nathaniel Hall, the two oldest buildings on campus, she recognized the beauty surrounding her. The cobalt sky behind the soaring oaks resembled a fake backdrop. The campus was pristine and she was finally awake to notice. Floundering in a sea of unanswered questions about Tim's life gave her new purpose. She needed to understand Tim's message and secret life without any resentment. She loved him so much; she did not want to believe he was not the man she thought he was.

Her eye stopped at the crest above Nathaniel Hall's main entrance. It was the college logo from 1867, the date the college was founded but something was different about it. She had never noticed this particular logo; it had thirteen stars around the top and the wings of an eagle in the middle of an open book.

She pulled out her business card. There were no stars or eagle's wings on the regular logo. She walked past this entrance a hundred times, and it never caught her attention. The ID card in Tim's briefcase displayed an unusual seal, and she searched online to find it without success. The seal resembled a combination of symbols from other agencies. The Defense Intelligence Agency crest had thirteen stars in a semicircle across the top of the seal, and the Central Intelligence Agency exhibited the wings. She took her iPhone out, snapped a photo of the crest, and walked through Nathaniel Hall, a building she traversed hundreds of times with fresh eyes.

She inhaled the smell of time. Old buildings…captured and held tight an aroma in their walls. The gritty smell reminding Kendall of dampness, woods and sweat. This post Civil War structure absorbed almost 150 years of changing environments, weather, and souls. She climbed the empty steps, and placed her key in the lock to the conference room. Andrew's key, bestowed on her when he retired, passing on the responsibility of finding a new co-chair for their unofficial committee of like-minded people and sharing ideas.

The hundred and fifty-year-old wooden door creaked as she pushed it open; it had been six months since Dr. A retired. She smiled as she closed the door, and looked out the window. She drew in the air, thinking to herself she could smell his after-shave and he would magically appear in the doorway. She rolled out the four pages of blueprint, trying to connect each sheet like a puzzle.

It resembled a series of tunnels. One tunnel appeared to be under a large building not connecting to the others. The other three were long and narrow, a hallway with classrooms or offices on each side. They overlaid each other as if they represented the first, second, and third floor. On the fourth sheet she noticed stars, wing symbol, and numbers on the bottom of the map. Longitude and latitude coordinates. She was sure of it. She looked up those exact sets of numbers.

She pulled out her phone. She downloaded the latitude and longitude app last night, and she knew, before she entered the numbers, exactly what the location would be. The tiny red dot landed on the town of Westminster, 2 College Hill, Westminster, Maryland. Western Maryland College.

Frozen, her mind swirled. She rolled the blueprints and exited the building. It was time to visit her favorite professor. Just then her phone buzzed, and she could see the call was from Mexico. Scout?

"Hello, this is Kendall." She paused, looking down at her chest, as if she could see her heart beating a little faster.

"Hi Kendall, it's Scout." She pictured him standing in his dive shop office, a smile on his face, carefree in beach shorts and a cut-off shirt, with a baseball cap on and probably a little ponytail hanging out the back. "How are things in Maryland?"

"Things are interesting, but fine," she replied, laughing from nervousness. "I bet you're looking at the water right now."

"Yes, it's gorgeous, another beautiful day in paradise."

"I never knew you called, I mean I never got your message." She paused. "I would have liked to say goodbye."

Silence. "I would have liked to say goodbye as well." The connection seemed to be delayed, making it a little awkward, and they both started talking at the same time. Scout laughed. "You go."

Kendall waited, then began. "I wanted to ask you a question, about a location down there. I found some notes from Tim, with longitude and latitude coordinates. It appears it is marking a spot near Puerto Morelos, close to you but in the middle of nowhere, actually in the middle of the jungle. If I give you the numbers, can you look it up on your computer?"

Silence again. "Scout, can you hear me?"

"Yes, I can hear you, let me go over to the computer. What are the numbers?" She read him the numbers; again there was a long pause.

Scout started speaking. "Kendall, I don't know how to tell you this, but you know how I told you in my message, there was something I needed to discuss with you?"

"Yes?"

He continued. "Well, it's like this. I'm not sure how to say this…" Another long pause. "Tim…wanted me to take Ryder to a different cenote. When Tim and I met, he gave me a small, very old map of a cenote, I never knew existed. No one did. It's extremely remote and takes about three or four days to get back to, maybe longer." Another long pause. "On that first day, when you and Ryder showed up, Ryder didn't even know he was going camping. And both of you looked like you didn't even want to go camping. It would have been an extensive trip and…I made a judgment call not to take you to the difficult one. It was a poor decision on my part; I know that now. So, no excuses." Another pause. "It's been eating me alive. I wanted to tell you, a hundred times. But my offer is this, if you and Ryder want to come back down, I will take you to that cenote, the one I should have shown you in the beginning. And it's all on me, the plane fare, everything, your husband was more than generous with me, and I'm sorry, I'm sorry I didn't tell you the truth. Please forgive me."

Kendall was stunned, perplexed, and speechless. "Well, what's so special about that particular cenote?"

Scout answered, "I don't know…but that's the location you just had me look up."

Kendall managed to go through the motions of work. She telephoned Dr. A, and he agreed to meet her for a drink after work. She wanted to call Ryder, but she knew she needed to figure things out. *What is going on?*

The briefcase, the cenote, all of these secrets couldn't be happening to her—an average everyday normal college employee. It was as if she were watching herself on film, seeing what her next move would be. She experienced this distancing before. Days, weeks, even months after Tim had been declared dead, she would walk into a grocery store and look at the man in line in front of her, or see a woman laughing and jogging while she was walking Harvey, and she wondered, did they realize what was happening in her life? Was it written all over her face? An overwhelming sensation of being in the present space but being detached from it all and sure everyone could see it. Walking around in the world as an outsider looking in.

Her secrets were about to overflow and explode, she needed to release the pressure. Dr. A brought her back to the present.

In a quiet corner in the back of a Westminster café, she told him about the briefcase. He never took his eyes off hers as she described the video, the pictures, the blueprint, the longitudes and latitudes, and the neurosurgeon's card. She told him everything except for the "Lambie" code word in the video, and the existence of the old map. She understood why she didn't share the Lambie secret, but why she held back the existence of the old map puzzled her.

Dr. Andrew Lunardini was the perfect listener.

Chapter 35

Kendall's life resembled a movie. The genre of the film unclear. Possibly a thriller, an action-adventure flick, or yet another sad story of a lost woman trusting a husband who hides a deep secret, only to discover he is not the man she thought he was. How did she get here?

The tightness in her chest relaxed, the pressure less constrictive since sharing the secret of the briefcase with Andrew. He insisted she call him by his first name now that he was retired.

Head bent forward, eyes rapidly skimming over each document, Andrew was engrossed. He sucked in the contents of the briefcase, scribbling notes, searching the internet, comparing photos, completely entranced.

He handed the neurosurgeon's business card to Kendall without even looking up from his computer. "Call this Dr. Trailov first thing Monday morning at Johns Hopkins. Find out if he knew Tim." He was nonchalant. "It might just be a card or it could be a lead."

She thought Andrew was younger than his years, but this Andrew was full of adrenaline like a teenage boy on his last day of school before summer vacation. The look of an anthropologist who discovers a bone, digging faster, anxious to see what lies beneath.

He was alive again.

****

Kendall swallowed and took a deep breath.

"Go ahead, use it, it's a master."

It turned out, Andrew's conference room key was a master to the entire building. The lock turned and the basement door opened.

It was seven a.m. Sunday morning. Andrew's grin was contagious. "It's possible the map in Tim's briefcase is an underground tunnel system, accessed right here, in the basement of Lewis Hall of Science." A flushed appearance colored his face. "I've always heard rumors of a bomb shelter underneath Western Maryland College, some type of tunnel system which led to a secret bunker hidden somewhere deep in the Catoctin National Forest."

Andrew whispered. "It was 1962 and I had just arrived at the college. The hush-hush was Western Maryland had a secret place to hide Congress." His salt-and-pepper hair framed his handsome face, his hazel eyes shining with excitement. "Oh, there were specifics, it supposedly contained decontamination chambers, a communication area, a clinic, a full-blown cafeteria, and dormitories designed to accommodate at least a thousand people."

She followed him down the stairs to the basement of the building, when a memory came back to her. "I remember, an incident with one of the fraternities. The Bachelors, the oldest secret society on campus. One of their pledges talked about being locked in a tunnel. He wanted to confide in us about a hazing prank, but he was scared to death to talk. We tried to investigate it, but he denied everything and said he made the whole thing up. When asked about the tunnel, he was adamant there was no tunnel."

She recalled telling Tim about the oddness of it, and how fast the kid changed his story. Tim chalked it up to a fraternity prank, adding the pledge was probably blindfolded and made to believe he was in a tunnel.

Kendall's mind was buzzing. "So what is Tim's connection to this place, do you think he was part of a military division that secured it?"

Andrew turned, his head cocked to one side. "Perhaps, not a bad theory, maybe that's why all the secrecy, but it doesn't explain all the other coordinates and locations. Something has been bugging me about those pictures with the presidents. I know this sounds impossible, but the man in the pictures—he looks like the same man."

She stopped. The pictures spanned too many years. "Impossible, he would have been over 150 years old in the recent picture with Obama, and he can't be a day over fifty. It has to be members of the same family, members that look alike…grandfather, father, and son."

The basement of Lewis Hall of Science was eerily quiet and empty. This was not unusual for a Sunday morning at a college, most of the students were sleeping. Andrew stopped in front of a door marked Boiler Room, with a Hazard sign on the wall. "See if the key opens this door." He pointed. Kendall inserted the key and it opened. Inside a typical electrical room with two closets. Andrew went over to one and tried to open it. Locked. Kendall tried the key; this time the door did not open. Andrew motioned to the other closet. She easily opened this one; an unlocked storage closet.

Andrew examined the room, checking out the walls and corners. He was certain the map pointed to this end of the building. He pulled a flashlight out of his backpack and investigated each corner, leveraging his body on the floorboards.

Kendall attempted to open the locked door with a paper clip she pulled from her bag. "What else do you have in there?" he asked. "I didn't know you had experience in breaking and entering."

She laughed. "No experience, unfortunately... thought it was worth a try. I have a paper clip and this key card." She smiled. "Come on, don't you know how to open it with a credit card like in the movies?" She handed Andrew the key card, and he grinned. His posture charged, his hazel eyes twinkled, peering above his round wire rimmed glasses. His shaggy salt-and-pepper hair reminded her of Harrison Ford. *Well, we are on an Indiana Jones type of adventure.*

The enormity and complexity of what was actually happening in her life struck her for a moment like a screen door unexpectedly slamming. Indiana Jones, secret tunnels, really?

She shook her head and chuckled. Andrew jiggled the key card wedged behind the lock. His clothing seemed out of place, almost like a costume.

"What's so funny, don't I fit the profile of the cat burglar?"

She pulled on her long ponytail twisting her hair. "First of all, no one uses the term cat burglar anymore and yes, you don't fit the profile. This is crazy, right? I mean what are we looking for. I can't believe all this is happening."

Andrew sat on the ground, his back against the door.

Using both hands to get up from the floor with the key card in his hand, Kendall heard a click as Andrew's hand passed over the bottom hinge of the door. "Did you hear that?" On his hands and knees, he ran the key card up and down the doorframe and they heard a click again. He tried the knob; it was still locked. He ran the key card over the door again and there it was—another click. He put his hand on the doorknob and opened it up.

Old strong steel faced them, looking like the door of a bank vault. It appeared to be decades old. There was no combination lock, no lever, and no handle visible.

Andrew ran the key card up and down all around the door, and again a loud click. The vault door popped its lock. They pushed against the heavy door and heard the loud creaking of hinges.

They were both speechless, staring straight into the dark black nothing. He took his flashlight from his backpack and held it up close to his ear, creating a soft spotlight shining down a long dark corridor. It was a tunnel, definitely a tunnel, with wiring and piping running down one side, some type of lighting system overhead, and mechanical tracks etched into the ground.

Without a word being uttered, Kendall followed him into the tunnel whispering, "What is this? A tunnel to a bunker?"

He turned around, scooted past her, and unzipped his backpack.

"I think we should follow it, Kendall. See where it leads, but I want to put something in the door. The last thing we need is to get locked in."

"Okay, let's do it." She gave a timid smile and took the flashlight he held out.

They walked in silence, Andrew's flashlight leading the way.

"What do you think the tracks are for?" Kendall stared at the metal tracks that ran the length of the tunnel. Andrew shone his light on the ceiling and sides of the tunnel. "My first instinct is it looks like an elevator shaft." He pointed. "You can see the wires running the whole length of the tunnel on both sides but instead of the elevator going vertically up and down, it looks like it's going horizontally through the tunnel."

Kendall looked around with her light. "You're right! That's what it looks like—a sideways elevator shaft." He stopped walking. "What? What's wrong?" she asked, whispering. He put his backpack on the ground, unzipped it and took out an electronic device. "I'm not sure if this GPS will work underground but if it does, we will at least have an idea of where we are headed. My guess is north." According to Andrew, they had been traveling west-northwest for the last two hours. Kendall knew she could walk a fifteen-minute mile, so she calculated they walked about six or seven miles. Andrew kept a fast pace and made the time fly by with stories of bunkers and bomb shelters everyday Americans built in the 1950s. He was certain this was the infamous bunker he had heard whisperings and rumors about as an Associate Professor on campus in the 1960s. He studied the small GPS device in his hand.

"Well, this is strange…" He slowed his pace. Turning around, he showed her the location on the GPS.

"How can that be? It looks like the tunnel runs right through the cemetery." The Nathaniel cemetery was about ten miles as the crow flies from Western

Maryland College. Local families who worked in or grew up around the college were buried here. Tim's coffin was buried there, just as she would be one day since she bought a plot at the time of Tim's death for both of them.

"How deep below the ground are we?" she asked. "Do you think we're close to the surface?"

"No. I think we've been going at a slant, a slight angle downward for the last two miles. I'm not sure how deep we are, but I am amazed my GPS works. There must be some kind of wiring for telecommunications down here." He slowed his pace. "Look, over to the left, the tunnel splits."

Her head and her heart pounded. *Tim, what were you involved in? Why would you have a key card that worked on this obviously decades-old underground system?* Andrew turned left. "It's a set of stairs, and if my GPS is correct, it's going to come out right in the middle of the cemetery."

Unable to comprehend what was really going on, she forced herself to speak. "Do you think it comes out in a grave?"

Andrew placed his hand on Kendall's shoulder. "I don't know, Kendall, it doesn't make a lot of sense, why the cemetery? I'm going to mark this spot on my GPS, and we can go to the cemetery later and see where this exact spot is. But if you're up for it, I would like to see where the rest of the tunnel goes." He waited patiently, as though he were asking a simple question of whether or not she would like to stay a little bit longer at the coffee bar down the street. She admired him as a professor, a mentor, and a friend. She could do this, no, she needed to do this and he was willing to help her find the truth.

"It's not even lunchtime yet, and I brought snacks," she said. "Let's keep going."

****

Steel tracks, concrete tunnels, the same view for the last ten miles. Kendall sighed. "Are you hungry?" They stopped for a quick lunch break.

Andrew, fascinated by the vents in the wall, was on his knees. "There has got to be some type of high tech system in this tunnel—ventilation, communication— I'm surprised there is no security camera."

"Well, if we are on video don't you think someone would have stopped us? Maybe there's no video because then there would be evidence this exists. I guess it depends on how classified this tunnel really is." Unable to eat, she stuffed her lunch in her backpack. "Seriously, how could Tim be involved in this?"

The Professor studied her without answering her question. "We still must be pretty far away from the actual bunker."

They had walked a long time. Kendall knew he was in good shape, he ran two marathons, twenty-six miles was nothing to him, but she also realized they had no idea of the length of the tunnel system.

"If they took the time and effort to lay tracks for transporting people, whether it's an elevator as I suspect or some type of monorail system…" He touched the tracks. "Yes, I'm really thinking some type of monorail, you know Walt Disney had a monorail system designed and built in the late 1950s, so that's possible, he certainly had a secret connection to the government, actually even to Western Maryland College."

Kendall stared. *"Walt Disney?"*

Andrew stopped and took a swig of water, angling the flashlight to illuminate the area they were standing in. "I think we should turn around. I'm marking this spot on my GPS. We could get in the car and check out the coordinates and find out where it is above ground. I know the stairs were in the cemetery, but at this spot I'm just not sure where we are; it looks like the middle of the woods." Andrew paused. "I'm not sure what Tim was into, but I'm not giving up. Let's try to figure this out."

Reluctantly she agreed, disappointed they had not found the answers she so desperately wanted.

Chapter 36

Staring out at the curvy, tree-lined road heading out to Cunningham Falls State Park, Kendall was thankful Andrew was with her. After leaving Lewis Hall, they decided to call it a day and regroup in the morning. But Andrew knocked on her door at five o'clock declaring he wouldn't be able to sleep without driving out to the location of the GPS coordinates. He was certain the tunnel went underground by Cunningham Falls State Park. He figured it would be an easy hike and assured her they could be home before it turned dark.

So here she was, the Professor beside her analyzing Google map on his phone, and Harvey in the back seat, eager to run in the woods.

Cunningham Falls State Park adjoins Catoctin Mountain Park. Both green, forested areas with dark, rich brown soil, vines, tall trees and rocks. When she first moved to Maryland, she loved to hike in the park. It reminded her of the green and brown dark forests of Western Pennsylvania where she grew up with a passion for the outdoors.

Her phone buzzed. Driving, she ignored it, she was an advocate of no texting or talking while driving. The sun lower in the sky, most hikers were gone or trekking back to their cars.

"How much daylight do you think we have left?"

Andrew looked down at his watch and answered

matter-of-factly. "The sun sets at 8:05 today, so…we have a few hours left, and I brought flashlights." He pulled them out as in show-and-tell. "But the park does close at dusk," he said. "The only issue is, I don't think there is a trail to where we need to go, so it may take us a little bit longer to follow the GPS."

****

They were making good time, averaging about a fifteen-minute mile. Her legs ached. The first four miles they followed a trail—but now definitely off trail—walking over boulders and through bushes following Andrew's GPS.

"It's exactly what I thought."

"What is it?" Kendall asked.

"See this road; it leads to the perimeter of Camp David. That's where the tunnel goes into Camp David or it breaks off and goes to Site R."

"I never knew where Camp David was."

"Yes, it's hidden here in the forest. It used to be a camp for government workers until President Roosevelt took it over and converted it to a Presidential Retreat and changed all the access. He originally named it Shangri-La after the magical place in Lost Horizon. Too bad Eisenhower changed it, naming it after his father and grandson, I liked Shangri- La better."

"How do you know it leads to Camp David?"

"I'll show you." He walked out to the road turning in both directions. "There it is." He pointed at a sign. She walked the rest of the way with Harvey to the large square sign. It read, *No Trespassing, No Stopping, No Standing, No Parking, Violators Will Be Punished by Law.*

"After this road, there is a larger area of dense

woods and another road that is only opened seasonally if at all, and then more woods and then another road before the perimeter, which I am sure has cameras and security. I heard there is a line where armed guards pop out of the ground if it is crossed. I don't really know. But seriously, we need to keep walking."

What would Tim have to do with Camp David? Just then a rabbit ran past, surprising Harvey. He yanked to run, pulled loose, and his collar came undone. The rabbit was fast but so was Harvey; he took off through the woods like lightning.

They both started running. Harvey ran like a greyhound, gaining speed. Kendall screamed, "Harvey!" at the top of her lungs, but either he suddenly went deaf or he was too far away to hear her panicked cries. Soon they came to another paved road. "What is this," Kendall asked, panic in her voice. "The perimeter fence? Is it electric? I don't want him to get electrocuted!" She frantically called Harvey's name.

"I know there is a perimeter fence all the way around the property but I have no idea whether it is electric. I'm sure the rabbit will not run into the fence..." Andrew stopped running yelling Harvey's name.

Another country road appeared in the distance. They were definitely in the middle of nowhere and the sun was slowly going down behind the trees and the mountain. Was Camp David really this far out in the middle of rural America?

Her heart pounded. In the distance, another road emerged with a green belt and a tall black fence with cameras and security equipment attached. Behind that fence was a large area of green, and a third fence off in the distance. A towering, sinister fence at least one hundred feet high. Her chest tightened, waiting for the armed security to spot them on the camera.

Andrew looking at his GPS, seemingly oblivious to the threat of men popping out of the ground. He looked calm. "I'm definitely right, the tunnel goes to Camp David, but I need to erase my GPS memory; do you know how?"

"What are you talking about?" She continued yelling "Harvey," gasping for breath.

"They might confiscate my GPS so I want to erase the memory of Lewis Hall, the cemetery, and the directions to Camp David." He stopped pushing buttons on his GPS. "There's a way to do that on a computer, but I am not sure how to do it on the device."

"Take the battery out, I don't know…smash it…"

His face tightened in alarm. "Here they come."

A massive military vehicle came speeding toward them, with two commando dressed men hanging out the windows, weapons pointed. A commanding voice boomed out of the speaker. "Kneel down on the ground and put your hands in the air, you are trespassing on private government land. I repeat, kneel down on the ground, hands in the air, *now!*"

Kendall and Andrew instantly fell to their knees raising their arms, hands up to the sky. Terrified to look at the Professor; her heart beating rapidly, anxiety took over, her limbs shaking uncontrollably. Andrew whispered without making eye contact. "Don't mention Tim's briefcase. Trust me, Kendall, don't say anything."

As the Hummer drew closer, the men jumped out of the vehicle and immediately handcuffed the

Professor and Kendall. Out of the corner of her eye, movement, she glanced sideways, and Harvey was running toward her at full speed. She looked up at the military officer holding a gun, and shouted out a high-pitched sound—unsure it was her own voice—"Please, please, please don't shoot my dog." Harvey stopped running about twenty feet away and switched to a slow walk, his eyes darting from face to face. He stretched in mid-stride, in Downward Dog pose, as if he had all the time in the world. She silently pleaded with the man holding the gun, looked over at Harvey, and commanded, "Harvey, sit, Harvey, please sit."

Harvey plopped his tail and butt on the ground, cocking his head to the side with a confused expression. And like everyone else, he was instantly taken into custody.

Chapter 37

"What the hell?" Scout walked in, disbelief on his face at the wreckage of his office. Lily was sitting on top of a stack of messy file folders. Desk drawers were pulled out and emptied on the floor. Three file cabinets where Scout kept all his client information, scattered...everywhere. "What's missing?"

"*No lo se.*" Lily stood up and raised her hands in the air, cursing in Spanish before she switched to English. "I don't know, they were looking for something." She muttered a few more phrases in Spanish.

Lily picked up the phone. "You want me to call the *policia*?"

Scout pulled his ponytail, fixated on the mess. "No, not yet. Was the door locked?"

"No, wide open. But the satellite phone is here, so is your kayak." She opened the refrigerator door "Your cerveza..."

Scout went to his desk. The drawers were open and empty, their contents covering the floor. "How about the petty cash?" Lily walked over to the corner, picked up the cash box with the key still in it and closed tightly.

"Still here." She turned the key and opened the lid. "All the cash is still here."

Scout shook his head. "What on earth were they

looking for?"

Lily and Scout worked the rest of the afternoon trying to assemble the various file folders and return everything back to its proper place. It didn't make sense. As far as Scout could determine, nothing was missing. Scout speculated it was just a bunch of kids trying to wreck the place, and something stopped them in the middle of their destruction and they fled.

He couldn't shake the creeping suspicion the robbery or pseudo-robbery had something to do with Tim Jackson's cenote map.

Last week's strange conversation with a local cenote owner flashed in his mind. In rapid Spanish, the landowner told Scout about two gringos who were asking questions about a cenote. The old man asked Scout if he had a map. "Mapa?"

Scout tried to understand the translation. In Spanish, the old man told him men were looking for him. Scout tried to clarify, but the man kept repeating words he couldn't translate. Scout was fluent in Spanish, but the combo mix of Spanish and Mayan the old man was spouting was difficult to follow. He repeated the old man's last words as he walked away, words that stuck with him: "*Eso es tabu,*" in English, "that's forbidden territory."

Was someone looking for the cenote map?

He needed to call Kendall. Secretly, he wanted to talk to her every day, every hour, and as soon as he woke up. He found himself dreaming of her. Usually the dreams took place in the cenote where they had kissed, except his dreams were definitely Rated R.

It had been forever, a long time past yesterday, since a woman had taken up residency in his mind.

Moving down to Puerto Morelos freed him of the last serious, complicated, and disastrous female relationship. He had no desire to return to that state of confusion. Nevertheless, the essence of Kendall consumed his thoughts. He would hit play on the iPod in his Jeep; a song, even the first few notes, would transport him to riding in the Jeep with her, coming home from the cenotes. He would glance to the right expecting to see her ponytail coming out of her hat, drumming on her legs with her fingers, with that irresistible smile, her eyes sparkling. Just thinking about her got his juices flowing. Yes, it had been a long time since his feelings were stirred up. He wasn't sure he liked it.

Chapter 38

Kendall and Andrew were taken to a concrete block building and placed in separate interrogation rooms. Sterile, stark rooms, empty of any personal effects. If she had been blindfolded, she would guess she had ended up inside a deserted office building. Clean, sparse and plain.

Camp David; her imagination expected something different, something more prestigious. Instead, she was sitting at a long particle board table, in one of four uncomfortable relics of the 1970s' plastic chairs, staring at a large glass window that reflected an image of a woman she didn't recognize. *What was she doing?*

She tried not to look at the glass window; certain someone was watching her sitting at the table. She studied her blotched and shaky hands.

They rushed her into the room; everything seemed to be on high speed. Then it screeched to a halt and she waited alone in silence. It seemed like hours until she had an opportunity to explain what happened. When the two large men entered the room, her insides were so tight she didn't think she could talk correctly. Her anxiety squeezed the breath out of her. Instinctively, she knew to explain they were hiking, just hiking in the park with their dog, but...

Andrew had repeated the sentence three times softly, like a mantra without moving his lips as the

Hummer was pulling up. "We were hiking, Harvey took off after a rabbit, that's all." He whispered this right after he told her again not to mention Tim's briefcase.

Her belongings were confiscated. Her mind went instantly to the briefcase. She locked Tim's items, including the briefcase in her file cabinet at the college, this time using a different hiding place in the back office, but the key card from the briefcase was with her. Well, now they had it.

She wasn't sure what Andrew packed in his backpack, she hoped it wasn't his notebook full of observations and assumptions. Certain it would read like the work of a madman obsessed with a conspiracy theory.

Her heart raced erratically. Hot, anxious and sweaty; a light sheen covered her skin. Her foot tapped up and down on the floor and she was squeezing her fist tightly. She knew she had never looked more nervous. She couldn't control the thoughts spinning through her mind, or the alarming reality of where she was. *This is the Federal Government, not just any government office but the highest in the land. I'm outside of Camp David being interrogated by federal officers who protect the President of the United States.* Speculation and conspiracy ran through her head like a fast-forwarding movie. What if they asked her about Tim…What if they knew about Tim? She needed to slow her thoughts and think before she started talking. *Tim, what were you involved in? What is it you want me to know?*

****

The image in the mirror astounded Kendall. She let the water run over her hands, washing them repeatedly with soap, patting down her face with the rough paper towel. She realized how much she changed. Older. The small creases by her mouth and in between her nose. Determined. Yes, determined to find the truth. So much happened since Tim's death, but she realized she could survive. She would figure out what Tim was involved in. Standing in the federal office building in Catoctin Falls State Park outside of the elusive Camp David, she realized she would not stop investigating until she discovered what her husband was trying to tell her, what he was hiding. If he didn't want her to be involved, he would never have left her clues. *Lambie, I'm not giving up.* Harvey was okay. Led out to a lobby both she and Andrew were being released. Behind a glass window, a young military man was petting Harvey and trying not to smile as Harvey raised his paw and high-fived him.

She wondered what the soldier would think about the trick Tim had taught him. He would hold his hand like a gun and go "bang"; Harvey would drop down to his stomach and roll over. Hysterically nervous, the thought almost made her laugh.

Signing for her belongings, Andrew walked out into the lobby. "There's the culprit." He pointed at Harvey, bent down and rubbed his head. His expression unreadable. "The officers will give us a ride back to the car, looks like this misunderstanding has been properly cleared up."

The ride back to the car was in silence, with Andrew staring out the window at the dark woods.

It was late. The park now closed, the parking lot void of all life. Kendall waited until the military vehicle was no longer in sight. "Do you know if they looked at your GPS?" She was giving Harvey some food she had in a container she kept in the back seat, her hands still shaking.

Andrew leaned against the car. "I don't think so, did you tell them anything about Tim?"

She shut the door and it accidently slammed. "I didn't tell them anything, I told them exactly what you told me to say. We were hiking and Harvey chased a rabbit. The odd thing is they never asked me about Tim, not one question." She was rummaging through her backpack. "And here's the key card, nothing about that either. I don't even think they looked at my phone. They would have needed the password."

She picked up her iPhone and entered her password. A text message came up on the screen from earlier today. It was from a blocked number, the words made her hands shake. "Be careful who you trust. All is not as it seems."

Chapter 39

It was another typical day in Scottsdale, Arizona. Perfect weather. A sky of intense bright blue, with no clouds marring the canvas. Late spring in Arizona was the ultimate in weather.

The beautiful day didn't help elevate Ryder's mood. Ever since he returned from the cenote trip with Kendall, he had stayed off the drugs. But now his publicist and manager wanted him to audition for a spokesperson position on MTV. The thought of being on camera again instantly made his chest tight, causing sleepless nights and a case of full-blown anxiety. He wanted to say yes, but as soon as he began to text or call back, anxiety strangled his mind and heart. He was now ignoring their messages.

Unable to sleep, he hiked a six-mile trail at the back side of Dreamy Draw Mountain Park at seven o'clock this morning. He had been dreaming of his father. Diving dreams. Dreams where he would wake up and clear aqua water dominated his thoughts. Cenote water. In his dreams, he saw his father, alive and happy trying to urge him to come with him, to keep diving down, going deeper and deeper. He wasn't anxious in the dreams. Actually, quite the opposite; he experienced calm, peace, and serenity. Like the old days of diving with his father, he had the feeling of being exactly in the right place at the right time. He never wanted to leave.

The cenote dream stayed with him all the way through the hike. The color of the sky matched the water of his dream. He contemplated going back to the DUN playground and get some downers so he could continue to sleep and swim in the cenotes with his father. He fought the urge to take drugs since he returned from his trip. Not that it was easy.

His publicist warned him if he didn't jump on the bandwagon now, if he didn't take the opportunities given to him today, and continue to put his face up in the celebrity sphere, he would lose his status. He would become one of those ex-reality TV stars nobody remembers, until four years later when they show up on the front of the local paper for shoplifting or rehab.

Paradise Valley was airing its last season, and Ryder could barely watch his performance. Anyone who looked too close could see the anxiety. A noticeable difference from the previous season.

His new addiction was sex. Sure, he had met tons of girls since *Paradise Valley* started, but contrary to popular belief, he hadn't slept with any of them. Make out sessions galore, but with his schedule being so busy with the show and personal appearances, he never had the place or the opportunity to spend the night with someone.

He wasn't a virgin.

The summer before *Paradise Valley*, Ryder lost his virginity.

Girls and sex consumed his thoughts, but he had never gone all the way. He was driving down Interstate 10 to Tucson to pick up a piece of furniture for his mother. Traffic was somewhat light in the middle of the day, non-rush hour. A blonde woman in a silver convertible Audi passed him several times, smiling an ultra-white mouthful of teeth. She would pass him and then slow down. He would pass her, exchanging sexy smiles. Ryder was passing the time, but when she pulled in front, turned on her blinker and headed for the exit Ryder's hormones sprinted. He hoped it was an invitation but unsure where this would go. He put his signal on and followed her off the exit.

She was older by at least ten years, but pretty in a platinum blonde, fake tan kind of way. "Wanna go have a drink?" she asked, giggling. She stepped out of the convertible and walked over to his car. He looked around at the exit where they pulled off, Picacho Peak. Yes, there was a big peak jutting out into the sky.

"I don't think there is much around here," he answered instead of stating the obvious, he was under eighteen. She tore away her sunglasses studying him intently. "Well, that's okay, I happen to have a bottle of Grey Goose in my cooler. You in? Let's take a ride to the lookout, I'll drive."

Speechless, but only for a minute, he pressed the button to close the Ranger's window and opened the door. As he stepped out, she smiled her blindingly white teeth and looked him up and down. Her tangerine halter-top completely open in the back, with thin spaghetti straps holding a full front set of fake boobs in place. She threw him the keys. "Actually, how about you drive my car?"

Middle of the week, middle of the day, no one was around, which was a good thing. While Ryder was driving she was pouring red plastic cups of vodka and rubbing the inside of his thigh. His jeans stretched tight as he grew. When he finally stopped the car, she was all over him. She looked him straight in the eyes and said, "Let's fuck."

And they did, at fast pace, with her climbing on top, unbuttoning his jeans, and then once more, pushing the seat in recline way back, this time slower, her guiding the way. The conversation was minimal.

He was lost in disbelief this was happening to him.

Her phone rang and rang and rang playing "Let it Go" by Idina Menzel. She never silenced it, she just kept moving up and down on top of him.

It ended as abruptly as it began. "Oh" is all she said as she smiled and she opened the door and climbed out.

He couldn't help noticing her big diamond ring as she sat in the driver's seat, taking him back to his car. "What's your name?" she asked in a soft voice.

"Ryder," he answered, and she burst out laughing.

"Seriously? Well, I will never forget you, Ryder, take care of yourself and thanks."

And then she just drove away, with her sunglasses back on and a quick flash of her white teeth.

He never told anyone. He really didn't think anyone would believe him. He kept it to himself, because he liked it so much. It gave him power; he just didn't know what to do with it.

Now, without the drugs from the DUN playground, he was focusing his addiction on sex. It started down in Puerto Morelos, where he met three different girls late at night wandering around the resort and slept with each one of them in the same night. It was his substitute for drugs. It was an escape, an occurrence to pluck him out of the moment and let him forget his insecurities and his anxieties. Having a random one-night stand was like taking a drug for a night. He was never sure exactly where the high would take him but he knew it would take his mind off anything else. The thrill of determining whether or not someone would sleep with you without really knowing you, and the excitement of how fast it could happen, coupled with the overall physical pleasure, was a different kind of high.

When he returned to Arizona he went searching for places where he could do the one-night stands. He never realized it would be so easy. He found them in the unlikeliest spots. He visited branches of his gym, LA Fitness, in outlying areas in Phoenix. Sometimes he would drive thirty miles just to work out, but it paid off, because lonely women were easy. He liked married women best, because he knew they wouldn't come after him or leak a scandal story to the tabloids.

He was honest with them when they seemed to be on the same addictive track. Sometimes it was as easy as saying, "You're beautiful, you're married, and that's why I like you, I just want to fuck, no strings attached."

He used condoms and never gave his real name. It was the easiest, cheapest high he had ever experienced. The only problem, just like popping a pill, he wanted more.

Chapter 40

Steve Crawford wiped the sweat off his forehead. After presenting his holographic pass, a simple white key card, he was led into the first of three gates entering Camp David. He had been to Camp David twice before.

He remembered the second visit more vividly than the first. It was burned into his memory forever. He had entered Camp David from underneath the ground.

Tim was with him, and it was that moment, Steve could now confirm Tim was hiding something.

No one else would have noticed the peculiarity in Tim. The stillness of his eyes or the way his genuine personality slipped into the Intelligence mode when directly observed. Only someone who shared a college dorm room might catch the slight change in his presence, but he knew Tim was lying to him.

The deceit affected Steve mentally, zapped his self-confidence, and kept him awake at night.

So, yes he remembered his last visit to Camp David vividly, not just because it was one of the two times he entered Camp David but because of Tim's actions.

They had just returned from a government diving trip in South America where they found some interesting biological elements. They were called to Site R to meet with biotech staff for follow-up reports on their samples

Steve was excited, Site R was an amazing engineering feat. It went down multiple stories below ground level. Previously, they had only been on one level but had heard the talk, the whispered leaks, a tunnel ran from Site R to Camp David. The underground base was rumored to be so large, it actually qualified as a high-tech subterranean town.

But, on that particular day, he and Tim were taken to a different level of Site R, where they boarded a type of monorail and ended up in a tunnel, a back way into Camp David. The tunnel. The rumors were true.

Laboratories, one after another, labeled with numbers not in sequential order, lined the deep hallway. Most were box rooms with both clear and opaque bulletproof Plexiglas, giving a foggy glimpse to a sterile environment with stainless steel tables, trays of glass vials, and computer biotech equipment. No expense for lighting and technology was spared here, as the doors were fingerprint accessible. They entered Lab 139, following a robot-like man with no conversation skills.

Two white-coated scientists were absorbed in the large computer screens on the wall highlighting projected images from a computerized microscope. The taller of the two portrayed the typical mad scientist look—white lab coat, round rimmed glasses, wispy grayish-white hair styled in a partial Einstein look. The other had no striking features, just short brown hair, brown eyes, and no expression. As they walked into the lab, the taller one focused on Tim with laser precision.

Perhaps staring was an understatement. His eyes locked on Tim as if he were looking at a lab subject under the microscope. After introductions were made,

Dr. Thomas, the gawker, went back to the corner of his lab and started rummaging through files and paperwork. At high speed, he opened and closed file drawers. He picked up his tablet device and was rapidly flipping through touch screens, swiping picture after picture in rapid procession. The images were reflected on the wall. He was swiping them so fast, it was hard to catch any of the details of the photos on the wall, just groups of men in a jungle. Possibly one of Kennedy?

Dr. Thomas noticed Steve's observation of the wall, and turned the projected images to a blank screen. He was drumming his fingers, then running them though his frayed white glob of hair in a repetitive motion. But what was most disturbing was the constant turning, stealing glances at Tim.

The other scientist, Dr. Helsel, brought up photographs of the last dive trip on his computer, a touch screen on the wall. He zoned in on the topography. He wanted Steve and Tim to circle with the computer pen the different areas where they entered the water. He remembered spending many hours that day sitting in the lab answering questions about the exact location of particular samples. They looked at picture after picture of underwater rock, coral, and pinnacles Tim and Steve had photographed and clearly marked

Dr. Thomas, the Einstein twin, had abruptly left the lab about two hours into the meeting. Steve couldn't help noticing as he stepped out of the access door to leave, he turned around, his eyes locked on Tim. Tim turned and Steve was certain from the way Dr. Thomas held his tablet, he snapped a picture.

Finally, Steve caught Tim's attention, Tim returned his gaze with a slow shake of his head signaling silence.

He remembered thinking, *Why am I out of the loop?*

They were diving for a specific type of underwater bacteria. It's what they always were diving for. Most of their diving trips over the years had been in carefully selected areas of the world focusing on retrieving bacteria, plants, and minerals for any type of life that lived on or around the bottom of the sea. In the last few years, they focused on Belize, Mexico, and Central America. With almost seventy percent of the world being water, The Collective research scientists believed what lies beneath, what rests on the ocean floor, played a significant role in essential nutrients, beneficial pharmaceuticals, and anticancer agents.

Their mission, from the beginning, was to discover and preserve the valuable resources on earth, to find them before they were extinct, before people destroyed the very parts of earth that would save them. The Collective would collect and safeguard scientific research, in order for humankind to exist healthfully and successfully.

After several hours in the lab, their host, the non-talking, brown-haired, white-coated scientist, entered the lab to escort them back to the top of Site R. They were shuffled toward the tunnel with the monorail. The door opened and they all got inside. He could see the concentration on Tim's face; he was busy observing everything, the touchpad, the tracks, the doors. He had seen this look before. Tim's many talents keen observation and photographic memory; during his training in black ops, he could memorize the phone book.

Chapter 41

Scout picked up the phone, cursing silently. He despised cell phones. He didn't hate the technology, he just detested how the technology changed people. He had been leading dive trips for over twenty years and even though he understood the advantage to having a satellite phone for emergency purposes—especially stuck out in the middle of the Yucatán—he didn't agree with the obsession and addictiveness humans had with the iPhone, cell phones or the iPad. Why couldn't they put it down and talk to each other.

With the new satellite coverage in Belize and Mexico, he observed the obsessed, talking on the phone constantly, texting while hiking back to a cenote. What really got him, a mere five minutes after a beautiful dive, oblivious to the beauty of the world around them they would be back on the phone. Trekking through the jungle, a snake could be dangling down from a tree branch, and if they were on their phone they would keep walking until the snake hit them on the forehead. It drove him mad, in the middle of desolate beauty, an uninhabited, exquisite stretch of beach, and there would be a beeping every so many minutes, because somebody's phone updated.

He remembered the incident clearly. It was a group of five men, and as the night went on, the beeping continued on and on. Each time it beeped, a thorn was being pushed further under his fingernail. He found the phone and threw it in the ocean. As he was hurling it into the water, he turned around and said, "Now, the fucking fish will be pissed."

Since then, he included as part of his dive talks, a lengthy section on cell phones. Turn them off, keep them in a waterproof dry bag and use only for emergency purposes. He promised, "If I hear your phone ringing, beeping, whatever, in the middle of the jungle, it will be confiscated."

He knew this pissed divers off. Taking away a man's cell phone, his modern technology—to some it was like cutting off their hand, so dependent were they on this extension of their arm, they couldn't function without it. Frankly, he didn't care. The real world was waiting for you to be in the moment.

Yet, here he was, Mr. I hate technology, holding the phone willing himself to call Kendall. He couldn't stop thinking about her. He couldn't stop dreaming about her. He wanted her back in Puerto Morelos. He wanted to show her the cenote her husband wanted his son Ryder to see in the first place, not only because of the guilt of having lied to them, but hoping it would close the door of uncertainty. He wanted her to have closure so she could move on, put the past behind her. He wanted her. *If I help her figure this out, we might have a chance.*

He inputted her number.

The call went straight to voicemail. He hesitated, should he leave a message? It was certainly not what he was wishing for but he owed it to her. He told her about the break-in at the dive shop, rambling, speaking rapidly; he mentioned the possibility of it being related to the map of the cenote, her cenote. He ended with a few simple words. "Kendall, will you come back? It's my responsibility to help you carry out Tim's wishes."

He did not mention Ryder. He did not express how much he wanted her, thought about her, or that he missed her. He hated voice messages and texts as much as he hated cell phones. As soon as he left it, he wished he could erase the message.

He headed to the sea, lowering his body on the beach, peaceful, shimmering, the soft sugar sand with the curved low palm tree almost touching the water's edge, as if taking a bow. His mouth was set in a straight line, eyebrows scrunched together; he held the phone in his hand, ready to throw it in the sea.

Chapter 42

The dark circles under Kendall's eyes reflected back from the mirror. Up all night, again. It had been a long time since she kept such hours.

She remembered when she first met Tim how they couldn't get enough of each other. It didn't matter if they worked ten long strenuous hours, or how many minutes they slept the night before. The energy of their love and desire for each other's touch kept their nerve endings wide-awake. A conversation could start about what to eat for dinner and the next thing they knew, deep intimate discussions on the meaning of life and how they found each other in this world...born total strangers, living life as one. She wondered if she would ever feel that way again.

Irritated and frustrated, she stepped out of bed, throwing on one of his treasured sweatshirts, and walked over to the safe where she kept the zip drive. She was still uneasy after the break-in, so she locked it away carefully after each use. Turning on her computer, she started going through the files for the hundredth time.

Loneliness swirled all around her. She had pushed away her close friends one by one when Tim died. She didn't blame them for staying away. They continued to call for a long time, but finally when she never returned calls and blocked everyone from her broken heart, always turning down invitations, they backed off, they retreated. *They have forgotten about me now.*

Now, in the wee hours of the morning, she longed for someone to share her thoughts and space with.

Her mind wandered back to Puerto Morelos. She picked up her iPhone. She was amazed she had taken only six photos on the entire trip. The photo she continued to go back and look at, repeatedly, was a photo of Ryder, Scout, and herself by the Land Rover in the jungle. The photo cut off the very top of Scout's head, and it looked more like a candid action shot. Ryder looked tan, rugged, and nonchalant staring off into the distance, ready to walk away. Her head was bent down looking at the ground, but Scout was looking directly into the camera, mouth closed, with a sexy little smile. It gave her a funny feeling in her stomach.

The message Scout left her earlier about the break-in was troubling. She opened the safe, and rolled the map she had not shared with Andrew, out on the floor. She now knew it was a cenote, a cenote Scout confessed they did not see. The paper the map was drawn on was delicate and old, but it wasn't disintegrating. It was an original drawing on unusual paper.

She pulled out her iPad calendar; the students' graduation ceremony was coming up. She needed to be there for the keynote address by Conrad Nathaniel. She decided once the ceremony was over, she would go back to Puerto Morelos.

Would she be able to persuade Ryder? This was, after all, the real trip his father wanted to take him on. However, at this point, it was so much more than a father-son celebration. She knew, with or without

Ryder, she would follow this journey through and see it to the end.

Just the thought of trying to persuade Ryder to go back with her a second time seemed impossible. Nonetheless, for Tim she would do her best to convince Ryder.

She clicked on the slideshows of the various presidents with a group of men. The locations were always near water, but not in the same place.

The photos…what was she missing?

She printed the photos out to her air printer and arranged them in order of date, in rows and columns making a huge puzzle on the floor. She then rearranged them by similar location. Nothing new. As she ran her fingers through her hair and sat back on her heels, she picked one up studying the detail of the photo. President Bill Clinton was in this one. She took her magnifying mirror from her top desk drawer and began holding each photo up to the glass.

An hour later, she picked up her phone and tapped Ryder's name under contacts. Of course, his generic voicemail. "Ryder, hi it's Kendall, there is something I need to discuss with you and something I need to show you. Please call me back."

She set the phone down, then picked it up again. It was too late to call Scout in Puerto Morelos, but she clicked on his photo, wishing she could talk to him.

Back to the briefcase she opened up the other map. Definitely an architectural map, blueprints of something structural. She laid it out on the floor next to the map of the cenote. She pulled out her Spanish dictionary and tried to interpret the infinitely tiny words on the cenote map. The words did not translate; they were not

Spanish, but unquestionably similar. Perhaps Maya.

Andrew might have a Mayan dictionary. It was curious, even to herself. She let him inspect every part of the briefcase, but not this map. She wasn't sure why. Something inside of her kept the map secret.

Her eyes settled on the business card lying on the floor. *Johns Hopkins Medical Center*, Dr. Peter A. Trailov, Department of *Neurology* and *Neurosurgery*. It was too late to call but she decided to Google him. Typing his name in the computer, she hit search.

Dr. Peter A. Trailov was the co-director of Adult Brain Tumor Consortium, a group of sixteen medical centers dedicated to improving treatments for adults with malignant brain tumors. His program focus was on clinical research and treatment of primary brain tumors, neoplastic meningitis, brain metastases, epidural cord compression, neurotoxicity, anticancer agents, and cancer pain management. The centers specialized in new drugs and treatments.

Why would Tim have his card? She did not want to jump to any conclusions but as the tears ran down her face, she could not keep her mind from going there.

It was getting late and after playing back Tim's video yet again, she wiped her swollen eyes, resigned to the fact she had to function tomorrow. She couldn't help herself. She was desperately trying to discover something she missed before.

Chapter 43

Kendall bolted up the stairs and opened the heavy glass back door of Decker Center. She was almost on time. As she ran/walked into her office, the Student Affairs office manager Nancy held out a thick stack of pink slips.

"Good morning, the top message is from Conrad Nathaniel. He wants you to call back right away as he is coming into town today." She could feel Nancy studying her appearance. "It's going to be warm today, it's supposed to hit seventy-five degrees." Kendall looked down at her black long-sleeved blouse and black pencil skirt, realizing the weather was the last thing on her mind.

She picked up the soft, pale gray sweater draped over her arm, and held it up with a smile. "Well, I guess I won't be needing my sweater." Nancy gave her a peculiar smile. Most of the employees and college students thought she lost her husband and her mind. *They might be right.*

She closed the door to her office holding the stack of pink message slips in front of her. She would get to them, but first, she pulled out the business card from her purse. *I need to know*, she dialed the number.

"No, Dr. Trailov is in surgery today. Is there something I can assist you with?"

"No, I don't think so, I wanted to leave my name

and number and ask him to give me a call back."

"What is this regarding?"

"My husband, Tim Jackson."

"And is he a patient of Dr. Trailov?"

She hesitated. "I don't know, can *you* tell me if he is a patient of Dr. Trailov?"

Silence. "You are asking me if your husband is a patient of Dr. Trailov?"

"Yes, Tim Cord Jackson—is he a patient?"

"I'm sorry, Mrs. Jackson, I cannot answer that question according to HIPAA regulations."

"Well, can you ask the doctor to call me back?"

The woman hesitated as if she wanted to say something else. "I will give the doctor your message." She disconnected.

The next priority, Conrad Nathaniel. She dialed his number and was surprised when he answered it directly. "Conrad Nathaniel speaking."

"Conrad, hello, this is Kendall Jackson, returning your call."

"Hello, Kendall Jackson." He chuckled. "Do you drink that wine?" He laughed again. "I'm actually driving on the 95 headed up toward Maryland this afternoon, and wondered if I could take you to lunch today?"

"Let me look at my schedule." She hesitated. "I'm sorry, Conrad, but I have several Commencement meetings today where I have to be present, although I'd really like to talk to you about the Commencement keynote. Could I meet with you later in the afternoon?"

Conrad's voice echoed as if he was speaking on a hands-free device. "Yes, let me take you out to dinner this evening and I'll tell you the story of how your husband saved my life and you can ask me all the questions you want about my keynote. I believe we made a deal when I agreed to be the keynote speaker, and now we will be even. Should I pick you up at seven?"

"No, that won't be necessary, I will be working late tonight, so let's just meet here at the school. Would you like me to make reservations somewhere?"

"Not necessary, Kendall, I'll make the arrangements, I know the perfect place. I'll see you at your office at seven, it's a date." And with that the line was disconnected.

The comment actually hung in the air, bordering on being inappropriate. It was most certainly not a date. She would use the time to gather some background information to help her students write the introduction to Conrad Nathaniel's keynote speech.

After returning the rest of her calls, and halfway through the morning she realized she wanted, no needed to call Scout. *I need to set the trip in motion before I change my mind.* Ryder had not returned her call—typical for her reality star stepson—so she left him another text.

She punched in Scout's number in Puerto Morelos.

Lily answered. "*Buenas tardes*, Scout's Dive Shop."

"*Hola* Lily, this is Kendall Jackson, is Scout there?"

She could hear movement and then static as if Lily had placed the phone down and run out to the beach. "Hello, Lily, hello, are you still there?" Another minute went by, and finally she heard someone picking up the phone.

"Kendall? Kendall? Are you there?" It was Scout. She smiled at the sound of his rough low voice.

"I'm here, did I catch you at a bad time?"

Scout was out of breath, breathing heavily. "No, no, not at all, I was just out with the boat on the beach." He took a deep breath in. "It's so nice to hear your voice."

Taken aback by the sincerity and the warmth in his tone, she spoke from the heart. "It's so nice to hear *your* voice, Scout."

A nervous silence filled the line. "I want to come see the cenote, Tim's cenote, the one he wanted us to see from the beginning." She paused. "I haven't spoken to Ryder yet...I'm not sure if he will be coming with us, but with or without him, I want to finish what Tim wanted. There are some things I discovered, that I really can't talk about right now, but I will explain when I come down. I need to see this through. I need to understand."

Her breath accelerated, as she shook her foot up and down in a nervous twitch. "Does your offer still stand? Scout, will you hike me back in there and take me to the cenote?" She ran her fingers through her hair, not breathing until he answered.

"Yes, I will take you. It's a difficult, longer hike in and out, more days of camping, but I can have everything ready by the end of the month. What date do you think you can be down here?"

****

After the phone call, she sat in her messy office staring out at an imaginary point, her mouth turned up in a genuine smile. She clicked on Facebook and sent Ryder a private message. She wanted this trip to be important to him. She had purposely withheld the contents of the briefcase. Now she needed to explain, she needed to share. He was Tim's son.

What held her back initially was the fear of Ryder's discussing it with his mother. She was sure if Tricia knew, she would go to the press, and make a publicity stunt of the briefcase, appearing on *20/20* to obtain fifteen more minutes of fame. She hoped she could persuade Ryder to keep it a secret.

Secrets, how did that become the word of the day. Late last night, when she was looking at the photos of the various presidents, she noticed something strange and she wanted to discuss it with Andrew. The idea of sharing the cenote map was also crossing her mind. She trusted him.

Then she thought of the text on the day of the Camp David hike. "Be careful who you trust. All is not as it seems." *Who sent that?*

****

It was six-thirty p.m. She looked down at her black blouse and skirt, and shrugged. She did not have time to go home and change but she would at least freshen up before her dinner with Conrad Nathaniel.

Even though she had not yet heard back from Ryder, she smiled. Her plan with Scout gave her new energy, and his last comment on the phone stirred up some pulse point in her lower region and a lightheaded feeling. Scout said softly before they disconnected, "Kendall, I can't stop thinking of you."

****

Andrew answered on the first ring. "Kendall, how are you? I've been thinking about you and wanted to share something I discovered." His voice sounded secretive.

"Really?" she replied. "I found something I think might be of interest to you as well."

He lowered his voice. "When can we meet?"

She wished she could meet him now; she wondered how long dinner would last tonight.

"Well, I have a dinner meeting tonight with our keynote speaker, Conrad Nathaniel, so depending on how late you're up, we could meet afterward at my place?"

Silence. A deep breath. "I'm not sure how to say this…" a long pause. "Be careful with Conrad Nathaniel. Between you and me, there's just something about that man I don't trust."

"Why? What are you referring to?"

Andrew cleared his throat. "It's nothing, probably just an over-active imagination of an old man. I always feel like he's hiding something. Just be careful; I'm sure the rumors are true about him being a ladies' man. You know he is supposed to be one of the most eligible bachelors in Baltimore."

She smiled, it was concern she heard in the Professor's voice. "Don't worry about me, it is strictly business, I won't let him take advantage of me."

Chapter 44

The city lights flashed by to a background of classical music, creating a sophisticated atmosphere inside the quiet, gray leather interior. Kendall was silent, inhaling the new car smell from the Tesla model X sports car. Conrad was on the phone

Speeding down Route 140, through Owings Mills, he was taking her to an old favorite dinner club in Baltimore, adding, "They have the juiciest of steaks."

Conrad smelled of old money, money passed on from generation to generation, perhaps piled up high in a corner of an endless attic.

She studied him. His perfectly cut, contemporary hair, strong chin, balanced face and gray eyes. Putting together his bio for the students' introduction, they were both June babies, two days apart, same year. She believed a natural connection existed meeting someone your exact age. Both introduced to the world at the same time, equal chances to win the same race, no generation gap, and society and historical influences equal, at least if you grew up in America.

She felt no such kindred spirit with Conrad. Certain they did not start the same race.

He grinned and hit a button on the dashboard; a panel turned over, and he took an object out, held it in his closed fist and offered it to her. "Hold out your hand."

"Excuse me?" *Why did he make her nervous?*

"Hold out your hand, please." She opened her palm; he dropped the copper coin. "Penny for your thoughts?"

She took a deep breath; her father used to say the same thing to her when she was a little girl. It was their special thing.

"I really wasn't thinking much."

He raised his eyebrows, she answered, "I guess I was thinking you and I are basically the same age, but extremely different."

His side profile reminded her of the actor Channing Tatum. She bit her lip, her thoughts going back to the days when she and Tim would play what famous person someone looked like. Intuitively, she still did this.

Conrad, perceptive, laughed, "What?…I didn't even respond yet so why are you frowning?"

He swiped a button on his dashboard. Bon Jovi's "Living on a Prayer" started beating. "Well, if we're both 80s kids then we should know this song." Conrad began moving in the seat, a strange but funny little dance that made her laugh. It was unexpected, almost out of character for the successful executive. He smiled. "John Bon Jovi, 1986, Richie Sambora on the mouth box."

She touched his hand, a strange sensation shot through her fingers, she placed the copper penny in his hand. "Your turn…"

He turned the music down slowly, and his eyes went back to the road, as he visibly abandoned whatever he was thinking of. "It makes me remember college, you know. Fun times."

Surprised by the answer, she asked, "University of

Southern California?"

"No." He made a left turn and she realized they were on Calvert Street, downtown Baltimore. "Western Maryland College."

They had pulled up in front of a restaurant, Prime Rib. Walking in reminded her of a throwback to a 1960s supper club in New York City. The wait staff all wore tuxedos, looked distinguished, handsome and glided gracefully around the room. The decor was upscale black walls with cream molding, vintage leopard carpet, and lighted individual paintings, giving an overwhelming romantic vibe. Throw in an owner who greets you by name, whisks you to a dimly lit back corner, and there was no doubt Conrad had been here before.

She caught the roaming eyes of men and women, who quickly looked away so as not to be seen staring.

She pulled a miniature silver tape recorder out of her purse. Conrad raised one eyebrow. "Would you mind if I tape your answers to my questions?" Without giving him a chance to answer, she continued, "I told the students on the Commencement committee I would tape our interview." Shoulders back and sitting up taller, she was trying to keep it on a professional level. Conrad raised himself on his elbows, clasped his hands together and rested his chin on his knuckles, looking directly at her.

"Well, how many questions do you have, Ms. Jackson?"

She took her iPhone out, pulling up her list. "Only ten; shall we get started?"

He leaned back in his chair, gazing first at the tape recorder, and then at her, swirling a glass of pinot noir.

"Let's do it this way, you get to ask me your students' ten questions and then I get to ask you ten questions before the evening ends. Deal?"

The electricity in the space between them intensified. "Well, I will certainly try to answer ten questions, but since I have no idea what topic you would be questioning me on, I make no promises. Deal?"

The corners of his mouth turned up. "Let's get your questions out of the way before our delicious juicy steaks are delivered."

Answering the formal interview questions, he slipped right back into the successful entrepreneur and man of science he was. The students had several questions on breathing underwater and he explained in great detail about the oxygenation of blood that allows humans to be alive. His invention used a type of oxygen micro particle that, when injected directly into the bloodstream, allowed a human being to breathe underwater for thirty minutes. A breakthrough technology for the private sector; the injection of oxygen could be lifesaving.

Conrad held a wine glass to toast, "Here's to a delicious meal with a beautiful woman. Now we can begin our date."

She swallowed uncomfortably, but clinked his glass. "A business date," she added with a smile and a nod.

He held his wine glass in the air before bringing the glass to his lips. "Okay, with that said, Kendall, here's your first question. Have you been on any date…in the past eighteen months?"

His straightforwardness and to-the-point attention

increased his attractiveness. She focused on her napkin, then directly into his eyes. "No. I have not been on a date since Tim passed away."

He did not look away; he didn't even look slightly uncomfortable. He delicately stabbed a piece of prime rib and continued eating. The space between them charged with electricity.

He wiped his mouth with the cloth napkin and remarked, "Well then, it's about time." He lowered his voice. "Let's just get the first date out of the way." His stare so intent, was he looking into her soul? He continued, "Kendall, young gorgeous Kendall, who has a whole life ahead of you, you have now been on a date as a widow." He smiled sincerely. "You can thank me later."

He appeared genuine. Most folks would not even utter the word widow.

She found herself engaged and enjoying the conversation. Conrad's other questions were lighter, focusing on her students, her position at Western Maryland, and then the subject turned to diving.

Conrad emptied the delicious pinot noir into both their glasses, and taking a sip, he asked, "Have you been diving in the last eighteen months?"

"I suppose this is one of your ten questions. What are we on, eight now?"

Conrad smiled lighting up his handsome face. "I see you're counting...But technically that was number seven." He returned to the last question. "Well, have you been diving, since..." he paused.

"Yes," She slowly answered. "My stepson and I just got back from Mexico, and we did a little diving."

"I love Mexico, especially the area around Playa

Del Carmen, beautiful white soft beaches, the color of the water is just a perfect aquamarine blue. Where did you go in Mexico?"

She hesitated; she wasn't sure why, but she lied. "We were in Cancun, staying in one of those all-inclusive resorts. You know, we just wanted to get away, try to keep the connection going between the two of us. Ryder, my stepson, is in a reality TV show in Arizona. He has quite the busy schedule, so it was fortunate we got to spend any time together at all."

Conrad smiled and seemed to be enjoying himself. "I promised I would tell you the story of how Tim saved my life...he never told you the story?"

She shook her head. Conrad continued, "I was interested in the sport of free diving, and we were in the Bahamas, training to see if I could compete. Tim was not interested in the free diving competition, although he could beat any one of us who were attempting to break each other's records. It's really more than a sport, it's where you hold your breath and go as deep as you possibly can on one breath and then make it back to the surface safely. However, it is so much more than that...it's about being in a place where nothing else matters. In that moment, underwater, you've taken one breath, your mind is focused on one thing; it's a mental sport as much as a physical, and the beauty and quiet are unimaginable. You can conceive how dolphins and sharks feel in that moment diving down." Conrad was getting lost in the memory. "I suffered hypoxia, the effect of not being able to think coherently, my vision was affected and then the blackout, the loss of consciousness. The next thing I remember was Tim...I didn't even know he was in the water with me, no one really noticed he reacted in a flash. He was so fast he actually gave me breath, which many people say not to do, but I didn't have any water in my lungs, I didn't suffer any damages. Tim saved my life."

Conrad spoke slowly. "He rescued me, and he gave me the drive to figure out how to breathe underwater, because I believe, Kendall, anything is possible, your husband proved that to me when they said it was impossible that I survived."

Staring at the features of Conrad's face, she spoke softly. "Wow, I've never heard that story. Tim was not one to be the public hero, I think he was a silent hero more times than I know." She paused, her thoughts going to his secrecy. "So, do you compete in free diving today?"

"No, I never competed after that day Tim saved my life, I still do some free diving but nothing intense, I'm not trying to break any records."

"Well, now if you just took one of your pills or your injections you invented, you could free dive and break all the records."

"Yes, my invention could change the whole sport of free diving, it would be like the baseball players taking performance-enhancing drugs to cheat the system. Now they will have to test free divers for drugs." They both laughed.

Kendall, without intention, was enjoying the charming company of Conrad Nathaniel. She may have been wrong when she thought they didn't have anything in common despite being the same age. His straightforwardness on Tim's death was refreshing. He did not look at her with pity, and he didn't play the avoidance game most people hid behind in conversation, afraid to mention the death of a spouse for more than two minutes. His story of Tim saving his life made Kendall love Tim even more.

Driving back to the college, where her car had been left in the faculty parking lot. He looked over at her and smiled, "I still have three more questions left."

She relaxed; his questions were easy. "Well, fire away."

He turned the music down. "So, tell me...what were you really doing at Camp David?"

It was as if someone had thrown a bucket of ice-cold water on her face. She was so shocked she couldn't respond immediately. Trying to get her thoughts in order, she blurted out, "Do you work for the government?"

He touched her hand. "I'm asking the questions, Kendall, remember, it's my turn." He flashed his charming look at her as if he were asking about her choice of dessert. "What were you looking for at Camp David?"

Her chest pounded. Random thoughts flashed through her mind. Possible scenarios of Tim and Conrad working together in some kind of secret service...Conrad trying to protect Kendall or Tim...or Conrad knowing about the briefcase. It didn't make sense.

She looked down at her lap and turned her face aside composing her expression, hiding her sudden burst of adrenaline, then looked directly at Conrad. "I was hiking, mushroom picking with Dr. A, you know, Andrew Lunardini, right? Crazy thing, we were accidentally up near the outside perimeter and my dog chased a rabbit, and the next thing we knew we were inside the perimeter of Camp David." She pasted a fake smile on her face. "Didn't get to actually see the complex itself, apparently we were way outside of the actual Camp David, near the private golf course. So, now answer my question—how would *you* know that?"

Conrad pulled into the parking lot behind the football field below the Decker Center. He was staring straight ahead, silent. He turned to face her, his eyes reflecting what appeared to be sincerity. His mouth was set in a serious line.

"I have a proposition for you. I would like to help you find what you're looking for."

Her mind was racing. Was Conrad friends with Andrew? She had told no one about the Camp David incident. Did her beloved Professor tell Conrad about Tim's briefcase? A darkness crept over her, an ominous heat started inside traveling to her face. She needed air. Her first impressions appeared to have been right, because right now she didn't trust him at all. She glanced at the door to figure out how to open it.

"I still have two questions left." His voice sounded serious. Kendall struggled with the door panel, trying to determine how to open the Tesla's falcon wings. She gripped the seat; her heart pounding.

"Kendall, what's in Tim's briefcase? I know it wasn't just his divorce papers, just some saved legal documents."

She found the latch to open the door; Conrad squeezed her shoulder. Her breath quickened.

"There's something I want to show you. Somewhere I need to take you, trust me; Kendall, there's something you need to see." His voice lowered, sounding sincere. "I know about The Collective. I know

Tim was part of The Collective, and so is Steve Crawford. I know what they've been searching for, I understand what they are after, and we mustn't let this get in the hands of the government. The government will keep it to themselves and mankind will never get to benefit."

Sweating, her heart beat accelerating, she had to get out of the car. Nothing made sense. *Trust him? He knows all this and he tried to use his handsome charm all night and now he brings it up?* Something was wrong, alarmingly off center.

His voice grew louder. "Do you understand the importance of this? Do you understand the magnitude of what I am referring to?" She jerked her shoulder away from his hand, stepped out of the car, and stood up, trying to take small measured breaths and hide her need for air to fill her lungs. She needed to get out of here.

"No, I have no idea what you're referring to…and I believe that's ten questions." She tried not to run to her car, but walked slowly; she didn't turn around to see if he would follow. She used the button on her remote control to start the engine and unlock the doors. The noise gave her some sense of normalcy as she opened the door and climbed in. The key clanged against the ignition, her hand shaking uncontrollably as she hit the door lock. In the rearview mirror he stood still beside his car.

Chapter 45

Kendall bolted the doors, yanked the blinds down and turned on multiple lights. Safer in the light. Grateful his master was home, sweet, shaggy, black Harvey ran up to her, jumping up, his paws on her shoulders as if to hug her.

Hugging Harvey with one arm, she grabbed her phone. It shook in her hand as she scrolled through the contacts, desperately trying to figure out who to call.

Was Dr. A involved? Was Steve Crawford working with Tim or was he working with Conrad? The words "The Collective" and "hands of the government" were flashing through her mind, repeating like a radio loop. Conrad's statement etched in her memory. "I know what they are after and we mustn't let this get in the hands of the government. The government will keep it to themselves and mankind will never get to benefit."

She yelled, "What will the government keep to themselves?" She buried her head in her hands. Tears ran down her face; loneliness and fear were thick in the room. Impossible, a lonely, widowed college administrator at a small private liberal arts school— involved in some type of government conspiracy? "Tim, what were you involved in?" She swallowed a massive lump in her throat. "What do I do?" She slumped to the floor.

****

It was at times like these she wished she had a family member to contact, even a best friend. With the loss of her father so many years ago, Tim had become Kendall's go-to guy—go-to person. Her mother, who still lived in Pennsylvania, was in the early stages of dementia. She would light up when Tim visited and she always knew who he was, but now when she called, she would ask how Tim was doing. She tried on several visits to explain Tim died in a diving accident; her mother would look at her with despair and grief in her eyes and repeat, "Why are you lying to me, Kendall? Tim is not dead."

So for the last six months, she would tell her mother what she wanted to hear, Tim was fine, just working or traveling. She hated the mantra of repeating it, saying the words aloud. When the false words came out of her mouth, she wanted them to be the truth. No, she could not call her mother.

That left a short list. She had no one to blame but herself for the world she had created, a world without close friends. Sure, she had lots of colleagues and acquaintances but she no longer had a best friend. Her childhood best friend had been long gone, replaced by Tim, now she had no one.

She hit Ryder's contact name on her phone. She knew he wouldn't answer.

"Ryder, it's Kendall," her voice cracked and she was holding back the tears as she swallowed. "I would really like to talk to you. Please call me when you get this message. It's important. It's really important."

Next she called Scout. As she listened to the strange ringtone signaling she was calling Mexico, she remembered something Conrad had said to her specifically. He asked what was in the briefcase, stating he knew it wasn't divorce papers, or some saved legal documents. Her face was burning up, she clutched her stomach. She used those exact words on a phone call or perhaps when she was talking to Steve. She dropped her iPhone as if she had never seen it before. *Someone is listening to my phone conversations.*

Just then Scout answered, "Hola." She scrambled to pick the phone off the floor.

"Hi Scout," Kendall paused, took a deep breath and exhaled. She knew what she must do.

"Kendall? Is everything okay? How are you?" Scout's voice was full of joy.

"Scout, I wish I could explain it to you…It's difficult; it just doesn't make sense even to me. But…I can't come to visit you, not now, maybe not ever—I just want to figure things out here, things I can't explain to you…I'm so sorry…" A tear was running down her face.

"Kendall, what's wrong? You don't sound okay, you can talk to me, tell me what's going on." Scout's optimistic voice had dramatically changed to a cautious, "dark side" voice sounding like he was on high alert.

She clenched her hands into fists. "I wish I could, Scout, but it's impossible, everything is just impossible. I am sorry. You take care of yourself, Scout…again, I'm sorry but I have to go," and with that she disconnected.

She scanned the beloved interior of her home. Had someone stolen her privacy? Bugged her home, her phone? Why? Nausea rose in her throat. She had no idea how to find a microphone or camera. In the James Bond movies, hidden microphones could be the size of a piece of pepper.

She ran to her laptop, to send Scout a message, her hand froze on the keyboard; e-mails were vulnerable as well. She wanted to throw her phone across the room, but thought of camera's, she hit play on her iPod, put down her phone, picked up Harvey's leash, and went out for a walk. She had some thinking to do.

****

For a brief moment Kendall forgot what had transpired the night before. Then reality set in, and paranoia took over, picturing hidden devices she showered and changed in the bathroom. She acted as if it were any other day. At about ten o'clock in the morning, she left a message for the Professor.

"Andrew, I have some things I need to talk to you about. Could we meet in our old lunch spot at noon today?"

At lunchtime Andrew was waiting for her outside the Lewis Science Center.

"Did you forget your lunch? You can share my turkey and cheese if you like." Andrew's smile usually warmed her heart. He studied her expression. "What's going on? Is everything okay?" He placed his hand on her shoulder.

"Let's walk." Kendall hooked her arm with his. "It's such a beautiful day, let's go sit outside the golf clubhouse and I'll share your sandwich with you."

The Rembert house, from the early 1800s, was the oldest building on campus and located right on the golf course. A few years ago, the Campus Development Office raised funds and with the help of sandblasting brought an historical building back to life in all its splendor. Beside the residence, a picturesque small park full of trees offered a bench.

She sat down, and rubbed her hands on her thighs. In a firm voice without hesitation she asked, "How does Conrad Nathaniel know we were detained at Camp David?" She searched his eyes, trying to determine whether he was someone she could trust. She prayed she could, she needed someone.

His eyes widened and he ran his thumb and index finger around his chin. "I have no idea, Kendall. I haven't told a soul."

"Think about it, Andrew. You didn't tell anyone? Maybe in a phone conversation, you mentioned it to somebody?" She asked gently.

He placed his hand on hers. "Kendall, I haven't spoken a word about Camp David or anything we've been researching or looking at." He paused. "Why? Did he ask you about Camp David?"

"He did, last night at our dinner. Well, actually, he asked me at the end of our evening. He wanted to know the real reason I was at Camp David." She scanned the golf course. No one was in the area; still she lowered her voice. "He wants to show me something, something he said I need to see. He said these exact words: 'I know what they are after, we can't let this get in the hands of the government. The government will keep it to themselves. Mankind will never get to benefit.'"

Andrew unwrapped his sandwich. He set it down and asked, "Do you have any idea what he's talking about?" He took a bite of his sandwich and swallowed. "He said mankind will never get to benefit?"

She studied the Professor's face and body language. Could she tell him she thought her phone or house was bugged. Her heart told her Dr. A was okay but just as she kept the old cenote map hidden, even from him, she held back her thoughts about being bugged.

"I don't know, Andrew, maybe this is bigger than me, maybe I should go to the police or call the FBI. Seriously, I can't believe I am talking about the FBI, that it's even part of my vocabulary. I don't know what to do." She stood up and paced in front of the park bench, twisting her hands.

He patted the bench beside him. "Sit down. Please. Tell me everything Conrad said to you. Let's talk this through before you call any authorities and certainly not the FBI, I don't know why everyone thinks of them first. There is something I didn't tell you yet as well; I figured out something interesting about the cemetery and the photos."

****

Her mind scattered like an unfinished jigsaw puzzle, she rushed back to the office. She had a meeting regarding Commencement weekend with the President of the College, she didn't want to be late. Her lunch hour became hours, while Andrew explained to her what he discovered about the men in the photos. Nothing made sense.

The idea came to her as she was sitting in the meeting. She asked Raj, a student worker for a favor, he was quick to return, handing her the bag from the drugstore. At the end of the day, she grabbed her new purchase and walked toward Harvey Stone Park. The sun's rays spotlighted the green leaves of the majestic oaks illuminating the walkway with life. Students lounged on blankets in the quad, their faces turned toward the warmth of the sun and the friendship of each other.

She unfolded the piece of paper with the name and number of the Palapa Bar down the road from Scout's Dive Shop and entered the international number on her new prepaid cell phone. The owner of the bar, Tony answered. She had met him briefly with Scout and hoped he would remember her. He did. He was another New Jersey retiree in paradise, living the expat life. She gave specific instructions for Scout to call this new number and not from his phone or dive shop. He said he understood without any questions.

Next call, Ryder's publicist, Courtney Clay. She always liked Courtney, who helped arrange for Ryder's time off for Puerto Morelos and after the fiasco on the trip, Courtney was still a fan of Kendall's. In Courtney's view, all publicity is good publicity.

"Hi Courtney, It's Kendall, I can't seem to reach Ryder. I can't explain it to you right now, but I don't want Ryder to use his phone to call me back. Could you let him use your cell phone and have him call me at this number? It's important."

"Kendall, what's going on? Is there something I should be informed about?"

In her most sincere flight attendant voice she whispered. "Courtney, that's why I'm calling instead of Tricia. I promise as soon as I can explain, I will. If you can do this for me, trust me, if there's any way to get good publicity for Ryder—and I think there will be—you will be the first to know."

"Consider it done, Ryder will call you back tonight."

Another call was coming in. By the strange numbers, it had to be Mexico. She hoped it was Scout.

"Kendall, is that you? It's Scout."

"Oh Scout, thank you for calling me back."

"Is everything okay?"

Her shoulders relaxed and her face grew warm. "Are you at the Palapa bar?"

"Yes, Tony was nice enough to let me use his phone, but what's going on?"

She took a deep breath. "I wish I could tell you...explain, but I can't right now. But the most important thing, I *am* coming down there, I just had to tell you something different last night. I think either my house or my cell phone is bugged...I wish I could explain everything to you right now but something I said in a conversation was repeated back to me from a total stranger who seems to know a whole lot about Tim's background and secret past."

Slow down. Breathe. "I'm thinking since my house was broken into, maybe they planted a bug, and since your dive shop was broken into, maybe they planted a microphone there or else they tapped our phones...Do they even tap phones anymore? I have no idea how any of that stuff works." She paused. "It's not my imagination. Tim was involved with something secretive with the government. I know this sounds crazy."

"Really..." Scout was speechless.

"Do you believe me, Scout?"

"I believe you. Do you think it has something to do with the cenote? Kendall, people from out of town were down here in Puerto Morelos, looking into the area of the cenote you, Ryder, and I went to. Apparently, they were asking questions," he whispered.

"Someone knew where we went. Who knows,

maybe they think there's a hidden treasure or something? The map I have from Tim, it's old…maybe it's valuable, worth some money. But don't worry, the map is safe," he continued, "and I'll make sure it stays safe. What can I do? I want to help you. Do you want me to come up there?"

His concerned voice tugged at her emotions, she held back the tears.

"I really am here for you, if there is something I can help you with, let me do it."

"Thanks Scout. Just talking to you, makes me feel better. I don't know who I can trust anymore, but I trust you. There's so much I want to share with you but it's smarter to speak in person." She added in a whisper, swallowing the lump in her throat, "Without anybody knowing, I need to find the cenote from Tim's map."

Before they hung up, they created a plan of action. She was not giving up. She would risk everything to find the truth. She needed to know what was going on, not just for Tim but for herself.

****

She raced over to the Lewis Hall of Science, and up to the conference room. Andrew was sitting there with his notebook in front of him.

"Busy day?" he asked.

She clutched a folder with the printouts of the pictures of the presidents. She laid them out on the table in chronological order.

"I want you to look at something I found." She pulled the magnifying glass out of her purse. "Look at his collarbone; what do you see?"

He leaned closer to the table with the magnifying glass. "It looks like a mark? Is it on the camera? Or is it a mark on his shoulder like a birthmark?"

"Look at the shoulder of every man without a shirt on in these photos." Andrew went from picture to picture with the magnifying glass examining each one.

"Well, it can't be the same person so what do you think? Some kind of tribe or family that has the same tattoo on their collarbone?"

"I don't know," Kendall remarked. "I just can't make sense of it." She didn't say what she really wanted to disclose.

She gathered up the photos and placed her hands on top of them, looking at the thousands of books that lined the wall. "You said you had something to tell me, something you discovered?" Andrew studied her face and pulled out his notepad and a map.

"Yes, the coordinates we found led to the cemetery, I went back there the other night, and it is the Nathaniel cemetery…It's pinpointed to a private mausoleum. It's possible there could be a tunnel underground from the mausoleum to, I don't know, maybe somewhere near Camp David?"

"Hmm…why, why do you need a tunnel from the Nathaniel cemetery to Camp David?" She chewed on the end of the pen, wrinkled her brow, she needed to ask, "Have you ever heard of The Collective?"

"The Collective? What is that?" The Professor looked up from the map, his full attention on Kendall.

"I don't know—it's something Conrad said the other night after dinner. He said Tim was part of The Collective and so was Steve Crawford. Maybe it's the name of a government organization they both belong to. The ID I found…" she was writing the words The Collective at the top of a piece of paper with the names

Tim and Steve Crawford underneath it, and an arrow going over to Conrad Nathaniel's name.

The Professor leaned back in his chair. "He said Steve Crawford?" She nodded. "When was the last time you spoke with Steve Crawford?"

"I've been keeping my distance," she said, rolling her eyes.

"Why, what happened?"

"Nothing really, I don't know it's a feeling I have…he's left me several messages and I've never returned them." She stood. "Maybe it's time I paid a visit to Steve."

Chapter 46

Kendall pulled her black Saab into the parking lot of Jackson's Easy. Steve's Porsche was parked in the back. She entered the code at the door and walked inside. Busy for a weeknight, executives and locals engaged in quiet conversations, filling the stools curved around the bar. Steve in the middle of a conversation, paused. "Be right back," and walked from behind the bar next to her.

"So this is how you return my messages—show up in person?" Steve smiled, leaning in to hug her; she stepped back.

"What time will you get out of here tonight? We need to talk." Kendall folded her arms.

Steve's big smile collapsed. "Well, I was going to go grab some dinner, would you like to join me?"

Kendall stood tall and replied, "Okay, I'll go with you. Across the street?"

About to say something more Steve closed his mouth. He walked around the bar and told Skip he would be back in an hour, then motioned for her to go out the back way.

They crossed the street in silence. Steve's hand grazed her shoulder. "Hey, what's going on with you? Is it about the other night?"

She kept walking several steps ahead. Steve caught up to her, gently pulling her back. "Kendall, I think we both were over-served the other night. Are you angry with me? What's going on?"

She snapped, her eyes blazing. "What's going on? *What's going on?"* Her voice cracked and went up an octave as she repeated the question. "That's exactly what I would like to know—what *is* going on?" A flood of emotions stuck in her throat, almost strangling her.

She huffed past the café and headed toward The Park, a memorial honoring Civil War dead. Steve kept her pace, silent. She didn't stop until she reached an empty clearing, then walked over and stood by a colossal oak. Her shoulders tense, her body posture rigid. She looked at Steve, took a deep breath and squeaked out, "I know about The Collective. I know you and Tim were part of The Collective. I hate you for keeping this from me, and anything you tell me right now I don't know if I'll believe. I don't trust you and I'm not sure if I can ever trust you again. So, do not lie to me. I'm sick of all the secrets. Sick of all the lies."

Steve's eyes darted to the tree line. He grabbed his chin, then ran his fingers through his hair. Silence except for the beat of their breath. He crossed his arms. "Kendall, I never meant to lie to you. It's not something I'm at liberty to discuss with you or anyone. The fact you are even asking me about this organization, scares the hell out of me." He grabbed her shoulders and looked into her eyes. "Where did you hear this?"

A tear slid down her face dripping off her chin. "It's true, isn't it! All these lies, secrets…Did you break into my house?"

Steve's face was still, expressionless. Silence.

Her chest pounded, she wanted him to deny everything, provide her with a rational explanation. "I need to know, Steve. I need to understand what is going on." Their eyes met, in his she recognized concern, a glimpse, a flash of Tim's best friend, the old Steve, the college roommates that would give their life for each other.

"Come with me, Kendall." He walked toward the street. "Let's take a ride." He stopped at her car, opened the door, took his cell phone out of his pocket and threw it on the seat. He didn't speak, simply motioned to her to do the same. She placed her iPhone on the seat. Steve closed her car door and walked toward his, saying, "You might want to lock your car."

****

The Gettysburg National Memorial Park driving tour was approximately two and a half hours long and open until ten p.m. in spring and summer. Driving toward the park, Kendall and Steve traveled in stony silence for the first twenty minutes until they reached the entrance. Steve's face took on a serious, hardened look. "What I am about to tell you can never be discussed with anyone and you can never mention my name or that we had this conversation." The words spewed out of his mouth. He confirmed he and Tim were part of a government organization nicknamed "The Collective." A classified organization that used ex-military, typically black ops soldiers. They were civilians to the outside world, but crucial to the military, possessing skills the government needed for confidential research projects. Steve emphasized the term research. Researching ways to better our country, ways to save dying resources, to discover hidden assets other countries had. All for the betterment of our nation, betterment of mankind. He stopped the car after speaking for thirty minutes straight. The moon disappeared behind the clouds, the night sky pitch black. No other cars were on the road. The perimeter of swaying trees closed in on her like soldiers, she wanted to run. Run from everything she was hearing.

"Did Tim tell you any of this?" Steve asked. "I need you to tell me the truth."

Her heart thumped inside her chest, finally she swallowed wondering if she could speak. "No, Tim did not tell me any of this." She grimaced, as if someone punched her in the stomach, swallowing the nausea. "I understand why it's classified, I know Tim loved his country, but to hide it from me for all these years, it makes me feel like I didn't even know him."

Steve's grim expression softened as he faced Kendall. He hesitated before speaking. "You knew him, Kendall. You knew him better than anybody did. The way he was with you...He loved you more than anything. It was like he absorbed you and you absorbed him. Being part of The Collective was not who Tim was, it was just something he did." Kendall listened to the sound of crickets from the field, focusing on controlling her breath. *I can't believe I never suspected anything*. Steve continued, "And he was incredible at his job, classified Intel, logistics, knowing the organization inside and out. Almost like a spectator watching over it...he got that from his Uncle Dan. He also worked on the DNA Project."

Stunned, she forced the words out. "His Uncle Dan was part of the organization as well?"

Steve shrugged and let out a breath of air. "Yes, good ol' Uncle Dan, was involved his entire life although we didn't know it either, until the end."

He grasped Kendall's hand in a fierce squeeze. "I'm concerned for you, Kendall. I'm worried about your safety. I believe before Tim died, he discovered something important. Some piece of the puzzle he didn't share with the organization. I think it involved a project we were working on, The DNA Project. Tim stumbled onto critical information, and even if I'm wrong, 'they' think he did, and others who want this information will stop at nothing to get it." He continued. "Was there anything in the briefcase that might be of importance to someone else, maybe something that doesn't make sense to you, anything?"

She turned to the window. The crickets tone now at a higher pitch. Even in the dim light the wide-open green fields became clearer. Right here, over 150 years ago, men fought each other, head on, charging one on one in civil war, battling for what they each believed in.

I don't know what I believe or who to trust. Nothing makes sense. She clasped and unclasped her fingers and squeezed her knuckles. "No, like I said before, it was just his old divorce papers, a few things, legal papers." The lie floated in the air like a neon sign.

Steve forcibly squeezed her hands. "Kendall, this is really serious. Please tell me if you find anything. Anything at all. The Collective is a classified organization for a reason. They've been around for over two hundred years…two hundred years without a word in the press, or a reference in a book. You can't speak about this with anyone; I mean erase it from your mind forever, do you understand?"

Steve Crawford, always so cool and level, looked anxious and agitated. His hair a mess; his age unfolded on his face as if she were looking at him through a magnifying mirror.

"I understand, Steve, but I need to know one thing, what is the objective?" She pulled her hands free, grabbed his shoulders. "I mean what is it they are looking for?"

He removed Kendall's hands from his shoulders and clasped them tightly, his eyes closed. The cicadas joined the crickets at a new octave, several minutes passed. Finally he said, "They're looking for what man has always been searching for. I'm sure there are many groups since the beginning of time all with the same purpose, the same quest. Searching, seeking, chasing…" Steve paused.

Kendall interrupted, "Searching for what?"

"A miracle, searching for the Holy Grail of nature, searching for that magical bacterium, that unimaginable plant that cures cancer and makes you live longer than humanly possible, an ultimate wonder drug."

She was shaking her head involuntarily. "Seriously? They actually think this cure exists?"

He let go of her hands and tightly gripped the steering wheel. "Well, maybe it's not actually a miracle, but yes, there is something out there that expands the life expectancy of humans and cures illnesses."

"They have proof of this?" she demanded. "They know something like this is real?"

He was looking in the rearview mirror and out the window as a sudden paranoia seemed to overtake him. "Kendall, I can't tell you anything else, this all classified information and I could be putting both our lives in jeopardy. Tim would never forgive me. He knew he could not share anything with you, as much as he never wanted to keep anything from you, but he did it to keep you safe, and here I am talking about details Tim would never tell you. The thing he most wanted to share but would not, and I can't say any more. I owe him that."

"But it's too late, Steve, I'm involved, I have questions, things I need to know."

His voice took on a gritty edge. "No, Kendall, there is nothing you need to know, you are not involved. Tim obviously understood this and now you know more than you should know. We're done discussing this. Promise me, we never had this conversation.

"Promise me, Kendall, for Tim."

"I promise."

He started driving again, following the Gettysburg trail of monuments, his mouth set in a straight line.

"I just have one last question to ask you." She had to know as a tear slid down her cheek. "Did his diving accident have anything to do with this…The Collective?"

He slowed the car down, and put his hand on her arm. "No, Kendall, absolutely not. He was diving the Blue Hole with non-classified guys. He wanted to take Ryder, remember? It had nothing to do with an assignment. It was just a terrible, terrible freak accident."

Chapter 47

Kendall ended the call. As far as she could see, the manicured green velvet golf course of WMC painted a picture of contentment and relaxation. Deep purple pansies and red and orange petunias vibrant next to the fresh cut grass. The opposite of all Kendall was. *Ryder may be more like Tim than I ever gave him credit for.* Today for an instant he was just like his father. Ryder listened, not saying much during the twenty-minute call where she did all of the talking. He asked a few sensible questions, straightforward and necessary, but allowed her to speak. He handled the news well. He didn't argue, he didn't sound uninterested and he didn't make quick responses or accusations about Kendall losing her mind or being paranoid.

He listened to the plan she devised, but at the end of the conversation, he made no solid commitment to join her on the journey to Puerto Morelos. He promised not to discuss it with anyone, and agreed if he was going to come he would follow her lead.

Before the call ended, he asked her, "What about Steve, do you think you could confide in him and maybe he could help?" She had not told Ryder about The Collective, yet. But his parting words interrupted her thoughts. "He was Dad's best friend and I know Dad trusted him."

Trust. She exhaled a loud sigh as she looked up to

the heavens, *am I doing the right thing, Tim?*

Walking across the quad, random thoughts bounced back and forth as she questioned her plan. A group of men in tightly-buttoned-at-the-neck shirts and suits emerged from the administrative building. Her pulse quickened and she forced her lips to curve up as Conrad Nathaniel emerged from the pack. His eyes lit up as his mouth widened into a grin. No need for a second opinion; he was a strikingly handsome man.

"Kendall, I was hoping I would run into you." He turned toward the group. "I'll catch up with you." He leaned over to kiss her on the cheek.

She stood still, her hands gripping her portfolio, studying Conrad's face. She rehearsed this moment in her mind. "I'm sorry about the other night, I didn't know what to say or what to think." She paused. "I'd like to talk. If the offer still stands, I'd like you to show me what you mentioned the other night, what I need to see."

He tilted his head to the side, analyzing her sudden change. "What time are you finished at work today?"

****

She didn't call anyone, didn't even text Dr. A. *Who can I trust?* She slid into the soft leather seats of the Tesla without anybody's knowledge or any witness seeing her go.

Dusk was falling but the air was still warm. The fireflies were out; lightning-bugs as she called them growing up in Pennsylvania, sparkling in the woods as they sped by. Conrad had classical music playing, and the melody by Chopin added to the mystery of where he was taking her.

He broke the silence. "You changed your mind.

Something happened." It was a statement, not a question.

She carefully chose her words. "I want to know what you know," she said. "I want to know the secrets my husband has been hiding from me."

Total blackness hugged the curvy country roads, streetlights and passing cars nonexistent. Conrad made a left turn and pulled up to a private gate. Nathaniel Cemetery was etched in iron across the masculine heavy barrier. He pulled out a card and held it up in front of the camera and the large mass of iron gate electronically activated, slowly opened.

Darkness cloaked the setting creating an eerie world; cemeteries conjured unsettling thoughts. Only the lights of the Tesla illuminated the hard-packed dirt road in front of them. Conrad opened the window and turned the music off; night sounds consumed the air. The locusts making their modern music were joined by chirping crickets and a few soft birdcalls. The tires of the Tesla the only noise coming from the electric vehicle. Kendall shivered, a silent creeping car added to the strangeness of the evening. Conrad parked in front of a large mausoleum. The falcon wings opened up to the night sky and she stepped out. The scene surreal: a futuristic car next to the centuries-old stone of the mausoleum.

Conrad approached her side of the car, closed the doors and offered his hand. "Ready?"

Butterflies who acted more like aggressive bees flew around in the pit of her stomach. "I'm going to leave here alive?" Her mouth curved into a shaky smile, she could feel the corner of her left lip quivering. "Right?"

Conrad's warm fingers circled around her hand. "Alive and enlightened."

Using the same key card against the age-old lock, the old mausoleum door clicked a modern sound. The lock and the handle never moved. It opened from the side hinge, resembling the door in the basement of the Lewis Science Center—an ancient façade hiding modern technology.

Inside the mausoleum three large drawers covered the wall, a gold name plaque on each one. Conrad walked over to the middle one and pushed the center. Another loud clicking sound, and behind the plaque a button appeared. He pushed it and walked over to the marble wall. When he pushed on the right side, the wall opened up.

"Seriously? What is this place?"

He motioned with his eyes to follow and led the way down the small tunnel ending at an enormous steel door. He flipped up a square plate on the wall, and looked directly into it. A retina scanner; in two seconds, the door opened.

"This place has been in my family for centuries. A place of respite for some, a place of enlightenment for others."

The downward steps led to a short tunnel. Through two more doors and a set of steps, the air temperature dropped. She rubbed her arms facing a corridor hallway with a dozen doors. The tunnel undeniably similar to the passageway she and the Professor had explored under the Lewis Hall of Science.

"Where are you taking me?" She watched Conrad use the key and open the middle door.

"Let me show you."

He led the way into a laboratory, hitting slider switches to cast lights in various areas and workstations. It was full of new technology, computers and high-tech microscopic equipment. The absence of dust unsettled her. Her eyes started in one corner of the room and moved in a circle, turning until her gaze stopped on a large photo on the wall. It was a bulletin board one would see on a police procedural TV show, with the detectives trying to figure out the suspect and all parties involved. One photo in particular caught her eyes, and then as her eyes traveled toward the bottom of the pyramid, her stomach tightened, a picture of Tim and below it a picture of Steve Crawford. She walked over to the wall, drawn to a picture she had seen before, a picture of President Obama, Hillary Clinton, and the man from the jungle.

Conrad moved behind her. He cleared his throat. "So, what do you know about The Collective?"

She continued looking at Tim's face, at his beautiful eyes, she put her fingers up to his face on the picture, and her voice was soft. "Is that why you have his picture on this board? Because he and Steve were part of something you call The Collective?"

Conrad inched closer, his body heat leaving little space between them. "What did Tim tell you about The Collective?"

"He told me nothing." She turned blinking back the tears. "Absolutely nothing."

Their bodies close; she could smell a hint of cologne mixed with an unfamiliar masculine scent. He touched her cheek to wipe the tear away. He leaned down, his hot breath on her ear. "I want to help you, no more secrets. You and I, Kendall, let's make a deal—no more secrets."

He stayed in her space, as if they were almost embracing. She held her breath. She wanted nothing more than to see sincerity in his eyes, to find the truth. He embraced her and she gently pulled away.

"Okay." Her shoulders back, her head lifted a little higher. "No more secrets? Tell me what you know about The Collective...Tell me how my husband was involved and why you're so interested? Explain to me why he would keep this from me."

Conrad silent a few seconds longer nodded. He moved away and flipped the bulletin board and pointed. "Your husband and Steve work for a centuries-old classified government organization. This organization's mission is to collect things, to research and experiment on things that may affect the American people, well, basically all of mankind..." He pointed to a world map on the bulletin board. It resembled electronic string art, lines in every direction around Central America and Mexico; and pin points marking coastlines and ports.

"My family has been following The Collective for over 150 years. My great-great-grandfather crossed paths with members of The Collective in 1865." He walked over to a flat surface and swiped it. It was the latest technology; the screen appeared on a regular tabletop. A picture filled the screen. A black-and-white photo of a shirtless man, a man who looked familiar to Kendall, standing in the jungle with two men, both in hats, white shirts, and light pants. "This is my great-grandfather, the original Conrad Nathaniel." He pointed to a handsome man not much older than himself with a serious look on his face. The resemblance to the man standing beside her, was evident, same cheekbones and eyes.

She had not seen this particular photograph. It was not part of the files in the briefcase. Her heart thumping, she asked, "Who are the other men?"

He pointed to the other Caucasian in the photo. "This is one of the first Navy SEALs, Jonathan Stadium. And this," Conrad pointed to the shirtless man, "this is a man we had in this lab two years ago."

Her eyebrows scrunched together. "What do you mean you had him in this lab, his body? Is he buried here?"

He leaned back against the table. "No, unfortunately he is not buried here. Although my grandfather would have liked that. He was very much alive when he was here. From all accounts and records from my great-great-grandfather, my great-grandfather, and my grandfather, he was approximately 175 years old."

He was watching her intently, waiting for her reaction. "One hundred seventy-five years old?" She took in a sharp breath.

He stepped away and started pulling up documents on the computer. Dates flashed on the screen, from the 1860s up to the 1960s, blood tests and medical reports.

"Yes, it's hard to believe isn't it? My grandfather was twenty-five years old when he met this man. His name is Tobias. He was conducting a study at the time, sort of in conjunction with the government. Researching native tribes in different cultures, comparing overall health and longevity, investigating which cultures were more susceptible to diseases. What he discovered, in one expedition near Central America, were the remains of a community of men and women whose ages were between 160 and 190 years old. It became my grandfather's quest to determine why this group of people could live so long. Tobias had a discernible mark, on his collarbone near his right arm. A birthmark almost resembling a circle, with four short straight marks underneath it and dots around the outside." He produced another black-and-white photo on the screen, an enlarged picture of the birthmark.

She had seen this mark before. She stared wide-eyed at the image, her breath quickened. "So what happened to Tobias?"

He tilted his head. "Don't you know?"

She shrugged. "Why would I know?"

"I brought you down here, Kendall." His voice tightened. "I am sharing my most sacred place with you, and you can return the favor by confiding in me."

"I have no idea what you're talking about. I know nothing about a man named Tobias."

His face darkened, the silence stretched out. "I thought we agreed no more secrets."

"I have never heard of Tobias or had knowledge of anyone living until they were 175 years old. I don't know what you think I know, but not this." She gestured with her hands, a trait she had tried hard to get rid of as an instructor, it reappeared when she was nervous.

He brought Tim's photograph up on the screen; a picture of him standing on the sand with a black wet suit pulled down halfway. Taken from a distance, Tim was not aware of the photo being snapped. He pointed to Tim. "He knew all about it. In fact, of all the research projects The Collective was involved in, Tim was the lead on Tobias. Oh yes, Tim knew more about Tobias than my grandfather did."

"Well, he never discussed it with me; he never even told me he belonged to a government organization."

"But you know now, don't you, Kendall. He may not have told you anything when he was alive, but he left you something. You know all about Tim being involved in The Collective. What did he leave you, what else is in the briefcase?"

She froze, her heart thumping against her skin, her breath quickened. "How do you know about the briefcase? From Steve Crawford?"

He moved closer to her. She flinched. "It doesn't really matter how we know, what matters is working together." His eyes grew large and he squared his shoulder. "We will pay you more money than you ever dreamed of, if you will help us. Help us find this cure, this bacterium. It could save millions of lives, it could cure cancer, it could change our age expectancy to double what it is now."

He paused. "The government," he paused again and went on, "if they find it, they will never let the American people have it. They are so worried about Social Security, economic distress, another recession, hierarchy of classes, the one percent getting hold of it…oh, they have a thousand reasons, but one thing I know—they will never let it be used to its full potential. We can change all that. We can save lives."

He put his hand over hers. "I believe your husband found the answer and I think The Collective terminated him because of it."

She moved and turned her face away steadying her breathing. "I need to sit down."

The laboratory was quiet except for her shallow breathing. Her face flushed, her hands sweaty and shaking.

Chapter 48

Scout met Lily at the Palapa bar, a wooden structure built on a pier overlooking the turquoise sea. Shiny silver fish swam underneath the deck, accompanied by a school of spotted eagle rays. One of nature's greatest canvas became the backdrop for Scout's new office. Lily with her lap top, set up shop facing a gorgeous view. If Kendall was right and his office was bugged, he would take no chances.

He extracted a notebook and opened to a checklist. "Were you able to secure the Lamanai tourist excursion?"

Lily was stirring a piña colada with her long colorful fingernails. They were blue today with gold sparkly flames at the tip. "*Si*, for two, the excursion to see a ruin in Belize and howler monkeys, lots and lots of howler monkeys. You land in a sugarcane field." Lily smiled. "It sounds *romantico*."

Scout did not look up from his notebook. "I just need it booked for one, just Kendall. And the boats—everything is secure with Jorge?"

"Yes," Lily answered. *Thank goodness for Lily.* She arranged a forty-foot Boston Whaler for the excursion. Jorge, the captain, was a childhood friend of hers and she assured Scout, she trusted this family friend who knew the sea and reefs backwards.

Scout, busy keeping up with his dive jobs and

making the arrangements for the trip, was anxious for Kendall to arrive. Lately, he found himself analytical and looking over his shoulder, a change from the free spirit attitude he usually portrayed. He had always been aware of his surroundings, of strangers around him, but in the past several days, he inspected everything and everyone with a cautious eye.

With the help of Tony at the Palapa Bar, he gathered and stored provisions for the big trip, strategically away from the dive shop. He was taking no chances.

If he could only talk to Kendall, perhaps his anxiety would be a little less. He decided to write her a letter instead. Not an e-mail or a text message but an old-fashioned snail mail letter.

Dear Kendall,

I'm writing this letter to let you know how sorry I am. It was wrong of me not to take you to the place your husband wanted you and Ryder to see. It was wrong of me to keep this from you. I have no idea what all this is about, but what I do know, is things happen so people can cross each other's paths. I wouldn't trade the days of our last trip spent with you for anything. I will make it up to you this trip; we will find the place your husband wanted his son to see. That I promise. I know how important it is to you. And I have to let you know you are very important to me. I think of our short time together constantly. It replays in my mind and in my dreams. I don't know if you feel the same way, but I don't want to live a life full of regret. I don't want to hide the way my heart feels. I've done that too much in the past, so I wanted to let you know how special you are. Kendall, you light up the jungle when you're

around. You elevate my heart and I am a better man to have met you. I hope we get to know each other.
Scout

He folded the letter in thirds and drew in a long breath. He couldn't send it yet, but he sealed it in an envelope and asked Lily to keep it somewhere safe. He would give it to Kendall after the trip.

Chapter 49

Steve was waiting outside Kendall's house when she pulled into the driveway. She hesitated and then opened her car door.

Steve's large strides brought him to the driver's side before she could step out. In a demanding voice he asked, "Were you just with Conrad Nathaniel?"

She forced a smile as she stood. "Nice to see you too…Steve, what are you doing here?"

He grabbed her shoulders. "Kendall, you cannot trust the Nathaniel family. What did you tell him?"

She stepped back, away from him. "Steve, Conrad Nathaniel is the keynote speaker at our Commencement ceremony and what we discuss has no relevance to you." She proceeded toward the door, car keys out and pointed at the lock. Harvey was jumping at the door.

His hand squeezed her arm. "I need to speak with you but we cannot talk in there."

"Why? Why can't we speak in there, Steve?" His face was easy to read. Nausea settled in her stomach. "So the government bugged my house? For how long, Steve? And my phone? My office? How long did you know this?" She grinded her teeth and opened the door. Harvey jumped, his outstretched paws reached her shoulder trying to hug her. "Hi Harvey, I know you've been here all day, let's take a walk." She stepped inside the house and grabbed his leash, ignoring Steve.

She headed toward the path through the woods, with Steve a few steps behind.

"We aren't the only ones listening to you," he said. "We have a trace on your phone. Someone else has a bug in your house. I tried to find it, but couldn't, it must be hidden well."

She kept walking. Trying to control her emotions. "How do you know somebody has a bug in my house?"

He was silent, while Harvey was taking care of business behind a nearby bush. "It's Conrad Nathaniel's people. They're very dangerous, watching every move you make. They believe you know something that Tim discovered before his death. At the college, I saw you get out of his car, please tell me you didn't discuss anything with him."

"I don't have anything to tell him, Steve, I don't know what you all are talking about, and you're certainly the last person I would trust to inform me whether somebody is dangerous."

"I know Conrad Nathaniel is bad." Steve paused, then added, "I know because he offered me money to find out what Tim was working on. He offered me money, a lot of money, to go against the government, to be a traitor, follow Tim and spy on him." Steve inhaled, shifting his weight from one foot to the other. "I said yes in the beginning, it was just one job and then I would be settled for the rest of my life. I could leave the East Coast and move to a warm green island. Live a simple life…" He crossed his arms over his chest. "But then I couldn't do it, I couldn't betray Tim. It was right before the trip to the Blue Hole, if I had taken the job I would have followed Tim, maybe I could have prevented something. I can't stop thinking about it.

Nathaniel is not to be trusted."

She tensed her shoulders, her voice rising as she spoke. "Prevented something? What do you mean *prevented something*, are you saying the government killed Tim? You told me it was an accident."

His eyes widened and his eyebrows arched downward. His voice softened. "No, Kendall, not the government, Conrad Nathaniel's people…I thought maybe they figured out what he had discovered and they killed him so he wouldn't tell the government."

Harvey sat down in front of Kendall's feet, making a barrier, aware of tension in the air. Steve continued, "But if they are still asking you questions and bugging your house, then maybe they haven't figured it out."

Color drained from her face. She stumbled over to sit on a tree stump. "What is it they are trying to figure out? I don't understand."

"It's like I told you, Kendall, they're looking for a bacterium, a plant, something that makes humans live longer, be free of sicknesses, it's partial immortality…but for Conrad Nathaniel's people, it's all about money. It's about greed. Can you imagine with an ingredient like that, what drugs they could put on the market and sell to the highest bidder? It won't be about saving the world, or helping those in need. No, if they find it, it will change the world forever and not in a good way. It will create a species of wealthy humans who will control the world, basically because they will be here the longest—and only because they can afford it."

He continued, his breath quickened, "The people of Mexico know something like this exists somewhere, they know the USA is searching for a mineral in their land and in Central America. The cartels, drug wars," Steve laughed an ominous laugh. "Everybody thinks it's all about the drugs crossing the border, cocaine, heroin or meth. We make movies about it, we splatter cartel warnings all over the front page of the newspaper, we have 24/7 news reports. That's just on the surface, that's what the government wants everyone to believe. What it's really about, is a battle to see who can find this resource first. The Mexican government wants the United States to stay out of their country, and stop investigating their land. They might not know exactly what it is, but they know the United States wants it. They want to find it first, figure out what we want so bad. Can you see it now? It would make Mexico the number one country in the world." Steve shook his head. "The Nathaniels? The Nathaniel family is the one that told the cartels. Anyone who thinks working with the cartels would lead to a favorable result for the world is not on the right planet. You have to be in agreement with that?"

She tugged Harvey between her knees and rested her head on his. Squatting on the ground, she took deep breaths to control her emotions. The silence stretched out for several minutes.

She stood up, and clenched her fists. "I wish I never heard of The Collective, I wish Tim just left the Navy SEALs and stayed a bar owner. But whatever Tim discovered, he didn't tell me, Steve. You need to fix this. As Tim's best friend, you need to tell them I know nothing, everyone needs to leave me alone. I just want to go on, live my life, try to move on the best I can without the love of my life." She marched back through the woods toward her house. "I need to get away from all of this."

He caught up. "Then let me see what's in the briefcase, Kendall. Show me everything and I will make this right."

She kept walking. Steve followed a few paces behind. When she entered the line of trees separating the woods from her yard, she stopped.

"I give you the briefcase and this is over for me?"

Steve nodded. "Yes, Kendall, give it all to me, then they will leave you alone. You can tell Nathaniel that you gave a briefcase of Tim's to me, and we can take you out of the picture. It will be between the government and them."

Silence. Breathing hard, her eyes squinted shut. "Okay, I will give you the briefcase," she said at last, "on one condition, get me out of this. I don't want to be involved in any way."

He let out a sigh. "Done."

"I don't have it at the house, but, I will get it. Meet me here Friday night after Commencement, and I will give it to you then."

"You're making the right choice Kendall."

"I hope so. I don't know what the right choice is. But, I just want to be done with this. See you Friday."

Catching her breath, she leaned against the closed door. Her suspicions confirmed; her phone and house…definitely bugged. She checked each window and door making sure they were locked, Harvey followed close on her heels.

The ring tone of her phone broke the silence. Dr. A. "Hi, what are you doing at this late hour?" She grimaced, she shouldn't be asking him questions on the phone. "Hey, would you mind if we talked in the morning? It's been a long day for me and I just need to go take a hot shower and go to bed." She cringed again, knowing someone was listening. *Did they have video? Again, she wanted to throw up.*

"Sure, Kendall, no problem. There is something I would like to talk to you about, could we meet for coffee before you go in to work?"

"She responded slowly, "how about our park bench at seven a.m.?"

"Sounds great," the Professor said. "I'll bring the coffee. And Kendall? Get some sleep. Good night."

Chapter 50

He's the only one I can trust. Kendall rushed across the quad to meet Andrew. He was sitting on the bench with two Starbucks coffees. He stood up and gave her a hug. She held onto his shoulders a little bit longer than usual.

"Everything okay, Kendall?" He patted the seat beside him holding out the coffee.

"I don't know how to answer that question," she gave a half smile, "but I guess I could tell you, because you're the only person I trust. I think I need to get away from all of this."

He rubbed his temple with his left hand and he drew in a long breath. He exhaled and turned slowly facing her, his shoulders slumped. "Yes, I agree, maybe you do need to get away from all of this. Go. Go somewhere far away, forget about it, put it behind you."

His voice. Something was off. She met his eyes. "What's wrong? Something's changed, I can hear it in your voice. What is it?"

He looked away, extended his hand, then looked down at the ground. "Kendall, this is bigger than us. I think you need to step back, step away from all of this."

She lowered her voice. "What happened, Andrew? Did something happen?"

Dr. Andrew Lunardini was silent, almost as if he wasn't listening. She knew intuitively something happened to drain the excitement and adrenaline from him.

"I made a mistake, I'm so sorry, Kendall, I'm so sorry." He squeezed her hand; his eyes glistening.

Her breath quickened. "What are you sorry for?"

"I'm sorry for my greed, my selfishness," He gripped her hand tighter. "It wasn't about the money, yes, money makes things easier, it was about the opportunity…probably my last hope before I leave this earth. My last chance to be a part of something monumental, a change in the world."

"I don't understand, what did you do?" she asked, whispering, terrified to hear his response.

"I told Conrad Nathaniel about the briefcase, I told him about Tim's video, the blueprint tunnel map, the photographs and the list of longitudes and latitudes. I told him we found the tunnel that led to Camp David. He knows everything I know, we know. Now, he wants the briefcase, the documents, the zip drive."

She ripped her hand free from his and covered her face, doubling over, as if someone punched her in the gut. She forced the words out of her mouth. "You…were…the only one…I could trust, you were the only one…"

He leaned over, speaking in her ear. "Listen to me Kendall. They already knew about most of it. They had your house bugged, your office, they wanted me to plant a device, a device I have now in my front pocket. They wanted me to plant it on the back of your iPhone under the battery—this morning. I can't do it, I'm not a spy, I'm a retired history professor."

He gently touched her shoulder. "Maybe you should give it to them, Kendall, just get rid of all of it.

They say Tim located an area where there is a bacterium that helps people live longer and healthier lives. It must be somewhere in that list of longitude and latitude coordinates. They're asking about a map. I told them the blueprint of the tunnel was the only map in the briefcase. They already knew Tim discovered the tunnel, and something about Tim and a man named Tobias? They told me the government knows all about it, too. Knows a resource exists to save lives. But, the government will never share it with the rest of the world. Big business, Wall Street, pharmaceuticals, hospitals, doctors, insurance companies, they'll never let them…it would destroy the economic system of our society. Social Security wouldn't exist, it couldn't afford to keep paying if people lived longer. The government is afraid it would destroy our society." He hesitated, then said, "Conrad Nathaniel's company would share it with the world. Develop a drug that would cure cancer, stop life-threatening illness. It would be like the Fountain of Youth in a pill. The world would change. Lives would be saved. Prolonging life would revolutionize everything."

She stared at the amazement in his eyes.

He took a deep breath. "And…they promised me," he hesitated before speaking, "they would help me…"

"Help you? How?"

He squeezed her hand. "Help me live longer. I have bone cancer, Kendall."

****

The campus was alive with sounds, colors and the smiling faces of students. Graduation was in two days, which meant new beginnings and endings, transitions in life, anxiety and excitement. Kendall stumbled through the throng of students, as if they were frozen in time and she was the only one with movement. She moved fast and made no eye contact. Several students stepped up to say hi but stopped short when they noticed the faraway gaze on her determined face. She had a target in mind. She walked straight through the lobby of the Decker Center into her office and closed the door.

Just for a minute, she put her head on the smooth cool desk, wanting to shut everything out. *No time to think, keep moving*. She went to work. She pulled the necklace out from under her blouse and over her head; the zip drive hung from the chain.

She had been extremely cautious with the contents of Tim's briefcase, changing the location every night and wearing the zip drive around her neck, hidden under her clothing. The most positive thing Andrew told her was they had not compromised her iPhone...yet. To her knowledge, no one except Scout knew about the cenote map. She was relieved; one secret was safe after all. Now without a doubt she knew what she had to do next.

Chapter 51

Kendall gave Harvey an extra hug, as she thought about what lay ahead. He let her hug him for an extra three minutes without struggling. She made sure he had enough food, toys, and treats, and the instructions for her neighbor, Lizzie, were all spelled out. Lizzie loved Harvey, and Harvey loved Lizzie. Harvey put on his gentle side with the soft-spoken eighty-year-old widow, following her around, lying at her feet, and keeping her company. Lizzie even had a dog door, left over from a dog she once had named Beauregard, lost and loved years ago. Asking her to watch him at a moment's notice was not an issue.

She whispered in Harvey's ear, "Wish me luck, Harvey, and let me figure out what your dad was trying to tell me, so we can put this behind us." She gave him one last hug, and told him her standard line as she was leaving the house, with her brown leather suitcase. "You be a good boy and I'll be right back." She packed two small bags and hid them in her trunk in the middle of the night.

The campus was at its best today, alive with excitement, tight with anticipation. A gorgeous May day at Western Maryland College, a perfect commercial for "why you should go to college back east."

With the towering oaks bright green and full of new leaves, and the meticulously cut lawn in front of the old red brick buildings, it was an Admissions' Director dream day. The air scented with fresh cut grass and flowers. Vibrant colors caught the eye and stimulating conversations filled the air. Students, friends, and parents lined the sidewalks, taking over the parking lots, walking together in packs, smiling and laughing, all here for graduation day. The beat of the marching band practicing added the perfect background noise.

She put on her best smile praying everything was in place for the Commencement ceremony. Conrad Nathaniel would be arriving any minute; she wanted to be ready for the next step. She took out her iPhone and snapped a few photos of the crowds and the setup of the ceremony about to begin. The Professor had agreed to plant the spying device in the back of her iPhone, upon Kendall's request.

When she showed up at his door, his eyes were full of shame. He was not a man upon whom betrayal sat easily. Disappointed with himself, deception made him sick with remorse. She explained she needed time to think, but she was almost certain she was going to hand everything over to Conrad, not the government. She needed the weekend to come to a final decision. Meanwhile, Andrew agreed to proceed as planned and place the device on her phone.

Writing a text, accepting invitations for the coming weekend, she smelled his cologne.

"Kendall, do you want to do a selfie?" Conrad laughed as he grabbed her phone and held it out for a close-up of the two of them.

She smiled for the camera. "You sound like one of the students."

"Well, I'll take that as a compliment, Kendall. I want to be able to relate to them in this graduation speech."

"I'm sure you'll relate, but I don't think they use 'selfie' anymore, that is so last year," she laughed. "They are really looking forward to your speech and your inspiration."

He lowered his head, his mouth near her ear, his scent in her nose and asked in a low voice, "Can we meet this weekend?"

She waved to a passing student; looking in the other direction when she answered. "Yes, I think we can arrange that, in fact I wanted to discuss something with you. I have some graduation commitments on Saturday but perhaps Sunday evening?"

He leaned down again whispering in her ear. "It's a date, and it's no longer the first one." He stood up tall. "Well, I had better go get ready for the speech." He flashed his charming smile and strutted away.

As soon as he was out of sight, she turned around and walked to the faculty parking lot, where she opened her trunk, placed her iPhone in it, and picked up her two bags. Her breath quickened as she walked down a campus path to the street, a taxicab waited with the engine running.

The Romanian taxi driver asked, as she threw her luggage in the backseat, "Are you the one called for a cab to the airport? Promising big tip?"

She put her sunglasses on. "Yes, BWI Airport please, as fast as you can."
****

She was flying from BWI to Houston and then to Belize City. She had no idea whether Ryder would show up in Houston or in Belize City, or if he would really show up at all, but she knew it was in his hands. She had shared enough information, he should want to come.

The briefcase sat in her living room, empty of all its original content. Inside she had put a zip drive and, thanks to a tech-savvy student worker, filled it up with several compromised fake files that would take effort to open. She left two pages of the original blueprints of the tunnels, but the other two pages, as well as the real zip drive and the cenote map, sat securely in her carry-on, under her seat.

Only Scout knew her plans. She had been extremely cautious in all conversations. She accepted invitations for graduation and made plans to meet Steve and plans to meet Conrad on Sunday night. With very little notice, the dean allowed her to take a week off after graduation, He thought she was leaving on Tuesday. The plan was in place.

They might come looking for her. She was not sure who "they" were, but she had a great head start and covered her tracks. She would leave a message using the new app *sly caller*, which would dial instantly to voicemail. She executed a solid plan and told anyone who mattered she just had to get away. If they looked into it further, they would see she had spontaneously flown down to Belize to spend a week in her timeshare at Captain Morgan's Resort.

After take-off, she leaned against the back of her seat and closed her eyes. An old memory surfaced, she and Tim walking the gorgeous secluded beach in Ambergris Caye. Soft white beaches and curved palm trees arching over the blue water, a hammock for two swinging in the breeze along the water's edge—a place she and Tim never wanted to leave.

After a few too many rum punches at ten o'clock in the morning, they bought a timeshare week in a beautiful little oceanfront resort in Belize. The resort, Captain Morgan's, was owned by the man who invented Tombstone pizza. They loved pizza and Belize and spent several vacations enjoying the cozy thatched huts and diving the beautiful reef.

She booked the condo for a week. She would check in tonight, leave some toiletries and clothes in the room, then book a two-day excursion to Lamania, a Belizean ruin on the mainland. She would never see the ruins. When she flew to Caye Caulker, the first stop on the excursion, she would step off the little Native Air twelve-seater, walk to Dock 5 and climb aboard a forty-foot Bertram named *Wanderlust*, hoping to find Scout and Ryder aboard.

Scout devised the plan. The Sherpas from the first excursion, Enrique and Roberto, his assistant Lily, and a boat captain named Jorge, apparently all trustworthy, assisted in the travel plans. To save time and be less suspicious, they planned to enter the land surrounding the cenote by sea and then hike in. Scout spent weeks getting everything together.

****

Kendall dug her toes in the white sand, happy to have completed Step One. So far so good. Tomorrow she would travel to neighboring island, Caye Caulker. Kendall made three Skype calls from the iPad in the Captain Morgan's reception area. Using her new app, the calls went directly to voicemail. Leaving short but sincere messages, she explained to Andrew, Steve, and

Conrad, she needed some time away and had forgotten her iPhone in the trunk of her car. She laughed as she said she was forced to unplug for a week.

Strolling back to her thatched hut on the beach, she stood tall, confident she was fulfilling Tim's last request.

Chapter 52

The sky full of orange, pink, and purple splashes resembled a child's finger painting, random colors thrown across a canvas, with glittery blue paint underneath. Caye Caulker was an adorable, hippie-influenced beach town full of culture. The locals, driving nothing bigger than a golf cart, held off the big hotel chains and tourism of neighboring island Ambergris Caye. Tropical trees lined the streets and palm trees hung over the shoreline.

Houses and cottages, painted a variety of bright and pastel colors enclosed by white picket fences, competed for attention with colorful hand-painted signs dotting the sand streets. Carrying her bags, Kendall strolled down two blocks toward white sands and the spectacular turquoise sea.

She studied a man in the distance. Scout. His stride gives him away.

Her mouth turned up in a wide smile. Even Scout's face couldn't contain the excitement. His blond hair appeared a little lighter next to his sun-kissed skin. Barefoot, wearing swim trunks and a light blue T-shirt advertising SNUBA, his hair hanging loose to his shoulders. Her hand on her chest, the cadence of her heart beat pulsated on her fingers. She dropped the suitcases and Scout was upon her. For a moment, they stopped a few inches apart and gazed into each other's eyes. He stepped forward his muscular arms wrapped around her. She hugged back and held on, closing her eyes for a minute.

"It's good to see you, Kendall, really good." He hesitated as if he wanted to kiss her but instead he stepped back and picked up the two bags. He cocked his head. "I have a surprise for you, and I think it's going to make you pretty happy."

Her cheeks ached from smiling, for the first time in months she felt safe as she walked beside Scout toward a long, skinny wooden pier. She exhaled a loud breath. Finally, someone she could trust. "Well, I'm feeling pretty happy right now," she said. "I'm not sure if I can get much happier."

At the end of the pier, a large white boat anchored next to the dock. The name *Wanderlust* stenciled across the stern. She spotted Roberto, from the cenote trip, organizing items on the boat, closing a hatch on the deck and loading supplies. He looked up and waved. Calmness; the sea shiny flat, a caressing breeze ruffling her hair. *I want to be here now.*

May was a perfect time to be on the Caribbean, Scout had assured her. Tim loved the sea and so did Scout. Their love for nature's vast miracle was attractive. Scout ahead of her turned around noticing her stopping for a moment and looking up to the sky.

She tilted her head and gazed at the dusk sky fading into night. "I miss you, Tim, with all my heart...I hope I'm fulfilling your request, doing what you want..." She whispered, "He's a good man I know you trusted him."

A new figure emerged on the deck of the boat. Kendall smiled, looked up to the sky again and whispered, "He came, Tim, your son is here."

She caught up to Scout in seconds, and stepped on the back of the boat, fighting back the tears with a grin. "It is so good to see you, Ryder," she said, hugging him, "your father would be so proud."

He limply hugged Kendall and quickly broke loose, widening the space between them.

"Well, that's why I'm here." He ran his hand through his hair, his shoulders back and head lifted. "I'm here for my father...Now I want to hear the whole story."

She smiled, ignoring the attitude she detected. "I'd like to tell you both; I need to tell you everything that has been going on."

Scout nodded to Roberto, who was untying the ropes to the dock, and headed toward the front of the boat, shouting back, "We have a good eight hours before we reach land, let's get situated and I'll show you where you can rest for the night, have some food, and you can tell us the whole story. We have plenty of time."

The boat glided across the flat seas at a good thirty knots. In the cabin, Scout and Ryder sat stiffly upright on striped cushions listening to Kendall, only interrupting to ask a few pertinent questions.

She started at the beginning. Slowly, and in detail, she told how she discovered the briefcase right before the first cenote trip. She tried to hide her innermost emotions of deep pain at Tim's deception. She described the suitcase and its contents in detail, and conveyed her initial bafflement about the old map.

She touched on her struggle with Tim's belonging to a government agency and never confiding the secret part of his life to her. She explained her interactions with Steve Crawford, the Professor, and Conrad Nathaniel. She told them of the tunnels beneath the college, and the Nathaniel Cemetery with a scientific lab hidden underneath. Scout interjected here and there, asking questions and adding another apology for not taking them to the right cenote. Ryder asked a few piercing questions, but continued to listen intently.

Both were silenced when she told them, "Others believe Tim found this bacterium, or plant, this thing everyone was searching for, that can prolong life, cure cancer and other diseases." She explained what little she knew of Tobias, the man who had been in the lab and was apparently 175 years old.

She added in a soft whisper, meeting Ryder's eyes, swallowing her tears, "Your father may have been killed because of what he discovered. His death may not have been an accident."

Ryder, firmly parked on the edge of the seat for the last two hours, crossed his arms over his chest. He had asked questions in an even, low voice. He jumped up and paced the small interior of the boat like a caged animal. His handsome features twisted in anger.

"I don't understand." He let out a harsh breath as he walked back and forth. "Who killed my dad?"

She placed her hands together and squeezed them as if in prayer. "I don't know, Ryder, I'm not sure who's more dangerous—The Conrad Nathaniels of the world or the government. What I do know, before I go back home I need to figure out who to give this information to. The government and Nathaniel both know I have it and I can't lead a normal life until I get it off my hands."

She hesitated, then spoke again. "No one knows, except for Scout and now you, Ryder, about the old cenote map. As far as I know, no one knows it exists. Maybe they're all searching for the map." She grabbed Ryder's hands. "I don't know how we would know what everyone is looking for…but I know the cenote is something your dad wanted to show you. Maybe if we find it we will understand why."

Scout took a deep breath and said, "I've heard old fishermen tell stories, legends if you will, of a tribe of people whose king lived an extraordinary long time. People of Mayan descent lived unusually long lives, and because of this their population doubled and tripled. Historians and researchers document the existence of over one million descendants of the Maya, and then poof, they dwindled to non-existence. Gone."

She propped her chin on her hands. "I remember reading something about that."

Scout continued, "There are many thoughts and conspiracy theories on how this large civilization vanished. Today 30,000 Mayan descendants live in Central America; if you talk to them, they will tell you stories about the disappearance of their people. One of the old Maya legends is about two kings. One found a way to live an unusually long and healthy life, the other had a village of sick and dying people. The king of the diseased people asked the other king to share his cure, his secret, but the powerful old king would not share, proclaiming it was sacred only to be used by the royalty, not common people. His greediness, his selfishness ignited violence among the tribes, destroying him and the secret of the cure. This is what many say caused the extinction of the Maya."

Scout took out a piece of paper and drew four symbols. "Hunkul Yax," he said.

Kendall looked at the drawing blankly. "What?"

"Hunkul Yax in Mayan," Scout repeated. "My drawing is not too good but I've seen it several times, and it looks something like this."

"What does it mean?"

"When translated to English, it means 'forever young'. A Mayan phrase passed around and used in reference to a specific tribe of Maya people who possessed an ability to lead exceedingly long lives."

Kendall and Ryder were transfixed. He went on, "Research exists documenting skeletons of women and men who lived to 150, 180, even 200 years old. The carbon dating of these skeletons has been disputed for years, but the majority of them found in burial grounds and caves in the Yucatán peninsula, are not too far from where we are going." He paused to take a breath, then added, "When folks talk about the ancient skeletons they are usually drawing symbols and using the words Hunkul Yax. It's a legend that's been around for centuries."

She pulled out her tablet, and inserted the zip drive she wore around her neck. The photos flashed on the screen. She repeated what she knew about the old man Tobias and Conrad Nathaniel's great-great-grandfather.

"I think Tim had something to do with helping the old man escape. I think they had him in the lab and then they didn't, and somehow Tim was mixed up in it."

****

Outside the boat's portholes, the glassy sea reflected the sliver of the moon. Light winds carried the boat toward its destination. Scout, Kendall, and Ryder poured over every document on Tim's USB drive, including the video message to Kendall. Ryder's eyes glazed as he watched his father in perfect health and totally alive on the screen. As soon as the clip ended, his hand reached out to touch the play button again. She stepped away from the computer and took a bathroom break, giving Ryder the privacy he deserved in watching his father on the screen. She could hear him play it several times.

****

Scout was mesmerized. Here was a man, whom he had met, so full of life and energy, talking to his wife, his voice echoing on the boat, as if he were eerily there. Tim brought Kendall and Ryder into his world. Because of him they were on this boat, caught up in this unusual situation. He watched the video in total silence, listening intently to every word, trying to decipher the meaning in it all.

He stepped out and made his way to the top of the boat. He took in a deep breath, his head tilted back, amazed at the star-packed sky. Roberto came up next to him and they stood in silence, the vastness of the sea and sky surrounded them.

"A few more hours to shore," Roberto said.

"Okay, then I guess we all better catch a siesta." Scout stretched. "We have a long journey ahead of us."

It was another hour before they took their sleeping berths and the lights went dark in the cabin. With Scout's head full of the what if's, sleep seemed impossible. The methodical slow rocking of the boat won the battle. For the sea that night was like a loving mother cradling her children in safe and strong arms.

In what felt like minutes, Scout's eyes slowly

opened. The night had passed silently, and the dawn's soft light snuck into the boat's staterooms and galley nudging him awake, alerting him the shoreline was close.

Chapter 53

Kendall's love/hate relationship with the sea was being tested yet again. The plan, according to Scout, was coming in from the ocean would save a few days of thick jungle hiking and make an easier trip back to the cenote. Ideas are not always reality. The gnarly reef guarded the shoreline with vengeance.

In order to cross the jagged reef without ripping the bottom or getting hung up, only two options existed. One was to find a natural opening where a boat could fit through without damage. Trolling back and forth for an hour, they found no opening, so, Jorge, the Captain, went to plan B. Timing the swells. As the waves came in, they counted in Spanish. Finally, Jorge went for it, as Kendall held her breath. The waves rolled them delicately over the sharp black teeth of the jutting rocks and landed them near the shore. Kendall exhaled a long breath and a squeal adding, "We made it!"

Once the boat was at anchor, it took a long time to bring all the supplies and tanks to shore in the dinghy. Anyone who happened upon the scene might have thought the boat was shipwrecked as they worked together transporting the supplies to set up camp on the minutest stretch of white soft sand, so fine Kendall named it sugar beach. Luckily, no witnesses existed, the sea was empty, no other boats on the horizon.

On the voyage over, Scout outlined the trek,

painting a picture of poisonous plants, bugs, and snakes. He described in detail how unmerciful the jungle can be. He wanted to make sure they understood the journey. *He just wants us to be prepared, and realize this is a completely different outing than their first cenote trip.*

There were no trails or roads leading into the destination pinpointed on Tim's map. Roberto and Enrique would lead the way with machetes, and they would help carry the gear.

Scout estimated with luck it would take four days and three nights to reach the cenote from the shoreline; coming in from the land would have taken at least a week, if not longer.

Fortunately, the weather was on their side, and the typical May humidity that starts creeping in and closing up the air was staying away for now. Their gear was checked and double-checked. Scout was a safety man and thanks to his new satellite phone and GPS, the well-planned and thought-out supplies, the five of them should be able to survive for at least fourteen days in the jungle.

Jorge and Lily would stay on the boat, anchoring in different coves each night but close enough to keep radio contact.

The first day went remarkably well, Kendall received a few cuts and scratches but the humidity stayed low and the group was determined to reach their destination. Roberto and Enrique found a suitable place to make camp for the night. With machetes, they chopped down a tiny circular area, large enough to set up three tents and an area for a semi-private bathroom. Scout hated chopping down clearings, Kendall could almost catch him wincing as the machetes in front of them destroyed the natural habitat of the jungle. He reminded them several times he wanted to leave the area with the least human impact.

As nightfall entered the jungle, the air teemed with background sound effects. Chirps, buzzing, and rustling of leaves and trees occurred in random order. An illusion of the sound of water filled the empty pauses. Even the sky seemed to press its own depth of thickness against the trees. The fire made by Enrique and Roberto warmed the small clearing. Scout mentioned it was necessary to provide light and to keep any curious predators of the night away from their space. Everyone knew it wasn't their space, but they were borrowing it from the Yucatán in order to experience its remote beauty and reach their destination. Even in the wildness of the jungle Kendall wasn't alarmed.

After a quick meal of vegetables wrapped in flour tortillas, Scout passed around a bar of dark chocolate. Enrique and Roberto were so excited by this that Kendall gave them her share. They were appreciative and their eyes shone with curiosity and warmth toward the only female of the group. After years of working with Scout, she knew they trusted him, but they carried a different cautiousness than in the last cenote trip. Their eyes constantly circled the jungle and they conferred in Spanish.

She and Ryder would be sharing a tent. Kendall was grateful. The idea of sleeping alone in the middle of the jungle seemed like the limit of lonely. It had been a long hot day, muscles were sore and sleep was inevitable. She lingered by the fire with Scout, giving Ryder some space in the tent, hoping he would be asleep when she turned in.

It was the first time they had been alone. She had been waiting for this moment, thinking about being together, seeing each other one to one after weeks of communication.

Her hands clasped around her knees, staring at the embers of the fire, she spoke softly, "It seems crazy, doesn't it? All the secrets and lies, a hidden map..." She turned and took in his handsome, rugged face. "And you're helping us, you're helping Ryder and me figure this out. Why?"

Scout gazed at her. "How can I not? I liked your husband from the moment I met him. I'm sure you have heard this many times. Tim was a unique and special human being. I believe what he wanted to show you and Ryder in the cenote will be special as well. One of my deepest regrets is I was not honest with you about the last cenote..." He paused as if he wanted to say something else. "I had no idea of all this." He ran his hand through his hair. "And I'm doing it for you, as much as I respect your husband, my heart hasn't felt like this for a long time. You make me feel emotions I almost forgot existed." He looked at her and swallowed. "I couldn't wait to see you again." He exhaled a loud breath and turned to face the fire.

She took his clasped hands in hers. "I don't know what to say, there are so many things going on, my life doesn't make a lot of sense, but I do know I'm so happy to be doing this with you, and you're here for me...for us." Kendall paused. "Thank you."

He sat still and looked at the fire. "I am here for you." He pulled one hand out of hers and placed it on the side of her cheek. The silence seemed like minutes as he looked into her eyes. He smiled and offered a hand to pull her up. "We should try to get some sleep, it will be another long hike tomorrow."

****

Morning in the jungle is alive with energy, with birds of different varieties cawing, chirping, and whistling, and a repertoire of buzzing insects completing the symphony. The early morning sun creates a hazy filter through the green trees, exposing shimmering cobwebs as it slowly wakes the untouched wilderness.

The smell of coffee floated through the air, nudging Kendall to an awareness of light and sound. Ryder was out of the tent, as she looked down at her watch surprised at what time it was.

After their jungle routine of waking up and quick personal hygiene, they consumed coffee and breakfast bars as Enrique and Roberto packed up the camp.

Today they would have to cross several rivers, reminding her of the river crossing on the last trip when Scout saved her. The group had a good rhythm. They traveled together for days before, but Ryder's attitude had changed and he was working together with an underlying excitement about reaching their destination.

Ryder asked questions regarding Conrad Nathaniel, the Professor, and the underground tunnel that led to Camp David.

"Do you think my mother knows about The Collective?" Ryder was walking behind her.

She thought about her words carefully. "I'm not sure, I doubt it—no one outside the government is supposed to know. Is there anything that would make you think your mother knew your dad was still involved with the government?"

He was silent for a moment as if he was thinking, the tone of his voice like steel. "No, nothing, she wouldn't have been able to keep it from me. I can't believe he never told me, his only son." For a moment the pissed-off Ryder emerged. "I thought I knew everything about my dad, or I used to." He swung his walking stick and cracked the branches beside him.

She understood. She stopped, placed both hands on his shoulders and looked him in the eye. He started to pull away but she held firm. "He was probably going to tell you. This was the trip for you and your dad to experience something that was vital to him, he may have just been waiting for the right time. He wanted this for your eighteenth birthday, maybe he thought when you were eighteen he could explain it all to you. You, his only son. He obviously wanted to share something special with you."

Ryder's unsmiling eyes were full of water. He looked away. "I just miss him so much," his voice wavered, "why can't he be here to explain all of this to me?" He wiped his face. Scout stopped up ahead and yelled back, "Is everything okay?"

She tried to give Ryder a hug but he stepped in front of her and kept walking. She yelled back to Scout, "Yes, everything is fine."

They were coming up to the second river of the day; this one was about four or five feet deep with pretty slow rapids. Enrique and Roberto were organizing the dry bags getting ready for the crossing. As Scout started out to test the depth of the river and make a safe path for everyone else, Ryder came barreling through the water, past Scout to the other side.

Scout turned and looked at her with a scowl. She shrugged and raised her eyebrows. Luckily, the crossing went easily and with Ryder in front and Enrique and Roberto following, she and Scout had a chance to talk.

"So what do you think they are saying about your sudden trip to Belize at the college?" he asked.

"Well, I think Steve Crawford is going to be upset I didn't meet him and give him the briefcase, and I think Conrad Nathaniel is too smart to think I just needed some time away. Then there's the Professor. I feel bad about not telling him but I just don't know whom to trust anymore. I think that's the worst thing of all—realizing I have no one to trust."

"You can trust me." His voice was softer. "I'd do anything I can to help you figure this out."

She glanced at Scout with his hair pulled back and a sincere look on his face. "I know, I believe that, and you are helping. I'm not sure if this trip will help me fill in the blanks about what Tim wanted us to know, but at least I honored his wish and brought Ryder to see his cenote and then I will be done with all of this. Well, sort of done, I just don't know whom to trust—the government or Conrad Nathaniel." She took off her sunglasses. "Do you think we would know it if we found it, what is so important?"

He answered the best he could, "I have no idea what we're looking for, but maybe we'll know it when we see it."

****

The sun was hanging low in the west and the sounds of the jungle were changing with the light. Enrique and Roberto stopped in front and put a finger to their lips. Frozen like statues in silence. The sound of the howler monkeys reminding Kendall again of the dinosaurs from *Jurassic Park*. A slightly human sound but eerily fierce as it echoed through the jungle. As in Africa when the lions roar in the distance, announcing the king of the jungle, in the Yucatán the roar of the howler monkeys is the sound of their king.

They found a small clearing up from the third river and camp was set up for the second night. Ryder, Scout, and Kendall decided to walk back to the river and take a bath. The humidity was moving in and the air was tight against their bodies. The mosquitoes so thick in the air, you could clear them with the palm of your hand.

Back at their small camp Enrique and Roberto were sweating profusely over the small fire grilling up vegetables. After two days of not eating anything cooked, the smell of onions, peppers and squash was delicious.

"Won't the smell bring in all the animals of the jungle?" Ryder frowned as he studied Scout.

Scout smiled. "Well, maybe, but with all those vegetables sizzling at least they would be vegetarians, we don't want to attract any meat eaters."

Ryder inserted his headphones and turned away.

The thick veil of darkness blanketed the jungle and the evening sounds filled the air. Enrique and Roberto were further away from the fire, but all five of them were sitting on the ground on tarps, Scout and Kendall talking about the next day, Ryder lying on his back with his headphones on.

A snap sounded in the distance. Enrique and Roberto stood searching through the thick trees.

Instinctively silence and stillness washed over them. Ryder rose, his earbuds in and Scout put his finger to his lips and motioned for him to turn his iPhone off. They were all at attention when they heard the snap again. Enrique and Roberto using hand signals slowly entered the jungle.

A shiny flash from the jungle, they both had knives.

Scout stood and crept to the edge of the trees listening intently. It went on like this for what seemed an eternity, and then Enrique and Roberto came back, nodding their heads and speaking in Spanish.

Ryder whispered, "What was it? Do you think it was a jaguar?"

Scout shook his head. "No, they are stealthy; it was probably just another animal checking out our fire."

He spoke with Roberto in Spanish and then turned to Ryder and Kendall. "Well, if it makes you feel any better, Roberto and Enrique will take turns staying up a little longer tonight and watching the fire."

Ryder shrugged. "Whatever, I'm going to sleep."

Kendall pulled the rubber band out of her hair, letting it fall loose around her neck. "I think I'll stay up with you for a little bit."

Scout went over to speak to Enrique and Roberto, then came back and plopped down next to Kendall on the canvas tarp. Enrique and Roberto moved facing the other direction, with Roberto lying down and Enrique propped on his elbow.

"What did you tell them?"

He moved his leg until it touched hers, whispering, "I told them I wanted to kiss you good night so would they please give us some privacy."

The corners of her mouth turned up involuntarily as her eyes widened and she gave him a stern look. "Really?" She leaned back on her palms with her legs crossed out in front. "I don't believe you."

He moved closer and kissed her softly on the lips. "Now do you believe me?"

Chapter 54

Kendall woke to the sound of a zipper clicking on the tent. For a moment, she didn't remember where she was. Ryder left the tent and she could smell burnt coffee grounds wafting through the air and see light green, dark green, and neon green leaves attached to thick brown branches through the opening. Tonight they should make it to the cenote, Tim's cenote.

She gave herself a moment. She took out her brush, ran it through her long hair and then put it in a quick braid. Her little makeup kit contained a mirror, refreshing wipes, some BB moisturizing cream with tint and sunscreen, lip moisturizer, deodorant, and vanilla lotion. She may have been in the middle of the jungle but she still had her morning routine. She looked at herself in the mirror not recognizing this woman. *Why can't you be here, why can't I ask you all the questions I so desperately want to know?* She longed for Tim to hold her just one more time; she knew that's why hugging Scout felt so good last night. He had kissed her and then they held each other for a long embrace; the problem was she wished it were Tim. It wasn't fair to Scout, she knew this was true but at this moment she had too many other things to deal with.

Scout, Roberto, and Enrique were crouched at the edge of the clearing, speaking rapidly in Spanish. When she approached the group, they stood up and stopped talking. She smiled. "*Buenos dias*."

Roberto and Enrique answered in unison, "*Buenos dias*," and Scout motioned for her to come to the edge of the clearing, where he squatted down and pointed to the ground.

"Roberto and Enrique heard some movement in the jungle last night; it was coming from over here. They think these are human tracks, not animals, and they're wondering if somebody could be following us."

"Following us from the shore?" Ryder asked. He had walked over and was listening.

"They're not really sure," Scout said, "but the previous night they thought they heard some noises, and now these tracks make them believe someone is following us."

Ryder looked around from right to left searching through the trees. "Do you think they're watching us right now?"

"If they are, they're keeping their distance. The guys walked around a pretty large perimeter this morning, but that's when they noticed subtle signs of somebody following us." He stood up. "I don't want to jump to any conclusions, but do you think a tracker from up in the States could be following us?"

She shook her head. "I don't know how I could have been followed. I changed planes twice, the boat ride, then in Caye Caulker I arrived and we left. You said yourself there was never another boat. We were so careful leaving Belize. Maybe we should radio Jorge and Lily and find out if there any boats out by the shoreline."

"Yes, I agree, that's my next step, let's see if Jorge and Lily have seen any boats or vessels on the radar."

He went to the dry packs and fished out the satellite radio.

****

The humidity now a tight wet blanket wrapped around them. Roberto and Enrique moved with ease. They didn't seem bothered by the rising heat. The hot air was sticky like a drying wad of chewing gum on the bottom of your shoe, annoying and coated with gnats and mosquitoes, but they pressed forward. Scout slapped the side of his neck.

Lily and Jorge assured him no boat had been on their radar or in the area for days. If one didn't come from the shoreline, the only way anyone could be as deep in the jungle as they were, would be to be dropped off by a helicopter. And a plane or helicopter that size, would have been clearly detected in the silence of the skies above the dense tropical jungle.

Scout prepared to accept the logic it was animals or locals living off the land, shrugged off the uneasiness in his stomach. This particular area of the Yucatán was all private land, according to Tim, who had written documentation allowing him access. Not that they had anyone to show it to. The staggering size of this parcel was thousands and thousands of acres of thick jungle and except for the wildlife appeared uninhabited.

Scout asked both Kendall and Ryder whether they had any concerns about continuing the journey; he knew before he asked, they were not going to turn back.

The canopy of the jungle appeared to be thicker, the closer they came to their destination. Hot and tired, they pushed through the brush, grunting and swearing, until an opening exposed a windy limestone river. The day had been a tough one. Ten long hot hours of hiking on rough uneven rock and shrub growth so dense at times they could not see Enrique and Roberto. Besides numerous bug bites, they suffered scratches, cuts, and stings.

The humidity had mysteriously disappeared. It was scorching hot, but dry.

Scout took a sip from his canteen. "In another hour we should be closer to the cenote, and we'll make camp. Everyone doing okay?"

Kendall nodded and Ryder kept walking. For the last several miles he and Ryder had been discussing cave diving, talking about the thrill of exploration and the newness of the sport in the Yucatán.

Ryder stopped to adjust his pack. "So, there are plenty undiscovered caves still out there?"

"Thousands unmapped, most inaccessible but the local people know about their existence. I've surveyed several complete cave systems, but many we have never found where they end."

"Have you ever named one?"

"Yes, Cenote Escondido nicknamed Mayan Blue." Time rushed by as he explained the surveying expedition to an attentive Ryder.

All the talk of cenotes and cave diving had Ryder full of excitement to find his father's cenote—which bore no name on the map. His thirst for the unknown familiar to Scout.

"Maybe we will be the first ones to explore it."

Chapter 55

"Sir, the resort in Belize states she checked in and unpacked, but they have not seen her since she left for the Lamanai tour she booked." The young agent handed him a thick folder bulging with documents.

"This tour your man states she went on, it was to the mainland in Belize?"

"Yes, she took a boat from the resort in Ambergris Caye to the small airport where she flew to Caye Caulker, for one stop to pick up passengers. Then the plane landed in a sugar cane field where a small group hiked in and then went on small canoes to see the Lamanai ruins. Our man lost her in the tour as he could not get booked on that particular plane."

"And he is sure she did not get off the plane at Caye Caulker?" He was holding a map of Belize, pointing to the small island of Caye Caulker, next door to Ambergris Caye.

"Well, sir, since he was unable to get on the same flight, he was there immediately after and he was assured no one stepped off the plane. She was still on the roster to go on the Lamanai tour." The young man was speaking rapidly, sweating profusely.

He was silent for a few minutes. He put the map in the file folder and closed the file. "I'd like to speak to Steve Crawford, and I mean five minutes ago."

"Yes sir." The agent rushed out of the office.

Chapter 56

The low setting sun, filtered through the dense jungle leaves, casting a lime-green light and slow-moving shadows. Exhausted, Kendall slowed her pace, wishing she could slump to the jungle floor. Scout, absorbed with figuring out his GPS, was attempting to pinpoint the exact location on Tim's map. As the light dimmed, an extremely dense barrier of shrubs and trees blocked their path. An impenetrable portion of the jungle, where thick vegetation created a border that continued as far as one could see on the left and on the right. A natural fence spreading in both directions on a parallel line.

"Well, I think it's beyond this dense barrier." Scout took off his hat and looked from east to west. Roberto and Enrique began hacking into a part of the natural barrier, using machetes, barely making an impact

"Almost looks like it was planted as a fence?" Kendall shaded her eyes.

"This specific kind of fauna needs a lot of water, so there must be some type of natural water feeding system in this area." Scout said. He attempted to push his hand through the mass.

Enrique called for Scout. He seemed excited, pointing toward the ground behind the machete path he had made. There, the remains of limestone rocks were visible, rocks that at one time had formed a wall of some type. It ran the entire length of the tree line on the other side, shielded from the dense vegetation.

"I've seen something like this at the Mayan ruins at Tulum." Scout said.

Ryder forced his lean frame through the opening in the shrubbery and got down on his knees clearing dirt and debris away from one area of the rocks.

"Hey, there's carving on this rock." Ryder motioned. Looking down at the rocks, raised symbols were visible, but hard to make out. Immediately Kendall went down on her knees moving dirt and debris away from the tablets. She sat back on her heels. "I bet few people know about this." She looked back at the enormity of natural fence covering the ground. "I wonder if Tim had ever been here."

Scout hesitated wiping the sweat off his brow. "No, he hasn't been here, at least from what he told me when we met. He stressed the point; he wanted to take Ryder here, a place unexplored, so maybe someone passed down the secret to him."

Ryder in manic motions, entranced by the sight of the ruins, continued brushing away ground and clearing off debris and dirt from a large area on the ground. Kendall noticed his fingertips bleeding.

Scout squeezed through the area Enrique and Roberto hacked holding his GPS. "We are apparently close to the cenote, but I really don't see any waterhole up ahead."

Kendall pushed through, the area in front of Scout a rather large flat expanse, somewhat cleared out. Compared to the dense shrubbery they just hacked their way through, it was sparse.

"I think we're less than three miles from the

cenote," he said. "The sun has set, so you have two choices, we can camp here for the night and find the cenote in the morning or we can try to go another hour and see if we can camp beside the water."

"How much daylight do you think we have?"

He looked at his watch and up at the darkening sky. "I think we only have about twenty minutes until it gets dark; we won't make the three miles by then."

She placed her pack on the ground, and stretched pushing her hands above her head. "Well then, I vote let's stay here for the night. We'll leave the excitement of seeing the cenote for tomorrow morning."

Ryder still on the ground was absorbed in sweeping away the rocks. "Fine with me."

Enrique and Roberto both nodded and started putting the tarps down, making camp. Tonight, they had a large clearing to construct a camp; Enrique and Roberto went to work making two fires on opposite ends of the outer ring.

"We can make a shower over there." Scout lifted the water they had been carrying from the last river.

Kendall smiled, overjoyed at the thought of being clean. "Well, that seems like a luxury!"

Scout nodded. "We're close to the cenote so we will get clean freshwater tomorrow."

Being together 24/7, the group bonded well, especially if they were clean. Besides the earthy jungle smells, body odor was a seasoning Kendall was happy to get rid of. Each had a task in setting up the camp and once completed, the sweat and bugs from the day were washed off. Ryder in a surprisingly civil mood, shared his batteries by turning on a classic rock playlist. Kendall almost felt normal. Scout brought out dry packed food, and each had a choice of pasta, Alfredo, Marinara or Pesto, and relatively fresh bread.

After a full meal of carbs, the muscle soreness of the day and zapped energy from the heat coated Kendall like a can of spray paint. Ryder, after spending an hour with his flashlight, clearing out earth and shrubs from the limestone ruins, was the first to retire.

No one discussed what happened earlier that morning; the something or someone being right outside their camp. As the light faded and the jungle noises filled her ears, Kendall couldn't drive it from her mind. Fear crept into her thoughts. *It could be locals living off the land*, she convinced herself. She was relieved Enrique and Roberto were keeping watch tonight. They smiled as they headed to the back of the campsite, leaving Kendall and Scout alone.

"Are you surprised to see the ruins?"

He cocked his head. "There are ruins all through this land. There were so many Maya at one time it's hard to imagine areas where they haven't traveled and made their mark."

She was leaning comfortably against a large pack. "I wonder if there are more ruins by the cenote, maybe that's what Tim wanted Ryder to see, a place the world doesn't know about." She could not get Tim off her mind. She studied Scout's profile from the side. She appreciated his rugged good looks, his kind heart, and the sacrifice he was making for Tim's birthday adventure for Ryder. She ached for a man's touch, but deep inside her heart, without a doubt, she still belonged to Tim. She didn't know how not to be his.

"We are in a sacred and special place." Scout placed his hand on top of Kendall's. "I feel

310

uncommonly lucky to be on this trip with you and Ryder, especially you." She did not remove her hand. Where his skin touched her there was heat. Desire flowed through her like liquid. She sat in silence, trying to sort through her body's reaction. A rustling, a quick movement on the other side of the fence interrupted her thoughts.

Scout stood; Roberto and Enrique walked toward the dense trees and bushes that served as a natural perimeter.

Roberto lifted his finger to his lips and Enrique stealthily squeezed through the opening with Roberto close behind. Scout motioned to her as if to say "stay" and walked over to the opening. In seconds, she was alone, focused on the spindly bushes and towering jungle trees and beyond. She held her breath and her body rigid, frozen in place, with her ear cocked in the direction of the fence listening. The jungle sounds became amplified—the chirping of the bugs, the humming of the locusts, even the buzzing of the insects. Her senses heightened. What did she think she was doing? She worked at a college, and here she was crippled with fear in a primitive jungle in the Yucatán.

She let out a sigh of relief when they returned to the camp area. It had seemed they were gone for a long time, but in actuality, it had only been ten minutes.

"Did you see anyone?" she whispered, trying to slow her heartbeat.

Scout was standing next to her breathing heavily. "It was probably just an animal. In the dark we were unable to see any tracks; if someone's out there, they're gone now. Roberto and Enrique are going to take turns on watch tonight and then wake me up before dawn.

It's probably best if we all try to get some sleep, morning will be here before we know it." Scout's tenderness had faded; he was back to being guide leader.

"Okay then, I'll see you in the morning." She pasted a smile on her face, clenching her hands together so he would not see them shaking.

****

Kendall woke up with knots in her stomach. Ryder was still sleeping, so she crept quietly out of the tent.

Nature was rising, the birds were singing against the buzz of insect noises creating an excited pulsing sound in the air. She tipped her head and looked straight up to the sky. Scout, Roberto, and Enrique were nowhere to be seen.

Scout's tent was unzipped and she tried to look inside to see whether she could catch him sleeping. Then a movement caught her attention out of the corner of her eye. She froze in place, adrenaline pumping and stared into the thickness of the green jungle, trying to focus on what she heard or glimpsed.

Nothing, and then she heard a crack behind her. She turned to see Scout, Enrique, and Roberto in the dense thicket of trees.

"You're up?" Scout walked toward her. "Did you sleep okay?"

She smiled, inhaling a deep breath. "I've had better. What were you guys doing?"

Scout forced a half smile. "We were just checking the perimeter, and you know, taking care of business."

"So, did you see any animal tracks?"

He hesitated. "We need to talk. Enrique and Roberto think someone has been following us, or watching us." He paused. "I really don't know what to conclude, but here are our options. Check out the cenote today, make tonight the last night of camp and haul it out of here as quick as we can first thing in the morning, or pack up and head back to the boat right now."

Her eyes widened, she gestured in agitation and demanded, "You are saying, just turn around now? We are less than three miles from the cenote and you just want to turn around now and head back because you think somebody's watching us?"

"That's one option, and then the other would be we came this far, no one seems to be threatening us in any way, so we spend the day exploring and we can head back tomorrow morning."

Ryder walked up behind her. "Well, I didn't come all this way, sweated, scratched and eaten alive…just to turn around and leave. My father wanted me to see the cenote; hell, it sounds like everyone wants to see it, I'm going to see it." He marched toward his tent, adding loudly, "With or without you I'm doing some diving today."

It was settled. She didn't know if she was alarmed or relieved. *Just do it.*

Enrique would stay at camp, and Roberto would accompany them to the cenote.

Chapter 57

Wild organic beauty erased the panic Kendall carried in her chest from last night. The water, mixed in with the rich dark soil and the right measure of sun and moisture, created a surreal vision. A land so pristine, so abundant and displaying every color of green imaginable, shadowed by deep browns and taupe. The closer to their destination, the splendor of the land magnified. The sky reflected off the deep greens, appearing turquoise in contrast to the leaves. Spectacular.

Immersed in the glorious landscape, the three-mile hike to the cenote flew by. Scout stopped, holding the GPS, trying to pinpoint their location.

"It has to be around here somewhere in this general vicinity, my GPS is acting strange." He checked the batteries.

Kendall wanted to help, she didn't travel this far for the cenote to elude them. She moved to the left trying to find an opening. She pushed through the trees, as far as she could see, primitive jungle, surrounded her, no clearing in sight.

She retraced her steps, she could no longer see Scout, Ryder or Roberto in front of her.

"Hey, Ryder! Where are you?" Silence. She listened for the sound of movement. "Scout?"

A yell. Not necessarily an alarming yell, but a yell

all the same. Was it jubilation, excitement, or anguish? "Scout! Ryder!" She took off running in the direction of the yell.

"Kendall, over here." Scout emerged from the thicket and directed her to the right, they pushed through a cluster of branches.

Roberto and Ryder were on their stomachs, peering over the edge of a massive hole camouflaged by the lushness of the jungle. Ryder turned around smiling, his eyes sparkling. "It's the cenote, it's Dad's cenote."

She lay down beside him, staring into the blackness; it took a moment for her eyes to adjust. The jungle canopy above moved slightly with a soft breeze and the sun hit a portion of the water. Iridescent blue sparkled in the sunbeams. She swallowed her excitement, this must be it. Her mind and heart were in amazement. The hole led to a shaft dropping down some two hundred feet.

She looked up at Scout. "How would we ever get back up?"

Ryder was standing. "How long is the ladder?" he asked. "And how much rope do we have?"

Scout spoke to Roberto in Spanish, and Roberto took off heading deeper into the jungle. He took his backpack off and brought out the treasured map and a magnifying glass hovered over a mark on the map. "I think this symbol is for River and I think there is a river nearby. If I'm right that river should flow into the cave below." They all studied the map. If they were facing north, it appeared the river should be to the east.

"How much further do you think it is?" she asked.

"If I'm reading this right, not far at all. Roberto is trying to find it."

****

Jubilant, Kendall placed her hand over her heart, the map was correct, just a short way down the trail Roberto found the river. A clear, shallow, winding river, with large rocks jutting out and it flowed into the mouth of a cave. Smooth large rocks unevenly lined the floor of the riverbank and vines hung from the hourglass-shaped opening. The hole stretched up to fifteen feet in height, curving in at the waist with rocks almost meeting in the middle. The gap in the center was only two feet side to side; the lower and higher openings about six feet across. Covered with a green drapery of moss and long hanging vines, five or ten dangling in varying lengths draped across the opening; it was as if a curtain was hiding the entrance. The water immediately outside the entrance of the cave was crystal clear, collecting in a small pool above a tiny waterfall. The pool filled with tiny silver and translucent fish, reflecting light and water and causing a shimmering shine. The river was more like a creek, only two or three feet deep.

Scout proposed, "We go in here, swim into the mouth of the cave with dry packs and snorkels, and if I'm right it should open up into a large wet cenote. Roberto is going to go back to the hole, and if there's a dry portion of the cenote he can lower our equipment down. Diagonally we should only be about a mile from the opening." He paused, then added, "Or if you'd like, let me test it out, go back to the hole and make noise and I can make sure it is possible."

"I'm in," Ryder said crossing his arms. "I want to be part of it, so Kendall can go back with Roberto and make some noise."

"I'm not sure, Scout, do you think it is safe?" She shifted from one foot to the other.

"This is part of the adventure, Kendall," said Scout. "We will use all safety measures going back in; don't worry—I've done this before." Like Ryder's, Scout's eyes reflected the excitement of the unknown.

"Okay, I'll go back with Roberto and I will let you guys see if that's the access." She ignored the pit in her stomach.

****

Scout peered into the entrance, a doorway into another world, a new frontier. He loved the rhythm of underwater breathing. The sound of his hollow breath calmed him down as they swam through tubes of total darkness. Scout led Ryder until they reached a narrow passageway; he swam in first making sure it was passable and then returned directing his movements. They drifted with the current in the cold clear water. Following a cave system for a short way, they squeezed between large boulders. Their headlamps bounced off the rocks like a submarine light as they crammed through the last of the small cave passageways, and the lights on their helmets revealed a large opening above. They surfaced to a spectacular cathedral foyer. They were on the inside of the cave looking up two hundred feet to the surface. They both let out a yell of delight in unison. Ryder glowed, his expression made it worth the trip.

Roberto and Kendall lowered the ladder, which hung in midair—not even close to the water. Then on a pulley system, they lowered down the gear to a dry platform slightly above the surface. Roberto lowered one of the large can lights to illuminate the incredible chamber.

Scout heard Kendall but could barely see her. She yelled, "I'm coming in."

****

Kendall had never before climbed down a rope ladder fifty feet into a two-hundred-foot hole. As she maneuvered down the narrowest part of the opening, the ladder lay against the rock until it ended, which left her hanging at the top of a massive cave chamber. Her chest rose and fell with rapid breaths she looked down, dizzy with the height above the open cenote. *You can do this.*

She screeched, anxiety building, "So how deep is it, do you think I can jump?"

Ryder and Scout were laying out the equipment on the dry part of the cave to the left oblivious to Kendall coming down the ladder. Wide-eyed, they tilted their heads.

"What the hell are you doing?" Scout yelled.

"Trying to get down to you," she called back. "How long a drop is it?"

"Kendall, it is about a fifty-foot drop from where you are. It would be much easier and safer if you climb back up the ladder and I can meet you at the mouth of the cave!"

"I could do easier." She paused for a moment, as if she was headed back up the ladder. "But I'm not going to." And with that she let go of the ladder and dropped straight down like a bullet into the clear blue waters of the cenote. *Can nature be more magnificent?* Every nerve ending on her body detected the rush of life. "Simply amazing," she said.

Scout shook with laughter as he dug out his copy

318

of Tim's map from the dry pack and laid it out on the rock platform.

"Ryder, It's your exploration; tell us which way you want to go."

Ryder studied the map. "I saw a large opening underwater over there." He pointed. "Wherever that passageway goes, that's where I want to go."

It was decided, Ryder would lead. The decision felt right to Kendall, even though her breath quickened. This is what Tim would want.

Scout drew a portion of the map on a waterproof clipboard. Ever the professional guide, he checked all their equipment and their air, and explained again the two-thirds rule. It was the classic guideline, meaning use 1/3 of the air going in and turn around with 2/3 of the air going out. Scout checked his dive equipment against a list, as a pilot checks his airplane before taking off. He went over his hand signals once more, then double-checked all the gear and the tanks. He took out the first aid kit and a few bottles of water from the dry pack, laid them out on the limestone platform, then rechecked all the lights.

As he held out a light, his face resembled a kid who had just won a golden ticket and was about to enter Willy Wonka's Chocolate Factory. "Let's do it." He beamed.

The main passage offered steep downward banks at the beginning, but they were not too difficult to maneuver. The sound of her breath reminded Kendall of a submarine ping. Slow and steady, she focused on the cadence as she followed Ryder. They approached a narrow tunnel and Ryder went first, signaling back to proceed. Their lights illuminated the brilliant white walls of an enormous room. Eye-catching decorations surrounded the three divers. Again, choices, with several different passageways going both upstream and downstream. Ryder chose the one to the left, clearly communicating to all on the clipboard. A narrow and long passageway, they swam single file for at least fifteen minutes. Kendall wondered if it would ever open up, her breathing accelerated.

She didn't like it. A constricting narrow tunnel with a difficult turn ratio. Kendall concentrated on the steady beat of her breath, like a metronome, it always relaxed her, but this time it was not working. Ryder seemed oblivious to any concern or danger, for diving and breathing underwater for Ryder was just like Tim, a second home. *Please let this open up*, she prayed.

Finally, the narrow tunnel spilled them out into a rather large area with a small air hole at the top. The decorations were stunning, with many formations and stalactites hanging all around. It was an elaborate, spellbinding display of what nature could create.

Scout signaled for their attention and pointed to the air hole at the top. They nodded, recognizing a safety chamber. They continued to the other side, swimming through a much larger passage, and entered a halocline, part saltwater and part freshwater, where they could see Swiss cheese perforations all over the sides of the rock.

The extreme beauty blurred time. Scout tapped Ryder on his shoulder and all three checked their air. They had used almost one third and knew it was time to turn back. Scout motioned, and Ryder pointed in the forward direction asking for another minute. He raced through a gaping hole of narrow rocks and immediately stuck his head back through, urging Kendall and Scout to join him.

Making it through one smaller tight passage, they found themselves in the mother of all caves. It was part wet and part dry and they could see the surface just above them. Swimming up, they emerged into the air. Looking up a hundred feet to the ceiling, they took off their masks in awe. The crystalline water and the visibility were perfect. Shining their lights on the inside of the cave, they could see dry smaller caves and what looked like tunnels on a higher level.

Breathtaking, staggering, and mesmerizing; Kendall inhaled the beautiful landscape.

"I believe this is what my father wanted me to see." Ryder floated on his back, his eyes scanned the ceiling. He pointed up to a dry ledge; something white glinted in the headlamp's beam.

"What is it?" Ryder asked Scout, who was shining his light capturing the same reflection.

"It could be anything, possibly bones, and artifacts…it has obviously been dry for a long time."

****

Ryder wanted to climb out and explore the dry ledge; he was fascinated. "Imagine the artifacts…imagine what we could find in here." Then he stopped dead, inhaling, staring at the wall above the small cave. He swam over to the ledge and tried to pull himself up. His mouth gaped but no words came out. *How could this be?*

Scout swam over beside him and said, "It looks like a Mayan symbol." He took out his board and drew the symbol.

Kendall gasped. "Oh my God," she exclaimed, "I've seen this before, I'm not completely sure it is exactly alike, but I've seen this. It has to mean something."

Ryder shouted. "You've seen it before—on me! It looks like my birthmark. Dad always thought I should put a tattoo over it."

Kendall's whirled around, her eyes wide. "Your birthmark? I never knew you had one—It's the same mark on the man in the pictures. The pictures on your dad's zip drive of the man with all the presidents..." She could barely catch her breath. "If you enlarge the area between the shoulder and collarbone, you can see that marking. Tobias has the same mark."

Ryder unzipped his wet suit at the neck and pulled it over his shoulder.

"Like this?"

****

There it was, a replica of what they could see on the wall. A light discoloration on the skin, unlike the darker one on the man in the photos. Kendall had attempted to draw the symbol several times at home. Ryder's birthmark was eerily similar, and it was on the same area between the shoulder and collarbone. She stared at Ryder's skin, then at the symbol on the wall.

"Do you know what it means?" Ryder asked Scout.

"I'm not sure," Scout said. "But I know it's a Mayan symbol."

Ryder hoisted himself up, trying to find a ledge to get closer to the dry cave.

"It's a sign. I just know it. We need to bring a rope and backup tanks tomorrow, we need to come back here and explore some more. Dad was right, this is epic!" It was the happiest Ryder had looked since his father died almost two years ago.

Kendall, still a little freaked out by Ryder's birthmark, blew out her cheeks. "Should we stay another night?"

Scout didn't look convinced. "We can discuss it. That's what I originally planned, at least two or three nights here. But, everyone has to be in agreement. It looks like whoever's following us doesn't seem to want to cause any issues, it's probably just some local hunters trying to figure out what we are doing here... So yes, if you both want to stay another day, I'll talk to Enrique and Roberto to find out if anything else was heard or seen today."

Scout checked the air supply in the tanks. "But for now, we need to head back, get the tanks lifted back up to the surface and swim to the mouth of the cave to get out."

Kendall couldn't wrap her mind around the coincidence of the Mayan symbol and the birthmark. *Did Tim know Ryder's birthmark was on the wall?* The road back was no less impressive as they were dazzled at each turn by colors and formations. Unable to discuss what she had seen, she tried to enjoy and be in the moment, but her breath sounded shaky in her head. When all the equipment was either stored on the platform or raised to Roberto on the pulley, they continued their trek.

Swimming and hiking through the wet cave to the mouth of the river with the hourglass opening flew by. The excitement of their discovery still energized their hike back to camp. Ryder was elated. Kendall's stomach was in knots.

****

Kendall could not get the symbol out of her mind.

323

She asked Ryder to show her the birthmark again on the trail back to camp. The brown pigment on his skin clearly resembled typical birthmarks, but it was the arrangement of the spots and shapes of the mark that reminded her of a faded henna tattoo, the kind one gets on the beach in Mexico for fifty pesos. A circular mark, not quite a perfect circle, with four short straight marks underneath it and a series of specks or dots around the circle.

"I never knew you had this." She touched Ryder's shoulder. "Did you know your father's tattoo was in that same area?"

He pulled back from her touch, his voice irritated. "Of course I did, he got the tattoo with the SEALs. He told me when I was little not to worry about the birthmark because he had a mark there too, his tattoo. I've always wanted to get the same tattoo he had to cover up my birthmark and Dad told me to wait until I was at least eighteen to make that decision, and we would do it together."

Scout spoke up. "We'll ask Enrique, he's part Maya. He might know what the symbol means."

****

When they arrived back at the camp, Kendall's anxiety seemed to dissipate as Scout chuckled, listening to Enrique explain his day. Enrique had not experienced any disturbances except for a wild howler monkey sitting up in the tree staring at him for several hours.

She laughed as she plopped down on the canvas tarp until she heard the low tone of Roberto's speech. She looked up, Enrique and Roberto spoke rapidly in Spanish. Roberto flinging his hands. Scout joined the conversation. Unfamiliar words blurred together as

Kendall attempted to decipher meaning.

"What's wrong?' she asked.

"Nothing," Scout said as he trotted over to his pack and retrieved his clipboard. He handed it to Enrique. His crude drawing of the symbol etched in marker.

"*Agua*." Enrique's eyes darted to Roberto's and they continued speaking in Spanish.

Scout turned facing Kendall and Ryder. "Water, it's the Mayan symbol for water. Enrique states water was sacred to the Maya; they believed the cenotes were spiritual passages to the underworld. And that's why over the years so many artifacts, jewels, and skeletons were found in the caves. The Maya believed water had special healing power and extended life. The reality of this belief is that they were right, because without water they could not survive."

****

Ryder rubbed his shoulder thinking of the birthmark he always wished wasn't there. He walked over to Enrique and pulled his shirt off to show him his birthmark.

Enrique's face changed, his eyes widened and his mouth was set in a line, as he examined the skin. He backed up, staring at Ryder.

"*Ay dios mio*," Enrique whispered.

Ryder knew enough Spanish from living in Arizona, it was an expression of "Oh my God."

"What? What?" Ryder asked. "Why is he saying 'Oh my God'?"

Scout, Roberto, and Enrique continued talking in Spanish, Enrique shook his head several times and gestured with his hands. Ryder could not understand what they were saying. Finally, Enrique and Roberto walked away, ignoring him.

"What? What was that all about?" Ryder asked, and threw his hands in the air. Something was wrong.

"They are going to get the tanks ready for tomorrow before it gets dark, and start the fires so we can get dinner ready." Scout rubbed his temples. "Enrique was explaining there is a legend that the people of the *dyznot*, meaning the cenote people, carry that symbol on their body. He is saying you might have part Maya in you and was asking about your father, and your grandfather."

"I never met my grandfather. He died when my father was young."

Kendall put down her water. "Seriously? Scout, what do you know about the cenote people?"

Scout shook his head. "I don't really know much other than the basic legend. Back in the heyday of the Mayan civilization, they lived near the cenotes and they were the guardians of the sacred water."

Ryder had his iPhone out and grumbled, "Shit, I wish we had Internet, I would look all this stuff up." Brightening, he asked, "Maybe this is what Dad was trying to tell me?"

Kendall smiled, "What, that you are a descendent from an ancient civilization? Who knows, maybe you're right. Maybe that's the purpose of the trip, something he discovered a long time ago and he wanted to share it with you on your birthday. I certainly didn't know your father's secrets." Kendall glanced at Scout. "What do you think, Scout? Do you think Tim and Ryder could be from a long line of Mayan descent?"

Scout gave a half shrug and cocked his head. "I suppose anything is possible."

****

In the privacy of her tent, Kendall unzipped a pocket in her backpack and unfolded a worn square of paper. Tim's kind eyes and warm smile met her gaze. She carried this photo for the last two years, opening it in private when she needed a fix, like a junkie with its drug. *What were you hiding from me? Why? Didn't you trust me?* She wanted answers. She needed the truth. Folding it back up into a square, she returned it to her pack, the back of her hand wiping the moisture from her cheek.

A cheesy aroma greeted her as she stepped out of the tent...dinner, freeze-dried macaroni and cheese. Scout stood up displaying two small bottles of champagne up in the air. He cleared his throat. "I breathe easier, now that I took you to the cenote your father wanted you to see, so I thought it would be worth having a toast and celebrating. Here's to discovering the right cenote." Scout unscrewed the lids, the bubbly liquid poured into each of their metal camping cups.

"And, Ryder, here's to your birthday present from your father, a remarkable adventure, and to getting to know both of you." Scout shot a quick glance at Kendall, then his eyes returned to the crowd.

Roberto added *"Feliz Cumpleaños."* Enrique mumbled the greeting and stared at Ryder.

After dinner, Ryder spread the cenote map out on the tarp. On his knees he hunched over, analyzing the drawing. He leaned closer and grumbled, "I wish you hadn't left the computer on the boat. I really would like to see the pictures of the old man's mark."

The birthmark. The symbol on the cave wall. Flashes of both consumed her mind the entire night during dinner. She wished she had the computer too, and could study the pictures of the old man. Her body ached from the intense physical activity of the day, but her mind ran on full speed, full of questions.

"Sorry Ryder, I wish we had the laptop, but I can't imagine carrying anything else, with all the gear we brought in. We will look at it first thing on the boat."

Ryder never took his eyes off the map. "According to this, it looks like there is another underground tunnel in that birthmark room, and if I'm reading this right, it opens up into an even bigger chamber."

Scout walked over and kneeled down next to Ryder.

"Birthmark Room, well that's a good name for it," Scout smiled and pointed to the map. "Now this map makes more sense, I didn't realize these lines were passageways and tunnels, but you're right, Ryder, this is where we came in...this is the second room and this is the third room. How about we name it, in your honor, the Birthmark Room. We just need to make sure we have enough air to go the whole way to here." He pointed to the area that so intrigued Ryder, a fourth room.

"We will," Ryder said. "We'll take the extra tanks and take breaks in the Birthmark Room for air. I know I can make it." He was transfixed on the map.

"Well, there certainly is a lot to explore tomorrow," said Kendall. "Let's say we all get some sleep and wake up at first light."

Eyes glued to the map, Ryder replied, "Go ahead, Kendall, I'm not ready for bed yet."

Shrugging her shoulders, she met Scout's gaze. Being in the water all day was taking its toll. "Good night, Scout." She knew he wanted to talk more, spend some alone time, but instead of giving in, she waved and unzipped her tent. Restless, her mind navigating dozens of theories, she heard Ryder enter the tent and listened to his steady breathing. Her life wasn't supposed to turn out this way. The love of her life wasn't supposed to be a liar. *Do I really want to know the truth?* She knew the answer. When sleep finally greeted her, she dreamt of cenotes, vibrant, clear blue water surrounding her, and blue eyes staring at hers, everything blue, blue, blue.

Chapter 58

Kendall woke up to a melody of chattering, whistles, and chirping outside the tent. The jungle was waking up with her, the birds on high volume, happily singing bubbly, cheerful jungle tunes, as if the birds were laughing.

Ryder's sleeping bag was empty. Her eyes adjusted to the light, and like a dimmer switch, the brightness slowly increased. She looked down at her Polar Loop exercise band, which tracked how many steps and swimming strokes she did during the day. It was 5:25 a.m.

Clang, Clang. Unzipping the tent, she stuck her head out. Ryder, ear buds in and *humming*, flipped burritos on the grill pan and stirred the coffeepot. In the early morning light he looked beautiful. The muscles in his face relaxed and the corners of his mouth turned up. This day was definitely going to be different, Ryder had never cooked for the camp or risen this early.

"Well, good morning, Ryder. I see you're up early. It smells great." His back to her she could see tortillas, beans, cheese, and powdered eggs, she touched his shoulder. He turned, took the ear buds out, and she repeated herself.

"Yeah, I wanted to get a good meal in us and then I want to get going. Roberto is going to pack us a lunch."

"Are the guys up?".

"They're checking the outside of the perimeter, but they're pretty much ready to go." Ryder's startling blue eyes shimmered with anticipation.

"You're really excited about this? It's good to see you so thrilled about something...your dad would be happy."

"I feel something here, a connection." He paused and looked away. "There's something down there. I know. There's something here, Dad wanted me to see. Maybe it was the marking on the cave, but whatever it is, I want to find it."

Scout, Roberto, and Enrique walked up to the fire. "Enrique's going to come with us today and Roberto is going to stay around the camp. There were no signs last night of anybody tracking us or watching us, so maybe whoever it was left." Scout poured himself a cup of coffee.

Roberto and Enrique exchanged conversation in Spanish. Scout translated, "Roberto thinks it could be local hunters who have moved on, but Enrique thinks they're still nearby."

"Well, they haven't tried to do us any harm, so I don't think it's someone who followed us from Conrad Nathaniel's group or even the government. I think it has to be some local hunters." She finally said out loud what she had been thinking for the last few days.

No one responded to her statement.

"Breakfast is ready," Ryder announced in a cheerful voice as if he were playing a role for the cameras; he handed out plates.

Scout chuckled. "Looks like someone's excited to start the day."

****

On the morning hike, time flew like the howler monkeys swinging across the treetops and before Kendall could sort out her thoughts, they were at the dark gaping mouth of the river. Scout swam gracefully through the entrance, his muscular build gliding, leading the way. Swimming in the cool clear water, climbing and pushing through rocks and narrow passageways, the trek through the cave seemed much easier this time around. In less than forty minutes, they were at the starting chamber.

"My underwater camera's gone," Ryder announced as the pinpoints of light from above illuminated the limestone ledge and Enrique was lifting the second orange tank down from the hole above.

Ryder kneeling on the dry platform, counted and lifted each supply item going left in the pack from yesterday. He set up a work light, casting a strange glow on the inside cave wall, highlighting the unique rock formations and massive decorations above.

Scout helped transport the tanks down from the top and rubbed his forehead. "Ryder, are you sure you left it here?"

"I'm positive." Ryder placed all the items left in the pack yesterday in a line on the ledge. "I know I left the camera here. When I was in the Birthmark Room, I was kicking myself for forgetting it on this ledge. I wanted to make sure I had it today to take a picture of the symbol on the wall. I'm one hundred percent positive I left it here yesterday."

Scout hesitated and shot a glance at Kendall. "I don't know, Ryder, there's no sign of anybody being here or coming through the wet cave. Is anything else missing?"

Ryder sighed then stood on the platform. "No, just my camera. I know I left it here and I put it in the dry pack."

Scout moved over to the platform and picked up each item: three small cans of fruit cocktail, granola bars and dried fruit all unopened, a knife, diving equipment, logbooks, and the first aid kit. "Well, that's strange, because nothing else is touched; I bet you find it back at camp."

"Or maybe we knocked it into the water." Kendall said. "Ryder, I have a small waterproof disposable camera and you're welcome to use it."

He stared at both of them as if they were crazy. "I'm telling you, my camera was here yesterday with the rest of the stuff and now it's gone. Somebody was here."

Scout finished the rest of the equipment checks, laying out the first aid kit and bottles of water for their return.

"Well, maybe some animal was up on the ledge and knocked it over and we will find it down below in the cenote." Scout tried to lighten the mood. "Maybe they will take some good pictures."

Ryder did not laugh, but grabbed the disposable camera Kendall offered, with an outstretched hand, without a thank you. The old Ryder was back.

****

The guide line Scout secured into place yesterday eased Kendall's anxiety and concerns about air supply. This trip they were pulling three extra tanks behind them. The steep downward banks and the tight restriction of getting to the first room seemed a little more congested, but the backup air supply was necessary to get to the third room, and allow exploration of the fourth room Ryder had discovered on the map. They needed additional air to get back.

The staggering beauty of the cenote was even more glorious the second time around. Today the decorations appeared more dazzling, in splendid statuette poses with the light shining upon the massive formation, the water crystal clear. A site so beautiful it seemed heavenly, not of this world. It made her think of Tim.

Once again, they snaked through the Swiss cheese formations and squeezed through the triangular hole in the curved narrow rock to get to the third room, the most astonishing of them all. They broke surface, heads back and chins in the air, marveling again at the stunning height of the room and shining their lights on the smaller caves up above and the tunnels on a higher level. Removing her mask the sound of her breath filled the silence. "It is truly spectacular." She turned around in all directions. "It reminds me of this place in Arizona, Montezuma's Castle, where the cliff dwellers built their homes way up high in little caves with different levels. It almost looks like that over there, like a few stories of a cave house." She pointed to the further wall to the right.

Ryder hoisted himself up on the ledge and removed his equipment.

"Are you getting out now?" Scout asked as he held onto the ledge. "If you want to see the fourth room, maybe we should go now and come back here to rest afterwards."

Ryder's back against the wall of the cave, he held a rope in his hands studying the upper tunnel. "I want to see what the white reflection is, and then I can come back and check out more later."

Scout was out of the water in an instant taking off his equipment. "Well, you can't do it by yourself, Ryder, let me give you some help." But before Scout finished, Ryder was securing clips and rappelling up the wall.

"Please be careful." Her words echoed back as she watched Ryder lift himself into the small passageway and disappear.

She took in a sharp breath. "Ryder? Ryder?"

Silence.

"It's pottery, it looks like a vase and has writing on it." Ryder emerged holding several pieces of jagged clay in his hand. "The cave goes back about fifteen feet and then it's blocked. I'm not sure if it's blocked naturally or intentionally, it looks intentional to me." Ryder disappeared and came back out to the ledge holding the camera in his hand. "There are symbols all over this wall, some kind of pictograms."

Scout was on his way up, and Kendall hoisted herself to the ledge.

With her head tilted back, she asked, "Did you take a picture of the writing on the wall?" She was shining her light as far as the beam could go up to the hundred-foot ceiling.

Scout yelled, "Do you want to come up and see this?"

"Later, when we come back this way. Then I'll take all my equipment off and explore a little...but if we are going to go to the fourth room, I'll wait until we come back through."

Scout descended, dropped to the ledge. "You're right, we should keep going to the fourth room, and then come back and take a rest before we go back through."

He handed her a piece of the pottery. She held it in her fingers, turning it over and looking at each side. A small imprinted stamp of what appeared to be a monkey, marked the clay. Jaggedly broken, she could make out part of a Mayan symbol. She lifted it to her nose and smelled it.

Scout laughed. "Are you smelling it?"

"I am smelling it, it smells *old*. It's amazing to hold something ancient in your hand. An object from a time gone by. I wonder how long it's been here, what's the story behind it, and why is it broken?"

Scout pulled out several more pieces and laid them on the platform. "Sounds like your inner Indiana Jones talking."

She smiled, trying to fit the pieces together like a puzzle. Ryder came down and added three more pieces.

"It's a type of vase, a jug with symbols on it." She guessed.

"It's hieroglyphics, the Mayan writing is using a set of glyphs." Scout added another section to the jug.

As the last fragment was put in place, the jug was almost complete. She gasped. "They are the same glyphs you tried to draw for us."

"Hunkul Yax," Scout said aloud "Forever young."

Kendall felt more confused, as she listened to the water dripping off their equipment.

Ryder traced the symbols with his fingers. "And what was the legend again?"

Scout cleared his throat, picked up a dry bag and carefully put the pieces into it. "The legend is this particular tribe of the Maya were called forever young

336

because they lived exceedingly long lives. There are documented cases of skeletons with a carbon-dated age of up to two hundred years old."

Ryder put his hands in the air to emphasize his statement. "That's it! Don't you see, that's what my dad was trying to show me. He found proof these people existed...The pictures of the old man, he found it...he found what *they* were looking for...whatever made this tribe live long—he found it."

Ryder scanned the cave in every direction. "It's in here somewhere, whatever it is it's in *here*. I just know it. I have never been so sure of anything in my life."

Kendall spoke almost in a whisper. "Maybe it has something to do with the bats." She pointed up to the ceiling. "There's thousands of them."

Ryder and Scout both tilted their heads back, staring at the black mass on the ceiling. Scout spoke first. "Well, there must be a way out through one of those tunnels up there, or there couldn't be bats, they need a way to escape." He paused. "But before we get too intrigued by the tunnels, we need to make a decision if we want to go explore the fourth cave, we need to start now. If we have time, we can come back and spend a while in here before we have to leave. Fourth cave?"

"Okay," Ryder said, "maybe we can stay another day and come back just to see if we can locate the tunnel that leads out, maybe we can find it, find what my father discovered." The glint of light illuminated his eyes.

Scout gathered his gear. "Okay, Indiana Junior, let's do one thing at a time. Let's go check out this fourth room, you wanted to see." As they all reentered the water, Scout turned to Ryder before putting his mask on. "Your adventure, you're first. Set the guideline."

****

Kendall followed Ryder with Scout in the back. She concentrated on the rhythm of her breath in her ears and the solitude and peacefulness of the underworld returned. After ten minutes, Ryder abruptly stopped and motioned stay. He squeezed through a small circular opening with rock cropping jutting down.

She waited with Scout, their lights illuminating the opening. She had no idea of the time, but unable to converse and staying in one place, Kendall was sure minutes had passed. She motioned to Scout forming an Okay sign with her fingers, her breath increasing. Scout motioned to wait, glancing at his watch.

The air bubbles appeared first followed by Ryder who motioned for them to follow. He led them through a small tunnel that opened to a large tunnel. Six people could easily fit side by side across the cave, it was the narrowing in the far distance that alarmed her. It tapered in like a funnel and before Ryder tried to go through the skinniest section, the three of them stopped. Scout wrote on his wipe-off board, "BC off." This meant they needed to take their tanks off and lead with them in front. Scout motioned he wanted to go first, but Ryder pointed to his own chest, shaking him off, affirming he was going to lead the way.

The tunnel was narrow, with rocks coming out of the sides adding to the claustrophobic atmosphere and difficulty of the journey. It was like blood going through a clogged artery, easy to pass through on the smooth parts, hard to get through where there was plaque built up.

Ryder was going as fast as he could, conserving air in their tanks. Kendall prayed, the map had to be right and the narrow tunnel would open up into a large chamber. There could be no other train of thought. Because if the small, winding limestone tunnel just continued to get narrower, there would be no place for any turn-around; no one could pass the other or head back in the other direction. Swimming backwards with tanks in front would be impossible. They were three sardines swimming upstream in a compressed narrow passage, slowly moving single file, hoping there was a way out.

Everything halted. Air bubbles filled the cramped space. Ryder's tank was stuck. Swimming methodically, carefully concentrating on her pace, the water became agitated. Something was wrong, terribly wrong. She cautiously moved closer to Ryder, her breath increasing in pace accelerating in volume in her head.

Ryder's hose snagged on a serrated spiky rock, and he was urgently trying to free the hose without ripping it. She tried to calm her pounding heart, concentrating on her breathing and trying to steady her air intake. Her panic was obvious in her jerky twitches, her legs flailing in desperation. She attempted to turn her body to get Scout's attention. Her anxiety built as she had difficulty controlling her breath. The tapered passageway seemed more constrictive than ever.

Scout, unaware what was exactly wrong, went immediately into rescue mode. He pulled his tanks in and tried to get in front of them to assist her.

As he yanked his tanks to fit behind him, they were

caught in the limited area of the passageway. With a strong sharp pull, he hit the yoke regulator connector on the top of his tank on a jutting stalagmite. She watched it happen in slow motion, her heart pounding against her chest, paralyzed by fear. A tremendous blast of air burst from the tank, knocking Scout's head against the wall and into a sharp point. She tried to turn to give him air. Blood colored the water and drifted toward her.

Blood. Red dark liquid drifted in the clear water. As it floated by her mask, she gasped for control of her inhalation. Her heart hammered on so fast and she could not catch her breath. The harder she concentrated, the tighter her chest constricted. *This is it* she knew with certainty, *this is it*. Trying frantically to control her breathing, made it worse. Tim. She could picture his handsome face, *I'm sorry, I'm sorry I can't save your son.* Scout. Poor Scout a wonderful man who was dying the same death as Tim.

Ryder, please save yourself, she prayed.

Out of the corner of her mask, a light illuminated the water in front of her. She could almost make out the outline of Ryder as she descended into blackness. *Maybe he's ok*, in her mind she was jubilant for a moment, *Ryder made it*. In blackness she envisioned Tim's beautiful face in front of her, swimming, his arms reaching out to grab her, and she knew then…she was dying and she let go, so she could be with him again.

Chapter 59

He was standing in judgement, in silence, meeting the blue-green eyes of the elder. He couldn't look away. Without words, disappointment clouded the older man's tan, stoic face.

"Sit," the elder pointed to the gentle curves of the beautiful hand-carved wooden chair.

He sat, shoulders back and chin up as he had been taught from his military days. He opened his mouth to speak, and the elder held up his finger to silence his words before they came out.

They sat in silence. The old man stared straight ahead, into the jungle. It was as if time stood still although the shadows from the sun moving on the jungle trees bore witness to its passing.

He finally turned his eyes unwavering from his. "You've broken the most sacred rule of our people." The elder paused, moving his hands away from his shoulders and unclasping his arms, the dark brown birthmark clearly displayed between the shoulder and collarbone. He continued, "I'm not saying I don't understand why you made the choice you did, but why was she here in the first place?"

"She was here, to bring him. She's the reason he even came at all."

The elder nodded. "And that was the only way the boy would come?" he asked.

"Yes, without me, I am certain it was the only way the boy would come."

The elder sat in a massive wooden chair made with loving curves and of the highest artisanship. He ran his hand through his long hair. "She can never leave, can you accept that?"

He walked over to the elder with his hands outstretched and the elder took his hands in his. At the touch, a loving look passed between the two men, one of understanding and gratitude. "Thank you, I understand."

Chapter 60

Ryder's eyes fluttered and then opened wide. The bright light blinded him and his hand protectively covered his eyes. His first thought, *I am alive.* He touched the soft sheet across his stomach.

He sat up, his head turning in both directions, and he muttered the words out loud, "Where am I?" The words echoed.

He was alone, on a low, small cot in some kind of thatched structure with one side completely open to the elements and the sun. He inhaled freshness. The jungle, he could hear it, smell it, and see the green. *How did I get here?* In the distance a cascading waterfall; the sound of rushing water was louder now. He tested his fingers, toes, and legs, he was not injured. Pushing the soft sheets back, he sat up and stepped onto the stone floor. He had his swim trunks on, but his wet suit and diving equipment were nowhere in the hut.

The other three walls displayed delicately crafted wooden artwork, and a vibrant blanket hung on the wall behind him, depicting a stunning water scene with beautiful fuchsia flowers and dark green foliage completing the background. A mirror image of the waterfall in front of him. Organic. Natural. *Where was he?* A large pitcher of water and a wooden cup sat on the table beside the bed.

A shadow blocked the light, as his eyes adjusted,

his heart accelerated in disbelief. "Am I in heaven?"

The man, with blue-green eyes that mirrored his own, smiled warmly. "No, son, you're not in heaven. You're very much alive." In one step, he embraced Ryder and held him tightly in his arms. Tears of joy ran down their cheeks.

****

"How? How is this possible?" Tim had directed Ryder to sit in the only other furniture in the room, two beautiful dark wood and vine carved chairs. Ryder stared at his father's face; he couldn't take his eyes off him.

"Am I dreaming?" Ryder pinched his arm.

"No. I have a lot of explaining to do, Ryder. I want you to understand who we are and where our ancestors come from. I want to make it clear why I had to leave without letting you know. Without allowing anyone to know. Not even Kendall."

"Kendall, Scout." Ryder's voice was raised as he stood up, realizing as usual he had only been thinking about himself. He gulped for air. "Did they make it? Are they alive?"

Chapter 61

The intoxicating smell was sweet and pure, like vanilla and eucalyptus, maybe with a bit of lavender mixed in. The aroma filled her nose, just enough to be relaxing, not overpowering. She inhaled and let out a breath of air, opening her eyes.

She had fallen asleep again and as her body and mind awakened, she remembered where she was. She was with Tim. She smiled at the flowers on the table beside her bed and touched her chest where she felt the tightness when breathing. The thunder of water. She looked out at the open wall and could see a beautiful waterfall in the distance. The birds were singing and the potpourri colors of the flowers were spectacular.

She had never witnessed such a magnificent display of nature in her life. If a picture could be a million words this would be it. She smiled slowly, and then her heart started beating rapidly and confusion took over. *Is Tim really alive? What happened to Scout and Ryder?* Her thoughts ran rampant through her mind, *did he really save me?* For a minute, she wondered if she had dreamed everything. Maybe this was heaven.

The single red and fuchsia flower lay across her sheet. It was exquisite, not just a flower but a work of art; it resembled a kind of orchid but with an unusually curly thin vine wrapped around a stem. She remembered, Tim had pulled it from the vase and given it to her the first time her eyes opened and she saw his face. Yes, she was indeed alive and so was Tim. He tried to calm her fears by telling her repeatedly how much he loved her, everything was going to be all right, he would never leave her again. Tender words spoken in a whisper as he held her face and assured her he would tell her everything, no more secrets.

His face moved closer and she could smell his scent. "It will all make sense, I need you to trust me one last time, trust in the love you know we have.

"Ryder is fine. Alive with no injuries." But, sadness drifted in his eyes, he lowered his voice. "Scout did not make it. They could not save him. He did not make it out of the cenote alive."

Ryder was alive. Scout was dead.

She heard him, and wanted to ask a thousand questions, but her eyelids were heavy and she couldn't force them to stay open. He whispered in her ear, as she unwillingly fell asleep, "Rest my love, it's okay we gave you something to sleep, mend your body. I'm not going anywhere."

****

The next time she woke up, darkness had crept into the room. A little groggy, she tried to control the thoughts racing through her mind. She was angry, confused, *what was real?* Her mind in the present, she wanted answers. Immediately. Getting out of bed, she attempted two steps and slumped down to the cold, hard floor. Her body weak, she was light headed as she sat on the smooth tan stone beneath her.

Just then, Tim and Ryder walked through the door. In a flash, Tim was down on his knees with his arms around her helping her up.

"Baby, are you okay?" His beautiful eyes were full of concern, tenderness, and love. Her heart constricted with emotion, and she knew then, she could never be upset with this man, the only man to own her heart. She was so happy to see him alive.

Chapter 62

If there was a heaven she was in it. Kendall leaned back on the hand-carved bench, inhaled the aroma of flowers and closed her eyes listening to the sound of the spectacular waterfall emptying into the small pond. Wearing a beautiful, soft cloth around her shoulders and another silky sarong wrapped around her body, she pinched her arm; she wasn't dreaming. Ryder and Tim lounged beside her, bare-chested, both wearing tan handwoven drawstring shorts resembling a line of ridiculously overpriced surf clothing from an organic, all natural, high-end retail shop. It all seemed surreal, with Ryder's birthmark and Tim's tattoo visible. The birthmark. Tim explained he tattooed over his birthmark before entering the Navy SEALs on the advice of his Uncle Dan, who was also of the cenote blood.

Silence finally filled the space, after talking for hours.

"I know it's hard to take in." Tim tucked a lock of hair behind her ear. A familiar gesture she had longed for, wished for and never thought she would experience again. She concentrated on the water hitting the pond. Tim was alive.

"So how have you been able to keep this place hidden from the outside world?"

He placed his hands over hers on the bench. "It's

private land, and there are others, just like Ryder and me, cenote people who live and work in the modern world, who protect it." He continued, "They knew the first time you stepped foot on the land. They were tracking your journey, and they let us know you were close."

"Did Scout know you were here?" She whispered, a sharp ping in her heart as she spoke his name.

"No, he had no idea, but I knew he was a good man from the day I met him. I'm sorry we had to lose him. I know you were close." Tim met her gaze. "He was kind to you, and Ryder; I wish I could have saved him."

She wiped a tear from her eye. "Without him, we would not be here. He brought me to you."

Tim squeezed her hand. "Then we need to make him a hero, he deserves to be called a hero."

The white noise from the waterfall filled their moments of silence for Scout.

"What about Enrique and Roberto? Are they going to be okay?" she asked.

"Yes, they are going to take you home, you, Ryder and Scout's body."

"Take me home? But what about you? I'm not leaving here without you." She placed her hands on each side of his handsome face. "I'm not losing you again, Tim, if you can't leave this place, then I'm not going anywhere."

He smiled trying to see behind her eyes. "If you stay here, then you can never return to the life you know. It would be an irreversible decision; you could never change your mind. You can never leave."

She sighed. It would be the easiest decision she ever made. "The life I knew was only a life with you and me in it together. I could never go back to living a life knowing you are here living yours and I am out there trying to live mine. Maybe I can help your ancestors fulfill their desire; find a way to introduce the nutrients of this place to the sick and those who need them, so they don't get into the wrong hands. I know this without any doubt. You have no idea how difficult it was for me to live without you."

"I'm sorry my love. It wasn't supposed to turn out this way. I took the chance marrying you because I couldn't imagine my life without you. I knew as we got older decisions would have to be made. I thought it would be me trying to live life without you."

"Whatever happens, my heart just wants to be with you for the rest of my life and my heart will never change my mind."

Tim stared at the waterfall cascading down into a clear pool of sparkling liquid. He took in a deep breath before he answered. "Well, that's another thing, the rest of my life could end up being an unprecedented long time."

Ryder joined the conversation. "How long is a long time?"

"Most cenote people live to the age of 175, even 200 years old. And it's only in the last fifty years of our life, our physical appearance starts to change. We hit the pause button on aging around thirty-five to forty years old. We keep our physical appearance at that age for many years. Basically, we simply don't age until the last fifty years. If you continue to drink the water, you will add years to your life and it will keep you looking younger longer. Kendall, since you have no cenote blood, it will be interesting to see how you react, how long you stay looking as beautiful and young as you are at this very moment."

She kissed him on the cheek and stood up, smiling mischievously. "So, let me get this straight, if I stay here I get to look and feel like I am thirty-six for another thirty or forty years?"

He smiled for a quick second, but his features turned serious. "Yes, that's what we estimate. We don't really know for certain, because it's been a long time since cenote people have given our water to an outsider."

Kendall rubbed her temples and sat back down. Was this really happening?

He explained, "The last time a person without cenote blood continuously drank the water, it ruined the Mayan civilization. It was the king. He was given a gift by the cenote people to heal the treacherous plague killing thousands of Maya. The cenote people thought they could trust him, he would take the water and save the people."

"But he didn't save them, right?" Ryder asked.

"Right, he didn't believe the water had magical powers, but still he tested it on two dying children and when they miraculously recovered, instead of sharing it and helping to heal those with disease, he murdered the children. His vanity and greed infested his body and mind. He kept all the water, building a temple around it, keeping it for his narcissist self, hoarding it, hiding it away from all the sick, dying Mayan people."

Tim stood and walked over to the ledge of rocks circling the magnificent waterfall. "That's how the cenote people ended up here. They were forced to go underground, separate themselves from the other Maya

351

to save and protect the water. When the Maya were sick and dying, tribesmen were poisoning other tribes' water supply so villages with large numbers of infected people would die. They were trying to cure the disease by murdering sick and healthy people. Families were scared and desperate to survive. Everyone became afraid to drink the water. Man cannot live without safe clean water. Desperation does strange things to good people; they lose their humanity, their goodness."

He returned to the bench beside Kendall and threaded his hand through hers. "The cenote people are good and loving people, they wanted to help all the Maya but because of the greedy king, much of the water was poisoned and ruined. It was their mission to protect and preserve the sacred cenote water before man and disease destroyed what little was left. So they went underground into the cenotes and started creating their own world, their little oasis, this hidden paradise." He held up his hands. "This is where we sit now. A garden of Eden. Nurtured for centuries by love and respect." Tim took a moment to look all around at the beautiful scene they were sitting in. "And, just wait until you see the community, this is just the perimeter."

"It can't be more spectacular than this," Kendall said.

"Oh but it is. With the nutrients in the water, crops plentiful, healthy people, we know little stress. Organic foods grown from the land mixed in with lots of love and happiness, free of disease, free of pollutants created by man. Peace and happiness do exist. It's real as you and I."

"So why would anyone leave?" Kendall grasped his hand tighter.

"To help the world and not end up like the greedy king." Tim twisted the wedding ring on his finger. "Those of us who were born from the Roamers, the ones who left this paradise to watch the world, do end up getting diseases and illness from processed foods and man's additives to our water and environment. But we can be cured with the return to our land and water. The water can cure most diseases, even cancer."

She held her breath. Cancer. "The neurosurgeon's card I found...do you have cancer?" She covered her mouth with her hand.

Tim gently moved her hand to his lips and kissed it. "I did, a brain tumor. I knew it was time for me to come home. I tried to do it for months without anyone knowing, but I was being followed round the clock. I am so sorry for the way I had to go. They were watching my every move, I couldn't return as I had planned."

Ryder interjected, "Do you still have cancer?"

"It's very unlikely. It's been two years, I'm sure it's gone."

"So, just because I have cenote blood doesn't mean I will live a long life?" Ryder fidgeted.

Tim patted him on the shoulder. "You will still live a longer life than most people, depending on what you eat and drink, but maybe we can change that, Ryder. You can help us find a way to introduce our nutrients to the right people so they can save lives without getting into the hands of privatization or controlled by the government."

Tim explained, "I've been working with The Collective, as my ancestors before me worked with the presidents of the United States and special interest groups. Trying to find someone to trust. Over the decades, we released small samples of nutrients found in our water to help them create vaccines for diseases— some you will never even hear about because they were cured by nutrients we secretly supplied. Over the years, the government got edgy, fear crept in…Greedy fear. They didn't know what would happen to American commerce if disease were eradicated. Everyone healthy would corrupt the Social Security system in America, health insurance, pharmaceuticals…they couldn't imagine the impact on the economy, worried it would collapse. Would the economy survive without the sick?"

"They didn't want it?" she asked, her voice taut.

"Think about it, if the government possessed the ability to cure disease—help people to live longer, life expectancy extended well beyond the imagination— how would they handle it or introduce it to the American public?"

"There's got to be a way."

"That's what we are searching for because the government resembled the greedy king."

Tim got up and walked over closer to the waterfall. "They weren't sure whom they would be willing to cure! They questioned whether they would be willing to cure everyone regardless of age, sex, race, religion, or national origin." He was pacing now, visibly disturbed. "Conrad Nathaniel's ancestors had knowledge such a nutrient existed. His great-great-grandfather was a good man, he wasn't afraid of the change in society and he was excited about all the new possibilities such a miracle could bring. He worked with our people for years, hoping a solution would be found. He was on to a solution, and figured out a way to introduce it without greedy hands getting on it. But he passed away in a questionable car accident. That's been the circle, the good ones die and the cenote people are left to begin again trying to find the one they can trust."

Kendall found it difficult to speak, she swallowed and inhaled. "So is Conrad Nathaniel one of the good guys?"

"I wish I could say yes, I saved his life one day for that specific reason, thinking he could be the one. But unfortunately, no...Somehow he knew I was involved. He had his men following me everywhere, I was afraid they followed me here. His men were at the Blue Hole the day I disappeared, they are the reason I faked my death."

Ryder was perfectly still. "Did you know before you went diving, you were never coming home?"

"No, I didn't know, until that day. For months one of our elder Roamers, Tobias, was being held by Nathaniel in a laboratory not far from Camp David. An underground military complex from the 1950s the Nathaniel family helped build and co-owned with the government. They were testing one of our people, they thought the nutrients were in the body. I helped him escape. I'm certain they knew I was involved. The only solution, especially in light of the cancer, was to come down here and make sure no one would find this place until the time was right."

"You know all the stories you hear about the fountain of youth? Did they come from here?" Ryder asked.

"Yes, most likely somebody, a Roamer over the ages let something slip, planted a seed in somebody's mind." Tim inched forward. "You're a Roamer, Ryder, you have to understand the importance of your role. You have to be careful about your television career. High Definition video can cause issues. Today's technology presents new and dangerous issues for a Roamer. The advanced inventions record day to day moments, actions, memories—dated, time stamped, in the Cloud, on Facebook and available for the world to scrutinize at the push of a button. If you continue to be on the television screen when you hit thirty-five or forty, people might notice you're not aging as fast as everyone else. This is what I wanted to talk to you on your birthday trip, explain our heritage, talk about your career on television. I'm sorry it never happened. Or at least the way I envisioned. Intuitively, I thought there would be a little built-in reaction to prevent you from doing television."

"Instinctive reaction?" Ryder rose from his seat. "Like getting anxiety every time the camera turns on."

"Exactly, your instinctive nature should kick in to protect you."

Ryder's mouth opened as though he wanted to say something, he sat down speechless.

It was a lot to comprehend. Kendall mentally exhausted, drank some water, staring at the liquid inside. Just when she thought they were done with the questions, they discovered more, talking until the late hours of the evening. The nutrients from the water energized them, healed them and kept them up all night long. During this time, they never heard or saw anyone else. Tim explained they were separated, because if they were not going to stay, the cenote people didn't want them to have any influence on the private community. He explained Ryder's role as a Roamer, asking Ryder if he was ready to fulfill his destiny. Emphasizing the importance of keeping the cenote people and the water sacred.

"No one can know, son. No one—that means even your wife if you get married someday. It is our oath, our promise. There will be times you'll be tempted, the Conrad Nathaniels of the world might seduce you with money, the government might watch you closely to see what you know. Resist the temptation. Make your life the best it can be. Find your passion. Go to college and work your way up to a man others would take seriously. Down the road you can be the one to help us find the right time and the right people. I know it exists. There's a way to help the world."

In the early hours of dawn, she slipped away. Tim and Ryder needed time. She would have all the time in the world with Tim. A long lifetime. It seemed like a dream. She finally drifted to sleep listening to their voices going back and forth in a melodic way, asking herself the question, do I want to live a long life? The answer was simple. Who could turn down an extended healthy forever with Tim. He was her life. She lost him once, it wasn't going to happen again.

Chapter 63

Decisions are life changing. Contentment is knowing it was the right choice. Kendall reflected on her old mantra, everything happens for a reason. The decision was made. Ryder would leave and she would stay. At morning light, Tim would take Ryder back through the cenote to an area where he could retrieve Scout's body and return him to the first chamber. Tim informed Kendall, Enrique and Roberto, had started a search for the three of them.

Time was of the essence to have Ryder return with Scout's body and be discovered by Enrique and Roberto in the morning.

Tim guaranteed to the elders that Ryder understood his role as a Roamer as Ryder attended a brief ceremony taking the oath of the ancestors. He would tell no one. Ryder would destroy all the maps and other contents of the briefcase and complete the cover story of Kendall's missing body and Scout's death. Tim assured Ryder, Enrique, who was Mayan, would help take Scout's body to another cenote, one not on private land. They would tell the tragic story of Kendall's death with Scout trying to save her, both perishing. Scout would be the hero.

Mayans did not want anyone searching on their private land, they still believed in the Hunkul Yax, their fountain of youth and hallowed land. They would keep the location of this sacred land secret until the day they died, hoping to discover it themselves, they would never disturb an artifact or tell the government about hidden caves, they too wanted to keep all intruders away.

When Ryder emerged with Scout's body it would be far from their current location. Ryder would explain, Kendall's body was unrecoverable.

She hugged Ryder, still trying to make a connection. This man-boy still indifferent to her even after all they had been through. She wondered if she would ever see him again. "You're going to have a wonderful life Ryder—I just know it. Please don't forget to contact Lizzie my neighbor, she can keep Harvey. I know she will love him." She was trying to reach Ryder one last time. "I love you. Take care of yourself, make your father proud. I know you can help change the world."

Epilogue

Two years later

Ryder pressed the glass button on the polished, dark wood elevator and rode up thirty-two floors all the way to the penthouse. Unconsciously, he rubbed his collarbone where his birthmark was, realized what he was doing and moved his hand away as if touching a hot skillet. When the doors slid open, a magnificent round office space greeted him. Glass, silver, and white composed the color scheme, with an outer ring walkway following the windows in a circle, looking out at downtown Los Angeles. The open lobby was in the center with windows all around, and fancy cubicles of glass enclosed employees busily talking on phones and working on computers at their desks.

After a second glance from all the women and a few of the men in the office, he was asked to wait in the high tech reception area, with video images playing on the glass walls and holographic movie clips of famous actors spouting historic one liners.

"Ryder Jackson, they're ready for you." Ryder got up, smoothed down his two-thousand-dollar gray suit and followed the attractive young receptionist into the boardroom. The table was slick natural wood carved into a modern high tech boardroom table. It gleamed of money. He could smell it. In walked Jonathan Koch, head honcho of Asylum Entertainment, and his right-hand man P.J. Abrams. They studied Ryder as most people do, probably wondering why he wasn't pursuing an on-screen acting career.

Quick introductions, then an edgy silence.

Jonathan Koch spoke first. "You have our undivided attention for five minutes, give us the pitch."

Ryder pushed his lips up into his award-winning smile and pulled out the manuscript. He had prepared for this moment. "What would you do if you discovered a water source that would extend life, cure disease, even cancer—would you give it to the world for free?" He paused, "Or sell it to the highest bidder?" He slid it across the table. "It's a one-hundred and twenty-page screenplay, a little adventure suspense with a twist of sci-fi. It's called *A Deep Thing...*"

A word about the author…

A. K. Smith is the author of *A Deep Thing*. Fascinated by the "what if's" in life, she still wonders if Shangri-La and The Holy Grail exist—hidden somewhere—waiting to be discovered. Her favorite question, "What would you do if you knew you wouldn't fail?" led her to both marriage and writing her first book. Her big loves are her husband, family, friends, and kindness. Her goal is to step foot on every continent on Planet Earth—she's slowly getting there.

Please contact her at aksmithbook@gmail.com — she loves to hear from her readers!

www.aksmithauthor.com

https://www.facebook.com/aksmithbook

Thank you for purchasing
this publication of The Wild Rose Press, Inc.

If you enjoyed the story, we would appreciate your
letting others know by leaving a review.

For other wonderful stories,
please visit our on-line bookstore at
www.thewildrosepress.com.

For questions or more information
contact us at
info@thewildrosepress.com.

The Wild Rose Press, Inc.
www.thewildrosepress.com

Stay current with The Wild Rose Press, Inc.

Like us on Facebook

https://www.facebook.com/TheWildRosePress

And Follow us on Twitter
https://twitter.com/WildRosePress